D0918781

FIC Tessier Thomas c.1
Tessier, Thomas.
Ghost music, and other
tales /

SEP ▊▊ 2000

GHOST MUSIC

GHOST MUSIC

and other tales

Thomas Tessier

CEMETERY DANCE PUBLICATIONS

Baltimore

❖ 2000 ❖

Copyright © 2000 by Thomas Tessier

Cemetery Dance Publications edition 2000
ISBN **1-881475-28-X**

Cover illustration copyright © 2000 by Erik Wilson.
Typesetting and design by Bob Morrish.
Printed in the United States of America.

Cemetery Dance Publications
P.O. Box 943
Abingdon, MD 21009
www.cemeterydance.com

To
ALICE

ACKNOWLEDGEMENTS

The author gratefully acknowledges the following editors, who first published some of these stories in slightly different form: Douglas E. Winter, Ellen Datlow, Thomas F. Monteleone, Stanley Wiater, Kristina Etchison, Dennis Etchison, Stephen Jones, Ramsey Campbell, David Sutton, William K. Schafer, Paul F. Olson and David B. Silva, Jeff Gelb and Michael Garrett, Paul Mikol, Barry Hoffman, Matt Johnson, and special thanks to Richard T. Chizmar.

CONTENTS

Food

"It's almost over now," Miss Rowe said, more to herself than to him. There was a faraway look in her eyes, but she smiled and her voice was bright with anticipation. "Don't worry, though. It'll be all right."

Almost over? What did that mean? Mr. Whitman would rather not think about it. As far as he was concerned, it was a typical summer Saturday. The August heat had eased off a bit, and there was a sweet breeze in the air. Other people would go swimming or shopping or would watch a baseball game, and Mr. Whitman and Miss Rowe would do what they usually did every Saturday afternoon, or so he hoped.

"But you aren't well," he was compelled to say. "I mean, it looks like you're in real pain now. I can see it."

"No," she replied without much conviction. "It's not that bad, honestly. I know what I'm going through better than you do, and it's all right." Miss Rowe quivered as she adjusted herself on the mattresses and tried again to change the subject. "What did you bring for me today?"

Mr. Whitman ignored that. "I do think you should let me get a doctor. You ought to be in a hospital, but the least you can do is have a doctor examine you."

"Absolutely not. If you do anything like that, I'll never speak to you again."

Miss Rowe said this not harshly, but more as a verbal pout. Unfortunately, Mr. Whitman knew it was also probably the truth. He was simply incapable of dealing with her on any terms other than her own. His sense of duty wasn't as strong as his fear of damaging the friendship they shared.

Mr. Whitman crossed the room, threading his way carefully through the piles of debris, and stood for a few moments by the open French doors. He enjoyed more of the breeze there, but the backyard was a distressing sight. The lawn hadn't been mowed in weeks. As if on cue, someone's power mower started up and whined steadily in the distance. The garden at the far end of the yard didn't quite exist. Mr. Whitman had cleared and spaded a patch for peppers and tomato plants, but he had never gotten around to putting them in. Now, the bare black soil sprouted a few weeds instead. But he had been busy, he reminded himself. Miss Rowe had taken over his life that summer.

"What have you brought?" she asked again.

"Oh, Balzac," Mr. Whitman answered distractedly. He had almost forgotten the book he held in one hand. Every Saturday afternoon he read a story to Miss Rowe. Balzac was one of her favorites, and his. Today he intended to recite "Facino Cane," a tale he practically knew by heart but which never failed to move him deeply.

He could see that Miss Rowe was pleased, but she was unable to speak. At that moment she was eagerly cramming a thick slice of Italian bread into her mouth. The sight was too distressing for Mr. Whitman to bear, so he turned to the volume of Balzac and flipped through its pages. It wasn't the bread, nor the generous layers of brandy pate and cream cheese that were slathered on it. Food, all food—that was the whole wretched problem. Miss Rowe was a compulsive eater. Most of her waking hours were devoted to the consumption of food. She was half his age, if that, and by his conservative estimate, more than triple his weight.

Their strange relationship had begun six months earlier when Mr. Whitman moved in and became her neighbor. They were a couple of solitary refugees from the outside world. They occupied the two ground-floor apartments in a converted Victorian house on the outskirts of Cairo. Not the Cairo in Egypt, but rather a country village in the central part of eastern Connecticut, where many towns have grandly incongruous names, like Westminster, Brooklyn, and Versailles.

Mr. Whitman had never married, but he had saved and invested his money shrewdly over the years, and when he reached the age of fifty he was finally able to retire from his editorial job in New York and leave the city behind him. He could please himself now, and do what he wanted—which was to buy and sell rare books. Mr. Whitman's specialty was crime, true and fictional, though he loved all literature. He had a respectable collection which he kept in the two-room shop he rented in the village. He also had a dozen or so truly valuable books in a safe-deposit box at the bank. Mr. Whitman didn't make much money at this business. He actually disliked selling any of his books and so he invariably overpriced them. But money had ceased to be an important factor in his life, and he was happy to spend several hours a day in his shop, surrounded by his collection, listening to public radio on the FM and tending to a very small mail order trade.

He discouraged off-the-street customers by keeping the door locked and the shades drawn. He was in the process of compiling a catalogue of his collection, but in a leisurely fashion. More often than not, he would push the lists aside and settle back to lose himself in a book. Mr. Whitman knew he would never be able to read everything he wanted to in one lifetime.

Miss Rowe was something of a mystery to him. She disliked talking about herself, but she did drop an occasional hint. Her only living relatives were a couple of cousins on the West Coast. However, Miss Rowe had come to Cairo from Boston, where something unspecified had apparently rocked her life about a year ago. An accident, an assault, some emotional trauma? Mr. Whitman had no idea. Perhaps she would tell him in time. Whatever it was, Miss Rowe had come to stay in Cairo with just enough money in the bank to pay her rent—and eat.

When Mr. Whitman first met her, she still moved around a bit, going out to buy what she wanted or to drive the back roads and take in the countryside. But now it was virtually impossible for her to leave her apartment. These last few months had seen Miss Rowe put on weight at an astonishing rate. Clearly she had gone past the six-hundred pound mark, and she showed no signs of slowing down. She had arranged for several local food stores to deliver groceries to her. Fresh supplies arrived daily.

Her apartment had been transformed into the nerve center for this remarkable consumption. Furniture was literally pushed out to make room for the essentials. A schoolboy with a perpetually dazed look on his face came around every afternoon to dispose of the piles of trash that Miss Rowe produced, while she spent most of her time reclining on an arrangement of king-size mattresses, stacked two across two, and an array of pillows. She covered her epic bulk with overlapping sheets.

Around her, within easy reach, like a ring of sophisticated equipment in the intensive-care unit of a hospital, she had a hot plate, a microwave oven, three small refrigerators, a toaster, a blender, a can opener, and shelves for paper plates and plastic tumblers, forks, spoons, and knives. Then there were the garbage sacks and cartons of food.

Mr. Whitman was used to all this because he had become a frequent visitor, as fascinated as he was appalled by Miss Rowe's extraordinary way of life. At first they had argued about it, often heatedly. He would tell her she simply had to go on a diet and get help—whatever it took to stop her from gorging herself incessantly. But Miss Rowe wasn't having any of that. She was happy, positively cheerful about her habits. Mr. Whitman took to reading to her from articles and books on the subject of bulimia, compulsive eating. But she refuted these expertly, pointing out that she never vomited, never purged herself with laxatives, and never suffered any attacks of guilt or depression. In short, she wasn't bulimic.

She enjoyed eating, pure and simple.

Mr. Whitman persisted, explaining to her over and over the dangers, the very real threat to her heart and health. But again Miss Rowe smiled at him and dismissed his warnings. "Your body tells you," she would reply calmly while devouring another can of spiced apple rings. "Most people really don't pay attention to their bodies, but I do. I really do. When it tells me to eat, I eat. When it says enough, then I'll stop." Her body, it seemed, urged her only, always, to eat.

Mr. Whitman then adopted a rather different tactic. He told her about his past travels throughout Europe and Asia, vacations in Mexico and the Caribbean. He went on eloquently and at length about the sights he'd seen and the people he'd met. But travel seemed to hold little interest for Miss Rowe, and in desperation he began describing some of the exotic foods he had eaten abroad. He didn't like doing it, but his reasoning was that if she were sufficiently intrigued she might want to do some traveling of her own, if only to sample foreign cuisine—and then she would have to impose some dietary discipline simply to be able to undertake any trip. That also failed, however. Miss Rowe loved food, but quite indiscriminately. The thought of toad in the hole, coq au vin, Arnold Bennett omelets, prawn vindaloo, Creole crayfish, and five-snake soup aroused no excitement in her. She was perfectly happy to zap three or four chicken pot pies in the microwave, and tamp them down with pickled herring, a few hot dogs, and a quart of applesauce. Miss Rowe was not averse to good food but she had no time for extraneous effort.

Although his concern never diminished—on the contrary, it continued to grow—Mr. Whitman began to concede the struggle after a month or so. The arguments were pointless, in the sense that they achieved nothing. Miss Rowe's confidence was perfect, unbreakable, her appetite supreme. Mr. Whitman could see himself turning into a nag, and that wouldn't do. Besides, by then he liked the girl too much to fight with her. He would still try, with a remark here, a caution there, to get through to her, but he had come to accept her as she was. He hardly realized it, but she had quickly become very dear to him. She was practically the only other person in his life.

The power mower continued to drone down the street, but the breeze had died away for the time being. Mr. Whitman sat on the room's only chair and found his place in the book. As always, a few words of Balzac healed much in life.

"I was living at that time in a little street you probably don't know...'"

Miss Rowe closed her eyes and listened contentedly. She chewed marshmallows because they were quiet. Books had never interested her, but she loved to hear Mr. Whitman read stories to her. He was very good, seldom stumbling over a word, and he could be dramatic without sounding hammy. No one else had ever read to her, not even when she was a small child.

"I don't know how I have been able to keep untold for so long the story I am about to tell you...'"

He lit a cigarette when he finished the tale. He had made a point of telling Miss Rowe the very first time they chatted that he limited himself to ten smokes a day, thinking she might find a way to apply his example to her own situation. She told him that she admired his willpower but she did not take up the suggestion. Now they talked about the story and the author, with Mr. Whitman carrying most of the conversation and Miss Rowe saying that "Facino Cane" was beautiful but so sad—and how many cups of coffee did he say Balzac drank every night? Finally Mr. Whitman was ready to conclude his visit.

"Please come back and see me this evening," Miss Rowe said when he stood up.

"Sure, I'll look in later," he promised. Then it occurred to him that there was something slightly odd in the way she had spoken. Some hint of urgency. "Are you all right?"

"Oh, yes," Miss Rowe replied, but with pro forma assurance. "It's just that I'd like to see you again. This evening."

"Fine. Well." Mr. Whitman started to go.

"Something's happening," she whispered breathlessly, to hold him there a moment longer.

"What is it?" Mr. Whitman asked. Now he was worried.

"I don't know. I just feel...different. Like something is changing inside me. But it's not bad," she added hastily. "It feels good, in a funny kind of way."

"You can't judge things like that by yourself," he told her sharply. "I really do think you need to see a doctor. It could be your heart. Funny signs often mean there is something not at all funny just around the corner."

"No, *no*." Then Miss Rowe made an effort to restrain herself and went on daintily, "I will not be poked and prodded and tested and otherwise treated like a freak. Next thing you know, I'd be in the *National Enquirer*. As it is, I worry all day and half the night that word will get out through one of the delivery boys and I'll be besieged by reporters, photographers, curiosity seekers, and self-important doctors. I couldn't bear it." She hesitated, then brightened. "Anyway, I told you: I feel good, not sick. In fact, I've never felt better. I'm tingly all over."

Mr. Whitman sighed unhappily. It would be nonsensical if it weren't fraught with danger. Tingly all over. He couldn't begin to imagine what that meant in terms of her general health. Or in any other way.

And the remark that something was happening—what on earth was he supposed to make of that? He knew that Miss Rowe had a penchant for the dramatic and was always trying to make something out of the sheer uneventfulness of her daily life. That's all there was to it, he tried to persuade himself.

But she did look somewhat different. Miss Rowe's face had a little more color to it than usual. She appeared to be slightly flushed; her cheeks were pink, whereas they were usually rather sallow because she spent all her time indoors.

Mr. Whitman and Miss Rowe touched each other rarely, and then only when their hands met to exchange something. But now Mr. Whitman had to be decisive. He sat down on the edge of the mattresses and held the back of his hand to her forehead.

"Are you running a temperature?" he asked out loud, to make his intentions clear.

"Oh," she said, perhaps a little disappointed. "I don't think so."

"Hmmn." Mr. Whitman marveled silently at the feel of her skin. Miss Rowe's head was not as large as a beach ball but gave the impression that it was. He expected it to be soft and spongy with so much fat, but it was surprisingly firm. Although there were layers of jowls pleated below the jawline, her forehead was smooth, nearly taut. The texture was almost silky, and supple. Mr. Whitman discovered he was reluctant to take his hand away. "Perhaps just a slight temperature," he announced, though he was not at all certain.

"I think you're imagining it," Miss Rowe said with a girlish smile. "But it's nice that you care. I don't know what I'd do without you."

You'd just keep on eating, Mr. Whitman thought sadly. But he smiled back, for he was truly fond of the young woman.

"Take it easy," he advised her. "You know, I wish you would eat more fruits and vegetables and go easier on that junk food." He had delivered this message countless times.

"Oh, but I do," Miss Rowe insisted enthusiastically. "Did I tell you that I made a nice big green salad this morning? I did, all by myself. Greens, and cherry tomatoes."

"Well, that's good," Mr. Whitman responded, his face forming an amused grin. She seemed so proud of herself for managing such a trivial feat. There was something endearingly child-like about Miss Rowe when she was in this kind of mood.

"I'm surprised more people don't realize how good a salad can be for breakfast," she went on.

"Yes."

Mr. Whitman left then; otherwise, he would be stuck there for a long and expanding rhapsody on salads, breakfasts, and food in general. He went directly to his shop in town, fussed around the shelves for a little while and then selected Rufus King's *The Lesser Antilles Case* and Kirby Williams's *The C.V.C. Murders* for his Saturday night and Sunday afternoon reading treats.

Back in his apartment, he filled a pilsner glass with cold beer and looked through the few items of mail he had found at the shop. There was nothing of much interest except a catalog from a dealer in St. Paul. He pushed the catalog aside and lit another cigarette.

Miss Rowe worried him. If something happened to her, if her heart suddenly gave out, he would be morally responsible. Now he wondered if he wouldn't also be legally at risk for failing to bring her to the attention of some medical authority. He had no idea what the law said, if anything, about a situation like this. Would he be liable to a charge of negligence? Or even negligent homicide? What was he supposed to do?

It didn't seem fair. Miss Rowe was after all an adult, and as such she was responsible for herself. She was compulsive but not mentally incompetent. Should his loyalty be directed to her as a personal friend, accepting her as she was, or to her health and well-being? The two should not be mutually exclusive, though in this case they seemed to be. Mr. Whitman thought that sooner or later he might have to discuss the matter with a physician—or a even lawyer. But he would mention no names, at least until he had received some guidance. It was now a matter that demanded clarification.

Later, when the sun had gone down but darkness had not yet settled in completely, Mr. Whitman tapped on Miss Rowe's door and entered her apartment. There were no lights on and it was hard to see, but he was aware of her stirring as the sheets rustled softly. Perhaps she had dozed off for a while.

"Turn on the lamp." Groggy, she struggled to hoist herself up against the pillows.

"Am I disturbing you?"

"No, not at all. Come in."

Mr. Whitman switched on the light and took his seat. Her eyes were somewhat puffier than usual, he thought, her complexion even more flushed than it had been that afternoon.

"Come closer," she said. He slid the wooden chair nearer to her bed, wedging himself between one refrigerator and the shelves of paper plates. "No, not there. Here. Sit next to me on the bed, please. I'm feeling kind of down."

Mr. Whitman perched himself cautiously on the edge of the mattresses. He was surprised that Miss Rowe didn't suffer blue moods more frequently. It wasn't right that a young woman in her early twenties should lead such a solitary, reclusive existence. And no matter how strongly she denied it, the constant eating had to take a psychological toll. Mr. Whitman wondered if her usual high spirits were finally beginning to weaken.

"You're so good to me." Miss Rowe took his hand, squeezed it, refused to let go. Her grip was warm and strangely inviting. "I wish I could thank you in some way."

"Oh, don't be silly," Mr. Whitman responded with a nervous smile. "The funny thing is, only a few minutes ago I was telling myself that I've really been quite negligent about you."

"That's not true. Far from it. You've been just the person I needed. Without you, I don't know if I could have...well, you have made all the difference, believe me."

"It's nice to hear that."

She squeezed his hand again. Odd, Mr. Whitman thought. It was almost as if she were comforting him.

"I must look awful," Miss Rowe went on. "I haven't looked in a mirror in ages. Do I...look awful?"

"No, of course not." She wasn't begging for a compliment, but Mr. Whitman naturally wanted to answer as positively as he could. "You do look tired, though, and as I've told you before, you need to make some changes in—"

"I *am* changing," she interrupted, looking away from him but also tightening her grip on his hand. "I *am* changing."

"Good. Well, good." Mr. Whitman didn't know what else to say because he didn't understand what she meant. He had a vague feeling that she was trying to edge him closer to something. "Can you tell me—would you like to tell me—what happened?"

"When?"

"In Boston."

"Oh." She looked at him again and smiled. "Does it make a difference? What if I told you that I killed someone, my family, for instance?"

"I wouldn't believe it," he scoffed. The idea was absurd.

"You see? It doesn't make any difference."

"But something did happen," he insisted. "You must tell me, Frances. It would be good for you to talk about it with a friend you can trust."

They rarely addressed each other by their first names, and Miss Rowe seemed touched. But she merely shrugged and gave him a bewildering smile.

"That's just it," she said quietly. "Nothing happened."

Mr. Whitman found that hard to believe, although there was nothing deceptive or evasive about her manner and tone of voice. On the contrary, they carried the weight of truth.

"I want to talk to someone about you," he told her finally. "I'm sorry if it upsets you, but I have to, and this time I mean to do it."

To his surprise, Miss Rowe didn't object. She nodded slowly as if to say she understood, and she even pulled his hand closer to her. "Not tonight, though," she said. "You won't do anything about it tonight."

"Well, no," he allowed. It was the weekend, after all, and he had no reason to think another day or two would hurt. "First thing Monday morning, though."

"That's all right."

It seemed too easy, and for a few moments Mr. Whitman wasn't sure that he'd actually said what he intended, or that Miss Rowe had fully grasped it. Not that it really mattered; he knew what he was going to do on Monday morning and already he felt a little better about things.

"Lawrence."

"Hmm?" He had to swallow to clear his throat. "Yes?"

"Would you lie down here next to me on the bed?"

Her voice was tiny and distant, painfully vulnerable.

"I just need you to be here with me and to hold me for a few minutes."

Mr. Whitman couldn't speak, but he felt an emotional surge that made his body tremble and his cheeks redden. He slipped off his loafers. She must be terribly lonely, he thought. She needs comfort, a little human warmth. He stretched out on the mattress and moved tentatively closer to her enormous bulk. Miss Rowe pulled him closer still, until the length of his body was pressed against hers. She handled him easily, almost like a toy doll, so that he had one arm across the expanse of her middle and his head resting on her breast. Then Miss Rowe seemed to sigh and settle, and they stayed that way for some time.

Mr. Whitman was glad that she was under the sheet and he was not. He was more or less paralyzed, caught in a state of diffuse but undeniable erotic tension. Maybe he needed this human warmth too, and the contact seemed all the more exciting because it was essentially chaste. He stopped thinking about it and let himself enjoy it like this, drifting along dreamily, half awake, until it eventually occurred to him that he had been lying in her embrace for quite a while.

The air was cooler now. The French doors still stood open, and it was dark outside. Miss Rowe's breathing was slightly congested but regular, and her arm slipped away from him when he stirred. She was asleep. He moved carefully, gathered up his shoes, turned off the lamp, and returned to his apartment.

He had another beer and smoked a cigarette. He couldn't sit in one place for more than a minute. His feelings were alarming, exciting, intense, and above all mysterious to him. Did he love her? Yes, but not as a lover—although he had to admit, there was a disturbing new physical element to it now. The feel of her body and her touch lingered on him like a tactile afterglow. He almost believed that if he looked in the bathroom mirror he would see it on his hand and cheek, a radiance, an aura.

Then a shocking thought came to him. She was *beautiful*. Miss Rowe—Frances. All six hundred-plus pounds of her. She was truly beautiful. And not in spite of her massive size, but because of it. The one thing about her that had frightened and even repelled him now struck him as nothing less than miraculous. Perhaps she did suffer from a dangerous compulsion, but wasn't it also a sign of her strength and courage, her character?

Mr. Whitman drank two more bottles of beer and didn't bother to count the cigarettes. His mind raced, uncovering pockets of illumination where there had been only uncertainty before. Yes, he did love her. In all ways. He would take care of her, more devotedly than ever, but without trying to change her. He would keep her alive, healthy, happy; there were ways. The discipline of love, a better diet.

Somehow it could be made to work.

And in some way, it seemed, he had to surrender to her for her to surrender to him.

Mr. Whitman glanced at the clock, but he didn't care that it was after eleven. He had to see her again, and tell her things. He had to be with her again—for the warmth and the great peace he had found in her embrace.

In the doorway of his apartment, he hesitated one last time. Was he making an idiot of himself, a pathetic middle-aged fool? Was he drunk, deluded, hysterical? He didn't care.

Mr. Whitman listened at her door and heard faint sounds of movement. He tapped, got no response, and then knocked a little louder. Still nothing—but those peculiar noises, muffled and unfamiliar. He turned the handle and went inside. The room was dark, but moonlight through the open French doors provided a bit of definition. His eyes began to adjust.

Miss Rowe was writhing on her makeshift bed like a person lost in an increasingly uncomfortable dream. She appeared to be asleep, but Mr. Whitman felt a shiver when he noticed that her eyes were half open, glassy, unseeing. She made sounds that were half-strangled in her throat. A fever, he thought. Convulsions? Something terrible was happening. He banged his knee against a refrigerator and crushed a carton of cheese crackers underfoot as he approached the bed, but Miss Rowe gave no indication that she recognized his presence. Her movements were becoming sharper and more violent by the minute, thrashing and jerking.

Mr. Whitman put his hand on her forehead and was startled to find that she was not feverish at all, but unnaturally cold. Her skin was slick with moisture, her hair smeared back on her skull. More than anything, he was frightened by how cold she felt—but there was something else. Her skin felt different. It was hard, layered, almost scaly.

"Frances?"

Then her head turned again and caught the meager light. Mr. Whitman saw that her eyes had changed. They were closed now, and swollen so tightly that it was all but impossible to make out the thin slits on either side of her nose—itself so broad and flat that it looked as if it had been pressed or squashed to her face. She continued to toss and squirm, but with her arms tight to her body and her legs rigidly straight together, as if she were bound in cord from her head to her feet.

The noises emanating from her grew in intensity, and as she struggled free of the sheet Mr. Whitman saw that her jowl-ringed flabby neck had altered. It melded smoothly into her shoulders, as if there were no real human neck there at all. And the skin, like that of her face, was so pale that it was almost a brilliant white, shiny as glass.

Mr. Whitman shook with fear, but he could hardly move. He managed to place a hand on her shoulder—the round slope where her shoulder had been—and again he was shocked at how cold she felt. He had to do something, but the idea was nothing more than a disembodied thought in his brain. Miss Rowe escaped the sheet. Naked, he realized dimly, she's naked. But her body had lost its features—breasts, hips, buttocks—and become a long, large, tubular thing. She was not Miss Rowe. She was something more or less than herself. Something—*larval*.

She struggled mightily on the bed, heaving and shrugging her entire body as if she were trying to escape from that place. Mr. Whitman clambered across the lower part of the bed as he realized she was trying to move herself away from him. It seemed that the most important thing was for her to remain where she was, and to get expert help. It was the only way she might overcome whatever terrible illness has seized her. But Miss Rowe would not remain still. She squirmed vigorously, rolling and flipping, advancing off the edge of the bed. She was so large—for an instant, Mr. Whitman was deeply frightened by the sheer, naked size of her as she reared up at him.

I love you, he thought hopelessly. He threw himself at her, arms spread wide, his legs pushing with all the strength he could muster. He hoped to embrace her and get through to her, to force her back onto the bed. Their bodies met and froze together for a moment, Mr. Whitman clinging to Miss Rowe.

"Frances," he gasped, dizzy with love and fear.

The moment lasted barely a second or two, but it seemed much longer to Mr. Whitman—it was his last. He thought that she recognized him in some way—his warmth, his physical presence, some part of his being. But then whatever forces held her drove Miss Rowe over him with irresistible power, and Mr. Whitman was bent back like a slender blade of grass as she surged and slid on her way. The appliances around the bed, the cartons of food and the shelves—now everything in the way was knocked easily aside like hollow stage props. Picking up speed, Miss Rowe moved into the night and was gone.

In the morning the delivery boy found the French doors wide open. There was a trail of sticky wetness across the back lawn, a wide unbroken ribbon that snaked through the dew on the grass to the unused garden plot. It looked like a tunnel had been dug there, and then had collapsed in on itself. A huge mound of soil had been turned up, and this dirt had the round, nodal appearance of digested earth.

Of Mr. Whitman, there was no trace.

BLANCA

When I told a few close friends that I was going to Blanca their reaction was about what I had expected. Why? they asked. There's nothing to see in Blanca. Nothing much to do, except disappear. Sly smiles. Watch out you don't disappear. Maybe that's why I chose it, I said with a smile of my own. It might be nice to disappear for a while.

For a travel writer who has been on the job ten years, as I have, it isn't so easy to escape. The good places have been done, the mediocre ones too. You name it and I've probably been there, evaluating the hotels, sampling the cuisine, checking out the facilities and amenities, chatting up the locals. It's a great job, but I was tired of the regular world. What I needed was a therapeutic getaway, to spend a couple of weeks in an obscure backwater doing nothing more than sipping cold beer on a terrace and reading a good book.

I knew people in the business who'd been to Blanca. It's boring, they told me. Miles and miles of rolling plains and rangeland. There was a dead volcano somewhere in Blanca, but it wasn't worth climbing. Yes, the towns were neat and the people were pleasant enough. There's never any difficulty getting a clean room and bed for the night in Blanca. But nothing happens, there's nothing to do. No monuments or ancient ruins. No lively carnival, no festivals or feasts. The nightlife is said to be fairly low-key, so if you're looking for that kind of action, which I wasn't, there are much better places to go. Blanca was cattle country, and the only good thing I ever heard about it was that the steaks were excellent.

Blanca is not a nation but a territory, overlapping several borders in that region of the world. The native Indians were crushed nearly two centuries ago. They still survive, a sullen minority now thoroughly domesticated by generations of servitude as cheap labor cowhands, meatpackers and household help. The European settlers tried to create Blanca as an independent state but numerous rebellions failed and it was eventually carved up by its larger neighbors. But Blanca is Blanca, they say, regardless of the boundaries that appear on maps.

Because Blanca has comparatively little to offer the visitor it is not on any of the main routes. I had to catch two flights, the second of which stopped at so many featureless outposts along the way that it seemed like days before I finally got to Oranien. With a population of nearly one hundred thousand it is easily the largest city in Blanca.

I checked into the Hotel des Vacances, which was within walking distance of the central district but just far enough away to escape the noise. My room was large and airy, and had a small balcony that overlooked two residential streets and a park. It was comfortable, and not at all like a modern luxury hotel. I slept for nearly eleven hours that first night, had steak and eggs for brunch and then took a lazy walk around the center of Oranien. The narrow side streets had a certain pioneer charm—the original hard clay tiles had never been paved over, and remained neatly in place. But the most remarkable feature of the city was its state of cleanliness. I began to look for a piece of litter, and couldn't find so much as one discarded cigarette butt. It reminded me of Switzerland, or Singapore.

On the top floor of a department store I caught a view of the southern part of the city, a vast stretch of stockyards, abattoirs and railroad tracks. All the beef in Blanca passed through Oranien on its way to the outside world. I'd come to a dusty, three-story cowtown, and it was the tidiest, best-scrubbed place I'd ever seen.

But then, I'd heard stories about the police in Blanca. They *were* the law, and if you had any sense at all you never challenged them. Littering ranked close to treason by their way of thinking, and while that might seem harsh to some I had no problem with it. I've seen immaculate places and I've seen squalor; on the whole, I prefer the former. Besides, it had nothing to do with me. I was on vacation, recovering from a personal mess, exorcising old demons (including a wife). The first few days I was in Oranien the only cops I saw were chubby little men in silly uniforms, directing traffic. They looked like stage extras in some Ruritanian operetta.

"Not them," Basma said quietly. "The ones you must worry about are the ones you can't see. The people in plain clothes. They are everywhere."

"Even here?" I asked, amused but intrigued.

"Yes, surely."

We were in the small but very pleasant beer garden behind the Hotel des Vacances. There were perhaps two dozen other people scattered about the umbrella-topped tables in the late afternoon sun. A few neighborhood regulars, the rest visitors and hotel guests like myself, passing through. Everyone looked fairly happy and relaxed.

My companion was both a foreigner and a local resident. Basma had taken it upon himself to join me at my table the day before, when I had just discovered the beer garden and was settling into *The Thirteenth Simenon Omnibus*. At first I resented the intrusion and tried to ignore the man, but he would not be denied. Finally I gave in, and closed my book.

We spent two hours or more, drinking and chatting, with Basma carrying most of the load. But he was easy company. A middle-aged Lebanese, he had reluctantly fled Beirut while he still had a cache of foreign currency. The city had become unbearable, impossible, and he believed he was a target of both the Christians ("Because I am a Muslim") and the Shiites ("Because they think all international businessmen are working for the C.I.A."). Besides, business had pretty much dried up. Basma had been in Oranien for the best part of three years, doing the odd bit of trade and otherwise depleting his capital. He was eager to move on to more fertile ground, but had not yet decided where that might be. By then I was tired and tipsy, and went to bed early. But we agreed to meet again the next day and have dinner in town, which is how we came to be discussing the police.

"Who, for instance?" I asked.

"Let's not be looking around and staring," Basma said softly. "But that couple at the table by the wall on your right. I've seen them many times and wondered about them."

A handsome man and a beautiful woman, both in their late twenties. He wore a linen suit, a white shirt, and no tie. He had dark hair and a strong, unmarked face. She was dressed in a smart, obviously foreign outfit—skirt, matching jacket and a stylish blouse. I imagined her to be the daughter of a local bigshot, she had that air of privilege and hauteur. They made me feel old, or perhaps just envious of their youth and good looks. "I don't care," I said. "I'm just passing through. All I want to do is relax for a couple of weeks."

"Of course." Basma smiled.

So that night he gave me the grand tour of Oranien, such as it is. After the mandatory steak dinner we strolled through the main shopping arcade, which was full of the latest European fashions and Asian electronic equipment, all carrying steep price tags. We took in a couple of bars, briefly surveyed a dance hall that doubled as an economy class dating service and then stopped for a while at a neon-riddled disco called Marlene's where the crowd was somewhat interesting. There the sons and daughters of local wealth came to dance, flirt, play their social games and get blitzed. Basma called them the second-raters, because the brightest of their generation and class were away in America or England, at the best private schools and universities.

By the time we'd squandered some money at a posh gaming club and had a disturbing glimpse of a very discreet place where you could do whatever you wanted with girls (or boys) as young as thirteen, I'd seen enough for one night. Oranien's dull and orderly exterior masked the usual wanton tendencies. It didn't bother me, but it didn't interest me.

Back in my room, I poured one last nightcap from my bottle of duty-free single malt and lit a cigarette. I'd had a lot to drink, but it had been spaced out over many hours, with a meal thrown in somewhere along the line. I wasn't drunk, just tired, reasonably buzzed. I know this for sure, because whenever I have gotten drunk in the past I've never dreamed, or at least I've never remembered it. That night I did have a dream, and it was one I wouldn't forget.

I was sleeping in my bed, there in the Hotel des Vacances. It was the middle of the night. Suddenly I was awakened by a loud clattering noise. I jumped out of bed in a fog. I was at the window, looking out on what seemed to be a historical costume pageant. It confused me, and I couldn't move. The street below, brightly lit by a three-quarters moon, was full of soldiers on horseback. They carried torches, or waved swords. The horses continued to make a dreadful racket, stamping their feet on the clay tiles. Every house in sight remained dark, but the soldiers went to several different doors, roused the inhabitants and seized eight or ten people altogether. They were thrown into horse-drawn carts, already crowded with prisoners. The night was full of terrible sounds—the soldiers shouting, men arguing or pleading in vain, their women and children wailing, a ghastly pandemonium. It seemed they had finished and were about to move on, when one of the soldiers, obviously an officer, turned and looked up directly at me. Now I was standing out on the little balcony, gripping the wrought iron tightly. The officer spoke to one of his comrades, who also looked in my direction. Then the officer raised his sword, pointing to me. I knew his face—but I had no idea who he was. A small group of soldiers, apparently responding to instructions, hurried across the street toward the hotel. Still, I couldn't move. A terrible fear came over me as I realized they would take me away with the others. The rest is sensation, the twisting, falling, hideous sweetness we all dream more often than we would like before it actually happens—our moment of dying.

I slept late—it was becoming a welcome habit—and woke up feeling remarkably cheerful and energetic. I remembered the dream, I thought about it all through my shower, over brunch and during my walk to the newsstand for the most recent *Herald Tribune*. I sat outdoors at a quiet cafe, had two cups of gritty coffee, smoked cigarettes and read the sports scores from a few days ago in my distant homeland.

It felt great to be alive. Any sense of menace or fear had dissolved out of the dream. It had already become a kind of mental curio that I carried around with me. Maybe I was happy simply because I knew I could never have had that nightmare in New York. What it seemed to say to me in the light of day was: *Now you know you're in Blanca.*

"It's local history," Basma agreed when we met in the beer garden later that afternoon and I told him about the dream. "You must have known about it before you came here."

"Sure. Well, vaguely." I lit a cigarette while an Indian waitress delivered our second round of beers. "I've heard the jokes about people being taken away in the dead of night, never to be seen again."

"Yes, but they are not jokes. What you dreamed is exactly how it used to happen—and by the way, it still does, from time to time."

"Really?"

"Of course."

"Well, that's politics, which never interested me. I'd just as soon get back to dreaming about sex."

Basma smiled broadly. "No need just to dream about it."

"Dreaming will do for now."

Basma shrugged sadly. I knew I was doing a pretty poor job of living up to his mental image of American tourists as people hell-bent on having an extravagantly good time. We had a light dinner together and then I disappointed him further by deciding to make an early evening of it. I was still a bit tired from our night out on the town, and I wanted nothing more than to read in bed for a while and then get about twelve hours of sleep. I had it in mind to rent a car the next day and see a bit of the nearby countryside, however flat and dull it might prove to be.

Simenon worked his usual magic. I was soon transported to rainy Paris (even in the sweltering heat of August, Simenon's Paris seems rainy), where Inspector Maigret had another nasty murder to unravel. It was bliss, but unfortunately I drifted off to sleep sooner than I expected. I woke up a little after four in the morning, still dressed, the paperback in my hand. I dropped the book to the floor and crawled under the covers. But it was no good. Finally I sat up and groaned, realizing that I would not be able to get back to sleep. For a while I simply stayed there, lying still.

I got out of bed when I noticed a strange flickering of light reflected on the half-open window. It came from the street below, a lamp-post or car headlights most likely. But when I stepped onto the balcony and looked down, I was paralyzed by what I saw. They were all there again. The horses, the carts, the soldiers with their swords and torches, the pitiful souls being dragged from their homes, the mothers and wives, the children. It was a repeat perfor-mance of the grim nightmare I'd had only twenty four hours ago, but this time I was wide awake. I forced myself to be sure: I took note of the cold, harsh wrought iron beneath my bare feet, I sucked in huge breaths of chilly night air, and I looked over my shoulder into the hotel room to reassure myself in some way. But when I turned back to the street below they were still there, the scene con-tinued to play itself out. I was awake, and it was happening.

I realized there were certain differences. Noise—there was none at all. The horses stamped, the soldiers shouted, the men argued and their families sobbed, but I heard none of this, I could only see it taking place. Silence ruled the night. And then there was the officer, the one in charge who had pointed his sword at me in the dream. I spotted him again and he still looked familiar to me, but I didn't know who he was. This time he never once glanced in my direction. He and his troops went about their business as if I didn't exist, though they could hardly fail to notice me standing there on the second floor balcony, the room lit up behind me. The fact that they didn't may account for the other difference, the lack of fear in me. The scene had a terrible fascination, I was transfixed by it, but at the same time I felt detached from it, uninvolved. I didn't know what to make of it. I felt puzzled rather than threatened.

Finally I did something sensible. I looked up the street, away from the scene, and sure enough, I saw the usual line of parked cars that I knew belonged there. It was a comforting sight. But then, when I turned back, the dream drama was still just visible. The soldiers and the carts had formed a wavy line and were marching away from me toward the main road, a hundred yards or so in the distance. I watched them until they reached the intersection with that broad avenue, at which point my eyes could make out nothing more than the bobbing, meandering flow of torch flames.

It took another few minutes for me to realize that what I was looking at was a stream of headlights. Then I became aware of the sound of that traffic; the silence was broken. The early shift, I told myself. Hundreds of workers on their way to the abattoirs, stockyards and packing plants on the south side of the city. The newsagents, short order cooks and bus drivers. All the people who open up the city before dawn every morning. Any city. I stepped back into the room, sat on my bed and lit a cigarette, wondering how yesterday's nightmare could turn into today's hallucination.

"Do you take drugs?" Basma asked me casually.

We were walking through the park, toward a bar I'd never been to in my life. It was about five that afternoon, and I'd blurted out the story of the hallucination—which was what I still took it to be—as soon as we met for our daily drink and chat. I laughed.

"No, it's been a few years since I did any drugs, and even then it wasn't much."

"You are quite certain that you were fully awake when you saw this—whatever it was?"

"Yes."

"And you were awake *before* you saw it?"

"Definitely. I was lying there, feeling sorry for myself for waking up so early. I saw the orange light flickering on the window—it's a glass door, actually, to the balcony."

"Yes, yes," Basma said impatiently.

"Well, like I told you, I sat up and went to the window, I stepped out onto the balcony, and there it was."

"I see."

Basma didn't speak again until we reached the bar, a workers' grog shop that offered only the locally brewed beer, Bolero. Once we got our drinks and I had lit a cigarette, Basma returned to the subject.

"So you think it was hallucination."

"Yes, of course," I said. "What else would it be?"

"Ghosts." Basma smiled faintly, not as if he were joking. "Perhaps you saw the ghosts of history."

"Oh, I doubt that very much."

"Why? It makes perfect sense. What is more, I think you may have been awake the first time you saw them, two nights ago. You only thought it was a dream, you were less certain because it was the first time and you had been drinking more—yes?"

"Yes, I had been drinking more, but I still think that I was dreaming. It ended in a panic and I was lost in sleep in an instant. No sensation of getting back into bed or thinking about it." I stubbed out my cigarette and lit another. I didn't like disappointing Basma again, he seemed as eager as a young child to believe in ghosts. "Besides, even if I were awake, that doesn't mean it was not a hallucination."

"The same hallucination, two nights in a row." Basma gave this some thought. "You have a medical history of this?"

"No, not at all," I had to admit.

"Then why do you think it should suddenly start happening to you now?"

I shrugged. "Maybe the stories I'd heard about Blanca. The emotional distress from the break-up of my marriage. Throw in the mild despair I sometimes feel at the approach of my fortieth birthday." I finished the beer and I realized how self-pitying I sounded, and it annoyed me very much. "To tell you the truth, I really have no idea at all why this kind of thing should suddenly be happening to me."

"Hallucination?" Basma asked again, quietly.

"That makes a lot more sense than an army of ghosts."

"As long as it makes sense to you."

It didn't, in fact, but I was fed up talking about it, fed up even thinking about it, so I fetched two more Bolero beers and then changed the subject. I told Basma about my day trip. I'd hired an Opel Rekord that morning and driven past miles and miles of cattle ranches, through small but impeccable villages, in a wide looping route north of Oranien. Altogether, I was out of the city for about five hours, and I'd seen quite enough of the countryside. There was nothing wrong with it—it was agreeably unspoiled rangeland—but it was bland, featureless, lacking in charm or interest. Just as I'd been told.

"Yes," Basma nodded. "I have heard that once you leave the city it's much the same in every direction for hundreds of miles. Although I've never seen for myself."

"You've never left Oranien, since you got here?"

"Why should I? There's nothing to see or do." His smile broadened into a grin. "Is there?"

"Well, no."

"Do you still have the car?"

"Yes, until tomorrow noon," I told him. "It's parked back near the hotel."

"Good. If you don't mind driving, I would like to show you something. Not exactly a tourist attraction, but I think you'll find it worthwhile."

He wouldn't tell me where we were going, but there was still plenty of daylight left when Basma and I drove away a few minutes later. I followed his directions and it was soon obvious that we were heading toward the south end of the city.

"The stockyards?" I guessed.

"Ah, you've seen them."

"Only from a distance." I told Basma about the view from the department store.

"Now you will see it all close up."

I was mildly curious. We passed through the commercial district, and then a residential area not unlike the one in which I was staying. The houses and squat apartment buildings became shabbier and more dilapidated the farther we went from the center of the city. The middle class in-town neighborhoods gave way to the worker-Indian tenements on the outskirts. I wanted to drive slowly so that I could see as much as possible, and in fact I had to because there were so many people out on the streets. Kids playing games and ignoring the traffic, grown-ups talking in small groups (men to men, women to women, mostly), and the old folks sitting stoically wherever they could find a quiet spot. Most of the local social life, including the cooking and eating of food, seemed to take place outdoors.

Almost before I realized it, we were there. The industry and the workers' lodgings had sprung up together over the years, without benefit of design or long-term planning. There were row houses right up to the open doors of an abattoir, apartment buildings wedged between a canning factory and a processing plant, and a vast maze of corrals holding thousands of cattle bumping against dozens of tiny back yards. After we had cruised around for a while I began to understand that these people lived in their workplaces—they would go home when their shift was finished, but home was hardly any different. The interminable stupid bawling of the cattle, the mingled stench of blood, raw meat and cowshit, the constant rattling of trains, the drumming vibrations of the factories—everything here, everything you saw or heard or felt or smelled was about decay and death. You could taste it in the air and feel it as a slickness that settled on your skin.

We reached the worst of it, a mean stretch where finally the people themselves seemed only marginally alive. They stood or sat about in front of their shacks, looking dazed. The streets, no longer paved, had become increasingly difficult to navigate. Ditches ran along both sides, and they ran red with blood from the slaughterhouses. In the absence of traffic and other human noises, the steady shriek of power saws carving animal flesh was piercingly clear. At every pile of garbage vicious cats and scarred dogs competed with huge brown roaches and gangs of rats for whatever was going. It was getting dark fast.

"I hope you know the way back."

"Yes, of course."

Basma gave me a series of directions and it wasn't too long before we were on a better road. Neither of us had spoken much in the course of our slumming tour. As soon as I caught a glimpse of the lights in the center of the city my stomach began to relax a little. I had been to some of the worst refugee camps in the world, but never felt so tense. Refugee camps are at least meant to be temporary, and there was always the hope, however slim, of eventual movement. The people I had just seen were never going anywhere.

"I suppose I've had Blanca beef many times, in my travels," I said, just to say something.

"I'm sure you have," Basma agreed promptly. "They ship it out in every form. Brains, tongue, heart, kidneys, liver, as well as all the usual cuts, prime rib, steaks and so on, all the way down to hot dogs and Vienna sausages. If it isn't tinned or wrapped in plastic, it's frozen."

We began to joke about becoming vegetarians, describing the best salads we could remember having, and we kept at it until we were comfortably settled with drinks in Number One, which was supposedly the better of Oranien's two topless joints. It was expensive but otherwise all right. That kind of bar, where the music was loud and the women occasionally distracting, was just what Basma and I needed, since our excursion into the south end had left us in no mood for serious conversation. We drank until the place closed, by which time we were both unfit to drive, so we left the rental car parked where it was and took a taxi.

I wasn't surprised when Basma got out of the cab with me at the hotel. I didn't know exactly where he lived but I assumed it was in the neighborhood because we'd met in the beer garden and we always said goodnight outside the hotel.

"Would you like to have a nightcap in my room?" he asked me as the taxi pulled away.

"No, thanks very much. I couldn't take another drink."

"Are you sure? I have a bottle of Teachers, pretty good stuff, and I live right there, across the street." Basma pointed vaguely to the first or second building on the opposite corner. "Come on, one more."

"No, really, thanks. I'm going to fall down and pass out, and I'd rather do that in my bed than on your floor."

Basma shrugged. "Okay. See you tomorrow."

"Sure. Good night." I turned away, but then stopped and looked back at him. "Hey, you know what? Your building is one of the ones those ghost soldiers raided."

"Don't be telling me such things," he said from the middle of the street. "I don't want to know that."

"Why? It's just ghosts and history. Right?"

"Don't be saying that."

Basma wagged a finger at me and kept going. I somehow made it upstairs, locked my door and even managed to get my clothes off before spinning dizzily into sleep. It was nearly noon when I opened my eyes again. The first thing that came to me was how nice it felt not to have had another hallucination, nightmare or ghostly apparition to brood about. I'd been truly out of it and I'd slept straight through, unbothered.

On the negative side, however, I felt terrible the moment I stood up. I took a long shower, which made me feel cleaner but did nothing for my head, and I was going to get some food when I remembered the rental car. I didn't want to pay another day's charges but it was already late. When I got to the car I found a parking ticket under the wiper blade. I shoved it in my pocket, wondering if I could safely tear it up or if the vaunted Oranien police would catch up with me before I flew out next week. The car rental agency wanted me to pay for the second full day, naturally, since I was well over an hour past the deadline when I finally got there. I had no luck arguing until I pulled out my *Vogue* credentials, at which point the manager became obsequious and sympathetic. No problem: no extra charges.

Then I got some much-needed food into my stomach. I went back to my hotel room, tore up the parking ticket and fell asleep again on the bed while trying to read the *Herald Tribune*. It was after four when I dragged myself down to the beer garden. I held off on the alcohol, cautiously sipping a flat mineral water while I waited for Basma. An hour later, I began to wonder if I'd made a mistake. We *had* agreed to meet in the usual place at the usual time, hadn't we? But maybe he had things to attend to elsewhere, and I'd misunderstood him in the boozy fog last night. I wasn't disappointed or annoyed, because in truth I really wanted a break from Basma's company, for one evening anyway. I stayed a little longer, out of courtesy, and then returned to my room. He'd know where to find me if he turned up later. But he didn't, and I had a very welcome early night.

The next day I felt great, and I did what I'd really wanted to do all along. I sat in the shade in the beer garden, reading Simenon. I had breakfast there, followed later by more coffee, then lunch, and, in the middle of the afternoon, lemonade and a plate of watermelon chunks. By five o'clock I'd knocked off both Maigret novels in the volume, and I was ready to allow myself a glass of cold Bolero beer. It was a very light pale lager, but I was beginning to develop a taste for it.

Where was Basma? I had a sudden guilty flashback to our drunken parting. I'd teased him about the ghost soldiers, as he thought of them, and now it occurred to me that I might have annoyed him. Perhaps that was why he was staying away. What you do when you're drunk always seems much worse when you reconstruct it later. I was tired of sitting there, but once again I stayed on for another hour or so, until it was obvious that my Lebanese friend was not going to put in an appearance.

I went looking for him a little while later. I started with the corner building diagonally opposite the hotel. Inside the unlocked screen door was a small entry foyer with a tile floor and a rickety wooden table. The inner door was locked, so I rang the bell, and kept ringing it for nearly five minutes before a heavyset, middle-aged woman answered.

"I'm looking for Mr. Basma," I told her.

"He go."

"When do you expect him back?" She shrugged, and shook her head at this. "Well, can I leave a message for him?" I took out a pen and a piece of paper I'd brought for that purpose. But the woman continued to shake her head.

"He go," she repeated emphatically.

"When will he be back?"

"Men come. He go with men."

Simple enough, and apparently the end of the story as far as she was concerned. I wasn't ready to give up, however.

"What about his things?"

"What."

"Things. Clothes, belongings." Most people in Blanca can speak English because the local dialect is one of those clotted, homegrown curiosities of limited use, like Afrikaans. But this creature's English was marginal at best. "His possessions, his personal—his *things*, damnit."

"Gone."

"When did he go?"

"Yesterday."

"Can I see his room?"

"Room?"

"Yes. Basma's room. Please."

"Room—yes, yes. Come."

It took a while to get there, because the woman moved only with difficulty. She showed me into the front room on the first floor. It was a dreary little place with a couch, a couple of chairs, a table, a hideous wardrobe and a single bed. There was a small bathroom and, behind a plastic curtain, an even smaller galley kitchen. The few items of furniture were old and worn, the walls faded and unadorned, the carpeting thin as newspaper. I went to the window and looked out at the park and the quiet streets. I looked at the balcony and window of my room in the hotel across the way.

"Nice view," the woman said.

I nodded absently. There was no doubt in my mind that Basma was gone for good. The room had been completely stripped of all personal items. What was there was what you got when you rented a very modest furnished room.

"Three hundred crown," the woman said.

"What?"

"Three hundred crown. One month." She waved her hand in a gesture commending the room to me. "One hundred U.S. dollar."

"No." I hurried away.

That night I slept by the balcony window in my room. I used the big armchair, and stretched my legs out on the coffee table. It was not a comfortable arrangement, but it wasn't unbearable, and I wanted to be there. It seemed important not to miss the apparition, if it should occur again.

I tried to read for a while but I could no longer keep my mind on the words. Basma wouldn't have left so suddenly without saying goodbye, I told myself. From what the woman had said in her skeletal English, he had been taken—and that surely meant taken against his will. But by whom, and why? It seemed highly unlikely that his Lebanese enemies would come such a distance to exact revenge, and he'd been so insistent in cautioning me about the Blanca police that I couldn't imagine he'd ever set a foot wrong here. Certainly not in the realm of politics. But Basma was an entrepreneur, so it was not impossible that he'd gotten involved in some shady deal that had landed him in trouble with the authorities.

Could I help him in any way? He had been good company, a friend. He hadn't tried to con me. He'd been a useful guide to the city. It seemed wrong just to shrug it off mentally and forget about him. But I couldn't think of anything to do, other than ask the local police about him—and I was reluctant to do that.

It was dawn when I awoke to the sound of car doors slamming. The first thing I saw was a silver Mercedes with black-tinted windows, parked at the corner across from my hotel. The car's yellow hazard lights were flashing. Four men wearing sunglasses and linen suits entered Basma's building. While they were inside a van with the similarly darkened windows pulled up behind the Mercedes and waited. A moment later the four men reappeared, with a fifth man in their custody—he wasn't even handcuffed, but it was obvious he was their prisoner. I stood up, swung the window open and stepped out onto the balcony.

"Basma."

I had spoken to myself, barely whispering the man's name in stunned disbelief. But the five of them stopped immediately and looked up at me. Basma looked terrified. I thought I recognized one of the other men. I was so shocked and frightened, however, that I took a step back involuntarily and stumbled, and I had to grab the window frame to catch my balance. Then the scene below was finished, gone as if it had never happened, and I was looking down at an empty street corner.

I sat on the bed and lit a cigarette. My hands shook, my head clamored. The smoke was like ground glass in my throat but I sucked it in deeply, as if trying to make a point with my own pain. I'd been so many miles, seen so much of the world, the best and the worst and the endless in between, but now for the first time in my life I felt lost.

Then I became angry with myself. My feelings didn't matter in this situation. Basma was the one in trouble, and I had to try to help, or at least find out what was happening to him. For all I knew, I was the only friend he had in Blanca. I didn't want to—it scared the shit out of me to think about it—but I had to do something. And now I knew where to start.

They came into the beer garden just after four o'clock that afternoon, as they had several times during the past week. The woman was as beautiful as ever, cool and formidable. The kind of woman you would fear falling in love with, but love to watch. It was her man, however, who interested me. The man in the linen suit. Basma had warned me about them. I was pretty sure the man was the officer on horseback I had seen twice. I *knew* he was one of the men I had seen take Basma away.

Dreams, nightmares, hallucinations, ghosts. Take your pick. But maybe the simplest, truest explanation was that I was in the middle of a breakdown, caused by the collapse of my marriage and my abrupt flight to this miserable place. It made sense, and I hesitated, clinging to my own weakness. But I was there, Basma was gone, and that man in the linen suit was very real. I got up at last and went to their table.

"Excuse me," I said. "I'm sorry to intrude, but I wonder if I could speak to you for a moment."

"Yes, why not. Please."

He gestured for me to take a seat. They almost looked as if they had been waiting all along for me to approach them—which made me feel even more uncomfortable.

"I've seen you around here almost every day since I arrived—I'm on vacation—and the thing is, I can't find a friend of mine. He seems to have disappeared. His name is Basma. He's a Lebanese businessman. He had a small flat in the corner building across the street. Do you know him?"

"I don't think so."

"Can you suggest how I might find out about him?"

"Go to the police."

They both seemed to regard me with an impossible mixture of curiosity and disinterest. I was getting nowhere.

"He thought maybe you were a policeman."

At last, something. The barest flicker of an eyebrow, then the man smiled, as if at some silly misunderstanding. The woman was keenly attentive now, and it was hard for me not to return the all-consuming look in her eyes.

"I do work in the government," the man told me. "I am not a policeman. But you are our guest here. Let me ask some people I know about your friend."

"Thank you."

"Of course, I cannot promise you anything."

"I understand."

"Are you staying here?"

"Yes." I gave him my name and room number, and told him I would be staying five more days. "Thank you for your help. I'm sorry to trouble you."

"No trouble."

Later, I felt disgusted at how deferential I'd been, all but grovelling for a scrap of information. The man knew Basma, knew the whole story far better than I did; he was a primary player. *Thank you for your help.* But how else could I have handled it? It would have been crazy to confront the man and accuse him of arresting Basma. It would have been absurd to tell him that history replays itself every morning on that street corner, and that I'd seen what he and his colleagues had done.

So the possibilities for action on my part were extremely limited. I'd done what I could. I began to think that I should let it go, that it was just one more thing in my life to put behind me. Basma was rotting in some filthy prison cell, if he wasn't already a ghost. In any event, nothing I could do would make the least difference. I might try to write about Basma and Blanca, something political with teeth in it—but not here, not until I was safely back in New York. I'd never written anything like that before.

I slept well that night and did very little the next day. I took a couple of short walks, but mostly hung around the hotel, reading and relaxing. The government man and his beautiful woman did not put in an appearance. I enjoyed another peaceful night, no dreams or ghosts. It was pleasant to idle away afternoons in the beer garden, sipping iced tea and nibbling slivers of chilled melon. I was actually glad that the man in the linen suit failed to show up for the second day in a row.

I did think about Basma now and then. I missed his company, but in my line of work I meet so many people, all over the world. Already he was slipping away from me. I had calmed down enough to realize I would never write that article. I wasn't equipped to do it properly. Tourism was my beat, not politics or ghosts or mysterious disappearances. To hell with Blanca. Maybe it was a surrender of sorts, but by admitting these things to myself I felt I was on the way to a kind of mental recovery, and that had been the whole purpose of the trip in the first place.

That evening I intended to find some new restaurant and have anything but steak for dinner. Then scout a few bars. I was in the mood for serious female contact at last. It was a little past seven when I stepped out of the hotel. At that instant the silver Mercedes braked sharply to a halt and the man in the linen suit jumped out. He came right at me. I was determined not to let this nasty little hood intimidate me anymore.

"Do you want to see your friend?"

"Yes, of course. Where is he?"

"I will take you." He gestured toward the open car door. "Please. It is still light."

I was aware that the other people on the street all stood motionless, watching. Calmly, at my own pace, I walked to the car and sat down inside. I was in the back seat, between the man I knew and another fellow, who regarded me warily. I wasn't too surprised to see the beautiful young woman in the front seat, along with the driver. She glanced at me once, then looked away. We raced through the center of the city. We were heading south, I knew that much. I asked a few questions but the only answers I got were vague and unsatisfactory.

The driver never slowed down. If anything, he pushed the car a little faster when we reached the crowded working class district. People and animals sometimes had to jump out of the way at the last second to save themselves. I could sense the others in the car trying not to smile. We passed the factories, the slaughterhouses, the tenements, the stockyards, the grisly processing, canning and freezing plants. We ripped through the sprawling shantytown and continued beyond the point where Basma and I had ended our exploration. Finally we were on a dirt road, crossing a vast scrubby wasteland. We had gone a couple of miles when I saw that we were approaching a cluster of vehicles parked with their headlights on, pointing in the same direction. They walked me to the edge of a long ditch, about eight feet deep. It was dusk, not yet too dark to see, but spotlights had been hooked up to a generator to illuminate the scene. It was all so bright it hurt my eyes. Perhaps a dozen other men stood about, smoking, talking quietly, taking notes and photographs. When my eyes adjusted, I forced myself to look carefully.

There were a lot of bodies in the ditch, I would estimate at least twenty. All the same: hands tied behind the back, the back of the head partially blown away, bloating features. I noticed the swarming insects, the ferocious smell. I stood there for a while, staring, but so help me I could not put together a single thought. A couple of men wearing goggles and masks were getting ready to spray the ditch with some chemical.

"Can you identify that person?" the man in the linen suit asked me, pointing to a particular corpse. "There."

"Yes, that's him." In spite of the puffed face, parts of which had already been nibbled at by animals, I had no difficulty picking out my late friend. "That's Basma."

"I am so sorry," he said quite casually. "It is a terrible way to die."

As if there are any good ones.

"Why did this happen to him?" I asked. "He was a harmless little man, a foreign guest in this country. Why should they," I almost said *you* but managed to avoid it, "do this to him?"

"Come here, please."

He led me back to the car, where the young woman waited. She looked smart as ever, this time in a tropical pants suit with a white blouse open three buttons deep. The man nodded to her. She reached into a leather briefcase I hadn't noticed and handed him something. He held it up for me to see. My eyes lingered on hers for a moment, but her look gave nothing away.

"Did you do this?"

I could feel the blood vacating my cheeks, then rushing back as I tried to muster a sense of embarrassed contempt. He had a large rectangle of cardboard, on which were pasted all the torn pieces of my parking ticket.

"Yes, we do that all the time back in New York. I hope it's not a felony here. I'm willing to pay the fine, whatever it is, and I'll pay it now, if you like."

"Did you refuse to pay a late fee to Bolero Rent-a-Car, and did you threaten to write negative comments about that agency in your travel articles in foreign publications?"

I took a deep breath, exhaled slowly. "I was about an hour late, but I explained the situation to them and they seemed to be satisfied. If they're not, I'd be glad to pay the fee."

"May I have your passport."

I gave it to him. "Why?"

"You can get in the car now. An officer will drive you back to your hotel. Thank you for your help."

"I need my passport," I told him. "I'm flying home in three days. Sunday afternoon."

"I know," he replied. "We will contact you."

I tried to talk to the driver on the journey back into town, but he ignored me. I was furious, but frightened as well. The whole thing was a grotesque charade. They didn't need me to identify Basma but they made me go through with it, knowing that I wouldn't have the courage to accuse them of his murder. Take a good look in that ditch, they were saying to me, this is the kind of thing we can do. They were toying with me, because it's their nature to toy with people.

What, if anything, could Basma have done to bring about his own destruction at the hands of these people? Perhaps he'd been involved in some way with a radical faction in Lebanon. Did the authorities here think they were eliminating a Muslim terrorist? Was he a crook or a smuggler, a charming criminal who had escaped from Beirut only to run out of luck in Blanca? To me he seemed a pleasant, fairly idle fellow with an agreeable manner and a taste for godless liquor. But, in fairness, I hardly knew him. We had a few dinners together, a lot of drinks, that was all. It was a brief acquaintance. Our backgrounds and our circumstances were totally different. They couldn't do *that* to me.

Common sense told me I had nothing to fear. The parking ticket and the rental agency were trivial matters that could be settled with a little cash. I was an American, a travel writer for a major international magazine. They might push me around, but they wouldn't hurt me.

All the same, I decided to take certain precautions. The next morning I tried to contact the nearest American consulate, which was some four hundred miles away. At first the operator of the hotel switchboard told me that all long distance lines out of Oranien were engaged. After an hour of fruitless attempts she said she had learned that they were "down," and that she had no idea how long it would be before they were working again. I went to the main post office and tried again—same result.

I tried to rent another car—at a different agency. I'm not sure what I intended to do with it—drive away, I suppose, right out of the country—but I was refused one because I could not produce my passport.

I didn't bother with lunch. I drank a couple of beers and smoked a lot of cigarettes. I wandered around until I found the railroad station. I bought a ticket on the next departing train, although I wasn't even sure where it was going. Then a uniformed policeman confiscated the ticket, smiling.

"We don't want you to disappear on us, sir."

Of course not. They got the parking ticket from the waste basket in my room. They had talked with the rental agency about me. They'd been watching and following me all the time. It was pointless to wonder why. I went back to the hotel and, as calmly as possible, I wrote a letter to my lawyer in New York, telling him where I was, that I had a problem with the authorities, and that if he hadn't heard from me—my voice on the telephone—by the time he got the letter he was to do whatever it took to get me out of Blanca—press conferences, congressmen, the State Department, the works. I wrote more or less the same thing to my editor. I used hotel stationery and did not write my name on the envelopes. The hotel was unsafe and so were the streets, but I thought my chances were a little better outdoors. I went for a walk and slipped the letters into the mailbox on the corner as inconspicuously as possible. I crossed into the park and sat on a bench for a while, smoking. Nothing happened. I got back to my room—just in time to glance out the window and see a silver Mercedes pull away from the mailbox.

This is my last night in Blanca. Tomorrow I am supposed to be on the noon flight out of here. I still have that ticket. I still do not have my passport. For two days and two nights I've waited. Nothing happens. I am waiting. There's nowhere to go, nothing to do, except smoke and drink and wait.

I think of them all the time, the handsome man in the linen suit and the beautiful young woman. Mostly I think of her, with her blouse open three buttons deep. Her breasts are not large because I saw no cleavage, but I know they are perfect. Her skin finely tanned with the faintest trace of sun-bleached down. I would like to have her, to lick her, but she is impossible to touch. You can only look at a woman like that, and wonder what it would be like to fuck death.

Tonight when I ask at the desk for a wake up call they smile and say yes, of course, and smile some more. No one writes it down. The

*porter says I don't look well. Would I like dinner in my room? Some
company? Clean, he adds encouragingly.*

*It'll be over long before noon. Around four or five in the morning
the silver Mercedes will arrive, the van right behind. The men in the
van are there to strip the room of my possessions after I'm gone. Some
morning in the future you can look out one of these windows and
see how it happened, too late for me—and for you.*

*I hope I'm not alone, I hope there are others. Many will be arguing,
begging, screaming, but some will walk out unaided, with quiet dig-
nity. If I have to, that's what I want to do.*

Not that it matters.

*I crush out a cigarette. I open another bottle of beer, reach for
another cigarette. I don't have to go to the window to see what is happening outside. There is light in the sky.*

Look for me.

The Banshee

He didn't mean to hit her—hard. But she went down like a toy made out of flimsy sticks, and she began crying in a loud and piercing screech. Even then she didn't stop talking. Bubbles of compressed words burst forth intermittently between heaving gasps of breath. Her features were distorted with anger and pain, her face corkscrewing tightly into itself.

"For the love of Jesus," Dermot muttered, turning away in a state of barely controlled rage. This is how murder happens. He finished the whiskey in his glass, poured a little more. She was still lying on the chipped lino, making noise. "I'm warning you, stop that racket."

"You hurt me."

"It was just a shove. You didn't have to fall down, you did that on purpose. Besides, if you don't shut up my flatmates will throw me out of here. And if that happens, I swear I'll fuckin' well kill you."

"They're not here," she pointed out infuriatingly.

"It's the neighbors," Dermot told her. "They'll complain to the lads again, and I'll be in trouble. They're fed up with this kind of carry-on. You can't keep doing this to me."

The noise diminished slightly. That was so typical of her, and so annoying. If he was reasonable, if he was willing to talk to her about it, then she quieted down. But there was nothing to talk about anymore. There never had been. So much trouble, and he'd never even been inside her drawers.

"Come on, now."

"No." Resentful. She made a disgustingly liquid sniffling sound. "I don't want to go yet."

"I want you out of here. Now."

"Dermot, please."

"I told you," he said. "It's pointless."

"*Dermot...*"

She began to cry again. He never should have let her in his door. Not the first time, not ever. But what could he do? Call the police? That'd be funny. And if he had to argue with her it seemed better to do it in the relative privacy of his room rather than out in the hallway. You couldn't ignore her. She would put her finger on the bell and hold it until you answered. She would pound the door with her other fist at the same time.

It wasn't his fault. True, he had smiled at her and chatted freely that first night she appeared at Dolan's, but that was all part of the job. True, when she began coming around almost every night he could see that she was developing a special interest in him, and he did nothing to discourage it, but they saw each other only at the bar and they never actually did anything together, so it all seemed quite harmless. You liked it when she told you you were the best barman in the best bar in Southie, didn't you? You silly great eejit. And yes, it was true that the time came when he invited her back to his place for a nightcap, but he didn't so much as touch her knee.

By then he knew something was wrong. She drank a little too much and spoke a little too forcefully. Her cheerfulness had the sharp edge of desperation, and he began to realize that she was a person with a problem. She was lonely. No crime in that, but it had apparently reached the point where it affected her mind. She would say something every now and then that was—wrong. And it made you think you were in the presence of a sick soul.

Dermot instinctively sympathized with her. He sometimes had his own bouts of loneliness and he often felt painfully homesick. But he decided not to get involved, perhaps sensing that he could never fill the emptiness in her life. Probably no one could. It had gone on too long now and was rooted in her.

Besides, she didn't really attract him, so he had no desire even to try. In the face of fearful odds, Dermot had managed to get to America. He had a job. He had a room. He had plans. He was there to make money, not collect problem hearts.

By then, however, it was too late. They talked for a while that first night and then she left. But she came back to Dolan's night after night. She usually stayed until closing time so that the two of them could walk home together. Like Dermot, she lived in the neighborhood. The rear exit of Dolan's led to a dead end alley, so he couldn't easily avoid her. He made excuses—going for a plate of spaghetti with the lads, a poker game—but there were too many times when he had to put up with her chatty company over the few blocks to home.

What kind of life did she have that she could stay out until three almost every morning? She claimed she worked in an office. More than that, Dermot didn't care to know: she might mistake his idle curiosity for significant interest. He occasionally walked her to her door; she always invited him in and he always declined politely. Most of the time he went straight to his place and she tagged along. The last twenty feet were the trickiest, from the sidewalk to the door. It required finesse or rudeness for him to get inside without her. He didn't always succeed, but a glass of whiskey and another forty minutes of forgettable talk usually did the job. If you satisfied her craving for company and attention, then you could ease her out.

The funny thing was, she never made a move on him either. A flash of leg was invariably accidental; the chair slid. When she bumped into him, breasts against his arm, it was the result of an innocent tipsiness. At first Dermot saw these minor incidents as erotic overtures, but he soon realized that they weren't. It was the hour, the booze, nothing more. She was happy just to be with him, to have his company. In his more charitable moments, Dermot thought of her as an eccentric.

"Get up, you stupid cow."

"I don't want to go."

"If you don't shift yourself, I'll drag you by the scruff of your neck and toss you in the gutter."

"Dermot!" A shriek, really.

"I mean it. Come along now."

She didn't stir. Whimpering, huddled to herself. Dear God, how did it get to this point? It was actually worse than if they were lovers, because lovers do split up and vow never to see each other again. The clean break sort of thing. Dermot's mistake had been to let this situation develop to the point where it was friendship, at least in her mind, and that was somehow harder to terminate neatly.

He had underestimated her every step of the way. How had he deluded himself into believing that he was in control? The alarm bells didn't start ringing until the first time she came visiting on one of his nights off. She had finagled his work schedule out of someone at Dolan's. The line was truly crossed. Dermot began calling her names, yelling at her, anything to drive the wretched woman away.

But his insults and verbal abuse didn't seem to matter. It was possible that she found some perverse pleasure in it, taking it as a form of attention. No matter what he did, he only seemed to implicate himself more in this imaginary relationship. Dermot felt helpless and trapped, and that made him angrier. If it took physical force to get rid of her, so be it.

"Come along," he said firmly, grabbing her by the shoulders. "Time to push off."

"You promised me a drink," she protested.

"I did no such thing."

"Why not?"

"Because I don't want to give you a drink," he said, hauling her to her feet. "I want you to go home and leave me alone. I'm tired and I have to write a letter to my father back in Ireland. He's not very well, and—"

"What about your mother?" she asked quickly, grasping at the slim conversational opening.

"She's fine, thanks. Come on now."

"My mother's dead."

"Ah, you'll be seeing her again soon enough if you don't get out of here in a flash, you drunken old sow."

She smiled at him. "Oh, Dermot..."

He opened the apartment door and gently started to steer her toward the hallway. She resisted, tilting in his direction. She had never really fought him before. Dermot regarded this gesture as an escalation on her part, a clear attempt to move things to a new level. It had to be squelched immediately. He yelled at her as he gave her a stiff-arm to the shoulder. She fell back, tried to steady herself, and pulled a picture off the wall. It crashed to the floor as she landed on a plain wooden chair—the back of it popped loose. Somehow, she straightened up on her feet as the chair cracked to pieces beneath her.

The picture was just a cheap print in a cheap frame, and the chair was worthless tag-sale junk. But they weren't his. Now he would have to replace them. Dermot gazed at the broken glass and wood on the floor. Enough is enough, he thought dimly.

She was about to say something, but he wouldn't let her. He grabbed her by the hair and yanked her out of the flat, through the front door and down the walk. She was screaming now. Dermot swung her by the hair and sent her reeling across the sidewalk. She banged into a car parked at the curb, and sank to the ground. The cries of pain continued, but the volume was down.

"And stay away, you stupid old slag."

Dermot turned and marched back inside. Mr. and Mrs. Thwaite glared down at him from the upper landing. He would apologize to them, but it was useless. They were the kind of people who would tell a leper it was his own fault when his lips fell off. Dermot knew they would complain to the lads, maybe even to the landlord. But he might survive—if your woman never came back.

He topped up his glass of whiskey and tried to calm himself. He sat down at the desk in his room and took out a sheet of lined paper. *Dear Dad*, he began. The old man wasn't well, that was an honest fact. Dermot hadn't written home in ages. No excuses, he just hadn't done it. There were times when his head felt like an anvil of guilt. He would fail again tonight. He was too jangled and distracted to concentrate.

If only he could ring them up on the telephone. Impossible. Dermot's home was on the outskirts of a small village a few miles from Kilkelly, itself no metropolis, in the bleak heart of County Mayo. There were still some places where the lines didn't reach, or the people couldn't be bothered to hook on. If you absolutely had to use a phone, you went to a pub in town. In all the years of his growing up, Dermot could remember about half a dozen such telephone expeditions.

Yes, it was a bleak corner of the world, but he did miss it. He missed the folks, his sister Naimh. He missed the grim beauty of the stark countryside. It was all so—empty. While here in Boston, everybody lived like matchsticks in a box. All he wanted was a few years here to raise enough money so that he could buy a decent pub back home. Then he'd be away like a shot. Of course, Dermot knew there was many an Irishman who said as much, and then never returned. They went to America and stayed. But he—

"Dermot. Derrrmmmmot..."

The voice was so close he jumped. She was in the side yard, outside his window. Not even six feet away from him, across the desk and on the other side of the wall. Jesus, Mary and Joseph. He couldn't move. His body shook. He saw a splash of whiskey on the barren page. Thank God the shade was drawn. Her voice rose, becoming a scream, and she hammered the wall of the house, but he didn't move. It soon got worse, much worse. If I move I'll kill her, Dermot realized, this time I'll fuckin' murder her.

The next thing he knew, the police were at the door. He let them in, catching a glimpse of the Thwaites outside. Trouble. A couple of cops had been scratched and bitten as they subdued her. She'd gone round the twist. The police knew her, it seemed. The one who talked to Dermot was quite sympathetic, and after a while it occurred to him that he was in pretty good shape after all. A statement would be required. Fair enough.

It got better in the weeks that followed. She had abraded a cornea, detached a retina and chomped a hole in a cheek. Not the kind of thing the police are quick to forgive. She got her licks in, give her that. She had no real job, she was a welfare cheat. When it came to psychiatric testing, she made a poor impression. They found a place for her, and Dermot was told that she wouldn't be turned loose for some little while.

It was the best thing, really. She was lonely, desperate, a disturbed person. She needed care and attention, and now she was going to get it. Perhaps not in the circumstances she would have desired, but it was care all the same. It was far better for her to be where she was, than to continue along the way she had been going until something worse happened.

When the machinery of the state took over, Dermot discovered that he didn't even have a walk-on role. It was surprising, but a relief. Events occurred on the strength of their own momentum. She was the only issue, who she was and what she'd done. Dermot had to remind himself that he had in fact once been involved. He wouldn't have been surprised to get a letter from her, or a bunch of them—lonely, impassioned, repentant, pleading, reflecting a new knowledge of her past weaknesses, some such approach. But he never heard from her again.

The lads seemed to think it was all good crack, and even the Thwaites acknowledged that he was not entirely to blame—he got a civil nod from them, at any rate. Dermot drew pints at Dolan's and gathered his tips, dispensing equal measures of genuine Irish nostalgia and nationalism to boozy Yanks who'd never been east of Revere. So it went until the morning the telegram arrived.

FATHER DYING / NIAMH / TOBERCURRY / EIRE

The back of beyond. He expected things to look different in some ways, and they did. But still, he was shocked. He had been in America for less than a year, and already home seemed so dark, chilly and cramped. His perspective had changed forever. But it was great to see his mother again. She was in fine form, as was Naimh, a lovely young woman of nineteen. And the kitchen was the same warm and cozy room Dermot remembered, the heart of the house where the fire never went out.

His father was not in good shape. The old man smiled at him but couldn't speak. There was barely enough strength left in him to change his position in bed. Dermot told him all about Boston,

Southie, Dolan's ("a bar, not a real pub") and the lads ("they're not bad for Kerrymen"). After a while he noticed that his father had fallen asleep, though his eyes were still partly open.

"Why isn't he in the hospital?" Dermot asked his mother over tea in the kitchen.

"They can't do anything more for him," she replied with calm and resignation. "He wants to be here when the end comes."

"He has pills to make it better for him," Naimh added.

"What are they, painkillers?"

"Yes, it's a morphine compound."

Dermot nodded. His sister had grown up so much in the last year. She had an air of efficiency and purpose now. No sign of the immature teenager. After two years of looking, she'd finally been lucky enough to land a regular job at a stationer's shop in Tobercurry. She owned a beat-up old Mini and she changed the oil and plugs herself.

Dermot went to bed early and slept late, recovering from the effects of jet lag. His mother cooked a grand breakfast for him: fried eggs, fried bread, rashers of real bacon (not that scrawny American rubbish), sausages, black pudding, grilled tomatoes and mushrooms, all washed down with plenty of strong tea. After that Dermot was ready for some fresh air and an eventual pint. He and Naimh went out for a walk, circling across the fields toward the village.

"How long can you stay?" she asked.

"Just the week." He'd told them that last night. "I had a hard time getting that. Things are nearly as bad over there as they are here."

He knew everyone in the village, of course. They were happy to see him back, and they told him they were praying for his dad. He also got a few nudges and sly winks, as if he had been away on a long weekend in Dublin with the lady representative of the Turf Board.

"Is that your Cadillac parked out front?" Gerry Byrne teased when they went into his pub.

"Of course it is. I flew it over in my Lear jet."

Last year Dermot and Naimh had gathered in Byrne's with some friends for farewell drinks. The jokes had been much the same—all about getting rich in America, fast women, buying huge houses with swimming pools, going to Disneyland. Good for a giggle, but now Dermot could see the black edge in such humor. It took three pints of catching up before he and Naimh were able to move to the corner table and talk alone.

"How long does he have?"

"Days," she said.

"Could it be weeks?"

"It's possible, but not many. And don't you worry about it if he does hang on a bit longer. You don't have to come back for the funeral. He's seen you again and that's the important thing. You were great with him yesterday."

"What about you?"

"What about me?"

"How long are you going to stay on at home?"

Naimh shrugged. "Until something better comes along."

That could take ages, given Irish courtship rituals. *If* she found someone. He knew the local routine. Saturday nights. The twenty-mile drive to the Crystal Ballroom, the one alternative to drinking in a pub. And even then, she would sit around for hours or dance with other women while the lads tanked up. And who were they? The ones not bright enough to go off to technical college, much less the university. It was a desperate business, in such a desperate place. Dermot didn't want to marry Naimh off in a rush but it pained him to think of her growing older alone, working by day and taking care of their mother the rest of the time, passing the prime of her youth in a barren place.

"You should consider Dublin, or at least Galway. And when I get established, the States. There's nothing for you here in the long term, Naimh."

"You could be right about that."

"I know I am."

When they got home they learned that their father had died. Their mother had gone into the bedroom to check him a few minutes earlier, and he was gone.

The next three days were busy with the wake and the funeral, and the other details attendant to an ordinary human death. When it was all over—the prayers said, the papers signed, the booze consumed, the old man in the ground, the last mourner departed—Dermot occupied himself with chores around the house. There were a lot of things that needed doing, things his father had not been able to do these last few months.

Dead at sixty. His mother not even that. She would want to stay on at the house until the day she died. There was no reason why she shouldn't, as long as her health was good. With a little financial assistance from Naimh and Dermot—not much, her needs were few—she'd manage all right.

If things went half-well for him, he'd be back in plenty of time to give her some grandchildren and look after her in her old age. And if he eventually changed his mind and decided to remain in America and raise a family there—if things went that well, then he could bring his mother across to live with them. And his sister, if she hadn't gotten married and had a bunch of babies in the meantime.

"Dermot."

His eyes opened in the dark. Chill air. Silence. It was a moment before his mind began to form thoughts. I am home, County Mayo, Republic of Ireland. Mother in her room and Naimh in hers. The peaty smell of turf burning, the fire still alive downstairs. The day after tomorrow—no, it would be tomorrow, in fact—he would get on a plane at Shannon and fly back to Boston.

"Dermmmmmmot..."

The bitch. Had her voice come from outside the window, or a window in the back of his brain? The sound of his own breathing. Nothing else. Dreaming—he must have been dreaming about that terrible woman. She was a good three thousand miles away, having all her neuroses and psychoses totted up by bored state employees who would move on to better things in due course.

Amazing, the quality of her voice. Like a moan from outside his window, and at the same time like a whisper in his ear. Real enough to wake him. It must have been a bad dream—he wouldn't have any other kind about that one.

The rest of the night was ruined. Dermot drifted in and out of sleep, never enjoying more than a few uninterrupted minutes of peace. Not that he heard her again, not that he'd ever heard her in the first place. He just kept waking, dozing, and soon waking again. Useless. Untracked. He grew more tired.

He must have slept again because at some point he opened his eyes and the room was brighter. Day outside, grey light: cloudy as usual. He felt as if he'd been in bed for a long time but the house was still quiet. Perhaps his mother had gone down to the shop for eggs or milk. Was Naimh returning to work today? Most likely. Life goes on—work, anyway.

Dermot couldn't move. Or it might have been that he didn't want to move yet. Some combination of the two, no doubt, inertia and laziness. His body was like a heavy weight, a solid material that encased him. He wiggled his toes a little—that's better. He tried to turn his head a little, and was surprised at how much effort it took to budge an inch. He felt okay. But then again, he didn't feel right at all.

A while later Dermot opened his eyes. Was I asleep? He had no desire to move now, no will to get out of bed and do something with the day. He had a foreign taste in his mouth, and his teeth tingled unpleasantly—as if he were biting tin. What was wrong with him, he wondered abstractly. It did seem to be a matter of interest, but not a real concern. Thoughts came and went, but he couldn't make anything of them. They were inconclusive, they had the random quality of accidents. Just thinking about what he was thinking about had the effect of exhausting him. Dermot realized his eyes were closing this time, and he felt happy about it.

He was drowning. He gagged, his tongue working furiously to retrieve something that was already halfway down his throat—he woke up spitting. It made a sound like dice on the lino. Dermot swallowed blood as he pushed his face toward the edge of the bed. He saw it on the floor across the room—a tooth. Yes, it's one of mine. The empty socket began to hurt, a deep, throbbing pain. What is this now, a toothache after the fact? Bloody unfair. It dug into him.

His face was wet. That was how he discovered that he'd been asleep again. The old woman was washing blood and dribble off of his chin. She was familiar. He wanted to tell her that she was in severe danger of scrubbing his skin down to the next layer but when she finally let go he was too weak to utter a word. Then he saw the man standing nearby. He looked unfamiliar, but he had to be a doctor. Of course—Dermot was sick. That explained a lot of things. He felt better. Still sick, but better.

Where were they? Why was he alone? They were here a minute ago, he was sure of that. He hadn't seen them leave, but now the room was empty. He was too alone. It was stifling, suffocating. He tried to sit up, but failed; the old muscle tone was somewhat deficient. He opened his mouth and tried to work up some saliva. He called out feebly.

"Haaaaaaa..." Almost a wheeze. They shouldn't leave him on his own like this. Dermot was aware of pain. His insides etched with acid. His throat choking him. Even his arse, God help him, felt as if it had hot coals embedded in it, from not being moved. He couldn't move himself, so it was up to them—and they'd done a disappearing act. He tried to think of anything else, to dodge the pain. Had they picked up that tooth? He was curious to take a look at the rotten bugger.

"Haaaaaaa..."

He looked up and the girl was holding his hand. By God, she was beautiful. He knew her. Naimh. Don't leave. Stay with me. Don't even let go of my hand or I'll fall off the edge. He tried to tell her these things but the words remained stuck in his mind and all he could do was look at her.

Then the boy. The boy? If he'd come such a distance, this must be serious. Oh yes. It had been a while, and he was happy. If only I could tell you that. The boy looked just like him. It was difficult even to understand what he was saying.

"...not a real pub."

Yes, yes, but it's work, it's real money, and you'll be able to build on it for the future. There's nothing for you here.

"...for Kerrymen."

Gone again. Everything goes so fast. You are left alone in a stark room with a view of nothing much. The pain scouring away at his insides had nearly reached the surface. Anytime now. And when it gets here, with any luck I'll dissolve completely.

Dermot's mind was flooded with clarity. This is dying. The hour, the minute. A surge of strength in his arms. He pushed up on his elbows, and then, painfully, his hands. He had to see, to see—but what? Not this mean, damp bedroom in which so much of his life had been spent. Out the window, away. Two people were walking across the field, toward the house. A young man, a young woman. Dermot and Naimh.

"Haaaaaaa..."

First their father, then their mother. It happened that way more often than you might think, when they'd been very close. Or so the doctor said. Dermot went to sleep, and she never woke up. At least with the old man it was expected. But this was a shock. He'd only had a little while to speak with each of them, and even then it was minor, trivial. Dear God. You've put us all in such a lonely, desperate country.

But that was a while back.

He moved. That is, he thought he moved. Dermot couldn't be sure about it. He was dreaming. The whole thing was just a long bad dream. *Yes, it often seems that way, doesn't it?* But Dermot knew better. He made an effort to move. He put his foot down.

Clutch in.

Shifted up coming out of the bend.

He knew this road. He'd had a few drinks, but that wasn't a cause for alarm. If the Garda stopped him, it meant nothing. He was Dermot Mulreany, bound for Shannon, bound for Boston. He had somehow gotten better, overcome tragedy and loss and reached this point in his life where he—

Clutch in.

Shifted down going into a sharp bend.

He knew this road. Another Saturday night at the Crystal. The band sang "Roisin Dubh," nearly as good as the Thin Lizzy version. The black rose. He would keep that in mind—it was a good old name for a pub.

You're so good-looking. So why do you live alone? Why do you sleep alone at night?

The lads reeked of stout and Carrolls cigarettes, as usual. They couldn't dance to save their lives, and all they ever wanted to do was get a hand up your jumper, but—

He glanced down at himself, trembling with sudden awareness. Female breasts inside that blouse. Stocking-clad legs, two knees poking out from beneath the plain skirt that had hitched up a bit in the car. He couldn't take his eyes off them, as if they were the most amazing thing he'd ever seen.

"Dermot..."

The car—watch out. Too late, the road was lost, the tree racing unnaturally toward him—no, her. No! his mind screamed. Not Naimh! *This time O God please let me be the one who dies not Naimh not Naimh let me die!*

Even worse, he lived.

He saw her on Boston Common. He wanted to turn and run when he saw her coming toward him, but his legs went stiff and he felt swamped with helplessness and inevitability. He simply could not avoid her. Hatred boiled up within him, but at the same time it was crushed with fear. It had to be two years now, more or less. Somehow she had got out. Done her time, had her treatment. They couldn't hold her forever.

He was the only one left.

She looked pathetic, shuffling along aimlessly. Raggedy old clothes, hair a mess, face wrecked by life. Still a young woman, for all of that. Dermot stopped. Couldn't move. She glanced at him. Their eyes met. She had the same look, searching, vacant, lonely, as if she peered out at the world from some awful place. Dermot shriveled inside. Sweat misted his face, turning cold in the sharp November air.

But she showed no sign of knowing him, not even a flicker of subconscious recognition. As if he were invisible and she didn't even see him there. Then she passed through Dermot like a sudden paralyzing spasm of anguish, and was gone.

Evelyn Grace

So Evelyn Grace was dead from a drug overdose at the age of thirty eight. Her body was found on the floor of the studio flat in east Los Angeles where she had been living for the last seven months. She had been a model, an actress, a singer, and she was unemployed at the time of her death.

Evelyn Grace. Dead. An accident, or so the coroner had ruled. But it was not impossible to imagine that Evvy had known exactly what she was doing with her last needle. Or that she had been murdered for some bizarre California-type reason. In fact, it was easy to imagine all sorts of things about Evvy. She had always been the kind of girl who made a guy's blood run away with his mind.

Tim LeClerc refolded his newspaper and set it aside. He lit a cigarette. He knew her, but they had never met. He and Evelyn Grace had been in the same graduating class at high school, back in the late sixties. They had been in different groups, however, and they didn't live in the same neighborhood, so for four years they passed each other in the corridors at school but their paths never really crossed. Tim had been aware of her, it was hard not to be, but she had probably never even known that he existed. In a class of nearly two hundred there were bound to be quite a few strangers, even after all that time.

Bitter early March, the land still frozen, locked up beneath steel clouds and day-old snow that was already tarnished with the grime of Utica. The wind hit Tim's face like cold fire as he ran from the diner to his car. It was then, while he sat huddled and shivering, waiting for the engine to idle down and the heater to generate some feeble warmth, that the idea came to him. He would go to Evvy's wake.

Why not? He was curious to see her again, even if she was dead, or maybe *because* she was dead, and that was morbid. But on the other hand her parents would appreciate the gesture. You can never have too many visitors at a wake. It was only about twenty miles away, in Rome. Besides, he had no one to rush home to, nor anything better to do with his evening.

That was how far he'd gotten, Tim thought. Twenty-odd miles in twenty-odd years. Never mind. He'd seen enough of the world when he was in the army to realize that upstate New York was the place for him. He came back alive and whole, and settled into a modest but clean apartment on the eastern edge of Utica. After a few false starts he had landed a decent job at the bottling plant and had been there ever since. Nothing to crow about, but it was a life and it did have its occasional moments, although Tim would be hard-pressed to enumerate many of them. When he wanted female company he could always find it. Somebody's neglected wife, or a divorcee on the wrong side of thirty, or any of the women at work who were still single because they were overweight or ugly or too crushingly dull to snag a mate. Nothing romantic, but the years had given Tim a rather functional attitude to sex.

His was just an ordinary life, but he never regretted it or felt sorry for himself. He liked it the way it was, uncluttered and straightforward, low-key but comfortable. At least he would never be shipped home in a steel box in the cargo hold of a jet plane while strangers drank cocktails overhead. Funny, how he'd been to Vietnam and escaped that fate, while Evelyn went to L.A. and hadn't. Poor Evvy.

Tim polished his dress shoes. He put on his best shirt and tie, and his only suit. He had second thoughts while driving to the wake, but promptly dismissed them. If he felt awkward when he got there he would just take a quick look at her, mumble some words to the parents and then leave. That's what he'd probably do anyway; no sense in sitting around once his juvenile curiosity had been satisfied.

But what actually happened was shockingly pathetic. Mr. and Mrs. Grace were the only people there when Tim arrived. He felt very odd indeed as he crossed the room and knelt down at the open casket. For a few moments he was occupied with Evvy. She looked lovely still, her face virtually unmarked by the years and events of her life. The mortician had done a good job, applying no more make-up than was absolutely necessary. Even now she retained her girlish good looks, the ghostly afterimage of a beauty you never forget once you've encountered it.

Tim was touched by her haunting appearance, saddened by the fact that her life had plummeted to this abrupt end, and he found himself wishing that he *had* met her when they were in high school together. How different everything might be now—for the both of them—if they had. It was an idle fantasy, of course, but Tim believed there was a kernel of truth in it. Don't all lives have at least one turning point that's flukey, or accidental, or capricious? Too bad, too bad...

At last he stood up and turned to Evvy's parents. Leonard Grace was small and wiry, with a scattering of white fuzz about his largely bare scalp. His manner was bright and alert, though he nodded his head too often, as if to emphasize his agreeable and understanding nature. Charlotte Grace was plump, with a moon face and a distracted air. It took Tim a few minutes to notice that now and then she would fade right out of the conversation, like a distant radio signal drifting in the ether. She had run the family for as long as it had existed, was Tim's guess, but now she was probably an Alzheimer's case.

Tim explained that he had been to high school with Evelyn, and her parents were very grateful to him for taking the time to come to the wake. He didn't actually say that he'd been a friend of their daughter, but they somehow got that idea and he saw no need to clarify the matter. It was such a sad situation, two old people, one of them not quite all there, alone with the dead body of their only child.

And hardly anyone came. The calling hours were from seven to nine, and in that time perhaps half a dozen people appeared to pay their respects. They were older folks, acquaintances of the parents, and none of them stayed more than ten minutes.

It was amazing, shocking, to Tim, who had expected a rather large turnout. A lot of people would have moved away over the years, but there still had to be plenty of former friends and classmates of Evelyn's left in Rome, so where were they? It was as if nobody wanted to admit knowing her. But why? Just because she'd been something of a bad girl, running off to California, living a wild, silly, rotten life? Because she'd met her squalid death at an age when she should have been organizing bake sales and ferrying kids to Little League games? *I see Evelyn Grace is dead. Tsk, tsk, tsk. Well, it was to be expected.* Smug, self-satisfied bastards. I didn't even know her, Tim thought, but I'm a better friend to her now than all those people ever were.

"She never wrote to us," Mrs. Grace said to Tim.

"Oh, she did too, Mommy," Mr. Grace put in gently.

"Never wrote, never called," Evelyn's mother continued. "We never knew where she was or what she was doing."

"She sent postcards," Mr. Grace said. "And she did call up on the telephone every now and again. Let us know she was okay."

"Once a year?" his wife asked challengingly. "Once a year, at best," she explained to Tim.

"Some people are like that," Tim rationalized. "Me, I can't write a letter to save my life."

It was a terrible choice of words, he realized immediately, but fortunately Mrs. Grace was already on another wavelength, and Mr. Grace merely nodded agreeably.

A few minutes before nine, when no one else had arrived for more than half an hour, Mrs. Grace whispered something urgent to her husband.

"Tim, would you mind hanging on here a minute while I take Mommy to the can?"

"Uh, sure."

No sooner had the old couple left the room than one of the young funeral home flunkies glanced in, checked the wall clock against his watch, and left. Charge by the minute, Tim thought sarcastically. He stood up and walked to the casket. It seemed very strange to be alone with Evvy—at her wake. Once again he was struck by how attractive she looked. And death shall have no dimension, he vaguely recalled, a line from a poem in high school English class.

Without thinking, Tim reached to Evvy with his right hand, knowing that his body shielded the gesture in case anyone came into the room. He hesitated briefly, afraid he would make a mess of the cosmetics if he touched her face, afraid her fingers would grasp at his if he touched her hands. Trembling, he let his palm settle on her breast. The experience was so confused between the real and the imagined that he wasn't at all sure what he actually felt, a pleasantly firm young female breast, or something harder and dead, a mixture of sawdust and embalming chemicals. When he removed his hand he felt a jangling rush of guilt and excitement, but he was more pleased than ashamed. He'd had his little moment of intimacy with Evvy, who had always been not only untouchable but unapproachable to him.

"You *will* be there tomorrow," Mr. Grace said when he and his wife returned. It was a plea, not a question. "Won't you."

"Yes, of course," Tim replied, although he hadn't planned to attend the funeral as well.

"We had to pay the funeral home for pall-bearers," Evelyn's mother said. "Twenty five dollars apiece."

"Mommy, please."

"I'll see you in the morning," Tim said, trying to smile comfortingly as he shook hands with them.

"Thank you," the Graces both said as he left, "thank you."

Tim called the bottling plant in the morning and told them he was taking a sick day. It was crisp and clear outside, with a hint of thaw in the air. He felt good, and had slept well, which Tim attributed to the kindness he'd shown Mr. and Mrs. Grace by sitting with them for two hours and promising to attend the Mass. It wasn't often he had the chance to do something nice like that for a couple of old folks. His own parents had died within three months of each other several years ago, and his only living aunt and uncle were in Scottsdale, Arizona. Mr. and Mrs. Grace needed him last night, and this morning, almost as if he were a son or a nephew, or an old family friend.

But it was not just altruism on Tim's part that pleased him. The bleak circumstances of Evvy's death, the fact that virtually no one came to her wake, the way her parents had *assumed* him into their tiny circle, and the feel of her breast in his hand—all of these things combined somehow to bestow on Tim a curious share in Evvy's life, and, however peculiar that might be, he genuinely liked it.

There were more people at the funeral Mass than had attended the wake, but Tim was sure that most if not all of them were just the usual band of daily churchgoers. One of the pall-bearers wore a green bowling league jacket. Aside from the funeral home crew and the priest, Tim and Evelyn's parents were the only ones at her graveside. Mrs. Grace turned wobbly and started to moan when it was time to leave, while Mr. Grace struggled to maintain a semblance of glassy-eyed composure. Tim helped them both walk along the gravel path to the cars.

"You will follow us back to the house, Tim," Mr. Grace said as he stood by the door of the funeral home Cadillac.

"Oh, no, thank you, but—"

"Please, Tim, come on along for a little while. We'll have some coffee and pastry." He put his hand on Tim's shoulder and gave a beseeching squeeze. "Mommy was up till after midnight, cooking. She couldn't sleep at all."

Tim sighed inwardly. It didn't seem right that Evvy's folks should have to return directly home alone. It was bad enough for them to have to forego the normal post-funeral reception with its sustaining presence of family and friends, but to have no one, no one at all, even to share a cup of coffee with, after they'd just buried their daughter—that was simply too much.

"Sure," Tim agreed. "I'll follow you."

The Grace home was a cramped little asbestos-shingled house of the working class thirties vintage. Not much, but no doubt it had seemed palatial, even miraculous, when it was built and first occupied during the Depression. Easy to imagine a girl like Evvy desperate to escape from here. But for Tim there was something nostalgically comfortable about it—he had grown up in much the same sort of place, and not nearly so far from this one as he had thought. When you go back to the old neighborhood the distances collapse, the yards shrink, and houses that once looked big turn into boxy chicken coops.

Tim and Mr. Grace sat in the living room and chatted, while Mrs. Grace brewed the coffee and prepared a platter of pastries. It was desultory, inconsequential talk about Rome, the old days, and the rapidly changing times that had overtaken everyone. Tim and Mr. Grace were in agreement that most of the changes were not really for the better. Astroturf, for instance.

It was not until Mrs. Grace had rejoined them, and they were all sipping fresh-perked coffee and nibbling delicious sesame-rum sweetcakes, that the conversation finally gathered itself around the subject of Evelyn. It was soon clear to Tim that there was a huge, aching mystery at the center of their existence and that it had to do entirely with the missing years of Evelyn's life, from the day she'd left home years ago until the day before yesterday, when she'd been air-freighted back to her parents. Everything in between was a cloud of unknowing, a dense fog broken only by the occasional spark of a phone call here, a postcard there—which, perversely, enhanced the darkness rather than illuminated it.

Evvy was a riddle to Tim as well, but he had been thinking about her quite a bit these last couple of days. Not logically, but intuitively, since they'd finally crossed paths only because of her death and his curiosity. There were some things he knew, others that he deduced or reasoned out for himself, and, most of all, there was everything he found himself wishing, imagining—it amounted to the same thing in the end. Evvy was in the purely residual phase of her incarnation, so it was up to him.

"I didn't want to go into it last night, at the wake," Tim said. "There wasn't enough time, and I didn't know how you would take it, but I do want to tell you. Evvy and I were good friends for many years. Ever since high school, in fact, and..."

"Evvy? Who's Evvy?"

"Evelyn, Mommy. Hush now, let the boy talk."

Mr. Grace leaned forward in the seat, every aspect of his presence fixed intently on Tim. Mrs. Grace was annoyed at her husband for his rare show of assertiveness, but she said nothing about it, and made an effort to pay attention.

"Well, what can I say," Tim went on hesitantly. "Evvy and I were good friends, ever since high scool. Of course, we did lose track of each other for while after that, but when I got out of the army I thought I'd stay on the West Coast for a while, see if I could find a good job there, and we ran into each other again. We went out a lot, had fun together, that kind of thing. She was busy trying to make a career for herself, and in the meantime I'd found decent work at a defense plant, but we still managed to get together a couple of nights a week, and on weekends. And...well, we got pretty serious, and there were times when I was sure we'd get married and settle down to a more normal life, you know? But something or other always seemed to get in the way of it. So, it was an off-again on-again type relationship, but even when it was off we were still great friends. I always loved Evvy, no matter what, and I think she loved me most of the time. I know she did. But we never managed to get it to the next stage. I wish that we had. We stayed in touch up until a couple of months ago, when I decided that it was never going to work out, and I was ready for a change in my life, so I made up my mind to move back here. We talked maybe once or twice on the phone, right after I moved, but that was it."

Mr. Grace's mouth was slightly open, and his throat muscles worked mightily either to shut it or to say something, but he did neither. Mrs. Grace appeared to be no less fascinated by what Tim had said, but she didn't look as completely surprised as her husband did.

Tim had paused to catch his breath—and his wits, he could only hope. He had said enough, too much, and it had taken off on him at once. It had seemed harmless enough. All he wanted to do was to give them something to cling to, a few dressed-up facts to fill in some of the vast blank spot that Evvy had left them. But no sooner had he started then the story took on a life of its own and became an account of *his* long love affair with Evvy. Is that crazy or what, Tim wondered.

But he had enjoyed it, too. Such an extraordinary thrill, to hear those things, to know that they were rising from a buried part of his brain. That they put him into Evvy's life, and Evvy into his. Tim marvelled that he hadn't contradicted anything he had said previously to Mr. and Mrs. Grace. But it was clear to him that they'd accept whatever he told them. They just wanted to hear as much as they could about their daughter, and that was the problem. Tim had merely opened the door.

"Go on," Mrs. Grace prompted.

"Yes, please, Tim. Tell us more."

Reluctant, feeling trapped by his own good intentions, but at the same time secretly delighted, Tim continued to elaborate his impromptu saga of Evelyn Grace's missing years. Her efforts to make it as a folk singer, then as a rock singer, finally as a country-and-western singer. Her two or three non-speaking parts in forgettable movies. The picture of Evvy perched atop a Harley that was used for the front cover of a biker magazine. Another one, showing her menaced by a man with a knife, that appeared in a true-crime magazine. The in-between jobs, waitressing in some pretty good restaurants and nightclubs, serving drinks in an L.A. airport bar, that sort of thing. The occasional respite taken in the unemployment line, recharging her batteries for the next time around. Nothing too shabby, nothing unrespectable, but never any breakthrough. The long hard road of a pretty young woman chasing her ambition down the years in Los Angeles.

Woven throughout, like a bright gold thread, was Tim's love for Evvy and her sometime love for him. Tim went on about how he was still sad that they'd never been able to make it a permanent relationship, a marriage, how he had learned to accept that. Now he consoled himself by thinking of the happier memories he had of Evvy and by reminding himself that in spite of her weaknesses and failings she had been a good person.

Tim wanted to finish there, on the kind of life-affirming note people strive for in funeral situations. He felt tired, and it seemed as if he had been talking for hours. But Evvy's mother and father were not quite through with him yet.

"The end, Tim," Mr. Grace said softly. "You have to tell us what happened to her at the end."

"Yeah, what about the drugs," Mrs. Grace demanded.

"Oh, well. Some of the movie people she knew, I guess they introduced her to cocaine somewhere along the line, and then the harder stuff. I tried to get her off it, but once you're hooked it's rough. You have to make a total committment, and Evvy could never bring herself to that point, where she was willing. That's the main reason why I had to give up, at last, and get out of the scene altogether. I couldn't change her, and I couldn't bear to watch what was happening to her, so I packed up my stuff and came back here. And she let me go. The guy who was supplying all her drugs meant more to her than I did."

"Did he use her?" Mrs. Grace asked. "They get them hooked, and then they use them."

"I don't know about that," Tim replied. He didn't like this because it tainted his own newly developed feelings for Evvy. It was probably unavoidable—she *had* died of a heroin overdose—but it seemed so distasteful. "All I know is I lost her. We all lost her in the end."

Mr. Grace looked subdued and thoughtful in the long silence that followed. Mrs. Grace seemed to be formulating some response but it never reached the stage of spoken words. Tim was about to leave when Evelyn's father took him aside.

"Come with me a minute," he said, leading Tim up a narrow flight of stairs. They went into a small bedroom. Obviously it had been Evvy's. "Tim, they sent back these two boxes of things with her. Personal effects. Not much, as you can see, but I was thinking maybe you'd like to take a minute and look through them. You might find something in there, some little keepsake, to take home and remember her by."

Tim was going to refuse, but it would probably be rude to do so. Besides, he liked the idea too much.

"Thank you," he said.

"Feel free, take your time," Mr. Grace added. "Come on down when you're finished."

"Okay."

Tim waited as the old man's footsteps faded away. Then he sat down on the bed, Evvy's bed. For a moment he pictured her as the most gorgeous girl in high school, the way she had been then. In this room. In this bed. He remembered seeing her at the lake on the day after the senior prom. She was with her crowd and she was wearing a bikini that would be demure by today's standards. No one had a tan in June. Evvy had snowy blonde hair, long pale thighs...It was sweet for Tim to pause there, to enjoy once again the permanence of her beauty.

Not much was right. The two cardboard cartons were filled for the most part with cheap clothes. Sneakers, jeans, T-shirts, socks. No dresses, no jackets, nothing very good. Evvy had had very little left at the end, her flimsy life stripped down to the minimum. He had to find something he could show to Mr. Grace and thank him for. The cheap plastic barette would do nicely—and it still smelled of Evvy's hair (or at least her hairspray).

Tim reached down to the bottom of the second box and pulled up a handful of bras and panties. Startled, he dropped them, but then he relaxed, smiled and allowed himself to examine them. Red and blue and lavender, not a white in the bunch. Evvy's bra size was 36C, for breasts that were ample but not excessive. Tim had been aware of that as far back as ninth grade and as recently as last night. He held a pair of delicate purple cotton briefs to his face— God in Heaven, they still had the delicious unwashed scent of her in them!

Tim quickly shoved the panties into his jacket pocket, and then carefully rearranged the other things back in the boxes. He held the barrette conspicuously in his hand and went downstairs. Mrs. Grace was still sitting where he had left her. She gave him a strained smile as he came into the living room. He started to say something to her.

Bong! and *Bong!* again, before he even hit the carpet. *Bong! Bong! Bong!* His hands were useless floppy things and his vision skittered away like marbles on a hardwood floor.

"The flat part, the flat part," Mrs. Grace warned. "Not the edge. That's my best skillet."

Tim's empty hands were bound together behind him with some sticky plastic stuff, packing tape, he realized dimly. And then his feet. His head wouldn't clear, but he tried to speak; it was impossible to put words together. He tried to focus his sight on the plastic barrette, which he was aware of, somewhere, near his face on the floor.

"Son of a bitch," Mr. Grace wheezed, his voice high-pitched, almost strangled, but with a nervous edge of triumph in it. "You could have saved her. You were the only one who could have saved her. We couldn't talk to her, we couldn't do anything with her. That's the way it is sometimes between parents and kids, you just can't do anything. No matter what you try, it doesn't work. But you could have saved her. You loved her, but you walked away and left her there to die. You left her there with that other son of a bitch, who was pumping dope into her."

"Least he could've done was make her call home once a week," Mrs. Grace remarked.

"Washed his hands of her, that's what he did."

Again Tim tried to speak, but as soon as he opened his mouth he was kicked in the jaw. His tongue hurt and he tasted his own blood. He felt the old man's hands on his body, emptying each of his pockets. Oh no, don't do that.

"Where's his car keys? Here we go...Look at this, Mommy, look. The son of a bitch was trying to steal Evelyn's underwear. Didn't want to bring *her* home, no. Just her underpants'd do."

"Whispering Jesus," Mrs. Grace responded.

Tim listened as Mr. Grace explained to his wife that he was going to drive Tim's car into downtown Rome, leave it there, and then walk back to the house. She was to do nothing until he got home, except hit Tim with the skillet again if he tried to cause trouble for her.

Move his car? That was bad. But I can get out of this, Tim told himself. Even if she is half gone, I can talk to her, I can distract her, confuse her, and work myself free. I should have known, he thought. The one thing he had steered clear of in his story was why Evvy had cut herself off from these people, to the point where she communicated with them only once or twice a year, and then by postcard or telephone. It had seemed too delicate to mention, and he had no idea of what might be involved, but now it came to him: Evvy might have had her reasons. Tim's mistake may have been to assume, like everyone else, that Evvy had been a bad child, selfish, uncaring, neglectful of her parents. Now he knew that there must have been another side to the story, Evvy's side, and he was stuck in it.

"Doesn't he need his car to drive home?" Mrs. Grace saw fit to ask as her husband was about to leave.

"He isn't going home. Tomorrow we'll drive him up to Canada and dump him there in the woods. I don't even want that son of a bitch in the same country."

When he heard his car being driven away, Tim looked at Mrs. Grace. He gathered himself, tried to clear his throat and speak.

But the old woman rose from her seat and approached him. She had the roll of tape in her hand.

"I don't want to see you," she said. "I don't even want to hear you, and I sure don't want you looking at me."

Ah, no, Tim thought as he saw her yank a length of tape from the roll. She bit it loose, and he noticed a couple of fugitive sesame seeds clinging to her dentures. She slapped the tape over Tim's mouth to keep him from talking. Then, at a more leisurely pace, Evelyn's mother began to wrap the rest of his head in tape.

He thrashed his body as wildly as possible, but he couldn't stop her, and when his head was done she proceeded on down around his arms, eventually securing his knees. It was a big roll of tape, and Mrs. Grace used all of it.

"Now, that's better," she said.

Grotesque, Tim thought, grotesque. He pictured himself as a kind of slapdash mummy, rotting away in the Canadian woods. Say, fifty yards from a back road—the Graces wouldn't be able to drag him any farther than that—but would he ever be found? It was such an outrageous and unreal image that Tim was, even now, incapable of feeling mere panic or terror. Instead, his mind was overwhelmed by a profound sense of exasperation.

If only his story had been true, and he and Evvy had been in love for a while. Then he wouldn't be where he was now, and Evvy would still be alive—because Tim never would have walked away from her. He never would have settled for an unhappy ending with Evvy, not in real life.

Tim's lungs felt like they were being clamped in a waffle iron, the oxygen slowly burning out of them. The last conscious thought he had was a rich and vivid recall of the last conscious smell he had experienced, Evelyn Grace's cunt.

In Praise of Folly

He drove north in air-conditioned comfort, a road map on the seat beside him, Satie's piano music rippling pleasantly from the stereo speakers. Thank God for the little things that make human life bearable when summer's on your neck.

It was August. The stagnant heat and humidity were so heavy they no longer seemed like atmospheric phenomena, but had assumed a suffocating gelatinous density. People moved slowly if at all, dazed creatures in the depths of a fungal deliquescence.

It had to be better up in the Adirondacks, cooler and drier. But Roland Turner was not just another vacationer seeking escape. He was on a mission of discovery, he hoped, a one-man expedition in search of a serious folly.

Roland was one of the very few American members of the Folly Fellowship, an organization based in London that was dedicated to "preserve and promote the enjoyment and awareness of follies...to protect lonely and unloved buildings of little purpose...unusual, intriguing or simply bizarre structures and sites." Roland first learned about the group two years earlier, when he came across an issue of their quarterly magazine in a Connecticut bookshop. The photographs were fascinating, the text charming and witty.

A typical English eccentricity, Roland thought at the time, the sort of thing that lasts for a year or two and then dies away as enthusiasm and funds decline. He wrote a letter to ask if the Fellowship was still going, and was surprised to get a reply from the president and editor himself, one Gwyn Headley. Not only was the Fellowship still active, it was thriving, with more than five hundred members worldwide (most of them, naturally, residents of the United Kingdom).

Roland immediately mailed off a bank draft to cover the cost of membership, a set of back issues of the magazine, a folder of color postcards and a copy of Headley's definitive work, *Follies: A National Trust Guide* (Cape, 1986).

There was something romantic and mysterious about monuments, castles and old ruins that had always appealed to Roland. He saw the past in them, and he loved to imagine what life had been like so long ago. Perhaps it was because his own day-to-day existence was placid and humdrum. Roland owned a printing company, a small outfit that produced trade newsletters and supermarket fliers for the Westchester County market. Over the years he had worked long and hard to build up a reliable trade, and now he presided over a solid, secure business operation. On the negative side, Roland's personal life was somewhat threadbare.

He'd been through a number of brief intimate encounters, but none of them even came close to marriage. Now in his middle age, Roland could take it or leave it. He enjoyed a good book, mainly history or historical fiction, as well as classical music, and he had a special fondness for follies.

A genuine folly was a building, garden, grotto or other such architectural construct that had been designed with a deliberate disregard for the normal rules. A folly was something literally "to gasp at," as Headley put it in his massive tome. Roland had not yet been able to travel to Britain, due to pressure of work, but he had managed to track down a few American follies, such as Holy Land in Waterbury and the Watts Towers in Los Angeles. He'd also visited a fully functional house that had been built out of beer bottles in Virginia, a four-acre Sahara located in the Maine woods, and a home designed as Noah's ark in the Tennessee hills. American follies tended to lack the air of lost grandeur that was the hallmark of classic British follies, but they often displayed a kind of heroic zaniness that was utterly endearing.

Roland could only look forward to the time in his life when he would at last be free to spend two or three months journeying around England, Scotland and Wales, leisurely inspecting some of the remarkable things he could only read about now—such as the rocket ship in Aysgarth, the "house in the clouds" at Thorpeness, Clavel's Tower, and Portmeirion, not to mention all the splendid follies that could still be found in and around the great city of London itself.

Follies are the dizzy, demented lacework on the edge of the vast human tapestry, Roland had written in a letter that for some unknown reason Mr. Headley had not yet seen fit to publish in the magazine of the Follies Fellowship. In his spare hours, Roland continued to hone his thoughts and write up notes on the American follies he came across.

Then, two weeks ago, the message had arrived from London. A "rather spectacular" folly was rumored to exist on the grounds of the old Jorgenson summer cottage in Glen Allen, New York. Would Mr. Turner be able to check it out and report back? If it proved to be a worthwhile site, photographs and notes would be welcome. Roland immediately faxed his answer: "Absolutely."

It took a while to find Glen Allen on the map. Apparently a rural village, it was some two hundred miles away, a little north of Big Moose Lake in the Adirondacks. Definitely a weekend trek.

Get up there and find a rustic inn Friday evening, spend Saturday investigating the Jorgenson property, and then drive back down to Rye on Sunday. Roland fled the office at noon, and a few minutes later hit the turnpike.

As far as anyone knew he was enjoying a short getaway in the countryside. Roland had mentioned his interest in follies to one other person, Patty Brennan, a robust divorcee who had worked for him briefly last year. Roland thought he fancied Patty, but they never got beyond the talking stage.

"You mean like Coney Island, or Grant's Tomb," had been her reaction when he told her about follies.

"Well, no, not exactly..."

Perhaps Roland had explained it badly. He decided then and there to keep the world of follies to himself, his little secret. Patty soon fell in love with the man who cleaned the heads of her VCR, and quit to take a position in his business. It was all for the best, Roland convinced himself. When you share something you treasure with another person, it's no longer quite so special; it inevitably loses a little of its magic aura.

Roland made fairly good time, but the actual journey clocked in at closer to three hundred miles, so it was a little after six in the evening when he reached Glen Allen. He passed by the Glen Motel on his way into town but found no other accommodation, and eventually circled back to it. A satellite dish, a room full of vending machines, three other cars parked in the lot. Nothing at all like a rustic inn, but it would have to do. Roland went into the office and paid for a room.

The middle-aged woman on duty took his cash, gave him a key and some brochures about the boating and fishing opportunities in the vicinity.

"Where's the best place to eat in town?" Roland asked.

"Bill's Friendly Grille, right on Main," the woman replied. "By the way, there's an electrical storm supposed to come through tonight. If the power goes out, you'll find some candles in your closet."

"Thanks. I was thinking of taking a look at the Jorgenson estate tomorrow. Is it hard to find?"

"The Jorgenson estate," she repeated carefully, as if giving the matter some thought. She was a large woman with bland, empty features. "No, it's not hard to find but it might be hard to get to. It's just a couple of miles up the glen, but nobody's lived there in about thirty years, so the private road's all overgrown. You'd have to hike some." Then added, "From what I heard there's nothing much left to see."

"Oh."

"Are you in real estate?"

"No, no, I represent the—well, it's a British fellowship, you see, and we're interested in neglected sites of architectural distinction."

He was upset with himself for hesitating and then failing to utter the word *folly*, but there was no point in trying to explain it to this woman. As it was, she made a vague sound and appeared to have no interest whatsoever.

"Well, I could be wrong but I don't think you'll find there is any architecture up there."

"None at all?" Roland asked in disbelief. Until now he hadn't even considered the possibility that he might have come all this way on a wild goose chase. "There's nothing left?"

The woman shrugged blithely, seeming to take pleasure in his distress. "Place burned down ages ago." She picked up the book she had been reading—a paperback account of some lurid murders in Texas—and found her place.

"Ah. Well..."

His room was adequate, just. There was mildew on the shower curtain, and the air had a damp musty smell that some city people regard as the authentic flavor of the countryside, but the sheets were clean and the air conditioner worked. Outside, the heat and humidity were nearly as oppressive as they'd been in Rye.

Roland decided not to linger in his room. He was hungry and a storm was coming. He left his overnight bag, still packed, on a rock maple armchair, left his camera locked in the trunk of his car, and set off to find Bill's Friendly Grille.

Glen Allen, what there was of it, had the peeling, outdated look of a town still stuck in the forties or fifties. It was not unpleasant—

the weathered clapboards, the old Flying Red Horse gas pumps, the rusty cars and battered pickups, the general store with a group of kids hanging around out front—a curious mix of what was genuinely quaint and what was merely Tobacco Road.

But it wasn't what was there, Roland realized as he parked. It was what wasn't there—no trendy boutiques, no video stores, no T-shirt joints, no fast-food chains, no blaring boomboxes, not even one odorific Chinese takeaway—that was somehow pleasing. The present had not yet arrived in Glen Allen, at least not with the full force of all its tawdry enterprise.

Roland sat at the bar and had the cheeseburger deluxe, which was suitably greasy and rather good. The fries were on the soggy side, but the coleslaw was tangy and delicious. Roland washed it all down with a large mug of cold beer—the first of several he would enjoy that evening.

There were a handful of other customers, regulars it seemed, who clutched their glasses, kept an eye on the Yankee game on the TV at the far end of the bar, and chatted easily with each other. None of them showed any particular interest in Roland, which was fine with him. Most of them were young and probably knew nothing firsthand about the Jorgensons. But Roland did eventually manage to learn something from Bill, the elderly owner of the place, who also presided over the bar.

"Old man Jorgenson made it big in steel, right up there with Carnegie. Lot of money. My father worked on the house when they built it, back in the twenties. Oh, it was beautiful. Wood from South America, marble from Italy, you name it. French furniture, big paintings on the walls. No expense spared. They lived there about two months a year, every summer. They called it a cottage, you know, because it only had about twenty rooms."

Roland nodded, smiling. Bill had a way of saying something and slapping his hand lightly on the bar as if to signal that he was finished. He would turn and drift away, tending to his other customers, but sooner or later he would wander back to Roland and continue, gradually filling in the rest of the story.

The Jorgenson clan came and went year after year. They kept pretty much to themselves. Nothing memorable happened until the winter of 1959, when the house burned down mysteriously. It was gutted, a complete loss. The only people there at the time were the caretaker and his wife, both of whom died in the blaze. Some people thought it was an accident, others that local vandals were responsible—the rich are always resented. There was a lengthy investigation, but no final verdict.

The place was abandoned, the Jorgensons never came back. It wasn't until a few years ago that the estate was in the news once more. A new generation of Jorgensons had seen fit, no doubt with tax considerations in mind, to deed the hundred-plus acres to the state of New York. The surrounding Adirondack forest had already reclaimed it, and now it was a legal fact.

"Weren't there any other buildings, besides the main house?" Roland asked anxiously. "Any other structures?"

"Oh, sure," Bill said. "There was a big garage, a gazebo, a few sheds, and an icehouse. And, uh, Little Italy."

"What?" Roland's hopes soared. "Little Italy?"

"Yeah, my kids used to play there when they were growing up back in the sixties. Crazy thing."

It was a folly, no question. It seemed that the old man had been in love with Italy, so much so that he decided to create a garden that featured miniature replicas of famous Italian sights: the Trevi fountain, Vesuvius and Pompei, the Blue Grotto at Capri and the Colosseum, among others. Jorgenson had added to it every summer for nearly three decades, and by the time of the fire the Italian garden was said to cover nearly four acres.

Roland was both encouraged and depressed. Yes, there was an authentic folly, but it had been rotting away since 1959, exposed to hot summers, freezing winters and the random violence of local kids. Whatever still survived was no doubt crumbling in the grip of the forest. It was sad, and Roland thought he would be lucky to get one halfway decent photograph. But it was certainly worth writing up—and publishing—it would be Roland Turner's first appearance in the pages of the Fellowship magazine.

It was well past ten when he finally left the bar. The heat had eased considerably and a breeze blew through town. The storm was closer. Roland could only hope it would be long gone when he went looking for the Jorgenson place in the morning. He caught a glimpse of lightning in the sky, but it seemed far away and there was no following rumble of thunder.

Main Street was now deserted, and Roland thought it looked a bit like an abandoned movie set. Signs swayed, windows rattled, leaves and dust swirled about, and everything was cast in the dim yellow glow of a few widely spaced streetlamps. The bright neon Genesee sign at Bill's stood out in welcome contrast.

Roland was about to get into his car when he first heard the sound, and he stopped to listen to it. Choir practice? No, this was not musical in the sense that it followed any pattern; it was not even human. Roland slowly turned his head, trying to figure out which direction it came from, but it was too diffuse, and the wind in the trees frequently overwhelmed it.

Back at the motel, Roland heard the sound again as soon as he stepped out of his car. It was stronger and clearer, yet just as hard to define as it had been in town. An Aeolian chorus that sang in the night, rising and fading, shrilling and moaning. The wind was part of it, but there had to be more, some unusual local feature that produced this effect. Roland actually liked it. He was reminded of certain ethereal passages from Debussy and Vaughan Williams. In his room, he turned off the air conditioner, opened a window and listened to it a while longer.

The storm passed by a few miles to the north, crackling and thundering in the distance like a transient war, and the village of Glen Allen took an intense strafing of rain. But it was gone in a quarter of an hour, and its aftermath was a humid, dripping stillness.

In the morning, as he was about to set off for the Jorgenson place, Roland spotted the woman who ran the motel. She came out of the vending machine room with a full garbage sack in one hand. Roland crossed the parking lot and asked her about the sounds he had heard the previous night.

"That's the wind coming down the glen," she told him. "When it blows a certain direction, you get that."

"Yes, but what exactly causes it?"

"The wind coming down the glen," she repeated, as if he were dense. "You don't notice it so much in the winter."

"Ah."

He stopped at Colbert's Store, a few doors up from Bill's on Main Street, to buy a grinder and a carton of juice for lunch. A few minutes later he nearly drove past what had been the entrance to the Jorgenson summer estate. As Bill had explained, it wasn't hard to find: about two miles up North Street, which was the only road north out of town, and look for it on your left. There were two stone columns flanking a single-lane driveway. Roland backed up and studied the scene for a moment.

The stone columns bore the dead pastel blue and green stains of lichen, and their caps were severely chipped and cracked. The wrought iron gate was long gone—only a pair of deeply corroded hinges remained. Then Roland realized that Jorgenson had planted a wall of arborvitae along the road in both directions. It could still be seen, but barely. It must have reached twenty or thirty feet high, but now it was a skeletal ruin, shot through with tall weeds, young maples, choke cherries, wild grapes, and other vines and parasites. The entryway itself was so thick with brush that Roland couldn't even park in it; he had to go another fifty yards before he found a grassy spot on the right. He slung his camera around his neck, took his lunch cooler, locked the car and walked back down the road.

The original dirt road to the house was thoroughly overgrown with weeds and field grass, but it wasn't hard to follow. Roland wandered off it twice and immediately noticed the change from the firm gravel base to a more yielding soil underfoot.

He passed through a tunnel of trees, a landscape effect that may well have been quite lovely once; now it was ragged, dark and gloomy, devastated by secondary growth. He came out of it on the edge of a large clearing, and sensed that he was now close to the site of the house. It was no longer "cleared" at all, of course, but the perimeter was unmistakably marked by the much taller pine trees of the surrounding forest.

Roland's pants were soaked. The sky was overcast, so all of the plants he waded through were still wet from the rain. But he preferred it that way to a blazing hot sun. He followed the road as it climbed a very gradual rise and then leveled off. Yes, he thought excitedly, this has to be it. Where else would you build a house? The three or four acres of flat high ground he stood on provided a gorgeous southern view.

Roland gazed down across the old clearance, looking for any human traces. There was a small lake—perhaps Jorgenson had it created for him—and the stumpy remnants of a wooden pier. The lake was nearly dead now, choked with algae, reeds and silt, but it must have been beautiful once.

Roland found it easy to visualize the Jorgenson children out on the lake canoeing, or jumping from the pier and swimming. The family might well have had picnic lunches in the shade of the big sugar maple that still stood by itself not far from the water. A view of the past. The lives, the dreams, so much effort to build a little world within the world. Were the Jorgensons haughty and unbearable, or decent and worthy of what they had? But it didn't matter, because what they had here was gone and so were they.

Roland turned and snagged his toe on a rock. It was part of the foundation of the house. He walked it, leaving his own trail in the tall grass and wildflowers. The fire, and the years, had left nothing but a rectangle of stones that barely protruded from the earth. The outbuildings had vanished as well; maybe some of the locals had dismantled them for the lumber and fittings.

Roland took a photograph of the ground on which the house had stood, and then another of the broad clearance, including the lake. He ate his lunch quickly, eyes scanning the landscape for a sign, a clue. If the Italian folly was hidden somewhere in the forest, he could spend a week looking for it. There was only one other possibility—somewhere up behind the house. Beyond a low ridge only a hundred yards away, the land seemed to hollow out as steep walls formed on either side. That was north. That was the beginning of the glen, or the end of it.

Roland trudged up the rise, and gaped. There it was, Little Italy, Jorgenson's folly. He was so excited he nearly broke into a run, but then he steadied himself and clicked off several shots of the whole panorama. There were all kinds of houses—country villas, farmhouses, squat urban blocks—scattered in clumps and clusters. There were statues, many statues, fountains, archways, piazzas, towers, churches, stables, barns and much more. It went on into the glen as far as Roland could see.

The land on which most of the folly had been built was low, but it was marked by any number of little hillocks that enhanced the visual effect. In addition, the walls of the glen had a way of jutting out and cutting back that created niches, defiles and recesses of varying size and depth. Every wacky detail somehow worked, and it all came together to create a remarkable illusion at first sight.

In fact, it looked its best at a distance. When Roland came down the slope to it and began to make his way through the narrow passages, the decay was all too obvious. Most of the structures had been built with cinderblocks, or plaster on chicken wire, and then coated with paint or whitewash. Tin roofs had been painted a reddish-brown to suggest tile. Cheap stuff for a rich guy, and it showed the effects of age, neglect and intermittent vandalism. Whole walls had been knocked down or worn away. Much of the tin was corroded, the paint blistered and peeling—what there still was of it. Statues were missing hands or heads, sometimes both. Everything was severely chipped or cracked.

Brambles and vines proliferated, often making it difficult for Roland to move about. But in that respect the folly had been spared worse damage. The ground was rocky and the soil thin, so not much else managed to grow there.

Roland advanced slowly, taking pictures as he went. He knew little about Italy but he recognized most of the famous landmarks Jorgenson had chosen to replicate. He was particularly impressed by a fifty-foot section of the Aquaduct high enough to walk under without ducking his head. It was broken only in three places and actually dripped a tiny residue of last night's rain. Roland had to smile when he noticed that the plaster Aquaduct was lined with cast iron half-pipe.

What really made the whole thing work was the dizzy range of scale—or rather, the complete lack of scale. A two-foot house stood next to a three-foot statue of a dog. Mt. Etna was somehow smaller than the Duomo, while the Spanish Steps were larger than all of Venice. Nothing matched anything.

That, and sheer quirkiness. Working only two months a year, Jorgenson obviously felt compelled to add a number of ready-made items to his dream world. The statues, for instance. And Roland especially liked the birdbath—a common garden birdbath—that utterly dominated St. Peter's Square. There were other birdbaths to be seen, as well as birdhouses that could be purchased in any garden shop or nursery even today; perhaps in the extreme reaches of his obsession Jorgenson saw an ideal Italy populated solely by birds. Roland grinned a few moments later when he came across a statue of Saint Francis of Assisi, surrounded by birdhouses that were mounted on sections of lead pipe—with the entire tableau situated between a *trattoria* and a bizarre little maze apparently meant to suggest the catacombs.

Roland came into a small clearing with a stone bench. Maybe this was where old man Jorgenson sat, pondering his extraordinary creation and dreaming up more additions to it. Roland rested his feet for a moment and changed the film in his camera.

It was easy to lose track of the size of the folly. Many of the structures were only three feet high, but quite a few were as tall as man, and with the gently undulating flow of the ground it was impossible to see ahead to the point where the folly displays finally came to an end. But it was also impossible to get lost, since the walls of the glen were always visible.

Roland had to keep moving. The sky seemed to be darker now, not from the lateness of the hour but from the appearance of more storm clouds. He hadn't thought to check the weather report, and he had no idea whether a new storm was due or it was the same one circling back. Roland didn't like the idea of having to hike all the way back to the car in a downpour, but it might come to that. He wasn't going to leave until he had seen and photographed every part of the folly.

Jorgenson had saved his most astounding flight of fancy for the last. Roland stepped through a gap in a wall, and he thought that he was standing in a courtyard. A stretch of ground roughly one hundred feet square had been covered with large paving stones that had subsequently buckled and heaved. Now the whole area was shot through with tufts of dull green weeds, laced with some kind of wild ground ivy.

There was a line of columns along the left edge and another on the right. They were ten or twelve feet high and some of them had fallen over, but they created a sudden impression that still had power. Roland found himself thinking of the Pantheon, but he had no clear mental image of the original to compare.

All this, however, was peripheral to the set piece straight ahead. Where the paving stones ended the ground rose up slightly before it leveled off, creating a rough natural platform. It was as wide as the courtyard, and it was full of statues. There were dozens of them. Roland stumbled forward.

Several interesting features, he thought in a daze. All the statues were positioned to face the center of the glen. They all had their arms raised and their faces uplifted, as if acclaiming the gods or seeking their merciful help. None of them had hands. They had open mouths but otherwise there were no facial features, not a nose or an eye or an ear in the entire assembly. They had no feet, unless they were buried in the ground, for the legs rose up out of the soil, converging in thick, trunk-like torsos. The statues were crude and stark, and yet they seemed to be possessed of a terrible poignancy.

They weren't presented as Romans in togas and robes. There were no gods or creatures of myth, not even a Venetian gondolier. They were like golems, clad in stone. Roland climbed the rise to inspect them close up. The surface was brownish in color, rough but firm in texture—like partly annealed sand. Perhaps there was an underlayer of plaster or cement. Roland had seen nothing else like it in Jorgenson's Little Italy. It was an improvement; these statues showed very little evidence of erosion.

But what madness!

Roland was in the middle of his final roll of film, snapping medium shots of the amazing statuary, when the first hand grabbed him by the belt in the small of his back. Then there were others on his body, pulling him down from behind. Something banged him along the side of the head, stunning him briefly.

How much time had passed? Roland's vision was blurred, and would not correct. His head throbbed painfully. It was dark and the air was somehow different. Maybe he was in a cave. He could just make out flickering firelight, and the busy movements of his captors. Roland couldn't move. They held him to the ground, his arms outstretched.

They were like kids—not yet fully grown, voices unformed. He thought there were about a half dozen of them. He had no idea what was going on, he couldn't understand anything. An unnatural silence alarmed him. Roland tried to speak to them, but they sat on his chest and legs, pinned his head in place, and stuffed foul rags in his mouth. Then he saw the dull glint of an axe blade as it began its downward descent to the spot where his left hand was firmly held. Same thing on the right a few seconds later, but by then Roland was already unconscious.

Searing pain revived him; that, and perhaps a lingering will to struggle and save his life. He was alone for the moment, but he could hear them—their squeaky murmurs, and a disturbing wet scraping noise.

Demented teenagers. Maybe some weird sect or cult. Or they could be a brain-stunted, inbred rural clan that preyed on anyone who was foolish enough to stray into their territory. How could this happen? Was the whole town in on it? What could they want? Perhaps in exploring and photographing Jorgenson's Italian folly, he had somehow violated their sacred ground. But it seemed most likely that they were insane, pure and simple.

Roland still couldn't move. His wrist-stumps were bandaged. The bastards had actually chopped his hands off. The realization nearly knocked him out again but Roland fought off total panic. He had to think clearly, or he was surely lost. The rest of his body from the neck down seemed to be wrapped in some kind of wire mesh. His mouth was still clogged with the hideous rags, and he had to breathe through his nose. He tried to lever his tongue to push the rags out, or to one side, so he could speak, but at that moment they came back for him.

They dragged him, and it became clear to Roland that some of the monstrous pain he felt was coming from where his two feet had been. They threw him down in a torch-lit clearing. They spread his legs, held his arms out, and began to smear some thick, gooey substance on him. Roland flipped and squirmed like a fish on the floor of a boat until they clubbed him again.

Fresh air, dusk light.

The same day? Couldn't be. But overcast, the wind whipping loudly—and that choral sound Roland had heard his first night in town. They carried him out of the cave, and the wailing noise seemed to fill his brain. He was in the center of it, and it was unbearable.

Only his head was exposed—the rest of his body now stone. It came up to his neck in a rigid collar and forced his head back at a painful angle. Roland caught sight of them as they propped him in his place on the third rank of the statuary. They weren't kids, they didn't even look human—pinched little faces, stubby fingers, a manic bustle to their movements, and the insect jabber that was all but lost in the boiling wind.

Like caricature scientists, they turned him one way and then another, tilting, nudging and adjusting. They finally yanked the rags out of his mouth. Roland tried to croak out a few words but his tongue was too dry. Then the final mystery was solved as his captors thrust a curious device into his mouth. He saw it for an instant—a wire cage that contained several loose wooden balls. They were of varying sizes, and Roland thought he saw grooves and holes cut in them. It fit so well that his tongue was pressed to the floor of his mouth. A couple of strands of rawhide were tied around his head, securing the device even more tightly.

A last corrective nudge, and then the wind took hold and the wooden balls danced and bounced. Another voice joined the choir. Satisfied, they went on to complete their work, covering the rest of his head with the sticky cement and then applying the exterior finish. Only his open mouth was left untouched.

Roland thought of insects nesting there. He pictured a warm mist billowing out on cool mornings as he rotted inside. And he wondered how long it would take to die. They must do repair work later, to keep the cages in place after the flesh disappeared. A strangely comforting thought in the giddy swirl of despair.

The wind came gusting down the glen. Empty arms raised, his anonymous face lifted to the unseeing sky, he sang.

A Grub Street Tale

"I still don't think he was that good," Geoffrey Wilson said as he charred the tip of a panatela. "Obviously he had a talent, but the fact is he never knew quite what to do with it."

"He's being compared to Hawthorne now."

"Ridiculous, isn't it." Geoffrey smiled and shook his head. "The same people who say that wouldn't deign to review his novels if he were still alive."

Judith Stockmann nodded hesitantly, as if she almost agreed with him. Geoffrey rather liked her, this dark-haired, dark-eyed young beauty. The perfect companion for a lovely summer evening. They were sitting on the terrace of a pub in Chiswick, discussing the short life and varying literary works of Patrick Hamm.

"You think he's overrated?"

"Oh yes, of course." Geoffrey flicked his lighter again and puffed until the cigar was properly lit. "No question."

"What was he like as a person?"

"He had a certain charm. We had some good times together in Soho, early on. He drank too much, needless to say."

"Especially in the last year?"

Geoffrey considered that. "All along the line, really. It did get worse toward the end, I suppose, but by that time Patrick and I saw very little of each other. Alas."

A sore point, that falling-out, but one that could hardly be avoided. It was a part of the unfortunate history. Geoffrey was reluctant to discuss Patrick Hamm with anybody, and at first he'd tried to fend off Judith Stockmann. But she had persisted, with notes or phone calls every week. Geoffrey eventually realized he couldn't put her off forever.

So he had agreed to this meeting on neutral ground. Dredge up a few moth-eaten tidbits for her critical biography of Patrick Hamm and try to cast things in a positive light. Geoffrey didn't care about her project, but why not see what Judith Stockmann was like in the flesh? So far, she seemed fair and objective. Quite attractive, as well.

"Were the two of you friends before—"

"No, it was strictly business at first. Our friendship grew out of our work together, over the course of time. I had serious hopes for Patrick and I genuinely liked him as a person. When he wandered off-track I did my best to help him right himself. But it's difficult for an editor and an author to hang together when there are serious disagreements."

Judith nodded again. "Commerce and creativity?"

"That was one part of it, yes," Geoffrey replied, "but there were other problems. Patrick could never bring himself to decide exactly what kind of writer he wanted to be."

"Don't most writers work through that?"

"It isn't easy to market an author who jumps from one genre to another and mixes them together. Booksellers have a hard time dealing with that, and so do readers."

"But the consensus now seems to be that Hamm found his true voice toward the end, with *The Lime-Kiln* and *The Varna Schooner.*" Judith sipped her wine. "He was only forty-one, you could say he was just hitting his stride when—"

"I know, I know," Geoffrey cut in. "Everybody seems to love those two books, and of course it's all very tragic, the way that it ended. But I thought at the time that those books were really very pretentious, and I honestly still do."

"You prefer his earlier work."

"Yes, I do. *Our Lady of Heavenly Pain* and *Nightmare in Silk* are my two favorites. I published them both, and I believed that Patrick was onto something new. It was brilliant erotica, it was elegant and stylish. It used elements of the thriller and horror fiction to good effect. I loved it, and I can remember thinking, he can't miss." Geoffrey shrugged sadly. "But he did."

"Critics now tend to see those works as potboilers," Judith said. "Efficient, but limited. Finger exercises, part of Hamm's mastering the craft of fiction."

Wilson scowled. "They would, wouldn't they."

"After the first two books—"

"That's when he started to drift," Geoffrey answered before he heard the rest of the question. "He wrote that ill-conceived family gothic, *The Weybright Curse.* God, I hated that. I'd just moved up to Pell House then and I was eager to bring Patrick with me. But I couldn't accept that book. He stayed at Bingley, they published it, and it promptly sank like a rock."

"Were there hard feelings?"

"Some, yes." Geoffrey reflected for a moment. "But I still wanted to publish Patrick, so I encouraged him to get on with the next novel. *Ill-Met by Gaslight*, which I did publish. It was an odd book, a modern murder mystery with time travel, but it worked in some bizarre way, and he was back with me."

"Was that about the time he turned to short fiction?"

She had an exquisite neck, Geoffrey noted. Honeyish tanned skin set off by a brilliant white blouse and tiny pearls.

"Yes, and it was infuriating. Nasty little stories, full of disagreeable people doing disagreeable things. He put together a volume called *Micronovels of the Dead*, and that was soon followed by a second one, *Tales of Extreme Panic*. But nobody would touch them. Patrick eventually lost his agent over that short fiction. No one knew it at the time, sad to say, but he was well into his final phase by then."

"Now those stories are highly regarded."

"Patrick would appreciate the joke."

"Did he discuss the last two novels with you?"

"Oh yes, and I advised him as best I could. But there were some serious problems to overcome." Geoffrey put his cigar down on the ashtray. "You see, by that time his name and sales record in the book business meant nothing. He'd frittered away whatever identity he had managed to create for himself. He was getting to be old goods, a maverick, and nobody cared. Career-wise, Patrick was in big trouble."

She had gorgeous legs, long and slender. Geoffrey could see and enjoy them properly, now that Judith was leaning back on the sofa in his sittingroom. They'd had a couple of polite drinks at the pub, and then she accepted his invitation to dinner. He took pride in his cooking ability and he intended to broil two superb Wiltshire steaks—assuming they got around to food.

He could dole out boring old Patrick Hamm anecdotes for days if that would keep her happy. Days, nights. First, he dug out a file of old letters from Patrick. Harmless stuff, often amusing, none of the final anger and anguish. Judith scanned them quickly and murmured with delight at certain passages. She gave Geoffrey a warm smile when he offered to make copies for her.

She knew the books quite well, but not the man's life. Her knowledge of personal details was limited to the kind of material that had appeared often in the press. Geoffrey was the first of Hamm's personal acquaintances that Judith had approached—so he had clear sailing and could set the tone. They had more wine as he talked and she listened.

The Soho clubs, Hamm's assorted and equally hopeless lovers, a brief stint working in an East End soup kitchen, Hamm's writing habits, his appalling taste in food, his uninformed love of music and art—Geoffrey told Judith all sorts of odd details as they came to mind. It might not be significantly illuminating of the man's work, but it certainly had the authentic feel of firsthand experience. Geoffrey could see that Judith was loving every word of it, and that pleased him.

"To get back to his books," she said. "He did stop writing the short stories and started a new novel, *The Lime-Kiln*. And he showed it to you as he was working on it, didn't he?"

"Yes, that's right," Wilson replied. "I thought it started off in very promising fashion, but at about two-thirds of the way through it Patrick lost the thread. I don't think he liked his own characters. He killed them all off, every one of them, which resulted in a book that ended as a damp misfire. What was it all supposed to be about, and who cared anyhow?"

"What did he do then?"

"He went back over it from scratch, just as I suggested. It wasn't the plot so much as the characters, the heart of the book. And the ending, of course."

"But that first version is essentially the same one that has since been published and acclaimed everywhere."

"Oh yes, yes." Wilson still ground his teeth at the notion. "After his suicide, all of that gloom and despair no doubt seemed more convincing. You could say it gave him literary credibility. I know that must sound awfully cynical, but that's how the world works sometimes. If Patrick had remained here in the land of the living, the living would have continued to ignore him."

It was sickening, really. Three years after Patrick's death *The Lime-Kiln* was published to sudden acclaim. A year later, *The Varna Schooner* followed to an equally enthusiastic response. The collected stories. And the literary community embraced a corpse, made a fallen hero of him. To Geoffrey it was all so hypocritical and crass. Trading on the dead. Sickening.

Patrick's suicide had occurred a decade ago, and the bubblet had diminished somewhat in recent years. It was bound to subside even more in time, Geoffrey was convinced. Patrick's writing was often interesting, striking and disturbing, but it was not great. Not truly classic. No matter what anyone said.

"You didn't publish the second version either," Judith said. "Can you tell me about that?"

"It was no better," Geoffrey replied promptly. "And in some ways it was actually worse. Revision was never Patrick's strong suit, and he was almost relieved when I suggested that he set *The Lime-Kiln* aside for a while and start something new."

"*The Varna Schooner.*"

"Yes, and a great idea it was. The full-length treatment of an episode merely hinted at in *Dracula*. What went on aboard that ship carrying Dracula's coffin to England? What if there were a few passengers, as well as the crew? I loved the idea. But once again, Patrick had problems. He had a very hard time getting the period atmosphere right. He wouldn't do the research, he had no interest in the kind of details that would make a book like that convincing. Instead, there was more of that fancy philosophical talk, endless pretentious babble. The same thing that I believed was the cause of all the trouble in *The Lime-Kiln*. It got in the way of the story, just totally flattened it." Geoffrey continued quickly, "Now, I know what you're thinking. That what I disliked is exactly what people now praise in those books, it's what makes them so good. Right?"

Judith smiled. "Well, that is true."

"Yes, it is." Geoffrey turned his hands palms-up and gave a helpless shrug. "What can I say? Perhaps I was wrong. Mistakes do happen in the book business. Eighteen publishers rejected *The Day of the Jackal*. Everybody knows DeGaulle wasn't assassinated, so who cares? Twenty publishers rejected *Watership Down*. Nobody wants to read about a bunch of bloody rabbits." Judith laughed. "So, those things do happen."

"And that was when the two of you had your final break?" she asked cautiously.

Geoffrey nodded tightly. "It was an honest disagreement. I told Patrick that his characters weren't real enough. He was too interested in using them as ideas, as symbols. That and the lack of attention to period atmosphere ruined both books."

"For you."

"For me, yes," he agreed reasonably. "If I could just give you my capsule view of Patrick's last two novels, I honestly feel that they fall between two stools. They're too sophisticated and good for the commercial market, category fiction, but they're not quite brilliant enough for literary acceptance."

"Hmn." Judith appeared to consider that.

"Patrick didn't care whether he was a commercial success and made a lot of money, or achieved literary stature. But he wanted one or the other, if not both, and that's the sad part. He never experienced either of them in his lifetime."

"That's certainly true."

They were in Geoffrey's study. He had remembered a box of old photographs from his days at Bingley and he knew that several of them showed Patrick. The Thursday afternoons when some of the house authors would drop by and the booze flowed, the fierce talk about literature and the book trade. Great times. Unheard of in this new era, with the business driven by accountants.

Judith loved the snapshots and thought one of them might be reproduced satisfactorily in her eventual book. Geoffrey agreed, happy to please her. It might never happen, anyway. Most books died before they reached hardcovers, and he was far from certain that there was enough event in Patrick's gloomy life to justify a proper critical biography. But why discourage her?

Geoffrey sat close to her on the sofa in his study, looking down her blouse while he explained who people were in each photo. Very minor writers, most of them, sorted out and silenced by the marketplace over the years. Decent folks, and they all had their two or three published volumes, now yellowing on a shelf at home, to comfort them in the genteel failure of their advancing years. Even one forgotten book—is still something.

"Did he—"

"Enough," Geoffrey interrupted softly. He took the box of photographs and set them on the coffee table. "I think I've done enough talking for one session. We can always return to Patrick Hamm another time. I'd like to hear more about you now."

"You would?"

"Yes."

Judith smiled. "But should I tell you?"

"Yes, you should."

Patrick caressed her cheek with the back of his fingers, and she liked it. She didn't do anything but he could see it in her eyes, and he suddenly thought: she may be in love with a dead man but she will sleep with me tonight. Judith smiled at him, rested her head on his shoulder and then gazed absently at the wineglass that she still held on her lap.

"Where to start?"

"It's your story. Anywhere you like."

He felt her laugh silently and managed to use that moment to slip an arm around her shoulder. Geoffrey thought he noticed her body respond by settling closer against his.

"We came from Russia. It was quite an adventure, actually," Judith said. "But at the time it was very frightening."

"Is that so?"

"Oh, yes. Our family name was Bronstein but my father took the name Stockmann, from Ibsen's *An Enemy of the People*. He was opposed to the government, he wrote pamphlets and tracts, he went to prison twice, they beat him. We lived in constant fear, never knowing when the police might come. But father was a man of real integrity. He was an anarchist, in the truest sense of the term. An idealist, really."

"A Russian anarchist," Geoffrey mused. "Fantastic."

"Anyhow, the regime was very shaky," Judith continued. "My father believed that real change, revolution, was bound to happen soon. Perhaps my father went too far in his papers and speeches, or it was just another crackdown. The Tsar's secret police had my father's name on a list of people to be arrested, and everyone knew that this time the accused would never come back from prison alive. So we had to flee the country."

"Good Lord." Still, something was not right there.

"There was no time to spare. We left everything behind, and had to sneak out of Moscow in the middle of the night."

"And you made it, thank God."

Geoffrey stroked her neck lightly, tracing lines down toward the collar of her blouse. The Tsar? She meant the KGB, clearly, but this was not the time to play editor.

"Only just," Judith said, "and not all of us. We managed to get across the border, into Romania, and then on to Bulgaria, but police agents stayed on our trail. We had a couple of very close escapes along the way."

"Of course the Romanians and Bulgarians would cooperate with the Russians, wouldn't they."

"Or at least look the other way, yes. But we made it to the coast and my father had enough money to bribe an official and buy passage for us on a cargo ship to England."

"Aha. Very good."

"Can you guess where we sailed from?"

"I have no idea." Geoffrey laughed at himself. "In fact, I didn't even know Bulgaria had a coast."

"It's on the Black Sea."

"Yes, yes, of course. The Black Sea, the Caspian. They're all somewhere in that neck of the woods, aren't they."

"We sailed from the port of Varna."

"Va—you're joking." With his free hand he took Judith's chin and turned her face so that she was looking at him. She was smiling, but not as if she'd made a joke. "You weren't serious, were you. Varna? Really?"

"Yes," she said simply. "It really happened. I know it's incredible, but it is the truth."

"Incredible? Not half. Ah, now I understand it," Geoffrey went on. "You grew up here in England. Later, you saw Patrick's book, *The Varna Schooner*, and so you read it because you'd passed through Varna. That's how you first came to know Patrick's work, you fell in love with it, and—here we are."

"That's not entirely wrong."

"What do you mean?"

"You're right—here we are."

God, sometimes he was bloody slow on the uptake. There she was, lips parted, eyes half shut, offering herself to him, and he was still trying to carry on a conversation. Nitwit! He quickly pulled Judith closer and kissed her. It was long, slow, deep and utterly wonderful. Geoffrey's hand slipped inside her blouse and touched skin that felt like warm silk, like some rare gold liquid that seemed to welcome and embrace his own flesh. Her whole body seemed to melt into his and that somehow made him feel profoundly alive, vastly more aroused.

Her tongue—no, a tooth, surely—entered his tongue, and it was like smooth sex, a painless, exhilarating penetration. He was puzzled and startled by it, however. He opened his eyes as he tried to pull back a couple of inches—and he couldn't move. It was as if Judith held him by the tongue, with some part of her mouth. Her eyes were locked on him, but she didn't appear to see him. His tongue throbbed, but not unpleasantly. Geoffrey had an odd sense of his mind slipping out of focus, drifting hazily. It was difficult to form thoughts, they seemed to keep falling beyond his grasp. He didn't mind. Much easier to drift, to float along in a delicious fog. It was so comforting.

He didn't hurt, but he felt weak. He was still on the sofa in his study, but now he was lying flat on his back. Judith sat on the floor beside him. The golden glow of her cheeks was now suffused with a faint pink blush. He felt so tired. He smiled, glad she was still there with him, though he wasn't exactly sure what had happened between them.

"You never even read *The Varna Schooner*," she said almost in a tone of regret. "You thought *The Lime-Kiln* was a waste and you were sure *The Varna Schooner* would be just as bad."

"No, I read it." Now he knew something was wrong.

"You didn't even remember my name," Judith told him.

"Years ago. Ten, at least. More."

"Patrick gave me life," she continued. "He created me, and at the end of the book he saved my life. I lost my entire family on the schooner *Demeter*, and the crew died as well. Patrick gave them all to Dracula, who came out of his coffin in the hold. But Patrick allowed one person to survive, a child, a little girl. I escaped ashore at Whitby."

"Mad."

"But there's a price to pay for life," Judith went on. "Any form of life. Patrick made me one of those who live forever. He was a good man, strong in many ways, but hopeless at dealing with the outside world. Hopeless at career-building. He trusted you, in spite of the times you let him down. And when you had no use for him or his last two books, he finally gave up. He knew he'd done his best work, but he had no hope left for it."

"He was a baby."

Geoffrey felt good saying that. It took all his strength to get the words out. He could barely move.

"I won't take all of your blood. That would be too easy. I can keep you this way for days." Judith smiled at him. "Days on end. Until you eventually die of hunger. Like Patrick."

"Compound organ failure," Geoffrey corrected stubbornly.

"Brought on by malnutrition. Starvation. When Patrick died in that awful flat in Hackney, he had no money, nothing."

"It was a Simone Weil stunt," Geoffrey railed angrily. "The ultimate career move. He had friends he could have gone to, he'd done so many times before. And he had money."

The exertion nearly knocked him out.

"Friends?" Judith said. "You were the only one, and you let him down. Money? He had seventeen pounds, that's all."

"Enough to eat. To work, to live another day." He tried to push himself up on one hand. He was shaky, but he thought he was beginning to regain some of his strength. "He didn't have to die the way he did."

"No, he didn't."

"He had friends. I told you. He had money."

"Yes, Geoffrey." Judith smiled again as she leaned forward, her mouth approaching his. "And I'm sure you do, too."

INFIDEL

"And how is me dear old friend Andy these days?"

"He's fine. He's in good health, and he said to tell you he plays golf at least once a week."

"Tsk." Monsignor Comerford shook his head in mock annoyance but couldn't keep from smiling. "It's a grand racket, the parish priest. Marry 'em and bury 'em, and count the weekly take. Tell Andy I said that, would you?"

"I will," Caroline replied.

"Did you know Andy and I were in college together in Dublin? University College. That was ages ago, of course."

"Yes, he told me that's where you met," Caroline said. "And UCD was where James Joyce went too, wasn't it?"

"That's right, Earlsfort Terrace. Great writer, Joyce," the monsignor added perfunctorily, as if he did not quite agree with his own statement. "A fine feel for the city back then, I'll say that much for him."

Caroline reached into her purse. "I took this snapshot of Father Andy a couple of weeks ago," she said as she passed it to the elderly priest.

"Ah, will you look at that chubby little bugger," Monsignor Comerford exclaimed with glee as he took the photograph. "He was always first at table, now that I think back on it. Mind you, he never shied away from a gargle either, but you'd better not tell him I said *that*. He might worry about his image. Parish priests tend to fret about such things in America."

"You can keep it, Monsignor," Caroline said as he attempted to return the photograph. "It's for you."

"Thank you very much." He set the picture down on his desk, next to the letter of introduction that Father Andy had written for Caroline. "But let's skip that 'Monsignor' business, shall we? Gerry will do nicely." Caroline smiled and nodded. "Good. Now then, how long have you been in Rome?"

"Four days."

It came as a mild surprise for Caroline to be reminded that she was sitting in an office in Vatican City, not in a rectory in some leafy suburb of Dublin. Monsignor Comerford, she knew, had been stationed at the Vatican for nearly two decades, but he was still thoroughly Irish in his appearance, accent and manner. The pink, well-scrubbed complexion, the curly white hair, the steady cascade of Carroll's cigarette ash down the front of his black jacket, the gentle singsong voice—all seemed to belong more in a cluttered Georgian sitting room with peat blazing fragrantly in the fireplace and a big bottle of Powers on the sideboard than in this obscure corner of the papal bureaucracy. Caroline had no clear idea what the monsignor *did* at the Vatican, but neither did Father Andy.

"And it says here," tapping the letter, "you're a librarian. Is that right?"

"Yes," Caroline answered.

"Very good, and what exactly is it you'd like to do?"

"I'd love to spend some time just looking through the books, the archives. It probably sounds silly, but I've always dreamed of having a chance to explore the Vatican library. I love books and manuscripts, all forms of writing."

Caroline hoped he wouldn't ask if she had been to Trinity or the Bodleian or the Sorbonne, because she hadn't. How could she explain to the priest that it wasn't just books, but the Vatican itself, that had drawn her? She really did dream of the Vatican—bizarre images of capture, of anonymous torture, of being trapped forever in an endless maze of barren hallways. Nothing was ever said, there were no signs, but somehow Caroline always knew that she was in the Vatican. At times she wondered if the recurring dreams were a form of sickness, but they never frightened her; on the contrary, she had come to feel almost comfortable with them.

"Is it the dirty books you're after?" Monsignor Comerford's eyes had turned steely. "We've a regular army of these so-called scholars that come trooping through here, most of them American I might add, and all they want to do is study the dirty books. Why we even keep them is beyond me, but nowadays destroying a book is almost a mortal sin. To some folks, anyway."

The monsignor was apparently finished, so Caroline answered his question. "No. History and the history of the faith, are my favorite subjects." Faith, she thought, and the loss of it.

"Ah, that's a welcome change." The monsignor beamed at her. "If all the fine young women of the world felt that way, there'd be a lot less bother taking place."

There was a barb in the compliment, for Caroline noticed how the monsignor glanced at her unadorned ring finger. History and books were all well and good, but he believes I should be married and taking care of a bunch of babies, she thought. That was fine with her. Caroline might disagree with Monsignor Comerford as to what a woman should or should not do but she was actually pleased that he was a priest from the old school. She hadn't come to the Vatican looking for trendiness or progressive attitudes. Her own faith had been blasted by the winds of modernism swirling through the Church in recent years.

"Well, you'd better get started," the monsignor said, rising from his seat. "You can have the rest of the afternoon, just get yourself back here by five. That's when I leave, and I wouldn't want you getting lost."

"Neither would I."

"And if you haven't had enough, you're more than welcome to come back tomorrow. There's so much of that clutter downstairs a person could spend years poking through it all, if he had nothing better to do with his life. And contrary to what you might have heard, none of it is off limits." The priest paused, then winked at her. "Of course, it's not everyone that gets in."

Monsignor Comerford left Caroline with Father Vincenzo, who was apparently in charge of 'the collection.' A short, thin man who wore wire-rimmed glasses and spoke excellent English, Father Vincenzo showed her some of the noteworthy documents and volumes in the official library. Air-conditioned, computerized, it was a completely modern operation in a centuries-old setting. And yet, it was a good deal smaller than Caroline had expected. But then Father Vincenzo took her on a tour of the three main levels below ground, where one room grew out of another and the number of them ran into the dozens before she lost count. There were books and manuscripts and tottering heaps of papers piled on every inch of shelf space, from floor to ceiling. Tiny corridors appeared, and then abruptly ended. On the third and lowest level the floor was made up of large stone slabs, long since worn smooth. The rooms were small and boxy, and seemed to have been carved right out of the earth. The passageways were quite narrow and the only lights were strung along the low ceiling with electric cable.

There were no labels, no numbers, no signs, nothing at all to indicate order. If you wanted to find something, where would you start,

Caroline wondered. But she was delighted, because she finally felt she had arrived where she was meant to be.

"These are the oldest stacks," Father Vincenzo explained. "Everything valuable or important has been removed, but otherwise it is not very organized."

"There's so much of it," Caroline said.

"Yes, it extends under most of Vatican City. The equivalent of two or three square blocks in New York City, I think." Then a smile formed at the corners of Father Vincenzo's mouth. "You are a book-lover. This, I think, is what you came to see."

"Oh yes, yes. I'm amazed. It's so much like I pictured it in my fantasies." The word seemed too personal, almost sexual in its intensity. Caroline felt her cheeks flush, and all she could do was add weakly, "But more so."

Father Vincenzo brought Caroline back to the stairs in order to show her how easy it was to find the way out, and then he left her alone to pursue her curiosity. She appreciated the fact that he didn't feel it necessary to warn her against damaging, copying or tracing over anything.

Caroline wandered aimlessly for a while, stopping to look at one item or another, and then moving on. Her knowledge of French and Latin was excellent, and she had a smattering of Italian, but most of the pages on the third level were handwritten, and sooner or later the calligraphy defeated her. Caroline simply could not concentrate, her mind refused to focus. What am I doing here?

Somewhere in a far corner of the third level, Caroline found a battered footstool in one room. She sat down on it, and leaned back against a wall of large, leathery tomes. She was tired, and her feet ached, the usual tourist curse, but she felt very happy. Pennsylvania seemed a billion miles away. She let her eyes close for a moment, and she sucked in the musty air. To Caroline it was like a rare and delicious perfume.

Books were the center of her life, and it had been that way ever since she was a small child. She liked to believe that she could still remember fumbling to open her very first picture book of nursery rhymes—but Caroline knew that was probably more her fancy than an actual memory. Books were mysterious, frightening, thrilling, disturbing, uplifting, nurturing, endlessly available and always accommodating. Caroline had dated many men over the years, but she had yet to find one who offered the same array of valuable qualities. Most of the time that didn't bother her. If you had to have something other than a relationship for the focal point of your life, what better than books?

Books, and belief. But belief was an increasingly elusive notion. For years it had been a natural part of Caroline's life, but lately it seemed irrelevant, or not even there. Nothing specific had happened to cause this change, yet it seemed as if the deep well of her faith had gradually evaporated to the point where it was now not much more than a thin, moist residue. But you can't control faith, anymore than you can choose your dreams.

Caroline stood up and resumed her wandering. In one large room she came across signs of fairly recent activity. There were stacks of bound papers on a table, many more on the floor around it. A prospectus announced the publication of the *Annals of the Propagation of the Faith* in five hundred volumes over a period of twenty years. Caroline knew that the *Annals* were regular reports to the Vatican from Catholic missionaries all over the world. It was a staggering thought. How many centuries of this tedious and obscure paperwork had accumulated by now? And yet, Caroline was sure that some of it must be quite fascinating. However, clipped to the prospectus was a laconic handwritten note, dated November, 1974, which stated that the project was abandoned because of the bankruptcy of the publisher. And of course the Vatican wouldn't squander its own funds on such an improbable commercial venture, Caroline thought, smiling as she left the room.

She walked until she came to the lowest (the floor had a way of gradually winding down into the earth) and most remote corner of the third level. Certainly this was where the overhead reach of electric cable and lights ended. About twenty feet away, just visible in the gloom, was a stone wall that marked the end of the passageway. The books and manuscripts, stacked from the floor to the ceiling on each side, were wedged together so tightly and had been undisturbed for so long that they appeared to have hardened into a solid mass, and Caroline was afraid she would damage them if she tried to remove any one item for scrutiny. She started to turn away, intending to make the long climb back up to the street level, but then she stopped, as she thought she noticed something odd about the far wall.

It was an optical illusion, aided by the feeble light. Yes, she realized, moving closer. There was not one wall, but two, at the end of the aisle. The outer wall, which came from the right, stopped just short of the stacks on the left, and the inner wall receded almost imperceptibly behind it. Caroline approached the gap, barely a foot wide, and peered around the corner.

Total darkness. She reached into it, and felt nothing but cool air. The passage continued. Caroline didn't know what she should do. She wanted to follow it, to find out where it went, but she had nothing to light her way. She could trip and tumble down a hole, or walk into a den of snakes or vermin—too many bad things could happen. Buy a flashlight and return tomorrow.

Yes, but first...Caroline slid her foot along the ground and edged herself behind the wall. Just a step or two, she promised, to see if it ends abruptly. Her outstretched hand bumped against something hard, not stone. A metal bar. Caroline gripped it and harsh rust flaked loose in her hand. It had to be a gate, which meant that the passage *did* go on. Caroline shook it firmly once, and the whole thing broke free. It was too heavy and unwieldy to control, so she shoved it away from her. The sound that came in the darkness told her that the gate had hit a wall and then slid down to the left. Firm ground, and a turn.

Caroline worked her way along the narrow passage. The wall swung back to the left, as expected. She moved cautiously around the turn, probing the air with her hand. Caroline stopped. This was as far as she could safely go without a light. She stared at the uniform blackness ahead of her. Beyond this point she could easily get lost in a maze of passageways. Okay, she thought, you found something interesting; come back tomorrow with a flashlight and a sack of breadcrumbs.

Caroline hesitated, her mind dancing with possibilities. It could be a long-forgotten catacomb, or a burial chamber that held the mummified remains of ancient Romans. She might even discover some manuscripts that dated back two thousand years. She should discuss it with Father Vincenzo, and together they could organize a proper exploration. But even as Caroline considered this, she found it impossible to turn back. The priest's office was so far away, such an enormous climb—and Caroline felt too tired. The cumulative effects of travel and touring and the miles of walking had finally caught up with her. The dead air didn't help either. She would have to rest for a few minutes before leaving.

As she stood there, leaning against the wall, Caroline began to notice the quality of the darkness. You could say that it had no depth at all, or that its depth was endless. But it was not a perfect darkness, she realized. Somewhere in it, close by or off in the distance, there was—not light, but the subtlest texture of light. I must look like someone on drugs, Caroline thought as she stared ahead. Pupils dilated wide as drift nets to sweep any random photons across the threshold of visibility. I look like a freak, but that's okay because it's a freaky situation. Caroline felt dizzy and disoriented, as if she could no longer tell which way was up, and yet there was nothing she could do—except fall down, if that's what was going to happen—because she was just too tired, too damn tired to care. But she was not wrong. There was light, or something like it.

Caroline was aware of the fact that she was walking. Toward the light, into the dark, it didn't matter which. She felt oddly detached from what was happening, as if her body had decided to move and her mind was simply floating along with it. Probably no one still alive in the Vatican knew of this hidden area, Caroline thought dreamily. Which means, *No one in the world knows where I am now.* But that didn't frighten her. On the contrary, she felt caught up in something of real importance out on the boundary of faith and uncertainty, and dreams.

A suffusion of light infiltrated her right eye, knocking her off balance. It wasn't that strong, Caroline saw as she steadied herself and her eyes re-adjusted. It was a glow, a hazy cloud of cold light some distance away, too weak to illuminate this place. Yet it had confused her for a brief moment. Caroline crossed the intervening space and walked into the faint light. She looked at a flight of crude stairs that coiled down and away from her, deep into the chilly earth.

For just an instant Caroline's mind slid toward the idea of leaving, but just as quickly it skittered away. Her body had no strength for going back now. It was as if she were caught on an electric current that carried her only forward, and down. And so Caroline descended the wet and slippery steps, pressing her hands against the close walls and bending her head beneath the low rock ceiling. Count the number—but the numbers bounced around like a flock of billiard balls clicking in her brain, and the momentum of her descent increased rapidly, flooding her with apprehension, so she couldn't.

Almost brightness. Caroline's knees sagged as her feet hit bottom suddenly and there was nowhere to go. She had arrived in a small room, really nothing more than a landing. Then she saw the gate, another gate. No, it was a door. Through the bars, a square cell, empty but for the old man lying in the middle of the floor. A clutch of tattered rags. The man looked ancient. What light was this?

Ah, child.

—Who...are you?

The words formed in her mind but never escaped her lips. It didn't matter. The old man smiled, and it felt, disturbingly, as if he somehow made Caroline's face smile with him.

Mani.

—What?

Caroline's brain swirled sickeningly, and it took an effort of the will to remain on her feet. The old man kept smiling that near-death smile. A sack of dead skin. But the smile, and those eyes were very much alive. He moved slightly, the muted sound of dusty parchment rustling.

Ma-nee.

The first syllable prolonged, the second quite crisp despite the long vowel. Caroline shook her head slowly.

—No...

Manicheus, if you wish.

Impossible, Caroline thought. It was all wrong and she knew she should leave at once, but instead her body sank down the wall until she was sitting on the bottom step.

—The holy man?

Paraclete. Yes.

—No. Manicheus died in 275 A.D.

Was put to death.

—As a heretic.

Yes, as a heretic.

The old man's laughter simmered uncomfortably in Caroline's brain. This is crazy, she thought, I'm hallucinating, the dreams are pushing up and breaking the surface.

No.

She struggled to recall what she knew of Manicheanism. It was one of many heretical sects that had sprung up in the early years of the Church, and perhaps the most dangerous. The Church had spared no effort to wipe out the Manicheans, although some of their beliefs still lingered on in the despair and cynicism that permeated so much of modern life. They claimed that the universe was made up of two equal forces, light (good) and dark (evil), in eternal conflict. God was good, but God did not reign supreme in this universe. If you put evil on a par with good, then all else is permanently diminished and faith becomes a matter of arbitrary choice. Human beings were just insignificant players in a cosmic struggle without beginning or end. So the gap between the Church and the Manicheans was a vast theological chasm that could never be bridged. But it was an issue of purely academic interest now, or at least it should be, Caroline thought.

—How could you be here?

They brought me back and locked me in this place.

—But why? Didn't they kill you?

Yes, but to them I was a heretic.

—I still don't understand.

The laughter came again, rippling through Caroline's mind in a very unpleasant sensation.

They believed that heretics return to this world, possessing terrible powers. The power to draw the lifeblood of faith out of other souls. To control the feeble human mind. That is why they burned heretics, and tore the bodies to pieces.

But that was another time, centuries ago, and now not even the Church believed in such things. Beliefs change, but do they ever matter?

The Pope had to see me, to see for himself that I really was dead, and so they brought me back from Persia.

—And put you down here and forgot about you?

Oh, they played with me a while, using their knives and hot irons. Dry laughter, like whistling sand. *But then the old Pope died, and yes, I was forgotten.*

—When did you last...

See someone? A charming young novice in the 13th century. I haven't been able to move from this spot in about perhaps three hundred years now. Easy to find souls, but not to bring them all the way into this place.

The old man was crazy, Caroline had no doubt. But whatever the truth about him might be, he obviously needed care, and maybe medical attention. He certainly did not belong down in a clammy dungeon. It was a miracle he wasn't already dead. He looked so frail and helpless, and there was such sadness in his eyes.

—I'll get help.

Don't leave me, child.

—What should I do?

The door. Come to me.

Caroline approached the cell door. The hinges looked as if they wouldn't budge. She put her hands around one of the bars in the center of the door, and shook it. The hinges held, but there was some give inside the lock. Caroline shook the door again and the corroded latch crumbled steadily beneath the pressure. Rusty flakes showered down to the floor. The hinges shrieked painfully as Caroline forced the door open.

The old man looked up hopefully as she slipped into the cell and went to him. She wasn't sure what to do next. He looked too weak and fragile to move.

Hold me.

Caroline sat down on the floor beside him, took him by the shoulders and carefully lifted him up. His head lolled against her shoulder, then slid a little, resting over her heart, and he smiled gratefully. Caroline had no desire to move.

Touch me with your skin.

Caroline stroked his cheek lightly—it felt cool and dry, like one of the old manuscripts she had examined. Regardless of who he was or why he was there, the old man responded to her hand on his cheek. His eyes brightened and his features became more animated. He was certainly old, but so small and shrunken, like some lonely, withered child.

I need to be closer.

Caroline didn't understand. Her mind felt tired, lazy, and remarkably tranquil. She didn't want to move at all. She hugged the old man closer to her.

To your warmth.

Her mind couldn't follow a complete thought anymore. Nothing mattered but the moment, and her part in it. Caroline unbuttoned her blouse and the old man quickly pressed his face to her skin.

More.

Her bra was in the way. Caroline pulled it down, uncovering her breasts. The old man rubbed his face against them, burrowed between them, and then she felt his tongue, like fine sandpaper, seeking her nipple. Caroline was paralyzed with delirium, dazed with a sense of giving. It felt as if her body was a vessel full of precious liquid, a kind of inner sea of living warmth that was now flowing through her skin into him. But there was nothing to replace it, and Caroline's heart quickened with a sudden surge of useless alarm.

—Holy man...

Once.

—You brought me here?

In a way, yes.

—You spoke to me in dreams...

In dreams you spoke with yourself, and I am what you found.

—You took my faith...

What we let go, was never there.

—Help me...

Become what you become, as I did.

—They were right...

Well, yes.

—You became...

What they made me.

—God help me...

And who is that, child?

Caroline reached up to touch her own cheek and was amazed to find that it already felt as cool and dry as onionskin. Too weak to move, Caroline rested her hand on the man's bony shoulder. She was vaguely aware that she ought to push him away. There was no muscle strength left in her arm. Then Caroline was unable even to remain sitting up, and she fell back flat on the floor. She felt so light there was no pain when her head hit the stone. The old man moved lower and rested his face in the warm softness of her belly. He left no mark on her, for the touch of her skin was enough. An image flickered across her mind—she was buried beneath a million books, and it was not an unpleasant experience. Then the books began to fall, tons of them raining silently down through the darkness, and Caroline fell with them, a fading ribbon of liquid heat that spun and swirled as she flew gloriously out of herself.

She wakes in darkness. Disoriented for a moment, she shoves the dead bones off her bare skin. Now she knows where she is and what comes next. She stands, buttons her blouse and leaves. She knows the way. So much time has gone by. It's late, and she has a million things to do.

La Mourante

"You need something new," Lawrence said.

"Yes, but what?"

Alex had been a member of Feathers for more than a year when Lawrence made the suggestion. They were sitting in the piano bar just off the grotto, wrapped in towels, their hair still damp. A lovely little nymph brought them Sapphire martinis.

Feathers was one of the most exclusive private clubs in the world. You couldn't buy your way in. You had to be nominated by a current member, and membership was limited to four hundred very wealthy individuals who were profoundly devoted to the pursuit of pleasure. In the age of AIDS, the club was both an ark of safety and an Eden of erotic license. It was located in a sedate brick building near Park Lane, London W1, but its members came from all around the globe to check their fears at the door and to unleash their transcendent fantasies.

Alex couldn't believe his good fortune when he learned that his membership had been approved. He and Lawrence had known each other since their schooldays together at Charterhouse. They were an unlikely pair, Alex the restless Yank from Westchester County and Lawrence the jaded last son in a played-out line of Wiltshire landowners. But they got along well and stayed in touch over the years. Lawrence made a fortune in the City and Alex did at least as well on the Street. Now in their mid-thirties, they each had the freedom and the means to do whatever they desired—and they suffered no illusions to hold them back.

Alex had just been complaining about the fact that he seemed to be running out of exotic places and females to try. Last year he'd done the hill tribes of India and Southeast Asia, and it was for the most part a disappointment. As he'd found so many times, reality can't compete with the imagination.

Which, of course, was why retreats like Feathers existed for those of privilege. But the urge to travel and explore, the need to test himself against raw experience—were powerful forces in the composition of Alex's character. Thus, the constant weighing of new possibilities, however dubious.

"Do you know about a place called Fado?"

"Fado." Alex shook his head. "Never heard of it."

"Aha." Lawrence smiled. "It's an island, somewhere off the northern coast of South America. The Caribbean, or perhaps it's out more in the Atlantic, I'm not sure which. Anyhow, it's very private, very hush-hush."

"What's the attraction?" Alex had done island paradises two years ago: the Andamans, Polynesia, East Africa—enough.

"Well." The smile on Lawrence's face had turned into a foxy grin. "Have you ever made love with a dead woman?"

"No. It sounds revolting."

"Yes, it does," Lawrence agreed. "But apparently it's not. In fact, I'm told by very reliable sources that once you've tried it, nothing else will do."

"I was told that about the Bushman girls in southern Africa. And other women, in other places. It's never true."

Lawrence nodded. "Still, you have to wonder."

"I'll pass."

But the idea wouldn't. Necrophilia. Ugly word, it conjured up grisly images of dead meat splayed on a cold slab, stiff limbs and pale waxy skin. How could anyone possibly sell that, and who (aside from a few demented souls) would want it?

Lawrence provided a name and an address on a scrap of paper, typical of the kind of highly prized information that passes from one hand to another in a place like Feathers. Alex still had no intention of actually going to Fado, but he was curious enough to visit M. Alain Gaudet in an anonymous office on a pleasant street not far from the center of Lausanne.

M. Gaudet extracted a good deal of information from Alex and provided very little in return. He described Fado as unique, an island resort privately maintained and operated, dedicated to the enjoyment of "individual practices unfettered by national laws or treaties or international conventions."

Fado was located off the coast of Blanca and was protected by the military government (for a price and perks, no doubt). In addition to the staff, it had a small permanent population with a mixed background: English, Dutch, Portuguese, Italian, French and African. The island was only a few square miles in area, but had "features of great natural beauty."

So far, so boring. M. Gaudet promised nothing. He allowed a few questions but answered them evasively. There was something in his expression that seemed to suggest that Alex should use his imagination. Alex was good at that.

Two months later, presumably after he'd been investigated in great detail, Alex was notified that he had been cleared to visit Fado. A local New York resident, a Mr. Worboys, could handle the arrangements. But did Alex want to go? Mr. Worboys proved to be only a bit more forthcoming with information.

"There are several hundred women on Fado, all shapes, sizes and shades, and they're all available to you at any time, in any number or circumstance you want. Some will be otherwise engaged at any given moment but you'll have as much variety and choice as you can handle. There's also a wide selection of living quarters to choose from—bungalows, cottages, cabanas, suites—you can change them as often as you like. The facilities operate day and night, you can have dinner at four in the morning...."

Alex listened patiently until Mr. Worboys was finished, and then asked if it was true that Fado provided for even the rarest and most peculiar tastes, as he'd heard. Mr. Worboys was silent for a moment, gazing evenly at him. He glanced briefly again at the papers on his desk, as if to reassure himself that Alex had indeed been properly cleared.

"Behavioral guidelines will be issued to you on arrival, but you can take my word for it that they're minimal." A tight smile flickered at the corners of his mouth. "None of the clients I've dealt with— and there have been a good many of them—has ever expressed the slightest hint of disappointment."

"Is that a yes?"

"Let me put it to you this way, dear boy. If you don't know why you're going to Fado, you shouldn't go."

Alex took that as a yes.

As the helicopter rose and quickly swung back toward Blanca, Alex sat in the lounge and studied the glossy arrivals kit he had just been given. How to get about. Living quarters. A detailed map of the island and its many delights. Restaurants, bars, some intriguing theme houses, woodland trails, jungle paths, caves and ornate gardens, a crater lake, waterfalls and black sand beaches.

All of which was fine, and predictable.

Alex then came across the behavioral guidelines Mr. Worboys had mentioned. There were only two of them, printed on a plastic card attached to a small round keyholder.

* *Respect your fellow guests. Do not violate their privacy or interfere with their activities unless specifically invited to participate. Disputes to be settled by staff.*

* *Respect those who serve you. Mutilation, decapitation and dismemberment are prohibited, and will result in severe financial penalties and expulsion.*

Alex smiled faintly. He rode a jitney from the heliport to an Iberian-style village square. Along the way he saw only a few guests and staff members, but plenty of women. Most of them were young, though some were a little older. Most of them were pretty and attractive, though some had average or even plain looks. All were nicely dressed in a variety of styles and outfits.

They didn't stand around, vacantly posturing. There were no lewd gestures, but most of them did seem to notice the jitney and its handful of passengers—with a glance and an innocent smile. Welcome, stranger. Yours for the taking, Alex thought.

They all looked very much alive.

Alex chose a simple three-room bungalow nestled in a wooded pocket just off a hillside trail. He sipped a drink and nibbled some fruit while he unpacked, then he took a shower and dozed for a couple of hours. It was late afternoon when he opened his eyes at the sound of someone singing softly nearby.

There was a small garden at the rear of the bungalow. Alex saw a young woman with long dark hair and golden skin. She sang to herself and occasionally clipped a flower, which she put in a wicker basket. She was dressed in a flimsy sleeveless top and a short pleated skirt, both white. Her back was to Alex, who stood at the window and watched her for a moment.

The young woman glanced briefly in his direction and smiled when he stepped outside. She continued to sing, though her voice was so muted and indistinct that it amounted to little more than a light melodious humming, a lilting murmur—but Alex was quite enchanted; he'd never heard anything quite like it before.

He crossed the patch of thick lawn and placed his hands on her shoulders. The woman leaned back against him, eyes shutting, her face half-turned toward him. She put the pruning shears into the basket and let her hand fall to her side, brushing his thigh. The air was full of a delicious scent, a subtle perfume from this lovely creature mingling with the smell of the flowers.

Alex kissed her hair and neck. He stroked her breasts, felt her nipples responding through the thin fabric. He put his other hand beneath her skirt, encountering silky flesh, sleek and firm, and baby fine hair. When he kissed her open mouth he didn't want to stop because she tasted so sweet and felt wonderfully cool and moist.

There was a cushioned wooden bench tucked beneath a wall of arcing shrubs, and Alex took her to it. He put the basket on the grass under the bench as they sat down. Her eyes were deep brown and had delicate hints of amber. She sat patiently, waiting for him to say or do something, but there was a lively brightness in her eyes that suggested playful anticipation.

Alex put his fingers to her lips and pushed gently, and she gave him a wide smile—he saw that her teeth were very white, but not perfect; they were her own, unstraightened.

He held her hand in both of his for several moments, but he could find no pulse. He slid the thin straps off her shoulders and admired her breasts—they were round and neither too large nor too flat, but they weren't flawless. Alex moved closer and rested his head on her chest. She held him there, stroking his hair, and he concentrated—but heard no heartbeat.

Alex sat up again and looked at her. "What is your name?" But she merely gave a slight shrug and a wordless rolling murmur of sound. "You do understand me," he said. She nodded once with a quick smile. "But you don't speak." Again, the faint murmur, and this time Alex noticed that her throat and mouth barely moved as she made it.

He wasn't sure what to think. He knew that there were some languages, Thai among them, that consisted largely of vowels used in extraordinary combinations and tones. These languages sounded like flashing water, and were very difficult to master unless you learned them from childhood.

Perhaps that was it, but Alex didn't think so. The strange sounds this woman made seemed almost older than language itself. Besides, if she could understand what Alex was saying then surely she could manage a few words of English in response. But if she were not breathing, if there was no significant passage of air to cause and convey voice—

Alex took her hand and pinched the fleshy spot between her thumb and first finger. The skin didn't turn pale, nor did color rush back into it when he let go. It stayed the same.

Alex was vaguely aware of his own heartbeat, increasing at a rapid pace now. His hand shook as he reached down to the basket of flowers and found a rose. He turned it carefully, located one thorn that looked large and strong enough, and jabbed it into the soft pad of the woman's thumb. She sat patiently, watching him. She didn't flinch or show any trace of pain. When Alex withdrew the thorn, the small wound it left was clearly visible but there was no spot of blood. No blood at all.

The surge of desire within him was deeper and richer than he had experienced in a long time, blinding in its sudden intensity. He took the woman in his arms and pulled her to the ground. They rolled over once, to the edge of the grass, and Alex dimly sensed the nodding ferns and shrubs touching his back as he wriggled out of his pants and pushed into her. He hadn't known such youthful eagerness in years. It was almost a new experience for him. His orgasm was so powerful and hallucinatory that Alex felt as if he were driving into the earth itself. Dazed, barely conscious, he rested in her comforting arms, his head between her breasts. The barest whisper of a happy sound emanated from her—but her body didn't rise or fall with a single breath, there was no heartbeat. She seemed perfectly still, at peace.

At first he tried to explain it to himself, to make sense of it in a way that seemed plausible. Alex was certain that she was not some kind of robot or android. The technology involved would be too advanced and sophisticated, in several different areas, to keep secret. From his work on Wall Street he knew about robotics and artificial body parts, he knew what the best companies could do at present—and not do. They made advances all the time but they were still light years from constructing a mouth that could kiss like this woman's mouth did. Alex had no doubt that she was entirely human—in body, at least.

Nor did he believe for an instant that a microprocessor had been implanted in her brain, somehow controlling everything that she did. The necessary hardware and software might be possible, but not the incalculable linkage to brain and body.

A much simpler and more plausible answer came to mind. The explanation had to be pharmacological. Alex knew that drug firms spent a good deal of time and money seeking useful new compounds in the unique plant life of the world's rapidly diminishing rain forests. There was a theory that the zombies of Haitian legend, people who were dead but still ambulatory and who could carry out certain basic functions, were in fact the product of a drug which had its origins in ancient African medical lore.

That was possible. The necessary refinements were possible. With the right resources, one lab with a small staff could do the job. Thus, the knowledge could be controlled and protected, even as it was put to use in a pet project as large as Fado. This was a line of thought with extraordinary implications but Alex had no particular interest in pursuing them.

He didn't care. It didn't matter *how* a woman could be dead but somehow still living. It was enough that *she was*.

He had sex with her twice more that evening, before travel fatigue caught up with him and he fell asleep in her arms in bed. She was awake when he opened his eyes the next morning, ready and available, still sweet. She sang to him as his body sang inside her. The sound she made was so tiny and elusive it almost seemed like a ghost in his mind.

Two days later, they were still together. They had gone out only to take short walks, to make love in a mossy clearing in the woods and later in a stream-fed rock pool. Alex was satisfied to remain with her at the bungalow most of the time. The world fell away, and he didn't miss it.

When his meals were delivered, she sat patiently with him. She dipped large raw prawns in a fiery sauce and fed them to him, but she neither ate nor drank anything herself.

Enough time had gone by, and Alex had to face the new facts of his life. He loved having sex with this woman, and his desire seemed to increase every day. This was a complete turnabout from his usual experience. For years he'd been quick to lose interest and move on in search of something, someone new. Now Alex wanted to keep this woman to himself. He felt no urge to sample any of the others on Fado. Besides, if he went off alone she might hook up with another guest, and then he might never get her back. She was sufficient, she was everything Alex wanted and needed—that was the other huge change in him.

It astonished him that the sex was never the same. The best experiences in his long sexual history now seemed like the merest biological asides. Compared to what he enjoyed with this woman, they vanished in significance. It was as if a previously unknown part of him was suddenly revealed, a primordial dimension of vast power and richness.

"Gina," he said to her. "I want to call you Gina."

She cocked her head and smiled. He was ready again.

He seemed to be flying into her, into the earth and beyond, into space and glittering dust. It was as if he were witnessing the birth of stars and galaxies, the universe itself, a million universes—through the window of his body and Gina. Then Alex would swirl together again within his body. There was something sweet and wonderfully sad about it. His whole being felt blurred and hazy. He would find himself in her arms again, tears in his eyes, his face nestled on her breasts. And he thought—if God had sex, it would be like this.

The world continued to fall away, and he didn't miss it. He had a lot of money back there, somewhere. He had done so much on the Street, and could do so much more—but it meant little. It was numbers flickering on a screen, it was nothing.

There were people in his life. A lot of them, in fact. But how many of them did he care about? They were acquaintances, not true friends. Colleagues, mostly. Women? He went through them on a regular basis, but none had ever tempted him into what might be termed a relationship. His life for the most part was made up of glancing encounters, by his own choice.

Until now. How could he continue—after Fado? Was there anything left worth his doing? Was there any place on the planet worth seeing that he hadn't already visited? Alex thought of his splendid apartment on Manhattan's East Side, and he was not happy at the prospect of returning to it. His adult life could be seen as one long, restless search for the new and the exotic, but Alex was tired of that now. Tired of always being driven by pointless expectation to ever diminishing returns.

He didn't travel to visit museums or stare at scenery. Alex went places to have women. Where next? Who next? But now there was no itinerary, no next stop in the quest—because the quest was over. No other women beckoned in his mind. The awful hunger was gone, replaced by a need to keep what he now had, regardless of what the cost might be.

There was only Gina. Sex with Gina took him right into the secret heart of this world, and beyond, and Alex couldn't bear to think of losing it.

▲ ▼ ▲

He tried to get Gina to write, but she apparently had never learned how. He gave her a blank pad and a pen, and asked her to show him where she was from. She drew a crooked circle, and Alex assumed that was meant to be Fado. He kept at it, but she had no skill and very little understanding of what he expected from her, so he soon abandoned the attempt.

It didn't matter. He seldom spoke to her because it seemed as if he had nothing truly worth saying. Besides, they had found their own special language—eye contact, facial movements, the subtle varieties of touch and gesture—which served them better than words ever could. And it wasn't long before Alex started to answer the occasional burbles of sound that Gina made with little clicks and murmurs of his own.

Time was running him down. He could stay on Fado until his funds were exhausted, and then go back to the world, rebuild his fortune and hope one day to return to Gina. But would she still be there—for him? The magic might be lost forever in the long interlude. It might be just as good with any woman on Fado, but he was almost afraid to find out. And the work, the need to make money and do business, would be so much drudgery—assuming that Alex could still concentrate on the task, which was by no means a sure thing anymore.

Or he could stay on Fado permanently, by becoming like Gina. That would force their hand. They could hardly risk letting him wander around back in the regular world if he'd been *transformed*. No doubt they'd be unhappy, no doubt they'd find work for him to do. But Alex would still be on Fado, he'd still have Gina.

The funny part was, it seemed more like choosing life than a form of death. He thought that Gina, in her own way, was so much more alive than he'd ever been. The years spent making money he never cared about, *that* was a zombie-like existence. The dreary hours spent hanging out with people like Lawrence in places like Feathers, how vacant and pathetic it all seemed. His quest, that sad and lonely search from Mexico to North Africa to Taiwan and a hundred other forlorn outposts, looking for the next thrill, the next 'ultimate' erotic experience—pointless, all of it.

He'd had everything that world could offer. It would not be hard to give it up: he no longer had any use for it, anyway. The real thing—the true *ultimate*—was right in front of him. In a way, his whole adult life had been a rehearsal for this moment. If Alex could make the leap. The decision was easy.

"Gina, would you like me to stay here with you always?" Her face lit up and she snuggled closer in his arms. "You must help me become like you." She looked up at him, uncertain, perplexed. "It's the only way," Alex said. "You must."

She was gone when he awoke the following day. He stayed in, had brunch and a couple of drinks, and waited for a member of the staff to come along and explain to him that his request was quite out of line, impossible.

But Gina returned alone, late in the afternoon. Alex was so desperate for her by then that he felt like a cloud of fire as he flew across the room to take her in the doorway.

A while later, Gina reached into the pocket of her discarded skirt and came up with a vial of oily brown liquid.

Dear Lawrence, he would write if he could be bothered to sit down and write, *It's true. What I've found on Fado is far better than words can tell. To live forever—abandon life! It isn't hard to do and the next level is the last—is GOD. And YOU are that GOD. Believe me. And God is sex and the sex is fantastic! Of course it takes loads of infrastructure but that's all laid on here—no bother at all.* Alex started laughing, and he couldn't stop for several moments. Gina didn't know what it was all about but she joined in his mirth. She smiled so strenuously that she ended up burying her face in his lap. *Tell the crowd at Feathers I said: Get a death! Adieu and adios Lawrence old chum. It was fun. Or so it seemed for a while. But the next world is not the hereafter it's the HERE and NOW. Honest!*

Alex drained the vial. Butterscotchyish. He looked at Gina and smiled, but she had her hands clapped over her eyes.

Seventy four paces to the corner.
Seventy three the last time.
He would get it right one of these days.
Hey, no big deal!
Alex turned the corner and walked the next lane.
A breeze and a blue sky and always the sun.
But no, sometimes there was a sudden downpour.

Nice shade trees down this way.
Always something new to notice, very nice too.
Let the breeze whistle through your teeth.
And sometimes it will, for fun.
Nod hello, why don't you.
A nod and a smile, hello.
Well done, very nice too.
Eighty seven paces.
A different matter, this lane.
Hullo hullo, what's this.
Coming his way—Gina?
A nod, a smile, hello.
They pass by each other.
Used to know her, didn't you?
Around another corner, the road.
Aha! Aha! Aha!
A jitney, women getting off.
When you've had a live woman, nothing else will do.
But they like the younger ones.
Smile and nod, hello in hope.
A breeze and blue sky and always the sun.
But no, the night too, the dark.
A nod to the live women.
A smile to the live women.
Me! Me! Me! he sang in the breeze.

1 Remember Me

Glen came out of the building on Park Avenue South and stood on the sidewalk. He wasn't sure what to do. A couple of men out by the curb noticed him, and exchanged words. One of them walked briskly toward Glen. Ah yes, he would be a pointer.

"Cab, sir?" the man asked politely. "Or directions?"

"Yes," Glen replied. "A cab, please."

The pointer raced to the curb and waved at the passing river of traffic. The other man stood by with an approving look on his face. He would be the pointer's pointer. No doubt the pointer's pointer's pointer was on patrol nearby. They did an amazing job, moving millions of people around Manhattan every day. But now the man came back, visibly upset with himself.

"What was it again, sir?" he asked sheepishly.

Glen looked at the piece of paper he discovered in his hand. "A taxi," he read aloud.

"Gotcha this time."

The pointer turned back to the road and resumed his attempts to flag down a vacant cab. A few moments later, he had one.

"Thank you," Glen said as he got into the vehicle.

"You do have your destination, sir?"

"Yes, thanks."

"Thank you."

The pointer closed the door and bustled away. Such a polite man, Glen reflected. He handed his piece of paper to the driver, who nodded gravely and consulted a plastic chart that was mounted on the dashboard before he finally entered the destination. Then the taxi accelerated smoothly, edging into the flow. The driver, meanwhile, settled back with a gaudy tabloid. Glen could see the headline on the open page: I EVEN FORGOT HOW TO MAKE LOVE!!!

As the street signs went by, Glen recognized them. But when they passed an expanse of wooded land he suddenly felt uncertain. It was big, and rather attractive. The leaves had such brilliant colors. But what was it? Glen asked the driver, who was unhappy about being disturbed.

"Central Park," he replied a minute later, when he spotted a sign that said Central Park West.

I thought so, Glen told himself. A park that big could only be Central Park. He had known all along—you can know a thing, even if the name for it slips your grasp. It was nothing to fret about, it didn't mean you were stupid or sick. Everyone has such lapses from time to time. It was—but Glen was too tired right now to think about it.

Just past 99th Street, the taxi swung around boldly and came to a stop in front of a large apartment building. The driver sat up and looked around.

"Here you are."

"Thanks."

Glen paid the fare. Money was still fairly easy, because it had numbers on it. Numbers went deep. Money went deeper. Money would last until the end, no doubt about that. He put his wallet back into his jacket pocket, and caught sight of two words penned in blue ink on the inside of his wrist:

GLEN BARNES

"And you are?" the doorman asked.

"Glen Barnes," Glen announced calmly.

The doorman checked Glen's face against the house photo bank on the desk terminal. Apparently everything was in order, as the doorman soon looked up and smiled.

"Yes sir, Mr. Barnes. You're in apartment eleven-twenty, as I'm sure you know."

"Yes, of course. Thank you." Glen hesitated, searching the wide lobby with anxious eyes. "The, uh—"

"The elevators are around there, to your right," the doorman supplied helpfully.

"You haven't moved them since this morning," Glen said in an attempt to make a joke.

"Couldn't be bothered," the doorman shot back, breaking into self-appreciative laughter. "Nice to see you again, Mr.—"

"And you, Jimmy."

"George."

"George, yes. What happened to Jimmy?"

"Jimmy? There's no Jimmy here, Mr. Glen."

"Really? I am sorry. My mistake."

"You're thinking of another place," the doorman named George suggested considerately. "Where you work, maybe."

"Yes, yes, that must be it."

What a strange man, Glen thought as he stepped into the open elevator. Eleven-twenty, wasn't it? He noticed he was sweating. It would help if everybody wore name tags. But there were others who said that would only make matters worse. Glen didn't see how that was possible.

He found a card-key in his wallet and tried it on the door. It worked. He went inside. It was a pleasant-looking apartment. It was his. And hers. She smiled at Glen, came and gave him a kiss on the cheek.

"Hi, Glen," she said sweetly.

"Hello...dear."

A lot had changed with the coming of The Flu.

Glen sat and watched the news on television. Glen's wife was in the kitchen, doing something. Glen had a small notebook in his hand. He flipped through it discreetly and in a few minutes he found the page he was looking for. Her name was Marion—but he knew that, of course!

"Marion," he called out.

"Yes?"

"How are you, Marion?"

"Fine...dear," she called back to him.

Glen quickly scanned the rest of the page, and saw much that was immediately familiar to him. You see, he thought, it's still all there. She

* has a mild case of high blood pressure
* is a lapsed Catholic
* works at a shelter for teenage girls
* likes icky French pop singers
* but does not speak or give French
* and is generally lazy in bed
* reads historicals
* likes microwave cuisine
* drinks one spritzer at night
* hates smoke
* except her father's pipe
* (her father is Phil, mother invalid)

Glen slipped the notebook back into his briefcase and looked at the television again. The economic news was very good. There was virtually no unemployment now, thanks to the pointer program.

There was a dark cloud attached to the silver lining, however, as it seemed that the demand for pointers would continue to grow for the foreseeable future, the need far outstripping the supply. It didn't take a genius to see what was coming.

There was also news about The Flu. The news was that there was no news, just a new statement to the effect that its symptoms were still believed to be transient in nature, and not permanent, deteriorating alterations. A doctor told the newsperson that six years was not too long a time for symptoms to persist. Good God, Glen thought. Don't tell me we've had The Flu for six years now. That is a bit much. He got up and went into the kitchen to raise this point with—his wife.

She hastily closed a notebook she was studying and shoved it into her handbag.

Glen emerged from his apartment building and stood there. A pointer soon appeared to help him, but had trouble finding a cab. You could try to flag one down yourself if you knew that was what you needed, but the drivers gave preference to the pointers. The thing to do was to cooperate. Everyone had to change and adjust, otherwise nothing would work anymore. As he waited, Glen heard a loud metallic voice coming from the park.

When the light changed, and there was still no taxi, he went to see what was going on. A crowd had gathered around a man who stood on a red plastic crate. He had a megaphone.

"The Flu is not a virus," he shouted. "The Flu is not just a bunch of bacteria. The Flu is a single organism. The biggest, most vicious creature alive on this planet. It sweeps across the continents and oceans as if they were nothing, and it feeds on us like locusts on a field of corn. It decimates us, and with every new feeding season the disaster grows far greater. Soon the dark process will be complete, the final changes wrought, and—"

"How do you know all this?" a heckler cut in.

"I know, because I worked for the government. I learned the awful truth they're trying to keep from you. I—"

"Yeah, but how do you remember it?"

This produced gales of raucous laughter. Glen smiled. What was he supposed to be doing? He had a piece of paper in his hand and he was wearing his suit for work. He made his way out of the crowd and headed toward the street. A young man approached.

"Need a cab, sir?"

"Yes. Are you a pointer?"

"Yes sir."

"Don't you have a badge?" Glen asked. "Or a uniform?"

"They abandoned that idea, sir," the young man said gently, as if speaking to an idiot. "Negative psychology. Where are you going?" He took the destination chit from Glen's hand and peered at it briefly. "Downtown. You're in luck, sir. I've got a taxi here with a couple of other downtown passengers, and there's room for one more. Hurry up, they're ready to go."

"I don't want to share a ride."

"We've all got to cooperate, sir," the man said sternly. "I hope you're not one of those selfish people who refuses to pitch in and make sacrifices like the rest of us."

"Well, no..."

"That's the spirit. Here you go."

Glen slid into the back seat of the taxi. There was a burly fellow already there, and another soon followed, sandwiching Glen in the middle. No one said anything. The taxi moved away, and a short while later it swung onto a road that ran through the park. The dying leaves had wonderful color now—it was that season of the year. Glen wished he had a window.

The man on his right suddenly hit him in the face. The man on his left began hitting him in the stomach. They kept hitting, and Glen never had a chance to say anything or resist. His mouth was full of loose teeth and blood, his vision was blurred, and he couldn't breathe. Then something hit him on the head, and he had only the vaguest sensation left in his body. He was being moved, he flew in the air—landed, fast and hard.

His briefcase was gone. His pockets were empty. His hands were empty—and bleeding; Glen must have landed on them when he hit the pavement. He wandered about for a while after coming to, and now he was sitting beside a pool of water. His head and body ached tremendously. He took off his tie, dipped it in the water, and cautiously touched his face with it. His skin stung, he knew his lips were swollen, and his teeth felt wobbly. The usual host of people moving about; they ignored him. He lowered a hand into the water and then began to pat it with a dry patch of tie. Glen sponged off some of the grit and gravel. Where the skin was only blood-stained, not torn, he rubbed harder to get clean.

Then he saw the faint ink marks swirling off with the blood, vanishing in the water—and he froze. My name was there, Glen realized too late. A few traces of ink remained, but they formed nothing. Not even a single complete letter.

This could be very bad, he told himself, but don't panic too soon. He knew a lot about himself. He had a job, he had a wife, he had an apartment. His job was downtown—that phony pointer had said so. These simple facts were hardly conclusive, but they were good to know and he was determined to hang onto them.

A little later he saw a policeman, who listened patiently to his story. The policeman explained that such muggings were quite common nowadays, and that the streets were full of people who had more or less lost their identities this way. Glen wondered if he had heard about it on the news and then forgotten it.

"What can I do?" he asked.

"You don't remember your name, not even your first name?"

"Not at the moment," he said. "I hit my head, and..."

"Yeah," the policeman said, nodding sadly. "Same thing with your address and place of work?"

"Yes."

"Okay, here's what you do. There's an Identification Center in the Plaza Hotel. That's the nearest one to here. If you ever had your fingerprints taken, or if you have any kind of criminal record, they'll have it on the computer and then they can confirm who you are."

"Otherwise?"

"Otherwise, you got a problem. There's talk about creating a national identity program but that's probably a couple of years away. In the meantime..." The policeman shrugged.

"This is terrible."

"Makes you wish you knocked over a gas station when you were a teenager, don't it? Hey, cheer up. Maybe you did."

"Why didn't they tell us it was this bad?"

"They been telling us for the last few years," the policeman said after consulting a fact sheet. "You just keep on forgetting about it. That's how this thing works."

"God, it's fiendish."

"Damn right it is. You don't notice until something happens so you get pushed off your spot, and you can't get back."

The policeman pointed him in the right direction and wished him luck. As he walked along he became aware of the large number of people who seemed to be wandering about aimlessly. Perhaps he was just imagining it as a result of his current state, but where was the sense of purpose in their stride, the glimmer of focus in their eyes? He was disturbed by the presence of so many bodies on the ground. They were lying everywhere, on the benches and in the grass, some were even sprawled on the sidewalk. Some of them almost looked dead, but surely the situation hadn't reached that point yet. Dead bodies rot, they smell, they cause disease. But he had to admit that the signs were not good.

The line of people outside the hotel was enormous. It would be hours before he got inside. The line didn't seem to be moving at all. He might have to come back tomorrow or the next day. As far as he knew, he'd never broken the law or been fingerprinted, but it was apparently his only chance. He moved along, looking for the end of the line. Then a short man took him by the elbow and leaned close.

"Looking for an I.D.?" the man asked.

"I'm looking for mine, yes."

"I got just what you need," the man went on. "Credit cards, keys, Social Security, addresses, phone numbers, everything a guy needs to get going again. The whole package."

"But is it mine?"

"You gotta start somewhere, pal."

"I don't have any money."

"Then what're you wasting my time for?"

The little man disappeared into the throng. It took a while to realize how unsettling that exchange really was. Identities for sale. But what good would it do? You couldn't just take the contents of someone's wallet and pockets, and gain the benefit of their identity. An interloper was bound to be exposed at home or at work. No, this was a scam, pure and simple. First you robbed some unfortunate person, and then you sold their useless personal papers to someone desperate enough to try anything.

There was one more aspect to this that particularly worried him. What if you walked into another person's home and the wife didn't recognize you as an impostor? She had forgotten what her husband looked like, and she had no photographs—or she thought they were photographs of someone else. You had the key, you were acting as if you belonged there. Would she accept the wrong man? Was anything like that possible? No, of course not. But when he tried to form a mental picture of his wife's face, he could not fill in any details.

Late in the afternoon the air turned very cold, a nasty wind set in and the sky was grey with wintry menace. He was in line but had advanced only a few yards, or so it seemed. If he had to come back tomorrow, where would he spend the night? He felt weak and sluggish, and it occurred to him that he was hungry. But how could he get anything to eat without money? If he had somebody's credit card at least he could get a meal in a restaurant. If the card still worked. But if he had cash to buy a card he could buy food more easily. The grave implications of his predicament were pressing in on his mind.

"This is all because of The Flu?" he asked the man tottering vacantly beside him in the line.

"What flu?"

"The Flu. You know. The Flu."

"If you say so."

It was pointless. He had to think. Perhaps he could find a safe corner in the bus station, or the train station, a doorway sheltered from the wind. Something like that. People lived that way, and survived. What shocked him to the core was how suddenly it had happened to him. One minute he was being driven to work, the next he was literally thrown away like garbage. And from the moment he came to in the park he could feel the awful change that was taking place. Terrible new facts assailed his brain. He was losing the will to resist, he could almost feel it leaching away. Helplessness was rooting itself in him.

"Mike?"

The breathless voice of a plain young woman. He had noticed her approaching, studying the faces in the line. Now she stared at him with frantic eyes.

"Oh my God, it *is* you," she exclaimed. "Mike, oh Mike."

The woman threw her arms around him. She hugged and kissed him, and told him how she had searched and searched for him. She had almost given up hope of ever finding him.

"This just happened to me today," he told her.

"That's what you think," she replied with an understanding smile. "But how do you know that the way you remember is more accurate than what you've forgotten? Besides, don't you think I know my own husband?"

"Tell me your name," he said.

"Roberta. Roberta Stone, and you're Mike Stone." She shook her head with amused delight, and laughed. "I bought that shirt for you at the Smartfellas shop."

Mike. Stone. Surely it would come ringing back to mind, if that was his name. But maybe it was symptomatic to draw a blank. There were no rules in this new situation, you had to play it by ear all the time. Mike was a short and simple name, and in that respect it did feel somehow right.

"What should I do?" he asked her.

"What do you think you should do, silly?" She put her arm through his and pulled him out of the line. "You should go home. Where you live. Now. With me."

"Should we get a taxi?" he heard himself asking.

"What're you, made of money?"

"I don't have any money," he had to admit.

"So what else is new?"

Home was a rather drab basement apartment on West 54th, near Eleventh Avenue. Roberta had the address tattooed to the back of her left hand. She had her name on the heels of her feet. There were hot dogs for supper, and a warm bed later. The next morning she took him around to Skinpainter, who made sure that MIKE STONE would never lose track of his life again.

"What can I do?" Mike Stone asked Roberta Stone.

"You were unemployed before you got lost."

"What about you?"

"I don't work."

"How do we pay the rent and buy things?"

"Interest from the sale of my mother's house."

"You mean we don't have to do anything?"

"Neat, huh?"

Until the French-cut stringbean fiasco. There was big news about a shipment of frozen French-cut stringbeans into Manhattan. Food had become a problem. Either the farmers forgot to plant it or harvest it, or the middlemen forgot to process and deliver it. Something was always going wrong, it seemed. But then a few tons of French-cut stringbeans arrived. The government had found them in a freezer. Roberta bought as many packages as she could grab. So did Mike Stone.

He was watching the news on television. The news was about how no one had heard from Europe in a long time. Well, they said it was a long time—but how could they be sure? Perhaps it was just the day before yesterday.

There was also news about The Flu. The news was that there was no news, but a doctor explained that the symptoms "continued to persist." He said that was not very unusual, even after eight years. Good God, Mike Stone thought. Have we had The Flu for as long as that? Eight years.

He got up and went into the kitchen to raise this point with Roberta (whose name was tattooed along the right side of his left index finger).

She had a wrapper in her hand. There were a couple of green blocks on the counter. Frozen French-cut stringbeans, glistening with moisture. She looked very unhappy, at a loss. He knew that something was wrong, so he didn't mention The Flu.

"What's happening?"

"I don't understand," she complained.

"What?"

"What do you do to get this stuff ready?"

"It's right there on the wrapper," Mike Stone said. He took the foil-paper from her hand and studied it. There was a picture of piping hot stringbeans with butter melting over them. "That's how you do it. Fluffy, like that."

"That's how you eat them," she said. "But how do you get to where they're like that?"

He looked at the directions. "Put them in a pot with a half inch of water. Heat to a boil. Cover, turn down the heat. Then let simmer until tender. That means test them after five minutes or so, to see if they're done. Okay?"

She nodded, but a while later he discovered that she had put the covered pot in the oven and baked it. The handle melted, and then began to burn. The beans were a dead loss.

The next day he took her out for a walk. A very long walk. He lost her in the crowd. There were crowds everywhere now. But he wasn't worried. She could find her way home if she could read her tattoos, or get someone to read them for her and give her the right directions. There were so many pointers available.

Of course, if she forgot to read the tattoos, or forgot what they meant, that would be a different matter.

Roberta failed to return. After a few days it seemed likely that she would never come back. Which was more or less what he, Mike Stone, had expected.

He managed quite well without her, and the time soon came when he stopped thinking about her at all. He had more important things to worry about by then.

Some other people moved into the apartment with him. A gang of young women, and a couple of tough men, one of whom claimed to be the actual owner of the building. He had no documentation but that was not surprising because paperwork had been in decline for a while now. Mike was allowed to sleep in the tiny front hallway every night, as long as he brought back food or firewood. It was a fair compromise, he decided.

This arrangement worked for a short while. One of the young women began to show an unusual interest in him. This was quickly discouraged by the two men, who spent most of their time each day herding the women about on mysterious missions to unknown places. When they went out, Mike had to leave too. Once, when he forgot to bring any food or firewood, they made him sleep outside in the stairwell.

That was the day he came across a storefront office that had been converted into a branch of the Federal Identity Network. It was dark and empty inside, but a great many people stood about on the street as if expecting it to open for business again.

"What's the problem?" he asked someone.

"I don't know."

Mike waited a while. Nothing happened. Then a car sped by, drawing considerable attention since there was hardly any traffic anymore. Nothing else happened, so Mike left.

The next day he saw a man hanging by the neck from an awning pipe. Pinned to his chest was a piece of cardboard, on which the letters DR had been hand-printed.

"What does that mean?" Mike asked someone.

"He was a doctor."

"How did they know?"

"I don't know."

Some little while later, on a similar day, Mike did not find his way back to the apartment. There was never a pointer around when you needed one. But then, there seemed to be less people on the streets, so the pointer program might have been discontinued. The warm weather had arrived, fortunately; shelter was no longer a major problem.

He was sitting on the curb, eating peanuts, when a woman sat down next to him. She was about his age. He offered her some of the peanuts. She took them, watched what he did and then did the same thing. They smiled at each other.

"What's your name?" she asked.

He looked at his finger. "Roberta."

She looked at her hand. "I'm Carl."

"Hi, Carl."

"Hi, Roberta."

They shook hands. They spent that night in an empty office. They hugged and kissed and did it, and he felt better than he had in a long time. But when he woke up in the morning she was gone, and so were his shoes. Why had she taken them, he wondered. You could find shoes easier than food. Besides, he was sure that she had her own shoes. He tried to picture her, and he concentrated on her feet. Well, maybe she didn't have any. Shoes.

He watched a man standing by the curb. The man swayed as if he were caught in a windstorm, though the air was calm. The man looked up the street, then down. Then up again, and down. There was no traffic to worry about, but the man stayed on the curb. A minute later, the man fell to the sidewalk.

This park overlooked the water. The big buildings were back behind him. He liked the place. There were only a few people on the ground. A nice breeze, the taste of salt in the air. A very high blue sky, some puffy white coulds, a warm sun. He bent over and snatched a stalk of tall grass. It was like a miniature tree with leaves and branches sprouting from the top of it. He placed it between his teeth—not because he was hungry, but because it was a naturally irresistible thing to do. He found that he could twirl it around easily, without opening his lips. You must have done this before, he told himself.

It was more pleasant to sit down than stand. Just for a few minutes. Then he would have to get up and do something. He knew he had something to do, somewhere to go. It had slipped his mind just what, but it would come round again. The sun felt wonderful on his skin. He hoped it would fade the peculiar markings on his hands. He had no idea how they'd got there in the first place, and they were a nuisance to think about. He studied his fingers, as if he were seeing them for the first time.

"Remarkable," he said aloud.

He stretched out on his back and twirled the stalk of grass, imagining that it was a tree growing out of his mouth. The earth was warm beneath him. Sooner or later it would rain. He thought of the rain washing him into the ground. Yes. Warm rain, sun, a deep blue sky far above. While I melt away like snow.

"Time to stand up," he says, but he does not stand up.
"Time to get up and go."
He does not.

The Last Crossing

Even when you know it's likely, when you have lived with the fear and uncertainty for weeks, it still comes as a terrible blow to be told that you no longer have a job. Dale Davies had been a trader on Wall Street for more than twenty years. He was a quiet but efficient man. He had risen to a certain level and then held his position. He was never a threat to the ambitions of his more aggressive colleagues. He was not brilliant, but the only people who seriously lost money with Dale were those who would have lost it anyway.

There is a kind of poetry of money, a rhythm to finance that generally follows the heartbeat of society at large. Everyone in business knows that there will be highs and lows, steady periods, slumps, occasional jolts and shocks. Through it all, the market goes on like life itself.

But this new slide into stagnancy was particularly worrying. It was longer and steeper, and for the first time in memory there was no bottom in sight. Dale sensed early on that it might prove to be a transforming moment, such as happens only once in every two or three generations, when things change fundamentally. If that were the case, he had no doubt that sooner or later he would find himself among those culled from the herd.

He was smack on fifty, a dangerous age: too far from young, too close to old. He believed that his best work was still ahead of him, but Dale knew he was probably wrong. All he wanted to do was carry on where he was for another twelve or fifteen years, to last the course.

He didn't. It was not his fault. Nothing to do with him or his performance. The firm was downsizing, and Dale was downsized out. The same thing was happening everywhere, a slaughter on the middle ground. The young wouldn't go, because they are young and in touch and cheaper to keep on. The old men on top wouldn't go, because they were after all on top. So it was Dale, and others like him, who were thrown onto the street.

He was given his notice on a Friday. He tottered out of the building and hesitated. He should go straight home to New Jersey and break the news to Cynthia, his wife. But he wasn't ready for that yet. Cynthia was a woman with lingering social pretentions. The hard fact of Dale's unemployment would not go down well with her, and sympathy would not be her first response. Joanne, their youngest child, had celebrated her nineteenth birthday last month by moving in with a heavy metal drummer in Hoboken. Things were tense all around. Dale went into Gallagher's. He needed time to think and calm down. He needed a drink.

Call him old-fashioned, but he believed that the dry martini was a divine creation. It seemed to go from the mouth right into the bloodstream, with welcome effect. But there was still a grim reality to be faced. Good Lord, Dale thought, what is happening? All that wariness and anticipation had failed to weaken the blow. It hurt, worse than he ever expected.

He had grown up reading novels about the exciting, ruthless, high-stakes world of business, and he had longed to be a part of it. He studied through the silly sixties, pursued his dream, and finally achieved it. Twenty years—but where did they go? The world had changed so much, and yet here he was, sitting in a fine old gin mill around the corner from the market, feeling just like a character out of Sloan Wilson or John O'Hara. His life nothing but an empty cellophane wrapper.

There was no future, no job waiting for him elsewhere. Dale was at his peak, but in the marketplace he was finished, or would be by the time this slide ended. A desk in a small brokerage out in the suburbs was the best he could hope for, and in itself that would be a kind of death. His clients wouldn't leave the firm to go with him— not for Dale Davies. He was finished. It was all over but the paperwork.

He hit a few other bars, heading vaguely west, away from the financial district. Too many young Turks gargling happily. They were on the escalator going up, alive with their futures. It was not their fault, Dale told himself. They, too, would eventually take it on the neck. Still, he hated them.

It was dusk when Dale realized that he had wandered all the way to the Hudson. The lights of Jersey City were fuzzed by fog. Over there, in the clean suburbs beyond, was his home: across the river, to hell. Not yet. The night had barely started, and Dale was in the mood to cut loose. Let me get robbed, or beaten. Let me be thrown in the gutter. Let me flirt with some pretty, young lady in a dangerous joint. Let there be an operatic moment in my life, and let it be tonight.

The immediate prospects were not encouraging. Dale was in a shabby dockside area full of rotten old offices, warehouses, meat packing plants and dubious shops cluttered with second-hand junk. But then he found a place, and almost at once he knew that it was the place he had been looking for all his life. There wasn't any name on the small sign overhead, but the flashing lights promised a BAR and GIRLS, and that was good enough for starters.

He went through a narrow doorway, down a flight of creaking stairs, and paid five dollars to a guy with no neck. Then he was allowed into the main room. He banged his right shoulder against a post thicker than a telephone pole—there were a few of them scattered about the big cellar, he saw when his eyes adjusted to the gloom. There were faint lights strung along the stone walls, a long bar off to one side, some rickety tables and chairs placed in dark corners. The music was loud but not unbearable.

Dale made his way carefully to the bar. He bought a gin and tonic, asking for extra tonic as it was a good time to slow down and pace himself for a while if he was going to make a real night of it. There were quite a few customers: men on their own, as he was. And there were a lot of fairly undressed young girls out on the floor—some dancing, some lounging around with disinterest, others working the crowd.

Dale saw stockings with garters, thong bottoms, string tops, gym shorts, hot pants, tiny tennis skirts, halters, T-shirts that were cut off to leave the breasts partly exposed, as well as some skimpy or filmy pieces of lingerie. The girls, who included the odd black and Asian in their number, had good bodies, and some of them were strikingly pretty. The place was kind of a dump but it was definitely no dog pound, Dale thought.

"Mardi Gras?"

She was blonde, with layered curls. She was short and cute, with a thin tube top that barely covered her breasts. Below, she had V-shaped panties that were cut high on each side. Dale found himself thinking of a babysitter they had used for a while, years ago. It wasn't the same girl, of course, but the association was quite pleasant. Lisa, as he recalled.

"What?"

"You want to Mardi Gras?"

"I'm sorry," Dale said. "I don't know what that is."

"Mardi Gras. It's, like, lap-dancing."

"Lap-dancing? What's that?"

"Okay," the girl said, smiling sweetly. "We'll go sit down on one of the couches, where it's nice and private, and you give me five dollars when the next song comes on, and as long as that song is on I'll sit on your lap and wiggle around and rub you up and down and cuddle you. You know? Like that." She tugged down the top of her blouse a little, an artfully nonchalant gesture he appreciated. But still Dale hesitated. "I can tell you one more thing," she went on. "They play long songs here. Not like some places I know, where it's two and a half, three minutes. All the songs on this album are like four, five, six minutes long."

"Really?"

"Sure." The girl moved closer, pressing her soft upper body against his arm, and at the same time placing her hand just below the small of his back. "Come on, give it a try anyway. Then, if you don't like it, at least you'll know."

"I can touch you?"

"If you're nice about it."

"Okay."

Dale put his hand just below the small of her back, and they made their way across the large room to a dark alcove where there was a battered couch. He noticed that the girl was wearing thick white cotton socks on her feet. That's why she was so short; the other girls, most of them, were in high heels. He preferred the socks. They were suburban, New Jersey, wholesome, and yet somehow more wicked.

Why didn't Cynthia dress like this? Why didn't she act like this once in a while? Well, nowadays she would neither look nor sound anywhere near as appealing as this fine young creature. It was a shame—even years ago, when she could have done this sort of thing with great success, Cynthia never had. It had to be his fault, for never telling her, teaching her. He never asked. The two of them had failed each other. Well, she had, anyway. Where was Cynthia's natural lust, her creative sexiness? But where was his, come to that? He had been timid all his life, in the office and at home. In bed. He had taken life as it came to him, which is what Cynthia had done. In some ways, it had never arrived for either of them.

Dale felt so sad that he had a moderate erection even before the girl settled on his lap and began using her body to play with him. He had his feet up and was sitting back against one arm of the couch. She spun around gently, put her face to his belly and slowly slithered up his chest. Her tube top was pulled down, and her bare breasts—not large but firm, buoyant—brushed across his face, and he kissed them. She took his hair, and pressed his face to one breast, then the other. Dale's hands moved down over her back, gliding to her bottom, her taut thighs.

She stood up on the couch, and suddenly she was in his face. He put his mouth against the thin cotton fabric. She turned, and deftly bent away from him, her fanny still in his face. He moved his head forward, touching her there. And that was the moment he didn't want to end, not ever. The smell and feel of her sent his mind swirling off in a dozen dizzying spirals. She touched Dale, her hand stroking him lightly, but that wasn't what mattered. It was this closeness—she was a stranger, he didn't even know what her name was—this sudden profound intimacy, much more intimate precisely because it was not the act of sex itself, that made him tremble and ache. In the cellar of this dead factory, warehouse, whatever, to have this contact, this moment.

"I love you," he said faintly.

"The song's over, honey."

But she didn't move. Dale extracted a twenty, put it in her hand. She touched him again. He ran his tongue along the inside edge of her panties. He tasted her. Pushed his tongue into her. Anyone watching? He didn't care. Everything was on the line.

"Oooh...honey...hey."

He gave her some more bills.

"Oh, God."

"What?" she asked quietly, not moving.

"You have to be home."

"It's okay, I told them I'd be late," she replied after only a brief hesitation. "My folks are asleep by now. Don't worry, I won't wake them when I get in."

"I'll be late getting back."

"You stopped for cigarettes, or milk. Gas."

"I—love—you."

"Mmmmmh..."

Suddenly he splashed her face.

"God...help me."

A murmur, but she caught it.

"You don't need any help now, honey."

"Lisa?"

She laughed softly as she moved off of him. "Samantha," she corrected. "Sammie. I'm here from four till midnight, everyday. You're sweet. You must eat right. I hope you come again."

"Yeah..."

"Look for me?"

"Yes, I will."

"If you don't see me, ask."

"Lisa."

Laughter. "Sammie."

"Right. Sammie."

He stumbled around, found his way, lost it, wandered again. The fog was worse now. Rare to see it in Manhattan, and never as thick as this. The streets were choked with mist, the buildings gauzed. It had the effect of dimming all lights, giving them the weak glow of oil or gas lamps. The cars and trucks inching along cautiously seemed like vehicles from another century.

Dale somehow made it down to the pier and got the passenger ferry to Jersey City. As usual, just later and drunker. Though not too much later, and not nearly drunk enough. He had lost the desire to have a roaring great night on the city. The romance in it, spurious at best, had vanished somewhere. Besides, he had to navigate his car home. He could drink more at home. Rip through the night and then pass out. Why the hell not?

The air was damp and raw, but Dale stayed out on deck as the ferry slowly pulled away. Amazing, how little there was to see! The bright lights of the city were feeble specks beneath the fog. Too bad it wasn't daytime, the whole of Manhattan would look like some ghastly cocoon, he thought. It would look like a dead thing but it would be teeming with tiny insect life.

Dale went inside. There were only a few other passengers in the ferry. Business types going home, sitting apart from anybody else, each in his own bell-jar of solitude. A tipsy young couple standing in a corner, bodies tight, a pint in a brown bag passing discreetly back and forth.

Dale sat down opposite a girl who was on her own. He looked across at her just long enough to register that she was fourteen, maybe fifteen, somewhere in that area. But she was staring right back at him, so he glanced away. Schoolbooks. It wasn't smart, a youngster out alone at this time of night.

His eyes drifted back to her legs. Pretty. She was wearing a denim jacket and a short skirt. Her legs parted. Bare thighs. Her legs parted a little more. White panties, just a tantalizing glimpse of them. Dale stared for some minutes.

He looked up at her face. Pretty, very pretty, and somehow familiar. She smiled at him, but it was shy, not the bold smile of a blatant come-on. He looked down. Her jacket was open, and her blouse was unbuttoned to the fourth button. Was that really the curve of her breast? She shifted slightly on her seat, as if to help him see that it was, but then she straightened up and the shirt flapped and that exquisite vision was gone. Her legs moved back and forth slightly. Peekaboo.

Dale gazed at her face again. She was still smiling at him, but there was puzzlement in it now, as if she expected him to say or do something and couldn't understand why he didn't. Where had he seen her before? The more it eluded him, the more certain he was that he knew this girl.

"Sammie?" he asked quietly.

She said nothing, but her head tilted a fraction of an inch and her eyes seemed to narrow with interest.

"Lisa?"

The ferry docked with a bump. People were up and moving to the exit. Dale waited until they were all gone, as did the girl. Then he rose from his seat and took one step toward her.

"Do I know you?"

"Do you?"

Dale didn't know what to say. Then she got to her feet, and stood in front of him. Waiting, apparently, for him to make some kind of move. She adjusted the schoolbooks in her grip.

"Do you need a ride?" Dale asked. "My car is parked in the lot outside."

"Thanks."

The night was clear, the fog blown away by a sharp wind from the northwest. Dale felt the chill, but it didn't seem to bother the girl. Her long sleek legs flashed as they hurried toward his car, and her blouse hung open in the harsh air. He turned on the heater, watching her intently as he waited for the engine to idle down. She put her books on the floor and sat back, smiling.

"Where do you want to go?"

"Where do you want to take me?"

"Home."

"Sounds good."

"My home," Dale said.

"I know."

It was so outrageous it made perfect sense. Dale could see exactly how it would play out. It was late. Cynthia would be up in bed, sound asleep. Probably snoring. And when she slept, she really slept. Dale would bring the girl in, take her downstairs to the now seldom-used family room, make her a drink and then see what happened. Later, he would drop her off wherever she had to go. It was like a movie. It was delicious. He accelerated, and soon Jersey City fell behind them.

"I'll make you a drink."

"Thank you," she said enthusiastically.

"How old are you?"

"Fifteen."

"I'll bet you've never had a martini."

"No, but I'd love to try one."

"The martini is one of the man's greatest achievments."

"Mmmm. Sounds good."

She took his right hand and placed it on her thigh. So warm and soft, yet firm, and gloriously bare. It was such a beautiful feeling that Dale nearly had tears in his eyes. He looked across at her— blouse open, now revealing a lot of breast, those dream legs that seemed so amazingly long, the girlish smile, the finger held to her lips—such a vision. When you find such beauty you can't just walk away from it. Before this night was finished, he would lay his face on her flat belly and cry. With sadness, yes, but also with joy—for being granted this moment at all.

Twenty miles flew by. The house was dark, a very good sign. He pulled right into the open garage, so that no snoopy neighbor would see the girl on the way into the house. She left her books on the floor of the car. They went inside through the breezeway, through the kitchen and downstairs to the family room. He turned on only one small table lamp.

"Ooh, it's nice and warm in here."

"Yes," he said.

The girl threw off her jacket and then flopped onto the sofa like a child. She wiggled and stretched her legs, and her skirt bunched higher. She sat up suddenly, turned and leaned across to look at the books on the shelf nearby. They were Cynthia's. The collected works of Danielle Steele. But Dale was gazing with awe at the girl's backside, those legs and the way the flimsy panties clung to her heartbreaking fanny.

"Do you want that martini now?"

"Yes, please."

"First, take off your blouse."

She smiled. She undid the remaining buttons and slipped out of the blouse. Some cheap gold chains hung between her so-lovely breasts. He went to her and touched one nipple with his cheek in an act of homage. She was still smiling, but with curiosity now, and he knew then that she had never behaved like this before, not with a boyfriend, never. It was new for her, too.

"Come on."

He led her to the bar at the back end of the room and showed her how a martini was made. There had been some noteworthy times in Dale's life, but nothing to compare with this, to have a sweet young thing standing there half-dressed while he fixed a martini. In his own family room!

"Take off your skirt."

She did so. He gave her the drink. While she tasted it, he came closer and ran his hands over her body—dizzy with wonder. She pretended not to notice, concentrating on the martini. Dale was awash with joy. Tomorrow might be the first day of a new era in his life, an Age of Lead, but still he had been given this one final moment of poignant, surpassing beauty.

"How do you like the martini?"

"Wow."

"Good. I'll be right back," he said.

"Okay."

She took her drink to the sofa and stretched out, waving her legs until they found a comfortable position. Dale knelt beside her and put his cheek on her belly. There had never, he thought, been a moment like this in my life.

"I"m going to lick you all over," he said softly.

"Cool."

"In a minute."

Dale went into the unfinished section of the basement, where he kept tools and stored things he didn't really want. He picked up a small hammer, the light little one he used for tapping nails in the walls when he wanted to hang a picture. Then he dashed up the stairs to the kitchen, then the half-flight to the top level, past the empty kids' bedrooms, down the hall to the master suite. The door was ajar. She was snoring. Well, it was more than just snoring. She sounded like a factory in western Massachusetts, in some previous era.

One good swing. It made an awful sound. But then there was a tremendous silence. Dale lingered. He became aware of wetness on his cheek. He pulled his shirt off, wiped his face and tossed the shirt aside. He left the hammer where it was.

Down the hall, down the half-flight, down the regular stairs again—suddenly there was so much motion in his life! Amazing. But when he got to the family room, the girl was gone. He looked around the empty room, catching his breath. Nothing, no one. He ran to the car, but the schoolbooks were gone as well.

Dale sat down on the sofa in the family room. He should be angry with himself, with fate and all of its nasty little indignities. But it was no use. A great lassitude came over him, and it was as much as Dale could do to finish the martini.

THE DREAMS OF DR. LADYBANK

A Divine Image

Cruelty has a Human Heart
And Jealousy a Human Face
Terror, the Human Form Divine
And Secrecy, the Human Dress

The Human Dress, is forged Iron
The Human Form, a fiery Forge.
The Human Face, a Furnace seal'd
The Human Heart, its hungry Gorge.

—William Blake

PROLOGUE

"It's an amusing thought, Ian, but..."

"Impossible."

"Well, yes."

"Science fiction."

"And weak on the science," Jack said.

"But doesn't the idea itself excite you?"

"Not really. I mean, what's the point? Everyone knows it's a dead end. Besides, even if it were possible, and I'm not for a moment admitting that it is, but if it were, you'd probably wind up with a raving psychotic on your hands, and that's not my idea of fun. Psychotics are very boring people."

"Psychosis is by no means inevitable."

"This is a splendid malt, by the way."

"Help yourself to more."

"Thanks, I will."

"The point you're refusing to acknowledge is the simple fact of communication, establishing once and for all that it really is possible. My God, Jack, that's a huge leap and you know it. You can't deny it."

"And you can't prove it."

"Perhaps I can."

"Well, I'd love to see it."

"What would you say if I told you I've found a suitable mind for the experiment?"

"I'd say she's probably young, impressionable, quite pretty, very malleable, and a great piece of ass."

"Jack."

"But I'm afraid that your getting her in bed and fucking her brains out will not be widely accepted as scientific proof."

"All right, I give up."

"Ah, don't stop now, Ian. I'm enjoying this. I haven't had such a good mix of booze and bullshit since college, when we used to sit up late at night, trying to figure out what the hell an ethic was, and how to get around it. We called those sessions the Utica Club, because that's all we could afford to drink."

"But I'm serious."

"Okay, you're serious, and you've got this, uh..."

"Subject."

"Right, subject."

"Two of them, actually," Ian said with a hint of smugness in his tight smile. "Two young men."

"Men, huh? You must be serious."

"Yes, and the fact that there are two of them should provide proof enough to justify continuing the research, don't you think? One might be a fluke, but two different people, who are strangers to each other, who respond and meet and interact *by design*—you would take that seriously, wouldn't you?"

"Sure, but come on, Ian. You can't do that with people. If you could, somebody would have discovered it by now. It's not as if we're completely ignorant of how the brain works. What it can and can't do—and I'll tell you one thing, it can't do that."

"The human brain does generate extremely low frequency radio waves, ELF signals. That's a well-known fact."

"Yes, but you can't do anything with them."

"If you say so."

"Not like you're talking about."

"We'll see."

"So, are these guys patients of yours?"

"No, they're just a couple of losers I met."

"And they agreed to go along with whatever it is you plan to try out on them, this experiment?"

"They don't know anything about it."

"What?"

"That would ruin everything, Jack. If they knew, they would expect, and expectation would contaminate their minds. Of course I haven't told them anything."

"Uh, have *you* ever heard of ethics, Ian?"

"Which one did you have in mind?"

"Oh, the one about not experimenting on people without their knowledge and consent. Seems to me there might even be some kind of a law about that."

"Tsk, tsk."

"What exactly is it you intend to do?"

"Nothing. That's the beauty of it."

"I don't understand."

"I'll just be thinking, Jack. That's all. Thinking of them and perhaps even for them."

"Ah, that's all right. Thinking isn't against the law, not yet anyway. But how will you know if it works?"

"I'm not sure, but I imagine it will become apparent one way or another."

"Well, if it does work, let me handle the legal side of it. Maybe we can sell it to Sony, ha-ha."

"That's a thought."

"I can see it now. Everybody will go around wearing a smart little beanie on their head, with an antenna sticking up. They'd sell like Walkmans—or should it be Walk*men?*"

By the time Jack finally left, after sopping up a good deal more single malt scotch, Doctor Ian Ladybank was almost sorry he had mentioned his little secret. But he had to tell someone, and Jack was the closest thing to a friend he had. You can't stumble across something like that and then not want to shout about it. Nor was it really a little secret; it was serious, major, an awesome challenge. He was sure it had in fact been discovered by others, in the past, although they might not have understood what it was the way he did. It was a skill, it had limits, and it was suitable only for personal purposes.

Amazing, how it had happened. Doctor Ladybank had given the matter a lot of thought over the years. The brain was his hobby, as well as his vocation. He read everything that came out and he even made a special study of radio science. His obsession wasn't his alone—there were other people active in the field. He was aware, for instance, of the theory that some UFO sightings may be triggered by localized disturbances in the earth's magnetic field that interfered with the wave cycles in the observer's brain. It was a matter of some significance to Doctor Ladybank—although few others seemed to consider it important—that the earth, the planet itself, was constantly broadcasting its own ELF waves, and that they were remarkably similar to those generated by the human brain. He devised his own mental exercises, instructing his mind to do what it had never done before.

All of this led nowhere until a young woman named Shelly had come to see him, not long ago. She thought she was stigmatic and she had the wounds to prove it. Her case was not as interesting as it had seemed at first glance but she was an attractive little creature. In his waiting room, as he was showing her out, Doctor Ladybank suddenly found himself wishing, or willing, that Shelly would reach up and touch her breast. A silly but typical erotic fancy, borne no doubt of mid-afternoon tedium. The girl did not respond, but her boyfriend, who had accompanied her to the office and was standing nearby, absently rubbed his Megadeath T-shirt at the spot where it covered his left nipple. The young man's blank expression indicated complete ignorance.

Stunned, Doctor Ladybank at first could not bring himself to believe what had apparently just taken place. It was too easy to be true. But yes, he had felt a tiny mental spasm at the instant the thought—wish, command, whatever—formed within his mind. Doctor Ladybank was flushed with a sense of accomplishment, happy as a boy who suddenly flicks his wrist in precisely the right way and at last manages to skip a rock across water.

He stood by the window in his office a few minutes later and watched Shelly and her boyfriend walk away down the street. When they were almost out of sight, Doctor Ladybank had a parting idea for them—and sure enough, the boyfriend's hand swung around to pat Shelly's ass. That evening Doctor Ladybank thought about the boyfriend again. *You need to talk to me. Urgently.* Less than a minute later, the telephone rang. He was Alvin Doolittle, but he preferred the nickname Snake.

The other one was sent to Doctor Ladybank, like many of his cases, by the juvenile court. Tony Delgado was only sixteen, but he had his own apartment, a trick pad near the river in the south end of the city. It was a decrepit neighborhood, full of rotting old tenements and abandoned factories, a tidal basin of foundered lives, but it provided all the tolerance and anonymity needed for Tony to practice his trade.

Doctor Ladybank quickly sized the boy up as innately Machian in affect. What Tony possessed was not quite a mind, but more of a constantly shifting panorama of received images and sensations. He learned little but survived, thanks to an underlying canniness that for nearly three years had helped him dodge both the law and the retribution of the streets. A minor stupidity had led him to juvenile court, which promptly fobbed him off on Doctor Ladybank, who within a quarter of an hour had the youth uttering numbers in German while tugging at his earlobes.

It was a discovery that should be important. It should give Doctor Ladybank power, fame, wealth—all the usual prizes. The only trouble was, he didn't know how to take the next step. What to do with this fantastic skill. How could he present it in such a way that would satisfy the scientific community? He could make videotapes of sessions with Snake and Tony, inducing all kinds of bizarre and unlikely behavior, but that would prove nothing. Not the least of Doctor Ladybank's problems was the painful fact that this skill of his simply didn't work with most people. He tried it with everyone he met now, but the original poor fools were the only two in the plus column. In spite of the odds against it, he was dogged by a fear that both of them really were flukes. Maybe it was just a freak of nature, devoid of any principle or broader application. But even if that were so, there was still a measure of personal satisfaction in what he was doing.

And it was early days yet. Doctor Ladybank was sure that he would learn much more as he pursued his experiment, and sooner or later the ultimate answers would come to him.

—ONE—

Tony Delgado thought he understood the problem. This Pied Piper, to give him a name, had a special kind of radio that he used to beam his infernal messages into Tony's brain. It had been going for a couple of weeks now, and the situation was only getting worse. Tony had tried to catch the Pied Piper several times before he realized that it was impossible. The Pied Piper was only about six inches tall, and could appear or disappear at will. Many times he was heard, not seen. There was no way Tony could get a hold of the little demon.

Tony was running out of possibilities. He had gone to Dom's Connection, the largest electronics store in the city, but they told him they didn't have any kind of jamming device that would do what he wanted. They suggested that he consider buying a good radio or stereo system, and just play loud music whenever he was bothered. But Tony had already tried that with the boombox he owned, and it didn't work. Static-ridden, distorted perhaps, the Pied Piper still got into Tony's head.

Now Tony had another idea. He rooted through the underwear in the top drawer of his bureau, and came up with the stiletto he had acquired somewhere along the line. It was his best weapon in the awkward moments that occasionally arose, not so much for use as for display. In Tony's chosen line of work it was sometimes necessary to introduce a deterrant factor, that slight touch of intimidation that prevents serious trouble, and the stiletto had never failed to chill a tricky customer. He was pleased to find that it hadn't lost any of its sharpness, though for the task he had in mind now all he would require was the very fine tip of the gleaming blade.

Tony Delgado lived in a small apartment in the heart of the south end. He was sixteen, and had been on his own for the best part of a year now. He had a perfect body, which he took care of religiously because it was his bread and butter. At five-ten, he was neither too tall nor too short. His physique was slender and boyish, and he avoided the muscular look, but he exercised enough to maintain a body texture that was both supple and firm.

He had one good room, the large one where he entertained his customers. Tony had invested a lot in that room, setting it up for the fantasy scenarios that were his trademark. He sometimes had to discourage mushy johns who wanted to use his personal bed or to stay all night. He preferred it that way, keeping the rest of his place, and life, off-limits. Tony's bedroom was small and cluttered, the kitchen bug-infested. The bathroom was modest but clean, and one way or another it saw a lot of use.

The trouble started more than a month ago. Tony had always been successful at avoiding the police until then. He had picked up a john at a bar in the neighborhood, but when they got outside the asshole lost his nerve. A patrol car happened to pass by as Tony was kicking in the rocker panel on the man's shiny new car. It should have come to nothing. The asshole naturally refused to press charges. However, Tony then made the unfortunate mistake of giving the cop a hard time, even shoving him away once. Since he was still a minor, Tony was sent to juvenile court, where some drip of a judge gave him a boring lecture and then ordered him to see a psychiatrist.

What a joke that turned out to be. For one thing, the guy had a funny name, Lady-something. Ladybug would be right, Tony thought, because the shrink was the crazy one. He was straight, and even beautiful, but as the interview went on Tony began to feel like he was stuck with a creep. It was no one thing the guy did that bothered him, just a very uncomfortable feeling that got stronger all the time. Tony had never experienced anything like that, and he had met some strange people.

In the end, the shrink talked pure nonsense. He told Tony to watch out for bright lights, bright colors, and, most of all, bright flowers. What kind of shit was that? Tony decided Doctor Ladybug was in bigger trouble than he was, and he nodded his head politely, agreeing with everything the shrink said.

It must have been the smart thing to do, because he was sent home to his mother, no additional sessions required. He was free of any legal obligations. Tony was back at work in his apartment that same night.

Tony's mother understood nothing. For thirty years she had worked at a dry-cleaning shop, and still did. Some people argued that the fumes were dangerous, and Mrs. Delgado did get headaches regularly, but it was steady work and there was a lot to be said for seniority.

She believed anything Tony told her. He was her youngest child, born when she thought her body was past all that. And he was the best when it came to calling her, visiting and giving her little gifts. So kind and considerate. She didn't like the fact that he lived away from her when he was still so young, but there was nothing she could do about it. Kids grow up quicker today, they do what they want, and Tony didn't have a father around to lay down the law. But at least the boy was good to her, and he lived less than a mile away.

So his first brush with the law had come to nothing, and his mother still lived in happy ignorance of his activities, but Tony faced other problems. AIDS had claimed or scared off some of his top customers, and to keep his income up he was forced to cruise the bars more often. That multiplied both his legal and medical risks. So far he remained clean, but business was tough, and getting tougher every week.

He had also developed a taste for coke. The good stuff, not that crack shit. But it cost money, and Tony was also convinced that it was one of the reasons he was so jumpy of late. However, these drawbacks were not enough to curb his appetite. They were simply new factors to bear in mind.

Worst of all, the Pied Piper had entered his life. At first Tony thought he was imagining things, or that it was some kind of weird side-effect of the drug. He would glimpse a trick of light or a play of shadows, but it was always on the other side of the room, and he always caught it out of the corner of his eye. When he turned to look carefully, there was nothing to see.

Then there were the sounds. Tony began to think of them as messages of some kind, though he never really understood them at all. They were like bubbles of noise that burst open deep inside his head. There was always a lot of static with it, which is how Tony finally cottoned on to the possibility that the Pied Piper was broadcasting to him. It was possible to pick out a few words now and then, sometimes a phrase or two, but none of it ever made any sense. Tony did get a certain feeling of urgency, and that only aggravated his distress.

Soon enough, the little man emerged tauntingly, letting Tony see him clearly—if only for a brief instant at a time. Now, a day never passed without one appearance, usually more. He never actually said anything, and his expression was always blank. The little fucker was a constant torment, even when he wasn't there. The only positive thing was that so far he hadn't turned up when there was a customer present.

Tony went into the bathroom and turned on the light around the mirror. He stood close to it, opened his mouth and found his targets. Tony's teeth were not perfect. Over the years he had accumulated a few plastic or composite fillings. They were okay, he figured. He wanted the two larger ones that were made of lead or silver, some kind of metal. It seemed obvious to him that the Pied Piper was using those fillings as built-in receivers for his transmissions. The metal picked up the beam and relayed it along the nerves in Tony's jawbone on to the center of his brain. So, if he could just get rid of those two fillings he might solve his problem. He had called three different dentists, but they seemed to think it was a set-up for a lawsuit, and turned him down cold. The only alternative was to do it himself.

It wasn't easy. At least he could get at the two fillings and still see what he was doing, but for the longest time the tip of the blade found no hold. Tony grew frustrated, then angry as the knife slipped off the tooth and jabbed his gums. He tasted a little of his own blood when he swallowed. His open mouth filled with saliva too fast, and some of it trickled down his windpipe, setting off a violent but useless coughing jag. Tony's eyes were bleary as he tried to refocus on the tooth. He was beginning to think it was an impossible chore, but then the point of the blade finally lodged in some tiny crevice for a second. It slipped off almost at once, but he was encouraged, and several tries later he found the spot again. Tony worked it carefully, digging the tip into the gap and trying to expand it. As long as the metal blade touched the metal filling it jangled the nerves in his tooth like a constant electrical charge, but he would endure that to get rid of the Pied Piper. Any pain would be worth suffering if it would end the daily nightmare visitations.

Tony's eyes continued to blur with tears and his jaw ached, but he was making progress. Now he had gouged enough of a crack to be able to use the knife as a lever. But whenever he relaxed or became careless, the knife would pop loose again and stab Tony in the gum or the roof of the mouth. The saliva that spilled out on his chin was distinctly pink. Worst of all, the goddamn metal filling seemed to be welded to the goddamn tooth. No matter how hard he pried at it, there was barely any movement.

"Come on, you fuck," Tony whined. "You're killing me."

Then he screamed and dropped the knife as he reached for the wall to hold himself against as a blast of pain shot through his entire body. The knife clattered in the sink. This is too much, he thought as he reached for it with trembling fingers. But then he discovered that the filling was loose. Yeah, he could move it with his tongue. It was still hooked in there, but when he poked it repeatedly it felt like it was rattling in place. Gasping for breath, Tony forced himself to re-insert the knife.

"Ein, zwei, drei..."

He increased the pressure, and the pain blossomed, weakening him so much that all the strength in his body seemed to be flying out of his pores. One last shove—the filling was at last torn free, but the knife blade scraped a bloody furrow across the roof of Tony's mouth at the same time. He nearly swallowed the jagged filling but managed to spit it into the sink. It bounced around like a deformed marble before coming to rest. Tony was dizzy and drained, and the hole in his tooth felt enormous, but he had done it. One down, one to go. He washed his mouth out, and then sat on the toilet lid for a few minutes to rest.

The second filling seemed to take longer, probably because he had little patience left. His arms and neck ached, along with his jaw, but somehow the pain bothered him less. Tony pushed on, desperate to finish the job, and eventually he was rewarded when the second filling slid off his tongue and joined the first one in the sink. He felt an enormous sense of satisfaction, freedom and accomplishment. He took the two lumps of twisted metal into the kitchen, opened the window, and threw them as far as he could out into the weed-choked, trash-strewn backyard.

Tony rinsed his mouth again, this time with warm salty water to stop the bleeding. Then he poured a large scotch, to remove the bad taste and soothe his nerves. He sat down in his one good room and sipped the drink carefully. God, he was still shaking. His arms and legs felt so weak. He let his tongue dance over the two holes in his teeth. They were huge. The edges were so sharp he would have to be careful not to cut his tongue on them.

But no dentist could refuse him now. Two fillings fell out when he was eating. Tough pizza crust, say. Or peanuts, or when he bit into a steak. It didn't matter what. That kind of thing happened all the time. Tony would insist they be replaced with plastic or procelain fillings, anything but metal.

He smiled faintly as he sloshed the whiskey around in his mouth. It stung his exposed nerves, but he knew that it was also beginning to deaden them. The pain was fading deliciously.

Zzzzzt.

Oh no, no.

Zzzzzt.

Tony put the drink down on the table because he was afraid he might drop it. This can't be happening. He looked around the room nervously. A glimmer of movement, then gone. A shadow that passed in an instant, as if a bird had flown by the window. Then the static cleared up beautifully.

—Ah, that's much better.

The words blared inside Tony's trapped mind.

—You can really hear me now, can't you!

—TWO—

"Hic, haec, hoc."

"Say what?" The bartender looked puzzled, wary.

"What?"

"You said something to me?"

"No," Snake replied. "I didn't say nothing to nobody."

"You want another beer?"

"Yeah, I want another beer," Snake said, his voice brimming with defiance. "And a clean glass."

The bartender brought the drink and the glass, withdrew some money from the small pile of cash in front of Snake, and muttered to himself in Spanish as he turned away. Lousy greaseball, Snake thought as he inspected the new glass. I'm sitting here, minding my own business, having a quiet beer, and this asshole has to get on my case. Say what? Say, fuck you, bro.

At least tonight Snake knew what he was doing in this place. He was waiting for the whore, Toni. Last night he had no idea at all why he had come there. The El Greco was a pisshole of a bar, buried in the unfriendly depths of the south end. But Snake went out last night, leaving Shelly behind alone and cursing, and he'd come straight across the river to this dump. He hated the place. It had the terrible smell of food you'd never want to eat, and it was full of jabbering spics. They all had the same look on their faces too, mean and vaguely pissed off, as if every damned one of them had to go through life with a splinter up his dick.

They wouldn't bother him, though, because Snake was wearing the colors. Sure, they could beat the living shit out of him if they wanted to, but they knew he'd be back sooner or later with thirty of the hardest fuckers around who would trash the El Greco, along with every spic they could get their hands on. Nor did it matter that Snake was no longer exactly in good standing as a member of the Legion of the Lost; he wore the colors, and that was all that counted in a situation like this. The colors commanded respect, or at least fear—which wasn't very different.

Last night he sat in the same place at the bar for nearly an hour, wondering what the hell he was doing there and why he could not bring himself to leave. It was odd, but then some odd things had been happening to Snake lately. Headaches, for one, the kind that ordinary painkillers didn't cure. And, according to Shelly, he was talking to himself more and more. But that was crazy. It stood to reason that a man can't go around talking to himself and not know it. Could he? What about that latest incident, the one with the bartender a few minutes ago? No, it was impossible. In a noisy place like this, the bartender made a mistake.

Besides, Shelly had her own problems. She'd gone quite pale and spotty in recent weeks. She also scratched herself a lot, so much so in fact that it had reached the point where she had these ugly open wounds in her hands and feet and on her body. Then, as if that weren't enough, she decided they were the marks of Christ on the Cross. Snake had to take her to the doctor, who sent them along to a shrink. Dumb fucking bitch. He ought to sell her off to an out-of-state gang, but the way she was now, her sales value was scraping along the bottom. Shelly was so bad that he didn't even want to touch her anymore—unless he had to hit her.

Maybe that was why Snake had come to the El Greco, to meet a new piece of ass. He had accomplished that much last night, when Toni sat down beside him and they got to talking. She was a fine item, all right. Cute fanny, long legs, pretty face. She could be a bit fuller up front, but Snake had never been all that keen on big tits. He liked women lean and—snaky.

It didn't bother him that she was a spic. Somehow, that was okay in a woman. Toni's creamy skin was such a pleasant contrast to Shelly's newsprint surface. And the eyes—deep, round, warm and brown, with flecks of gold. Snake couldn't remember the last time he'd looked closely at Shelly's eyes, but now he thought of them as washed-out blue peas adrift in a pinkish-white glaze. No question, Toni was an exotic gem in comparison.

It did bother him, however, that she was a whore. He didn't care how many men she fucked. The problem was that he lacked the money to buy her talents. Even if he had it, it would go against the grain for Snake to spend it on something he'd always managed to get for free.

He and Toni were eventually able to work out a deal based on non-cash considerations. She liked coke, and she needed Demerol. Snake had experience and helpful contacts in the field. He was strictly minor league, but he did know how to cut himself an edge in such transactions. It was one of the many ways in which he cobbled together an erratic income.

"Darling."

"Hey, babe." Snake smiled as Toni edged close to him at the bar. "You look great."

"Buy me a drink."

"Sure. What'll you have?"

"You forgot already. Tsk, tsk."

"Yeah, well...What was it again?"

"Red Death on the rocks."

"Right."

As there were no other barstools free, Snake gave Toni his. He signalled the bartender. Toni looked fantastic in a clinging black mini-dress. Snake could hardly take his eyes off her legs, but he did turn away long enough to watch the bartender carefully when he took the money for Toni's drink.

"You can take your sunglasses off."

"I like the dark," she replied.

"It's dark enough in this dump."

Toni sipped her drink. "Do you have something for me?"

"I told you I would."

"I know what you told me, but do you have it?"

"Of course I do."

"You're a darling. What is it?"

Snake leaned close to her. "God, you smell great."

"What do you have?" Toni repeated with an edge in her voice. "What do you have for me?"

"Demerol."

"Beautiful." Toni relaxed and smiled at him. "There is one thing I have to tell you."

"Yeah? What's that?"

"It's the wrong time to use my little pussy."

"That don't bother me, babe," Snake declared proudly. "In the Legion of the Lost we don't just poke bloody cunts, we hunker right down and eat 'em."

"Really?" Toni gave a dramatic shudder. "Sounds icky. And it would bother me, darling. But you know, I really have a great ass, and I'm sure you'd love it."

"Yeah, it looks good, and I bet it feels like velvet," Snake said. "But I ain't no butt-fucker."

"So there are some things the Legion of the Lost won't do," Toni said sarcastically.

"Damn right."

"Oh well. I guess—"

"Read my mind," Snake told her.

"I give great head."

"Right. You better, babe."

"How many pills do you have?"

"Put it this way. You owe me five blow jobs."

Toni looked rather disappointed. "But darling, you will be able to get more, won't you?"

"What do you do, eat 'em like candy?"

"I'm in pain," Toni said resentfully.

"You need somebody to look after you," Snake pointed out, a clever idea forming in his mind. Blow jobs every night. A great source of income. He would move her out of the south end and put her to work making real money, no more of this back alley boffing for bucks. "Yeah, somebody who'll take good care of you."

"I take care of myself."

"I mean a regular guy."

"I've got a hundred regular guys, darling."

"To protect you," Snake clarified firmly.

"I've never needed protection."

"That just means you're overdue for trouble."

"Oh." Toni didn't seem to care for what Snake had in mind, but then her face moved slightly as if she had just felt a twinge of pain, and then she smiled up at him. "Oh dear."

"Yeah, but don't worry about it, babe," Snake told her with a wide grin. "Now that I'm here you'll be all right. I'll take care of you and you'll take care of me, right?"

"You might decide you don't want me," Toni said. She had a peculiar smile on her face. "When you get to know me."

Snake laughed. "Oh, I'll want you, babe, you can be sure of that. Matter of fact, I want you right now."

Toni discreetly slipped her hand between Snake's legs.

"Mmm, so you do."

"Come on, let's go."

"Your old lady must not be treating you right."

"What old lady?"

"I can tell, darling."

"Yeah, well, she's on the way out," Snake said. "She just don't know it yet."

"No one ever does."

"Come on," Snake said anxiously.

"Let me finish my drink," Toni insisted calmly. "Besides, I can see that you like standing in the middle of a crowd of people and having me touch you this way. It's nice, isn't it?"

"Jesus, babe."

But she was right.

—THREE—

—Greetings, plasmodium.

"Hey, I've been looking for you."

—Stand by.

"Where are you?"

—Here.

"I can't see you."

—You can hear me.

"Come on out, man. Let me see you."

Tony had a large mayonnaise jar. If he could just get his hands on the Pied Piper long enough to shove him into the jar and screw the cap on...Into the trash...Into the landfill...But, only after Tony hammered a few nail holes in the cap and then steamed the brain-eating son of a bitch alive over a pot of boiling water for a couple of hours.

But maybe Tony wouldn't throw him away. Maybe he'd put the jar on a shelf in the living room and let his johns goggle at it. What the hell is that, they'd ask. Souvenir from the Caribbean, he'd tell them with a straight face. My voodoo chile.

—Slime.

"Where the hell are you?"

—Everywhere.

"Yeah? Where's that?"

—In your head.

"That's what I have to talk to you about," Tony said. "You have to let me call a dentist and get an appointment, because my jaw is killing me all the time now."

—No.

"I can't take it anymore."

—No.

"Fuck, man, why the fuck not?"

—He'll see what you did to your teeth and he'll think that you're crazy.

"I *am* crazy."

—He'll get them to lock you up.

"I'm locked up here most of the time, talking to myself."

—I am always with you.

"Then come on out and let me see you."

—See!

Suddenly Tony couldn't see anything but the Pied Piper. It was as if he were inside Tony's eyeballs, peering into his brain. He had an evil grin on his twisted face, and now his filthy hands came up and started scratching at the inner lining of Tony's eyes in an effort to shred through the membrane. Scraping, ripping, peeling the cells away with ridged fingernails that were as sharp as razorblades.

The pain was excruciating. Tony slid off the chair and fell to his knees on the floor, holding his head in his hands. He was too weak to scream, it felt like the breath had been sucked from his lungs. One hand groped blindly toward the small brown bottle on the coffee table. Tony had tried all the regular store-bought painkillers, but none of them helped. Finally he had scored some Demerol from a beautiful idiot named Snake, his new friend. The Demerol was fantastic, although it never really lasted quite long enough. Now Tony had just a few left.

—No.

The muscles in Tony's arm went dead. His fingers fumbled at the brown bottle but could not grip it. *Please*, came the whimper from the back of his skull. *Please let me*—but a shrill racket overwhelmed his feeble thought.

—Sorry.

Tony began to beat his head against the floor.

—Do you want the people downstairs to come up and find you like this? They'll call a doctor and he'll decide you're crazy. He'll have them lock you away forever.

Tony continued to bang his head on the hardwood floor in an effort to knock himself unconscious.

—Listen.

Tony could no longer lift his head; it rested face down in a smear of blood. But the pain had let up, and his brain began the laborious process of forming clear thoughts again. His breathing came back in short, shallow gasps.

—You can have your pill.

Tony tried to reach for the bottle, but couldn't.

—Not yet. Only when you have listened to what you must do for me.

"Yes."

—And accept.

The air was thin and liquid. It had a raw, unpleasant edge that reminded Tony of grain alcohol.

"What is it?"

—You must bring someone here.

"Who?"

—Someone you trust.

"I don't trust anybody, man."

—Nevertheless.

"How can I, with you hanging around?"

Business had fallen right off the table ever since the Pied Piper had taken over Tony's life. He couldn't dare bring anyone home when he longer had control of the situation. He had to go out at night all the time now, hustling quick tricks in toilets and alleys for prices he would have laughed at a couple of months ago. Tony's whole world had shriveled around him like the skin on a rotten corpse.

—You can.

"Can I take money from him."

—Yes.

"And do my job?"

—That is what you must do.

"I get it," Tony said, smiling faintly. "You can't see me when I'm outside, and you want to watch. Right?" For once the Pied Piper was silent. Tony chuckled. "That's okay, man, that's cool. But you have to understand." His voice took on a pleading tone again as he pushed himself over onto his side. "I can't go on living like this. It just won't work."

—Leave the living to me, plasmodium.

"I mean it, man. I'm dying in my socks. People will come to see what's the matter, why I'm not in touch. My family, like that, you know what I mean."

—Then deal with them.

"I can't handle it."

—Why not?

"I just can't. I'm afraid."

—Of what?

"You..."

—But, I'm you.

"The fuck you are," Tony protested. "I'm sick. I hurt all the time now. The only way I can face people is in the dark, and it's all because of you. *Not me*, I'm the one you're doing it to, and maybe I should be locked away somewhere. Maybe that'd be the best thing."

—Nonsense.

"You're killing me. Day by day, you're killing me."

—Ingrate.

"Come here, you little shit."

Tony had regained a slight measure of strength by now, so he lunged in the direction of where he thought the Pied Piper might be, but his fingers grasped empty air. The demon was gone. Tony knew it at once from the sudden lightness he felt, the release of his mind.

It was the worst attack yet. Tony's heart banged inside his chest, weak but frantic, and his skin was slick with sweat. His arms trembled, nearly buckling, as he made an effort to sit up on the floor. He looked at the thin patch of blood on the hardwood and felt a terrible anticipation of his own doom. This is how he would die, like an animal, like less than an animal. Like trash, like slime, unseen, all but invisible, stepped on, rubbed away, a smear, a tiny stain on the street.

Tony crawled up into the chair. He saw the brown bottle of Demerol, but he no longer felt the need for any. Save them. The ache in his jaw was dull and distant. If only he could manage to grab the Demerol and get it down his throat in the minute before the Pied Piper got a hold of him. It was the only thing that did seem to keep the demon from getting through, at least for a short while. But he would have to carry a loose pill all the time, or else have one installed in a special socket in his teeth, like some of the Nazis. Come to think of it, the holes were already there, waiting to be custom-fitted.

He needed more Demerol, that was the main thing. Enough to keep him safe day and night. It was so damn good, so much better than coke or weed or anything else he'd ever tried. Better even than sex. So what if it turned him into a placid addict, lolling about like a zombie? Anything was better than having that fucker inside his brain.

Tonight he would see Snake again, and he would make sure the guy was sufficiently motivated to get more Demerol. There was no way Tony could live without it now.

He noticed the mayonnaise jar on the floor, and it puzzled him for a moment. He picked it up and looked at it. The strands of mayonnaise left inside had turned into a greenish-black slime. Slime, the Pied Piper had called him.

Plasmodium. That was a word Tony knew for certain he didn't know and had never heard before. Until today. Where did it come from? Impossible. Unless the Pied Piper was real.

The pain began to swell like an infernal orchestra in Tony's head, and he reached for the brown bottle.

—FOUR—

"Where y'goin'?"

Snake looked over his shoulder. Shelly was still on the old couch, which sagged nearly to the floor. She looked like she was sampling coffins and had found one that suited her. She had been lying there most of the day. She was out of it, brain-blitzed on those pills the shrink had prescribed for her. Shelly discovered happiness when she doubled the original dosage and now she didn't scratch herself so much. She was also a lot easier for Snake to handle, although his feelings for her did not improve. Snake was hooked on Toni.

"Out," he replied curtly.

"Out where?"

"Fuck you."

Shelly struggled to push herself up on one elbow. It wasn't a pretty sight. Scrawny arms and legs. A whining, watery voice that came from a face resembling a tombstone. She also broadcast an odor that would pit steel. He looked away from her and put on his Legion of the Lost leather jacket.

"Snake..."

"Don't wait up."

Twenty minutes later Snake parked his beat-up Dodge Colt on South Freedom, hurried around the corner and entered the El Greco bar. The usual do-nothing crowd was on hand, drinking, yammering over the soccer table and sticking their chests out at each other like animals. Snake hated them all. They seemed to smirk at him and laugh to themselves whenever he came in, but not one of them had the balls to take him on because they knew he'd kick the shit out them. Snake knew about spic fighting abilities—they were game little roosters, but hit them in the body and they all break up like a sack of sticks.

Toni was there too, as she knew she damn well better be. It hadn't taken him long to straighten her out on that score. Snake was not to be kept waiting, not for one minute. You have to make sure a whore knows her place and toes the line, otherwise she'll piss all over you. Snake was pleased, but didn't show it, though he did tell her she looked sexy when she came and wrapped her arm around his waist. They got drinks and sat down at the far end of the bar, away from the crowd. Unfortunately, the El Greco didn't run to booths or tables.

Toni smiled, gave him little kisses, murmured in his ear and touched him secretly, but for all that she seemed tense and edgy. Her face was drawn and she toyed with her drink nervously.

"What's the matter, babe?"

"I'm in pain," she said.

"Drink your drink, and have another."

"You know what I mean."

"Relax."

"You got more?"

"Sure," Snake said.

"How much?"

"Jesus, you are jumpy tonight. Enough, okay? I have enough for you."

Toni settled down a little and stroked his thigh gratefully. Nice. Snake was pleased, but not entirely happy. His efforts to advance the situation in the last ten days had so far failed. He loved the blow jobs in his car, parked in a dark lot, and he knew he had a hold on Toni, but his control over her was only partial. She had agreed to consider working exclusively for him, but still would not commit to it. Snake's dream of free sex *and* free money hovered just beyond his reach. For the moment.

"But," he said quietly.

"What?" Toni's face tensed immediately. "But what?"

"I'm not happy."

"Why?"

"Take those sunglasses off."

"Pretend I'm a stranger, hot for you, and—"

"Take 'em off," Snake demanded. "It's dark enough here."

"Okay." Toni removed the shades and blinked, wincing. Then she smiled at him. "Whatever you want, darling."

"That's better."

"Besides, I'm hot for you anyway, you know."

"Yeah, well." Snake tried to look cool, but it wasn't easy to ignore her hand between his legs. "Listen to me."

"What's the matter?"

"I want you working for me."

"I know, but—"

"You don't belong down in this part of town. I can take you to better places, fix you up with guys that have more money. You can pull a ton, and I'll take care of everything. Everything you need, I'll get it for you."

"Sounds good," Toni said in a neutral tone of voice. "Maybe we could do that, but I'm not ready for it yet."

"No? We could leave right now, head on up to the Green Door and bag a half-dozen yuppies in no time."

"But not tonight, darling. I don't feel too good."

Snake shrugged his shoulders as if it didn't bother him one way or the other, but the expression on his face tightened. "There's something else."

"What?"

"I'm getting kind of tired of doing it in the car."

"Oh."

"Don't worry, babe. You're great. But I'd like to go back to your place, where we can take a little more time and really do it right. Slow and sweet, you know?"

Toni looked unhappy. Snake knew he was walking a fine line. She had already made it clear to him that she didn't bring anyone home, that it "wasn't convenient" for some reason which she would not specify. If he pushed her too hard, she might decide to drop him and take her chances with somebody else. Whores know so many people. It might take her a few days, but sooner or later she'd find another source of coke and Demerol, and Snake would be left out in the cold. Toni was too valuable to lose. It wasn't often that you found such a hot young thing, such an unusual beauty who really could perform. Toni was a sizzler.

But damn it, if Snake was going to be her one supplier, then he was entitled to more than he was getting. She didn't even let him touch her hardly at all, aside from a little ass-grabbing and an occasional brush with her nubby tits. Snake wanted more, much more. He wanted to roll around naked with her on a bed, to watch her strip, to splash around together in a bubble bath—the kind of things he did with Shelly, when she was human. Toni was great when she put her nose to the grindstone, but Snake was determined to strike a better deal.

"Darling, I will take you back to my place, and we'll have a wonderful time—many wonderful times."

"All right."

"But," Toni said, holding her hand up, "I have to get myself organized first."

"What the fuck does that mean?"

"I told you, I'm suffering the most monumental pain, from my dental problems. That's why I need the medicine."

"Right," Snake said wearily. He knew better than to ask why she didn't just get her dentist to write a prescription. She was a no-hope junkie whore, and it wasn't hard to figure out what the future had in store for her, but at least he had found her while she was young and still had a lot of tread. She was worth taking a certain amount of bullshit to keep. "How long will that be?"

"Next week."

"Really?"

Her eyes danced vaguely, avoiding him. "I hope."

"Jesus, babe."

"You poor darling," she said soothingly, caressing him again discreetly. "I'll make it up to you, just wait and see. I will, I really will. We'll have the most fantastic time together. And in the meantime, I'll suck your brains out, I'll drink you dry."

Talk like that dazed Snake. "God, you make me hot," he told her. "Let's get out of here."

"First."

Business first, was what she meant. Snake expected that and had prepared for it. In his pockets he had two packets of pills, a larger quantity in case Toni met either or both of his demands, and a smaller number if she turned him down. It was time to yank the leash. Snake slipped her the packet containing half a dozen Demerols. Without looking at it, her eyes widened in alarm.

"That's all?"

"'Fraid so, babe."

"Why?"

"Recession. Supply and demand. Things are tight. Remember when I told you it'd be a lot easier if we worked together?"

Toni was trying to look stern, but it didn't suit her. "You know I can find other sources," she said.

"It isn't wise to take business away from the Legion," Snake countered, falling back on his last serious threat. Not that the Legion gave a damn about him. However, Toni didn't know that, so the threat was as good as real. "It makes 'em want to go out and kick somebody's face in, that kind of thing."

"All I want is a little time," Toni said pleadingly.
"What I just gave you is a little time."
Toni sighed unhappily. "All right."
"Now, let's go out to the car."

—FIVE—

Tony couldn't stand it anymore. The pain was too much for him to bear. Three days ago he had finally gone to a dentist and had his teeth filled with some kind of plastic. It was a hideous session, lasting hours. The dentist obviously thought that Tony was crazy because of what he had done to his teeth, and for not removing his sunglasses. It cost a lot, and since Tony was not a regular patient and had no dental coverage he was obliged to fork over the money in advance. That was smart on the dentist's part, as Tony never would have bothered if he knew the fillings weren't going to work. They didn't.

At first he thought it was just a matter of time before the pain wore off for good, but after three days it was clearly there to stay. Perhaps he should have had new metal fillings installed to interfere with the Pied Piper's broadcasts, but the originals hadn't really done the job, and it now seemed likely that Tony's teeth had little if anything to do with the strength or weakness of the torment he experienced.

He hadn't actually seen the Pied Piper in some time now, but the messages still came through several times a day. They meant little to Tony, aside from the sheer pain and terror they caused him. It had reached the point where he spent most of his time in bed or on the couch, weak from the last onslaught, trembling with dread in anticipation of the next one.

The pain usually subsided at night, and Tony would go out to eat and then hustle up some work. He tried to do what the demon voice wanted. He brought several customers back to his place and performed magnificently. They were cheap bums who didn't deserve such royal treatment but Tony would do whatever it took to please the Pied Piper. When the voice returned, however, it was always dissatisfied, and the agony continued.

Worse, Tony hadn't seen Snake since the night before he went to the dentist. He needed more Demerol, huge amounts, to get him through each day and make life somewhat bearable. Tony stabbed a glossy fingernail at the ice in his drink. It looked as if Snake would not appear at the El Greco tonight. That was bad, because Tony was completely out of Demerol. It had occurred to him that unless he got some he might kill himself tomorrow—assuming the Pied Piper would let him. Tony didn't know what to do. He left the bar, planning to return later. In the meantime, he would hit a few other places and see if he could find Snake.

The bastard was jerking his chain, that's what it was. Tony wouldn't work for him, wouldn't take him home for a long night of sex. Well, there was a problem. Somehow, Snake had yet to grasp the fact that Tony was at least nominally male. Tony could work the straight side of the street, but that was nerve-wracking, and he had no appetite for it. Nor could he bring Snake home, as it wouldn't be long before the Lost Legionnaire noticed some little something taped flat between Tony's legs.

Tony pulled a couple of quick tricks in his wanderings, but he didn't find Snake. He eventually found himself crossing the bridge into Riverside. It was a poor working-class neighborhood, virtually identical to the south end but for the fact that there were very few blacks or Hispanics in Riverside. It was for the most part unknown territory to Tony, but for some reason he felt he was heading in the right direction.

He tried a few bars along the way, looking in, then turning to leave immediately. Tony had long ago developed an ability to recognize places where he was sure to get beaten up.

He had to work out something with Snake. He could tell him the truth, and probably get beaten up for that, but at least it would clear the air. The charade couldn't go on much longer, and it might be better to get it over with sooner than later. But he had to have something to appease Snake. A share of Tony's income from gays—that might do it. Why not? It was the same kind of deal Snake wanted, except that Tony would be working his regular beat, not the cash-laden yuppie straights at the Green Door. The money might be less but it was still money for nothing. And Tony would have his steady supply of coke and Demerol. Yeah, it might just work out.

Nonetheless, Tony shuddered at the prospect of confronting Snake with the truth. Was it really necessary? Tony had enough cash on him now to buy a few days' worth of pills. Do that, just pay for the medicine, take it and go. No sex, no promises. Keep it strictly on a business footing. And if Snake insists on more? Tell him it's that time of the month. No, Tony remembered he had done that only a week or two ago. Vaginal fungus? Snake might want to eat it. Tell him you've got the clap, and you're out of action for a while. Head, yes; anything else, no.

The rattletrap Dodge Colt—there it was. Tony was amazed. He had found Snake. Almost. The car was parked in front of an aged triple-decker. On one side of the house there was a vacant lot, then a bakery and some more shops. On the other side, there was a diner, now closed, and a bar that Tony had already checked. Across the street, nothing likely. It had to be this apartment house. But which of the three apartments?

Tony started on the ground floor. He pushed the doorbell, but it didn't ring. He was about to knock when, through the side window, he caught sight of an elderly man sitting in an armchair in the front room. Doubtful. Tony went up the battered stairs. The light was mercifully dim, a single hanging bulb nearly burned out, and the air was permeated with the compressed smell of stale cooking—decades of it. The apartment on the second floor was dark and the screen door was locked. Tony caught his breath, and then continued on to the top floor. Lights, a dull noise inside. Tony knocked. Nothing. He knocked again, louder. Still no sign of a response. He knocked hard enough to hurt his knuckles.

"Yeah."

The voice was faint and distant, but Tony was certain he had heard it. He tried the door, and it opened. He entered a narrow hallway. It was dark, but light came through an archway ahead on the right. Tony took a few steps and stood, looking into a drab living room. There was a girl on the couch.

"You must be the little woman."

"Who're you?"

"I'm looking for Snake."

"He's out."

"Where?"

"I don't know."

"His car is out front," Tony said. "Would he be somewhere in the neighborhood?"

"He went with Crabs."

"What?"

"Crabs. His friend."

"Oh." Tony felt uncomfortable talking across the room. He moved closer to the pathetic girl, who made no effort to get up. She was squeezing her fingers strangely. "Are you okay?"

"No. I'm out of medicine and I'm all fucked up."

"So am I."

Without thinking about it, Tony went to the couch and sat on the edge of it beside the girl. She looked awful.

"That's a pretty dress."

"Thank you." Tony glanced at the girl's hands again and was shocked to see that she was digging her nails into the palms, and blood was oozing between her fingers. She was gouging out a hole in the center of each hand. "What're you doing?" Tony cried in a voice strangled with alarm.

"It's Jesus," the girl said. "Jesus is in me."

"Jesus?"

"These are His wounds." The girl's eyes were brighter now, lit with enthusiasm. "Look at my feet."

Tony turned his head and glanced back. "Oh my God."

"Yes, yes."

"Honey, let me—"

"And look here."

Before Tony could do or say anything, the girl yanked up her T-shirt, revealing a pancake breast. That's not much bigger than mine, Tony thought. Then he noticed the running sore in the side of the girl's body, about the size of a silver dollar. The skin around it was streaked with dried blood. She must have picked at it for hours, days. It was terrible to see, but also fascinating and even exciting. Tony felt as if he'd walked into this girl's living, ongoing dream.

"Nobody believes me," she said sadly.

"I do," Tony found himself saying.

"You do?"

"Yes. I do."

The girl smiled. "You're so pretty."

"When is Snake coming home?"

"I never know."

Tony's eyes drifted helplessly back to the bloody wound near the girl's breast. The skin had not been allowed to form a scab. The wound had the wet, puckered look of a vagina, Tony thought in a fog of wonder. You have two of them and I don't even have one. He couldn't keep from smiling.

"Put your hand in," the girl said. "Just like they did with the Lord Jesus. Go on. Please."

"My hand won't fit."

"Your finger then."

Tony hesitated, but then was astonished to see his hand move toward the girl's body. His middle finger slid effortlessly into the moist wound. It terrified him to picture the long artificial nail, hard and sharp, pushing deeper into the girl's body, but he didn't stop until the finger was in all the way.

"Tell me your name."

"Shelly." Then, "No. *Jesus.*"

Tony felt as if he had plugged into a chaos of heat, turmoil and liquid. Shelly's body quaked violently, her eyes shining, an unfathomable expression on her face. Pain and peace, maybe. Her hands clutched Tony's arm, pressing it harder to her body.

The next thing he knew, he was in a squalid kitchen, washing his hands in a stream of tepid tap-water. Roaches huddled in the gap between the backsplash and the crumbling plaster wall, but he ignored them. Tony's mind couldn't seem to focus on anything for more than a second or two, and now the pain was starting to seep back in at the edges.

Where was Snake? But that didn't matter. Go away. Get out of here. Now. You can always kill yourself tomorrow, but if you stay here they'll come, and they'll think you're crazy. And then they'll lock you up, and it'll be too late to do anything.

In the living room, Shelly was still. Her eyes followed him as he approached. He imagined the faintest smile on her face, or maybe it was actually there. At the edge of his vision, where he could not quite look, he knew that Shelly had inserted her finger into the wound. Her hand twisted and poked. There was a lot of bright red, and it was spreading, but Tony looked away. Then he left as quickly as he could.

ENTR'ACTE

Doctor Ladybank chatted with Jack and his wife, Gloria, for a few minutes, and then took his drink out onto the terrace. The party was in full swing, and it was a little too hot and crowded inside for him. The evening air was pleasantly cool, sweet with a mix of fragrances from Gloria's flower garden. Nice woman, was Gloria. A bit too nice for a rogue like Jack, but they seemed to get along and had been together for years.

Doctor Ladybank normally didn't care for social gatherings, mingling with a lot of strangers, making forced conversation, but every now and then Jack threw a good old-fashioned cocktail party that simply couldn't be missed. This one came at a particularly good time. Doctor Ladybank needed a break. He'd been giving too much of himself to his experiment lately.

It didn't tire him, it wasn't stressful, there were no nasty side effects at all as far as he could tell. But it was utterly irresistible! In just a few short weeks he had become thoroughly caught up in the lives of his two subjects. He resented any time spent away from them. Work, eating, sleeping—the bulk of his normal activities had faded into dullness.

There were many problems yet to be resolved. First, was the lack of quality time with Tony and Snake. It was often difficult to get through to them, especially at night. When Tony went out, Doctor Ladybank almost always lost contact. The same applied to Snake. It was not an absolute rule, however. There were several times when he did reach them at night, including a few important moments. Doctor Ladybank had no idea whether that was because of the intensity of his concentration or merely the configuration of their surroundings.

By now he had a rough idea of the range of his effect on the two young men. It went from basically annoying them to generally influencing their behavior, and peaked at substantial control of their thoughts and emotions. It was dazzling, but also somewhat perplexing. He could hurt them, to the point of unconsciousness, but he had not yet learned how to make them laugh or feel sudden moments of spontaneous pleasure. Doctor Ladybank regretted that, as both Tony and Snake were doing so much for him, and they lived such unrewarding lives. But he didn't regret it very much; there was no place for sentiment in science.

Feedback was bliss. That was perhaps the most exciting part of Doctor Ladybank's discovery. How would he know if his efforts were really working? In practice, he found that he just knew, he sensed it somehow, without knowing quite how he knew. It was not as if he "heard" Delgado answering him, for instance. But Doctor Ladybank's thoughts and directives flowed intuitively, as if they were in fact conversing on some new level, and thus, when he held either of them in the strongest contact he was aware of what they were doing, how they responded and what his own next words should be. To Doctor Ladybank it didn't qualify as vicarious experience but there was certainly an intellectual thrill in it.

It was a bitter disappointment to him that in the four weeks since he had happened on the technique, as he thought of it, he had not found anyone else receptive to it. That was definitely a puzzle, apparently defying the laws of chance and probability.

The greatest mystery, though, was at the heart of the whole experiment. To what degree did he affect their behavior? Was it mostly his doing, or was he just providing an added mental shove, urging them along paths they would have taken anyway? So far, it was impossible to know for sure.

A mosquito buzzed close to his eye. Doctor Ladybank went in and got another drink. He was buttonholed by Margaret Zuvella, a lawyer with the Public Defender's office. She didn't fit in with Jack's corporate law crowd but she was young and very attractive, which made her an ideal party guest. Doctor Ladybank had met her on one of his court-appointed cases, and they'd encountered each other a few times since. What a subject she'd make, he couldn't help thinking. But when he tried the technique, it had no effect whatsoever on her. Sad. They chatted about a nineteen-year-old pyromaniac they had both tried, and failed, to keep out of prison a few months ago.

"He set a fire in the library," Margaret said with obvious delight. "Then he got the prison laundry."

"Splendid. Troy's a determined lad."

At that moment Jack horned in, looking loose and well-oiled, but not at all tipsy.

"Maggie," he said, smirking like someone about to explain an inside joke. "I have to warn you."

"About what?"

"Ian here. You better watch out. He can make you take your clothes off right here, in a room full of people."

A tendril of dismay uncoiled in Doctor Ladybank's mind.

"Really," Margaret said, smiling. "How can he do that?"

Jack tapped his forehead. "Brain waves. He beams them over to your brain and makes you do whatever he wants."

"Jack." Doctor Ladybank forced himself to chuckle and shake his head dismissively.

"I'd love to see it," Margaret said.

"Honestly," Jack continued. "Ian is conducting experiments on a couple of people, doing just that. How's it going, by the way, Ian? Got them jumping through hoops yet?"

"You're not," Margaret said.

"Of course not," Doctor Ladybank replied. "Jack and I were laying waste to a bottle of malt last month, and we were talking about clairvoyance, telepathy, that kind of thing. It was just a load of idle speculation, that's all."

"Ah." Margaret nodded.

"Oh, Ian, come on now," Jack protested. "You were damn well serious about it. I wasn't, but you were."

The silly crock was pushing it. Doctor Ladybank was shaken, but he maintained an expression of placid indulgence.

"It was the whiskey talking," he told Margaret. "Then, and now, in Jack's case, I'm afraid."

"I see."

Jack gave up, and the three of them laughed politely.

"I still think it's a good idea," Jack said as he started to leave in search of others on whom he could shower bonhomie.

"What is?" Margaret asked.

"If Ian gets you to take your clothes off."

"Jack, go away," she told him, trying to suppress a giggle. "Go away and behave yourself."

Yes, Doctor Ladybank thought. Go away, Jack.

—SIX—

For once in his life something had gone right. If he hadn't been in the right place at the right time the cops would have put the collar on him in a flash. They knew him, they'd busted him a couple of times in the last few years, though never for anything too serious. Yeah, they'd love to hang some hard time on his ass if they could, but Snake was covered.

It was a minor miracle, looking back. Half of his life, it sometimes seemed, was spent in transit, scraping around, looking for this guy or that, hanging out—unaccountable time witnessed by nobody who would ever remember. But on the night Shelly died, Snake fortunately had been with or seen by other people for every minute of the hours in question. More amazing, they all stood up for him when it counted.

He and Crabs had gone to Rudy's early that evening. The two of them teamed up to monopolize the pool table for several hours, winning drinks until nearly midnight. Then they decided to go to a nightclub called Ravens, on the other side of town. They were turned away at the door and exchanged mean stares with—of all people—a cop moonlighting as a bouncer. Snake and Crabs were both known to the cop; he'd thrown them out of Ravens a couple of months earlier. Retreating across the road to Cher's Plus Two, a titty bar favored by area bikers, Snake and Crabs met a number of other people they knew. They stayed until closing time, two a.m. By then they were in such good spirits that they decided to drink a nightcap or two at Snake's place. Instead, they found the dead body and promptly called the police.

What a way to go, Snake thought as he drove aimlessly around town. Shelly. She had her good side, a while back. But to die like that, to carve a hole in yourself with your own fingernails, and bleed to death...Jesus. It was enough to make Snake wonder how he had put up with her for so long. She must have been stone cold loco, so far off the wall that she couldn't even see it. To tell the truth, however, he had never imagined she was that sick. Weird, sure, and the laziest damn thing on earth. But not sicko sick. Maybe Snake should have paid more attention to that shrink who saw Shelly. Maybe they all missed something then.

Oh well. It was over now. Any residual feelings that Snake might have had for Shelly disappeared when he learned that he, as her common-law husband, had to pay to dispose of her remains. If she had any relatives, he didn't know who or where they might be, and she didn't leave much more than a pile of dirty clothes. She lived light and went fast, amen. Snake didn't hesitate to choose the cheapest available cremation (the "Bake 'n Shake," according to Crabs). Shelly's ashes were in the jar on the seat beside him now. It was time to find somewhere nice for her.

The ocean was too far away. A babbling brook would be nice, but then Snake considered the fact that any moving waters in this old mill city were bound to be thoroughly polluted. What about a park? Open air, a quiet setting, flowers—shit, he could strew her ashes right in a flowerbed. That would be perfect. But then again, it wasn't so easy. The two or three city parks Snake knew of had pretty much gone to seed, neglected, overgrown, dangerous. The best one was adjacent to the public library, and it wasn't so bad, but even there the winos used the flowerbeds as a toilet and a parade of fags stalked the shrubbery.

It wasn't as if Shelly deserved a spot in Arlington National Cemetery, but Snake felt obliged to do the best he could. He hadn't been much help to Shelly in what turned out to be her last weeks alive. Plus, she had spared him the aggravation of tossing her out, so he figured that he owed her something.

There it was! Snake knew he'd found the ideal place for her as soon as he drove around the bend in the road and saw the green expanse of a fairway in the distance. The city golf course. She would like it, he had no doubt. All he had to do now was find an attractive little spot off to the side somewhere, maybe beneath a birch tree in the rough. Hell, there might even be a clear brook in a place like this.

Snake parked the car along an open stretch of the road, took the container of ashes and walked quickly through the weedy grass toward the fairway. It was the tail-end of dusk, so if he didn't find a place soon he'd end up dumping her in the dark.

There was a foursome a hundred yards away, but they were on the way in, their backs to Snake. He jogged across the fairway. The woods on the other side looked promising, but when he reached them he found the ground unsuitable. More tall grass, rocks, and bare dirt where paths had been worn. At least at the library she would have had flowers. Damn it all anyway. He was looking for the kind of scene they put on greeting cards and in Disney films, but this was just a bunch of useless country-type land.

Snake pushed on. A few minutes later he came out on the far side of the woods, and he was startled by the sudden change. He was in someone's backyard. Nice looking house, must have cost an awful lot. Beautiful grounds, too. Snake hadn't tried burglary, but this would be the kind of place to start with if he ever felt like having a go.

He had other business now. His eyes had settled on a lovely rock garden just a few yards away. Snake hurried across the lawn to it. Oh yes, the perfect resting place for Shelly. There were cascades of delicate flowers, clusters of blue, purple and white, not much pink or red. Just the colors you saw at funerals, Snake thought as he bent over and started to scoop out a hollow in the rich soil. You'll love it here, kid. The kind of folks who live in a place like this will take real good care of you, or at least the garden around you.

"What do you think you're doing?"

Snake jumped upright. He had been about to unscrew the cap of the jar containing Shelly's ashes, but now he froze, gaping at the middle-aged man who stood ten feet away, hands on hips. Must have seen me from the house, Snake thought uselessly. He wasn't worried about having been discovered by the homeowner, but he was puzzled. The guy was a stranger, and yet seemed familiar. Snake could turn and run, and he knew he'd get away easily, but somehow the urge to flee had been transformed into curiosity.

"Who are you," the man demanded, his voice more threatening, "and what do you want?"

"Hey, Jack." Snake was surprised to hear himself say that. "How the hell are you, Jack?"

The man's head clicked back a notch. Then he stepped closer and peered at Snake.

"I don't know you."

"Sure you do, Jack. We used to hang out at the Utica Club, remember? *Agricola, agricolae, agricolorum.* Right? *Hic, haec, hoc, ad hoc,* in hock around the clock with bock beer."

Even in the gathering darkness, Snake could see the man's eyes widen as he tried to digest what he'd heard. Snake couldn't help him. He had no idea.

"Get out of here this instant."

"Jack, lighten up."

"I'll call the police."

"Why don't you crack open a bottle of Glen Grant? We can sit down and talk twat, just like the old days."

The man tottered, then turned stiffly toward the house.

"Jack, Jack..."

Snake scooped up a rock and caught the man easily. The rock crushed the back of his skull, creating a wreath of pinkish-grey jelly around the edges of the impact. The man grunted once, the last of his breath forced out of him. He hit the lawn and didn't move again.

Snake pulled the body over onto its back. Now the wife will have to sell this place, he thought. Who knows what'll happen to the rock garden? The new owners might well dig it up and plow it under. That wouldn't be right. You're going to get a real fancy burial, Shelly. Elegant casket, expensive plot. Can't beat it.

He unscrewed the jar, forced the man's mouth open, and began to pour the ashes down the throat. It soon filled. Snake tamped the coarse powder down with his fingertips. Believe me, Jack, if you saw Shelly at her best you *would* want to eat her. That would have been when she was about fifteen.

The cheeks bulged, Snake noticed when he was finished. Jack the Chipmunk. Best I could do. Time to take a *haec*.

So long, kid.

—SEVEN—

Tony washed down the Demerol with a gulp of Red Death on the rocks. Behind the shades, his eyes watered slightly, but he felt his body steadying. That was mental, since he knew it would take a good five minutes before serenity began to kick in and all was right with the world again...for a while.

"You look happy, darling."

"I buried Shelly."

"Maybe that's it. Where did you put her?"

"Somewhere out in the countryside," Snake said with a vague wave of the hand, as if he'd suddenly lost interest in the topic. "It's a pretty place."

"I'm sure it is."

Tony had heard about it only last night around this time, as they were sitting on the very same two barstools at the El Greco. It was boring. Tony didn't want to listen to another word about the stupid cunt who'd bled herself to death, but Snake was having a hard time putting it behind him. He kept pulling away from it, and then sinking back, like a car stuck in a rut. It was morbid, as well as incredibly tiresome.

Tony had his own uneasy feelings about Shelly. He imagined he had met her—or was it a dream? Anyhow, he had this picture of her in his mind, like he could see her dying. It was probably because Snake had given such a graphic description of what Shelly looked like when he found her. And it had stayed in Tony's head, making him feel very uncomfortable.

Part of the problem was that Snake kept him jangled up in a state of constant uncertainty, dishing out the pills in ones and twos like candy. Wouldn't sell a quantity, even though Tony had the cash. Snake wanted other things, and so he was making a move for absolute control. It was clear and simple, but Tony had yet to figure out a worthwhile response to it. Shelly's death was a minor week-long distraction that didn't really change anything in Tony's life.

The easiest thing, of course, would be to stop using Demerol or coke, period. Then Tony would be able to kiss Snake goodbye, and how sweet that would be. The big clod had lost any semblance of attractiveness he might have possessed. Not that he was ever anything but a trick and a supplier as far as Tony was concerned. The game was fun at first, but now Snake's mean and demanding way of treating Tony most of the time was simply unbearable.

And how could he get off the drugs? That was impossible, at least in Tony's present condition. They weren't drugs, they were medicine. They kept him alive. Whether that was a good idea was another matter, but as long as he wanted to survive all the pain and mental interference, he had to have his medicine.

Zzzzzt.

Oh God, no. Not now, not here. Tony had a terrible fear of the Pied Piper getting through to him in a public place. Even if it was only the El Greco, where some pretty weird things happened from time to time.

Zzzzzt.

Fucker. Get lost. Ignore him. But that never worked. The demon had continued to haunt and hurt Tony everyday over the past week, never letting up for long. The Demerol helped, but it was by no means a perfect immunity. All it did was keep the agony in moderate check for a while, so that Tony remained just this side of suicidal. The Pied Piper still got through.

—Plasmodium. Found you.

"Be right back, darling," Tony said to Snake. "I've got to make a trip to the little girl's room."

"Yeah," Snake muttered.

Tony slid off the barstool, wobbled for a second on his high heels, and then clattered quickly across the linoleum. Thank God the pisser was vacant. Tony shut the door and leaned against it, pressing his head to the blotchy particleboard.

—I want him.

"Fuck off."

—You heard me.

"For what?"

—Bring him home.

"It won't work with him. He's straight."

—Do it, slime.

"Listen, when he sees my *cojones* he'll go crazy. He'll tear them off and shove 'em down—"

Tony went blind and sagged to the damp floor, too stunned to make a sound as pain exploded throughout his body, abrading every cell in his nervous system. It felt as if sonic booms were being triggered inside his brain and the plates of his skull were about to crack open at the seams.

Yes, yes, okay. He couldn't even get the words out, but the torture died down immediately. Tony found that he could breathe again, he could think, he could see the slick of scummy water his face rested in on the floor. He was theoretically still alive, a fact of dubious value. Why is this happening? Why are you doing this to me?

—Because you are slime.

You got that right. "But you're me, right? That's what you said a while back, fucker. If I'm slime, so are you."

Silence. Relief. Goddamn, Tony thought as he struggled to his feet, I shut him up. I shut the Pied Piper up. At least for a minute or two. Turned him right off. Tony gripped the sink to steady himself and then looked in the mirror. His face was grimy and wet from the floor. He washed himself and applied some fresh make-up, regaining a little composure in the process.

It was no good. The Pied Piper was gone for now, but he had delivered his message. Tony had to bring Snake home tonight, and whatever happened from that point on—would happen. Might even be better if Snake did go berserk and kill him. That would put a stop to all this misery. He could see the newspaper stories. An anguished biker tricked by a transvestite—Snake might have to transfer to the Foreign Legion to live that one down. Meanwhile, Tony's tearful mother wouldn't believe a word they said about him and his queer life. She'd hand out pictures of him as a choirboy and talk about the perfume he gave her last Mother's Day (because she was still young and pretty).

Why the fuck not? Who the fuck cares anyway? When you live in the shadow of the curb, where else do you expect to die? Grab the best chance that has come along in years. If you don't, that little demon fucker will just come back and eat at you, rip away at you, until you do what he wants. Get it over.

Besides, Tony knew that the column inches, however lurid and distasteful, would be a kind of comfort to his mother. Maybe not right away, but in the long term. A front-page murder story was better than no obituary at all.

—EIGHT—

The place was a dump on the outside, but the living room was nice enough. In a spooky kind of way. The shades were drawn and the only light came from a large floor lamp with a fringed shade that cast the room in a soft golden glow. The air was humid and warm, but it had a sweet scent that added an exotic, mysterious touch, and the furniture was comfortable. It wasn't the way he'd fix up a room, but Snake decided that he liked it as he sat back in a big armchair.

Toni was on edge, nervous as a high school girl on her first date. What a riot. Snake wasn't going to make it any easier for her. Why should he? This was his payoff. He was going to enjoy every minute of it. On the way there from the bar Snake gave her explicit instructions. He was to be treated like a king, she was to wait on him, pamper him, baby him, indulge him, humor him, and above all, she was to tease him to the max. He couldn't wait for that to start. This was going to be the greatest damn fuck Snake had ever had, the one he'd dreamed of for years.

The whore looked good, real good. Her hair was quite short, and it was brushed and slicked back in a striking fashion, and it looked so wet you'd think she had just this minute stepped out of the shower. Tonight her dress was almost elegant, not at all the usual trashy glitter. She wore a white blouse that hung loosely on her flattish upper body, and a long wrap-around skirt that had a nice way of parting to flash her terrific legs when she walked. Toni was somewhat on the tall side, a sort of slum-pussy version of Jamie Lee Curtis without the front porch.

"What would you like to drink?"

Better already, Snake thought. Just being there had changed her tone of voice. Gone was the barroom hustle, replaced by such a sweet desire to please—God, he loved it. Toni was standing beside the chair, close to him. Snake liked that too. He placed a hand on her leg, just behind the knee, savoring the firm flesh beneath the fabric of her skirt. It was one of his favorite sexy spots on a woman's body. You could feel those wires—now, what the hell are they called, tendons, sinews?—that run all up and down the leg. Neat.

"Do you want a drink, darling, or...not?"

"Mmmm."

Snake's hand slid higher, taking the skirt with it, but Toni stepped aside gracefully, escaping his reach. As she did so, she contrived to flap the front of her skirt open briefly. Very nice little move, Snake thought appreciatively.

"Well?"

"Got any bourbon?" he asked.

"Of course."

"Okay, let's have a large glass of bourbon, on the rocks and with a splash of water."

"*Ein, zwei, drei.*"

"Huh?"

"What?"

"What'd you say?"

"I said it's on the way."

"Okay. Fine."

A little weird, but what the hell. Snake already had a good buzz on, so nothing was going to bother him. As long as Toni did her part. From where he was sitting he could see her in the tiny kitchen, pouring the drinks. At that moment, she put the bottle down and bent over. She opened her skirt and fiddled around with the catch on her garter. It took a moment for the significance of the navy blue ribbon and the bare skin to register. Oh Jesus, she's wearing stockings, Snake realized with joy. And now she's showing me. Man, this is just like being in the foreplay part of a porn movie. Scenes like this were the best—the teasing, the slow seduction—even better than the wild sex that would follow soon enough. But now Snake wasn't just another jerk-off watching the picture; he was starring in it.

The bourbon was good and there was plenty of it in the heavy crystal tumbler Toni brought him. She sipped a pale liquid from a glass about the size and shape of a lipstick holder.

"What's that?"

"Cointreau," she told him.

"Oh yeah." None of that Red Death shit here. She was doing it all right, no question. "Nice stuff."

"Snake?"

"Yeah?"

"Do you have any metal fillings?"

"Metal—what?"

"Metal fillings in your teeth. Lead, silver, like that."

"Oh, sure. Lots. I've got a regular scrapyard in my mouth, everything but gold. Why?"

"Do you get much static?"

"Just from people who don't know better," he replied with a quick laugh. "But I soon straighten them out."

"So...You don't hear anything?"

"Like what?" Like, what the hell is this all about?

"A voice."

"Just yours and mine, babe." Snake sounded calm, but he was beginning to worry. She looked nervous, close to panic, in spite of the fact that she was sitting on the couch, drink in hand, her thigh tantalyzingly visible. "Hey, relax."

As if on cue, Toni said, "Whatever they want."

"What?"

"Whatever they want."

"Who?"

"Men."

"Oh." This was an abrupt shift, but it was definitely a lot more promising, so he went with it. "Such as?"

"Come on my face. Come in my mouth."

Her voice was stiff, and her eyes seemed to be fixed on some remote inner point. However, Snake now thought he understood the game. She was going to tell him about the things she did. Dirty talk to turn him on. It was a little more open and blunt than he would have liked, but he was prepared to cut her some slack if it had the desired effect.

"That's pretty normal," he told her.

"Ride my ass."

"Some do like that. Not me, but some do."

"Tie me up. Blindfold me."

"Uh-hunh."

"Hurt me."

"Not too bad, I hope."

"Piss on me. Shit on me."

"Aw, Jeez." That was exactly the kind of stuff Snake didn't want to hear. How the hell could he lick her body now, with that stuck in his mind? "Where? On your back or stomach," Snake said hopefully. "Right?"

"And my chest. And face. And mouth."

"That really drags me down, babe." The script had gone into some other movie. Snake was not happy. The only thing that kept him from clocking her on the jaw was the fact that he didn't want to give up yet. There was still a chance Toni would snap out of her robot stare and get back on track. "I wouldn't treat you bad like that," he said. "I'd treat you like a queen."

Toni suddenly began laughing. Snake didn't understand, but he smiled at the improvement in her manner. She appeared to be much more relaxed again. He also liked that foxy look in her eye as she tuned in to him.

"Darling, would you really be a good boy?"

"Sure."

"I want you to do something for me."

"What?"

"Promise not to peek? Promise not to touch where you're not supposed to?"

"Well, I don't get it."

"Put your drink on the floor and sit forward on your seat."

"Okay."

When Snake did what she told him, Toni got off the couch and carefully stepped up onto the coffee table, inches from his face. Hey, hey, hey, Snake thought. This is more like it.

"Here," Toni said, handing him her glass of Cointreau. "I'd like you to rub it into my skin. Just the bare skin now, and you must behave yourself."

"O-*kay*."

Snake splashed the liqueur on his hand and then placed the small glass on the table. Toni pulled her skirt open, and cupped one hand modestly over her panties. The sight of that navy blue underwear against her golden skin was fantastic. Snake lovingly stroked her upper thighs, above the stocking tops.

"Mmmm..."

"Your hand is in the way," he dared.

"You don't touch there. Understand?"

"Yes."

"That's good. You're a good boy, aren't you?"

"Yes."

"And you're doing a good job. What does it smell like? You can put your face closer."

Snake went so far as to put his face between her thighs, his cheeks touching her. His forehead bumped against her hand. Toni didn't stop him.

"Oranges."

"Right." Now her fingers gently pushed his face away. "The back, too. Don't forget the back."

Snake poured the last of the Cointreau in his hand, and Toni turned slightly on the table. She pulled the skirt higher, so he had a clear view of the flimsy blue fabric stretched tightly over her ass. He rubbed the back of her legs gently and slowly, while his eyes were locked on target just above. Toni's other hand was still planted on her crotch, so deeply that her fingers curved up in sight from behind. Odd, but Snake barely gave it a thought as he had other things on his mind. His hand inevitably slid up and grazed her firm round bottom. She let him do that until he began to squeeze it energetically, insinuating his fingers beneath her panties, and then she spun around.

"I told you to behave."

"Oops."

"Never mind, you did a good job."

Toni stepped down from the coffee table and took her spot on the couch again. Snake took his drink from the floor and slurped a major mouthful. He smiled at her and let his eyes drift slowly along the length of her body, stretched out on the couch. As if responding to his gaze, one of her knees pushed up so the flap of her skirt fell away.

"Did you hear that?" she asked.

"What?"

"The voice."

"No." She was still a little crazy, he thought. "You hear voices, you better see the Doc."

"Which doctor?"

"The witch doctor, yeah," Snake said with a laugh. "Hell, I don't know. Go to a shrink, babe."

His eyes were on her legs and he didn't feel like discussing anything else. Toni's arm had fallen casually across her crotch, another peekaboo move that tickled Snake, and her thumb rolled in a small arc on her upper thigh. Lightly, back and forth. It was mildly hypnotic, very arousing.

"Tell me about him," she said.

"Who?"

"Your doctor."

"I don't have one."

"But you know one."

"No, I—"

Snake hesitated. Well, he did know one. Technically. He'd met Shelly's shrink, back a month or two ago. But he didn't know the man, in fact he couldn't even remember the guy's name.

"Go on."

As if to encourage Snake, Toni now stretched out completely on her back and raised both knees up straight. Then she let them loll open and she rubbed herself in a slowly escalating rhythm as her body squirmed with pleasure. Snake didn't know what he could say, but he didn't want to stop the show. He was caught up in it almost as much as Toni was.

"The Doc is okay."

"Yeah..."

"The Doc is good."

"Yeah..."

"He'll take care of you, but you have to trust him."

"Yeah..."

"And do what he tells you."

"*Yeah.*"

Her knees drove toward her chest, her hands worked in a last frenzied rush.

"I wish I could tell you his name."

"*YEAAAAAAAHH!*"

Her body rocked convulsively, then turned rigid. She puffed air in short bursts. You momma, Snake thought. He nearly missed his mouth as he tried to take a drink with his eyes frozen on the girl. You hot little whore momma, that was better than a sexpic. The way she had done it with her clothes still on somehow made it that much more real. It was like peeking through the window next door and watching your teen queen neighbor engage in self-service fun. Snake had a hard-on, and he was clean out of words.

Toni rolled over onto her belly, her skirt rumpled and still showing a lot of leg. Her face was pressed to the couch, her one visible eye peering brightly at Snake. There was the faintest of smiles at the corner of her mouth.

"You like to watch."

"Hey." Snake shrugged with a grin.

"You do, and you like to have someone do it for you. That's okay, darling, that's cool."

"Well, not always..."

"I'll do it for you. Special, because you're special."

"So are you, babe."

"Come on with me."

Snake followed her into the bathroom. It was dark, and Toni didn't turn on the light. Instead, she pulled the door so it was almost shut, allowing only the slightest illumination to filter in from the living room. She had Snake stand facing the bathtub and told him to unbuckle his belt and unzip his pants. She was right behind him, speaking in a low soft voice, caressing his back.

"Grab hold of the shower bar," she directed. "That's right, that's it. Now close your eyes and imagine you're in a luxurious hotel room somewhere, maybe Paris, or Rio. You're high up, maybe forty floors, and the view is fantastic. You stand at the window and gaze out at the spectacular scene. It's night, and it's like a dream, just being there. The city is far, far below, but it's all lit up like a million shiny jewels. Now, a young woman comes into the room. Women always come to you, so you don't even turn around, you just know she's there. For you. She comes right to you, her hands flowing over your body. You still don't turn, you watch the city below and you let her love you..."

Her hands snaking around him, finding his nipples, squeezing them through his shirt, then planing down, snagging his pants and taking them to the floor. Her face to the small of his back, her hands gliding up the front of his thighs. She takes his cock in one hand, cups his balls with the other, tightening her grip with expert care as her face burrows into his backside. She licks and explores until she finds the puckered rim.

"Ohhh-aaaah..."

She tongues it delicately while her hands play with him in front, the pace of her movements increasing steadily. Snake heaves with anticipation, his body shaking beyond his control, and she knows he is about to come. Her tongue plunges deeply into him.

"Oooooh-Gaaaaaahd..."

He shoots off. Little spattering sounds from the porcelain tub, but they're almost lost in the noisy rush of breath above. Snake can hardly hold himself up by the shower bar, he's so weak and dazed by this onslaught of pleasure. He still can't believe it, what she did to him. So good.

"Toni..."

She had backed away from him a little. When he glanced over his shoulder at her he caught sight of the swift movement, but he didn't understand it. Then he felt it, and it was the last thing he felt. The stiletto blade punctured his spine, paralyzing him. The tip snapped off, but she kept hammering the broken blade into his body, up and down, between the ribs, into his flabby midriff, blood blossoming in a spray of grey roses, his hands slipping off the shower bar, the slow dizzy fall through hot buzzing air, and still it came at him, that knife, *bam bam bam bam bam bam*, arcing at him, fixing him for all time, his shiny metal transport to the end of the night, *bam bam bam bam bam*, out of the grey, the gloom and the shadows and into the perfect no pain the perfect no night the perfect no light the perfect the

—NINE—

silence was terrifying.

Tony was shaking so violently that he had to hold onto the sink and the wall to keep from falling to the bathroom floor. He hit the switch and the ceiling light went on. It was temporarily blinding, since Tony didn't have his shades, and he whimpered in pain. The floor was covered with blood—such a vibrant red—he could see that much as he squinted through his tears. Tony breathed deeply, sucking air in an effort to hold off panic.

Snake was in the tub. Tony had pushed him into it when he saw that the guy was about to keel over backwards on top of him. Now the only thing he could think to do was to leave him there in peace. He's draining, Tony told himself. Let him drain. It was the best place for him.

But then what? He couldn't move a big body like that on his own, and he certainly couldn't get it out of this building or the neighborhood without being seen. Not even in the middle of the night. Impossible. This is bad, bad, bad. He hazarded a glance in the mirror. A savage stared back.

"What now?"

Nothing. The little shit. Tony noticed his stiletto on the floor, and saw for the first time that the tip was broken. Where was the other piece? The way his life was going, that would turn out to be the one little thing that landed him on Death Row. The two hundred-plus pounds of incriminatingly dead meat lying in the tub suddenly seemed as vast as a continent, and somewhere in that land mass was a vital scrap of metal. He had to find it and then get rid of it.

Tony edged closer to the bathtub. Jesus, why did he have to stab the guy so many times? But why did he even have to stab him at all? Dead, Snake looked merely pathetic. A nobody. Just one more poor stiff who wanted to live, and be loved by somebody, but who never quite got a handle on his life. Not all that different from me, Tony thought.

But, on to business. Tony picked up the stiletto and washed it under the tap in the sink. Then he wrapped it tightly in the hand towel, wiping it several times to make sure he didn't leave a fingerprint on it, and carried it into the kitchen. He dug up a plastic supermarket bag and put the knife in it, towel and all. He rolled it into a tidy little parcel, squeezing out as much air as he could, and he used the loop handles to bind it with several knots. He set it aside on the counter.

Tony wasn't ready for the next step yet, so he changed into jeans and a T-shirt, put on his sunglasses and had a large drink to settle his nerves. He didn't feel better, but at least he was somewhat calmer.

The silence was truly awful. Tony thought he could hear the cells beginning to turn rotten in Snake's body. Snake had become a factory, a death mill where billions of tiny forces worked away nonstop at the process of decay. Snake was sliming out, so there was no time to waste.

He mopped up the blood on the bathroom floor, and then began the awkward job of removing Snake's clothes. Why? It seemed the thing to do. In the pockets of Snake's cheap black pants he came across a wallet containing thirty two dollars, and a medicine jar that held fifty Demerol pills. Fifty of them! To think I almost felt sorry for you, you cheap bastard. I'm in good shape now, he thought gleefully. Tony burned the driver's license along with a few other papers in the kitchen sink, wiped Snake's wallet clean, and buried it in an empty milk carton in his garbage bag. He put Snake's clothes in another bag.

So far, so easy. Three ordinary parcels to throw away. But what about the big parcel in the bathtub? Tony needed help. The Pied Piper had gotten him into this mess, so where was he? Not a peep. The little fucker. I'll bring him here fast. Tony got on his knees and smashed his forehead against the kitchen floor. It worked immediately.

—Slime.

"Jesus, man." He struggled to his feet. The pain wasn't so bad but black spots peppered his vision for a moment. "You can't take me to a certain point and then leave me there alone."

—I can do anything.

"Then get rid of the guy in the bathtub."

—That's your problem.

"I might as well call the cops," Tony said. It was a bluff, and not a very good one, but it had just occurred to him that the Pied Piper needed him, or wanted him, in some way. He reappeared the minute Tony banged his head on the floor. For the moment, at least, it seemed to give Tony a slight amount of leverage. "I'll tell them he was a trick, and he turned nasty and pulled a knife, and I had to defend myself."

—That's the ticket.

The quick mockery worried Tony. "Why not?"

—You defended yourself by stabbing him all those times in the back?

"Well..."

—Remove the body, plasmodium.

"How do I do that?"

—Piecework.

"No way, man, no way. I'd rather call the cops, and take my chances that way."

—Yes?

"You bet yes. I'll do it right now."

Tony turned toward the telephone, but froze, and then sagged against the wall. It was as if invisible hands were wringing his liver, and at the same time a tiny neon worm burned like acid in the depths of his ear, eating its way into his brain.

—Yes?

"...No..."

—I own your mind, which means I own your body. Listen and hear, boy. I can make the acid pour into your stomach all day, I can dump adrenalin into your blood till your heart shivers so bad it knots up and can't send oxygen to your brain, I can bleed your eyes and ears. I can make your nose run so much you'll drown in your own snot. I can cover you with sores, I can make your skin itch so much you'll scratch it to bloody shreds, and I can bloat your balls so they're as big and foul as rotten apples, or I can make them as small and hard as orange pips. I can squash them, I can make you piss hot acid and ground glass, I can make your lips peel off like layers of parchment, and your muscles turn to mush. I can make you chew up your tongue and spit out the bits. I can turn the marrow in your bones to lava, I can fill your mouth with fungus and raise hordes of maggots in your arsehole. And believe me, I can keep you ticking along this way forever. Yes?

"...Yes..."

—Good little plasmodium. Now get to work. Use the Ginsu steak knives you got from that nig-nog limousine driver. They're tacky, but they'll do the job.

"You know everything in my life?"

—Your life is mine.

Then he was gone. Tony obediently got the steak knives and took them, along with every spare plastic bag he could find, into the bathroom. The pasty bulk of flesh was still there.

"Sorry man, but you're already dead."

Tony made a few tentative slices at one elbow, and promptly threw up all over the corpse. Jesus mother's tit, he'd never get through this. He made sure that the drain was fully open, turned on the cold shower and pulled the curtain around the tub. While Snake was being sluiced down, Tony went to the sink to pat water on his own face and rinse his mouth out. Then he took a Demerol, figuring it would help him through the ordeal.

A few minutes later, he hummed as he cut loose Snake's left forearm. The elbows and knees were trouble enough with all those wires to saw, but the shoulders were much worse, far messier. At least the head was easy. By then, however, Tony had filled every plastic bag he had. He would get more tomorrow, but for now the only thing he could find to put Snake's head in was the spaghetti pot his mother had given him. It had a lid. Tony squirted some wash-up liquid in with the head and added water until the pot was nearly full, hoping the detergent would delay the inevitable rot and stench. He placed the covered pot on the stove, where it did not seem too conspicuous.

He did as much as he could, eight plastic-wrapped items, the head in the pot and the torso still floating in the tub. When he woke up the next morning, Tony had to have a shower. He couldn't stand the feeling of dried blood on him, dried scum, and the bits of Snake's flesh that had lodged beneath his fingernails. He had fallen asleep as soon as the last package was taped up. The only way he could have his shower was if he had it with the torso too, since there was nowhere to put it. Reluctantly, that's what Tony did, heaving the ghastly thing as far back in the tub as possible and then standing directly under the showerhead. He had to clear the drain a couple of times, as it got clogged with greasy chunks of gristle and meat. Tony showered quickly, then sat on the edge of the tub and cleaned between his toes with running water.

As he had done the night before, he filled the tub until the torso floated, and sprinkled pine-scented kitchen cleanser on it. To be on the safe side, he added two-thirds of a bottle of Canoe, the last of his rubbing alcohol (which was also useful in certain sexual scenarios) and a blue toilet tablet. That should keep the smell down for a while.

Sleep had refreshed him somewhat. Tony didn't need the Pied Piper to tell him what he had to do. Fortunately it was overcast outside. He put on his sunglasses and went to the supermarket to buy the largest and heaviest trash bags they had. He also bought a couple of rolls of sticky packing tape, more detergent, rubber gloves, alcohol and disinfectant. The store's fluorescent lights were getting to him, even with his sunglasses on, so he picked up a pair of mirrored clip-ons that helped considerably.

Tony had a couple of ideas. He now thought he knew the best way to get rid of the torso, and in the back of his mind he had a rough notion of how to escape the torments of the Pied Piper once and for all. But he would have to approach it carefully when the time came, never quite letting his thoughts settle on it, or else the demon might tune in and foil the attempt.

It was a long day, taking four trips in all. A piece of arm and a piece of leg each time. He carried them in a gym bag, and he dropped them in litterbaskets, dumpsters, anywhere reasonably safe, where they were unlikely to be noticed and opened. He even managed to slip one forearm into the trash bin at Burger Billy's, along with the remains of his lunch. By the end of the afternoon Tony was exhausted from all the walking he had done, but he also felt enormously relieved that much of Snake was scattered around the center of the city. Out of my life.

Tony examined the trunk of Snake's car, to make sure it had enough room for the torso. Some people fill a trunk with garbage and then just leave it there, God only knows why. Snake's trunk had a well-worn spare tire, a jack and some small tools, and the puzzler: a beat-up copy of Elvis's *Blue Hawaii* album. Good place to keep your record collection, Snake. Tony parked the car right in front of his building.

He had a drink, though he didn't need it to relax. He felt serene, almost—*almost* in some kind of control of his life once more. Tony had sailed through this horrible day, popping Demerol whenever the wave seemed to falter.

What day was it anyway? Sunday. Time? A little after six in the evening. Good, perfect. People were eating, and in a few minutes they'd sit back to watch *60 Minutes*. There would not be many cops on patrol at this in-between hour.

Wearing the rubber gloves, Tony somehow got the torso into a large heavy-duty garbage bag. He knotted and taped it, then slid it into another one. Was a third bag necessary? Why not? There was no point in taking chances. Tony wiped a thin streak of scum from the outer plastic when he finished, and dragged the big sack into the living room. He removed the rubber gloves and carefully put band-aids on his fingertips. With the torso, at least, there would be no prints on the bags.

Now. No need to carry it, even if he could. Tony looked up and down the hallway outside his apartment. All clear, nobody in sight, no sounds of activity. Tony tugged the garbage bag by its plastic loop handles, dragging the load into the hall. He locked his apartment, and then pulled the sack to the top of the stairs. Still no one about. Gripping the loop handles firmly, he tipped the torso over the edge and followed behind, letting it bump down the stairs but holding it so that it didn't bounce noisily out of control. It was like walking the dog, Tony thought with a smile. No sweat. When he got to the ground floor he stepped over the bag and was about to drag it to the front door when Leo Jenks emerged from his apartment. He was okay, a middle-aged man who delivered bread for a local bakery, but Tony wasn't at all happy to see him at that moment.

"Hey, Tony."

"Leo, how's it going?"

"Good, and you?"

"Okay. Just cleaning up."

"Yeah? Whaddaya got there?"

"Newspapers and magazines. You want 'em?"

Jesus, don't get cute.

"Not unless it's *Penthouse* or *Playboy*," Leo said with a sly grin. Like everyone in the building, Leo knew Tony was gay.

"'Fraid not."

"The stuff piles up, huh?"

"Sure does."

"Let me give you a hand," Leo said, bending to reach for one end of the garbage bag.

"No, don't bother, Leo. It's too clumsy to handle that way, but no trouble to drag, you know? Just leave the front door open for me, will you?"

"Yeah, sure. See you, Tony."

"Yeah, thanks."

Fuck me pink, Tony thought when Leo was gone. If he had got his hands on it he'd have known right away that it wasn't a bunch of newspapers and magazines. But it was no time to stand around, worrying about a near-miss. Tony hauled the sack outside to the edge of the curb as quickly as he could.

"Jesus," he groaned, heaving it up and into the car. Fucker must have weighed a quarter of a ton. Tony banged the trunk shut and allowed himself a casual glance around. The old geezer next door was sitting on his front stoop, but he was busy playing with his grandson. There were other people on the street, but none of them seemed to be watching Tony. He straightened his sunglasses, got into the car and drove away.

"All *right*."

With the window rolled down and the radio playing, it wasn't bad at all, especially since the humidity had fallen. Tony liked driving but he seldom got the chance to do any, so it was a treat for him to be out like this—in spite of the load he had in the trunk. He cruised through the neighborhood, then headed into the center of town. He circled The Green, drove out to the east side and checked the action along the commercial strip leading to the mall. Nothing much happening. Well, of course. It was a Sunday night, and that's the way it's supposed to be. Quiet.

By nine o'clock Tony was ready to get it done. Better to do it while there was still some light in the sky. He drifted north into the woody hills near the highway, on the outskirts of town. There were few houses on these side roads that zig-zagged up the steep valley walls. A power company sub-station. A junkyard. A landfill transfer depot. Not much else. Aha, there it was, just what Tony was looking for: a clearing off to the side where folks dumped unwanted items. He stopped the car and got out.

Nothing, only trees for a hundred yards in either direction. Tony listened carefully, but there was no sound of an approaching car. On the ground: an abandoned sofa, several bald tires, rusty wheel hubs, a corroded hand-wringer washing machine, and the best sight of all, plenty of garbage bags similar to the one Tony had. People. Makes you wonder, Tony thought with a smile. There was a junkyard down the road, *and* a landfill station. They could bring their rubbish to either place, but no, they've got to throw it here, along this nice woody stretch of land.

Tony opened the trunk and took extra care not to rip the bag as he pulled it out. He dragged it across some of the other bags on the ground. Still no cars coming. He left the package behind a dirty but unscarred vinyl clothes hamper that had no doubt been discarded because of its ugly design.

Sorry, Snake. We had our moments, one or two.

The pot on the stove was a shock. For some reason, Tony had blanked it right out of his mind. But there it was. Okay, so he still had work to do. Tomorrow he would dispose of Snake's head, and then he would deal with the Pied Piper.

—TEN—

The windowshade appeared to be on fire, which meant it was extremely bright outside. The sun has no mercy, he thought. Men have no mercy—not much anyway, and not often. Everything was supposed to be better now, but it wasn't. Tony thought two days had passed, but it might have been three.

Where was his brain? The sun beat him, the moon laughed at him, nothing worked. He found it hard to keep track of anything. So much time, thousands of minutes, had been spent sitting still, trying to think, trying to focus his mind. Trying to find it.

The Pied Piper had got him once—or was it twice? Hard to be sure. The Demerol helped and Tony had found some silence, but the demon voice jarred him from sleep, pried open his brain when his guard was down. No mercy.

—Open a vein.

"Fuck you."

—Get it over with. Best thing.

Like that, juiced with spasms of pain meant to keep Tony in line. But he was learning. The Pied Piper couldn't be there all the time. Even in a fog of Demerol, Tony managed to organize his thoughts into a rough plan. There wasn't much chance it would do any good, but it was worth a try. Anything was better than going along with this shadow-life, twitching between drugs and torture, barely able to function.

He remembered how he had at first been plagued with a lot of static and garbled bits of words. That had been bad enough, but not nearly as bad as the clear reception he had been getting ever since he removed his metal fillings. The metal had not aided the broadcast, as Tony originally believed, but instead had actually interfered with it, at least a little. So, a lot of metal would block out the Pied Piper completely. Maybe.

The spaghetti pot was taken, unfortunately. Tony put on his doubled sunglasses and ventured outside. The glare was so fierce that his eyes were seared with pain from light leaking in at the sides, and he was nearly blind before he even got to the corner. The supermarket was three blocks away, too far to go. Tony dived into the cool, dark interior of the Sparta Mart, a neighborhood shop that carried groceries and a few basic items. Mrs. Bandana, the wife of the owner, sold a lottery ticket to another customer and then directed her indifference to Tony.

"You got any aluminum foil?"

"Bottom left," she replied curtly, pointing toward the rear of the store.

Tony took two overpriced boxes. He also found some rolls of masking tape, which he figured should not be as harsh on his skin as the sticky packing tape he had at home. He paid, and insisted on being given a plastic bag to carry his purchases. Tony needed it for Snake's head. Steeling himself to face the glare outside, he ran all the way back to his apartment.

He put the pot in the kitchen sink and removed the lid. The smell was horrendous. He turned on the hot water and let it pour over the head, gradually rinsing away most of the muck. At least there were no worms crawling through the eyes and mouth, nor any other nightmare surprises that Tony had feared. When the water finally ran clear, he dumped the head into the sink and put the pot aside on the counter.

You don't look so bad now, he thought. What was your name? Alvin Doolittle, according to the driver's license. How the hell could a person with a name like that ever get into the Legion of the Lost? Snake sounded better. In fact, he looked better dead than alive. A bit rubbery, but the color had washed out nicely. The skin had the bleached look of white marble, Tony thought, or a fish's belly. There was no sign of trauma in Snake's face. He looked calm, an admirable quality.

Something Snake had said. The Doc this, the Doc that, trust the Doc, do what the Doc says. Hard to tell if it meant anything at all, since the whole scene had been mad, sick. But Snake told him to go see a shrink, and that seemed important. Tony had been sent to a shrink by the court, the weird guy with the weird name. All my troubles started after that. Maybe he can help.

—Easy, slime.

Tony shuddered. "Go away."

—Poor little plasmodium.

"The Doc'll take care of you."

—Maybe I am the Doc.

Jesus, that was a thought. "Are you?"

—You've got two heads now. You tell me.

"I'll find out, one way or the other."

—Will you indeed?

"Believe it."

But the demon was gone, his parting shot a raucous laughter that erupted in Tony's head. It took a moment to clear. Oh yes, I'll kill you, he thought bitterly. If he could just get to see that shrink again, he might find an answer.

Tony took a large, empty trash bag and dropped Snake's head into it. Then he rolled the black plastic tightly, taping it to form a rough ball. When he was satisfied with his work, Tony put the head in the Sparta Mart bag and then picked it up by the loop handles. There. He looked like anybody carrying home a nice big cabbage or honeydew melon from the market.

—Die, you slime.

"Oh fuck..."

—Lie down and I'll help you die. It'll be easy, it won't hurt at all. Lie down. Now.

"No, no..."

But Tony could feel the demon taking hold of him. The blood in his veins felt like broken glass, slashing him apart, churning his insides into a massive hemorrhage. As he started to fall, he grabbed the box of aluminum foil from the counter, ripped it open and fumbled to unroll a length of it. He hit the floor, rapidly losing strength. He couldn't even tear the foil, but he did yank enough of it out of the box to pull over his head—

—and suddenly the Pied Piper was silenced. Not completely gone, for Tony could still sense his presence, but substantially muffled. He pressed the aluminum foil to his skull, adjusting it to fit more tightly, and then he waited anxiously. Was the demon voice merely toying with him, allowing Tony to think he had won, before unleashing the final assault? It would be just like the sadistic bastard to do that.

But nothing happened, and Tony gradually became aware of a distant, very faint static buzz. There you are, little buddy. A minor irritation, nothing more. No pain. No words. No torture. Tony laughed out loud, shocked with relief and joy.

"It works! It works!"

Now you know you can beat the guy, Tony told himself. It's always something simple, easy to overlook or misunderstand. Like the common cold that wiped out the Martians in that old movie.

Less than an hour later Tony was ready to go. You look like a crazy, he thought sadly as he checked himself for the last time in the bathroom mirror. But that didn't really matter because he would be walking through the South End, where half the people out on the street looked damaged one way or another. Maybe he should have kept Snake's car, instead of abandoning it in the lot at the train station. No, the car was a major risk. He'd done the best thing he could with it. Now Tony would just have to walk, and if people stared—let them.

Tony had fashioned an aluminum foil skullcap, which he kept in place with an ordinary headband. For extra safety he had tied a couple of dozen thin foil strips to the headband, making a long fringe that hung down as far as his jaw on both sides, and around the back.

It would be better to wait until evening, but he was anxious to get rid of Snake's head. Besides, Doctor Ladybank wouldn't be at his office later. Now that the Pied Piper couldn't reach him, Tony was full of good ideas. He'd looked up psychiatrists in the Yellow Pages, and discovered an Ian Ladybank. His office address was in the center of the city. That was the shrink Tony had been sent to, no doubt about it. He called to make sure that Ladybank would be in all afternoon, but he didn't give his name or ask for an appointment. It seemed a safe bet that when he walked in with this headgear they'd lead him right to the shrink.

Tony's doubled sunglasses did a pretty good job, but all the light leaking in at both sides was enough to wear him down fast, so he taped the shades to his face with masking tape, overlapping the strips until he had built up a thick screen that tapered down across each of his cheeks. That should do it, he thought. Block out most of the unwanted light and you'll be okay. He could hear the Pied Piper still clamoring to get in, but faint and far away. Oddly, it was good to know the demon hadn't vanished.

Tony walked a couple of blocks with no difficulty. The tape worked fine, his eyes were still okay. No sweat. Well, no, that wasn't exactly true. It was a hot day, very humid, and Tony was perspiring already. But that was a minor inconvenience. He felt good for the first time in ages.

Was he the only person on earth being tormented by the Pied Piper, or were there others? Strange, how Tony had felt a sudden urge to ask Snake if he heard the voice. A very strange thing to do—you just don't ask other people if they hear any mysterious voices. It didn't matter, because Snake had so much metal in his head that he most likely wouldn't hear anything even if the Pied Piper did broadcast to him.

That old movie came to mind again. Was it possible that the Pied Piper was really a Martian, or some other alien? Could this be part of a plan to take over human minds, Tony wondered. Drive us crazy, turn us into slaves? *Because*, he thought, if the voice came from me, if it was all just my own craziness, then how could the aluminum foil work? So the voice had to come from someone or something outside. Ordinary people can't do that, but perhaps it was a top-secret government project. Or aliens. Tony had seen a few stories in the newstand rags about this kind of thing, and he had always laughed about them in the past. But this was now. He knew a lot more, from bitter experience. Anything was possible.

What about Doctor Ladybank? The Doc. Was he in on it? Why did Tony feel drawn to see the man today? For help. But the Doc hadn't helped him at all last time. Just gave him some bullshit about watching out for—bright lights and colors. Jesus, maybe I was hypnotized, Tony thought. Maybe that's what this is about. If that's it, I'll kill him. Right there in his office.

How good it felt to be able to use his brain again! It had been so long since his thoughts weren't cluttered or twisted with the Pied Piper's invasive tactics. Tony felt human again.

But he was beginning to think he had made a mistake. He was approaching the center of the city and he still hadn't gotten rid of Snake's head. It was partly due to the fact that Tony had not found a suitable place to dispose of it, but even more because he was simply attracting too much attention. People—every rotten one of them—were stopping in their tracks to gawk at him as he walked along the street. How could he dump his parcel with a big audience on hand? Somebody would step up to open the bag at once and then they'd all grab him before he could get away.

To make matters worse, the aluminum foil skullcap and fringe were magnifying the heat and frying his brain. Tony was sweating like a pig now. He stopped abruptly and went into the department store he had almost passed. The air-conditioning came as a great relief. He wandered around for a few minutes, imagining that all the security people in the place were watching him.

Shit! what if they demanded to inspect his bag? He couldn't very well refuse, they'd just hold him until the cops came. Tony began to tremble with fear. Then he saw what he needed. He kept his shopping bag clutched tightly in one hand, and he went to the counter in the sports department. He paid for a New York Yankees baseball cap, which he put on immediately. It sat snugly on the aluminum foil. The clerk appeared to be in shock, but handed him his change and receipt without a word. Tony then strolled out of the store as if he hadn't a care in the world.

Brilliant idea, he thought. The fringe was still hanging in plain view, and there was all that tape on his cheeks, but he now felt somewhat less conspicuous. It would be a lot better if Tony could do away with the fringe, but that was too risky. If he let the Pied Piper back in, he'd never be free again. Maybe he could do without the fringe, maybe the skullcap was sufficient to block out the Pied Piper, but Tony wasn't about to take a chance.

Burger Billy's was crowded. Tony was pleased to see that he was indeed drawing fewer stares, thanks to the baseball cap, but there were still people watching him. He didn't feel comfortable enough to drop Snake's head in the trash bin, so he turned around and left the fast food restaurant.

The public library. That was the place. There was a large litter barrel (disguised as a piece of mod sculpture) in front of the library. Tony had already tossed one of Snake's feet into it and the newspapers had made no mention of its having been found. Best of all, it was located in the middle of a long sidewalk that went from the curb to the library, which sat back a distance from the street. That meant he could time it so that there was no one nearby when he walked past and dropped the dead man's head in the artsy-fartsy opening of the litter barrel. In spite of the heat, he pushed on in a hurry.

One more block, Tony thought. Then the park. He was sticky with sweat, tired but determined. I'm going to treat myself when this is over. A quick warm bath, followed by a long cool shower. Broil a T-bone steak, wash it down with that bottle of bubbly the TWA steward had given him, do a couple of lines and hit the bars. But tonight it would be for fun, not work.

"Hey, fuckhead."

Tony was only a little way into the park when the half dozen or so teenagers descended on him. Assholes, every one. They had nothing better to do with their time than hassle the elderly, the drifters and the gays who lingered in the park. Anyone they felt they could pester without comeback. They closed around Tony like an evil cloak, taunting him, shoving him, flicking fingers at his Yankee cap, snatching at the plastic bag.

"Fuck off, you little shits."

"Eat shit, fuckhead."

Some of them were a year or two older than he was, but that didn't matter. Tony strode on toward the library, poking elbows at anybody who got too close. They answered by bumping him, and then he was tripped. As he fell, cursing them loudly, he was hit on the head and his hat went flying. The aluminum foil skullcap was knocked loose. Oh Jesus, no. He clamped his hands on it and tried to adjust the headband. Somebody was yanking at the strips of foil that hung across Tony's face.

"Nice hair, asshole."

"What's in the bag?"

"Open it."

The kids were already pulling at the tightly wrapped parcel. Tony jumped up and lunged for it, but they pushed him down again. He had been sweating so much that the masking tape wouldn't stick to his cheeks anymore. Light flooded in, burning his eyes. Tony shrieked at them and swung out with his fists, but he didn't make contact. In return, he was pummeled from all sides. The doubled sunglasses were ripped from his face.

Tony fell to his knees, hands clapped tightly over his eyes. I'm okay, I'm okay, he tried to convince himself. But he already knew from the shouts and screams that they had discovered what he had in the bag. Now he was being kicked and punched, and when he tried to ward off the blows he was hit in the stomach so hard his eyes opened briefly. The color purple ravaged him—he was in a flowerbed full of violets.

Tony screamed.

"No! Don't touch that, not that! Please don't—"

But they did. They were ready to take his mug shot, and one of the cops calmly reached up and pulled off that stupid aluminum foil thing he had on his head.

Zzzzzt.

EPILOGUE

Life isn't disappointing, but people so often are. They may raise your hopes for a while, but sooner or later they'll let you down. People are...Doctor Ladybank pondered the matter for a few moments, seeking to find the right word. Yes, he had it.

People are unworthy.

He was not entirely sure what they were unworthy of, but the point seemed irrefutable. It was difficult to follow every train of thought to the end of the line when you were drowning in a sea of disillusionment. The gift—for that was how Doctor Ladybank now regarded it, not as a skill or a technique—was apparently gone. Radio silence. Day and night he tried to tune in someone, anyone, but he found no one.

What happened? Doctor Ladybank wasn't sure. For a few days after Tony Delgado's arrest, the boy could still be reached. But then he began to fade gradually, and after a month he disappeared altogether. It was not the effect of buildings and metalwork and power lines, or Doctor Ladybank never would have managed to reach across the city in the first place. Nor could it be a matter of distance, as he had driven the fifty-plus miles to the Bartholomew Forensic Institute, part of the state hospital for the criminally insane, where Delgado was being held pending trial. He parked in the visitor's lot and sat there for an hour, trying feverishly to regain contact with the boy. Nothing.

Doctor Ladybank wondered if the failure was his. But he did the same things with his mind, he hadn't forgotten how it worked, anymore than you can forget how to ride a bicycle. Of course, it may have been a gigantic fluke, a scientific peculiarity that had its brief moment and then passed. But Doctor Ladybank could not believe that. He still had faith in his gift. All he had to do, he told himself, was persist. It would come back to him. And he would connect. Believe. Persist.

His favorite theory about this temporary failure centered on the inadequacy of his two subjects. Snake had always been tricky to handle, a dim prospect. Doctor Ladybank had never enjoyed the same intimacy of mind with Snake that he had with Tony. To steer him out to Jack's backyard and then get him over the hump—that was like composing the *Gurre-Lieder*. Delgado, on the other hand, was ravishing in his openness and malleability. Great potential, unlimited opportunity. But something had gone wrong, and Doctor Ladybank feared that he had gone too far with the boy. Now parts of Delgado's brain had simply shut down and were incapable of any mental reception. How else to explain it?

Of course, terrible things had happened. But no, don't say that. Terrible is an emotive word that has no meaning. It would be more accurate to say that unfortunate things had happened. He couldn't explain it, but it was hardly all his doing. When minds meet and interact in such a pioneering way the results are almost certain to be unexpected. Two minds adrift in each other, it was like—and here Doctor Ladybank took comfort in the persistence of the musical metaphor—a vast orchestra lost in the aleatoric reaches of the night.

Besides, Snake and Tony were hardly innocents.

Fuck it, as they would say.

Doctor Ladybank stared at the papers in front of him, but he couldn't see the words. It was that time of day, when he usually summarized his notes on the patients he'd seen, but his mind just wouldn't focus. Such boring and squalid lives that people insist on living...Doctor Ladybank was glad when the phone warbled.

"Margaret Zuvella on the line for you."

I remember the bristols, but the face escapes me.

"Yes, put her through." Pause, click. "Hello, Maggie?"

"Hi, Ian. How are you?"

"Fine, thanks, and you?"

"Busy as usual, but bearing up."

Doctor Ladybank gave the obligatory chuckle. "Now, what can I do for you on this rainy Tuesday?"

"I was hoping you'd agree to examine a client of mine. He's indigent, of course, so it'll be at the usual lousy state rates. But he's convinced you can help."

"Oh? What case is it?"

"State versus Anthony Delgado."

"Ah."

"You know him, you saw him a while back on another case. He seems like a major league fuck-up, but what do I know? The state experts are picking his brain now, which is why we need you."

"Yes."

"Yes, you remember him? Or yes, you'll examine him?"

"Both."

"Ian, you're a doll."

Not really—but Doctor Ladybank didn't say that. The tide had come in, his boat was lifted off the sand, and he was sailing again. The time would come, he knew beyond the slightest doubt, when he would make contact, and *connect*, with some other person. When that happened, Doctor Ladybank would progress with the gift, exploring new territory, achieving the unimaginable.

But for now, thanks be to the void, he had a chance to learn more from one of his mistakes. Perhaps even to save it.

Tony smiled when he saw Doctor Ladybank's fountain pen, one of those fat expensive jobs. In happier times he'd had a couple of well-off tricks who used that kind of pen. Check-writers with skinny dicks.

They were in a small consulting room at Bartholomew. It was painted the mandatory institutional shade of pastel green, and it was stuffy from a lack of air-conditioning, but it was as good as heaven—compared to the ward in which Tony was kept. The guard stood outside the door, keeping an eye on them through the sturdy wire-and-glass window. Doctor Ladybank had brought Tony a carton of cigarettes from Maggie. Tony had never smoked before, but in a ward full of wackos it seemed a perfectly natural, even healthy thing to do.

The questions were stupid and boring, but Tony tried to give polite answers. There was something eerie and unreal about this. After so much time, he was still unsure of Doctor Ladybank's true role in what had gone down. Had he been directly involved in all of Tony's suffering? Was he partially responsible for the bleak future Tony faced? It seemed unlikely, because the same man was now trying to construct a "demon voice" insanity defense so that Tony would be spared hard prison time. Not that he relished the prospect of an indefinite committal to the nuthouse.

"One problem," Doctor Ladybank said, "is your assertion that the voice stopped communicating with you."

"Yeah, it did."

"When did that happen?"

"When I was still in the city jail," Tony said. "It took me a couple of weeks, maybe more, to get rid of it."

"You stopped the voice?"

"That's right."

"And how did you accomplish that?"

"By banging my head on the bars and the cement floor," Tony explained proudly. "See, it really bothered him when I banged my head on the floor at my apartment. He said the people downstairs would put the cops on me. But I figured, maybe he was afraid I'd shake up the works." Tony tapped the side of his head. "So that he couldn't get to me anymore. In jail, I had the time to try it out, to do it everyday, as much as I could take. And it actually worked. I could feel him getting weaker, and finally I couldn't hear him at all anymore. If I'd only done that at the beginning, I'd have saved myself— my life."

"I see." Doctor Ladybank put his pen down. "Do you have to continue this behavior, banging your head, in order to—"

"Hell, no," Tony cut in. "It did the job, and that's it. I never got a kick out of knocking myself senseless, you know. I'm not crazy. I just...went through *something* crazy. And I'll tell you this too: he's still out there, man. I know he is."

"Yes. Now, tell me—"

"Doc, I have a question for you."

"Yes?"

"Why did you tell me about bright lights and colors?"

"Pardon?"

"The first time you saw me," Tony said, leaning forward, his arms on the table. "You gave me some line about watching out for bright lights and bright colors."

"I'm sure I didn't," Doctor Ladybank insisted.

"Yeah, you did. It sounded weird at the time, and I didn't give it much thought. But later, when the voice came and all the trouble really started, lights and colors began to hurt me. They got so bad I had to wear sunglasses and dark clip-ons. But I was still in agony." Tony paused. "Why did you do that?"

"I can assure you I did no such—"

"What was it, some kind of test? Or were you just having a little fun with me?"

"Anthony, you won't help your case this way."

Doctor Ladybank was trying to sound calm, but he was clearly flustered. His cheeks had more color now and his eyes cast about evasively as he droned on about Tony's "willful and naive attempt to embellish the delusion," and other uptown bullshit.

"Doc," Tony interrupted. "I'm a whore. Maybe that's why I can always tell when I'm being jived. I thought it was the CIA, or aliens from space, or that I was just crazy. I doubted it was you, I really did. Until now."

"I'll speak with your attorney."

Doctor Ladybank was trying to look annoyed. He shuffled the papers on the table, picked up his pen and began to write. As if Tony were no longer there, and had indeed ceased to exist.

Writing about me. The subject. That's what you were doing. You weren't trying to read my mind, Tony thought, you were trying to write it, to script my life like a dream or some kind of movie in your mind.

"Plasmodium."

Doctor Ladybank looked up sharply when Tony spoke the word. A ghost of a smile formed around the psychiatrist's eyes, seeming to say *I cannot be hurt by you.*

The baleful, haunting expression on the man's face triggered a profound claustrophobia in Tony. It felt as if the world, the universe itself, and every cell in his brain, was shutting down, blinking off, closing forever, and all that would be left was his sense of awareness—perpetual awareness of the dark around him.

The room itself was being blotted out.

Write this!

Tony snatched the fat pen from Doctor Ladybank's fingers and in a single swift motion rammed it nib-first through the shrink's right eye. He pushed it as far into the demon brain as he could, and then sat back, experiencing a remarkable sense of clarity and peace of mind.

Doctor Ladybank's mouth opened slightly. Otherwise, he did not move. His left eye was still open, glistening sightlessly. He appeared to be considering the matter.

Lie Down With Us

Mia was the only child.

She and her mother lived in a small house at the end of the last street in town. The forest began at the edge of their back garden, and it spread as far as the rocky hills a few miles away. Mia kept to herself most of the time. She grew flowers and vegetables, and she loved to explore the woods. She did well at school but she was rather shy and had no close friends. Whenever she and her mother went into town Mia was disturbed by the crowds of people and the noise, and she always felt much better as soon as they returned home.

The forest was like another part of the house, a combination playroom and wild garden that offered numerous distractions. But unlike home, the forest constantly changed in so many small ways. Mia loved it. She knew where the good mushrooms grew, and which were the ones to avoid. She knew which berries were sweet and tangy and delicious, and which ones would make her sick. And she knew where many of the animals lived—owls, shrews, mice, red squirrels and raccoons. At night Mia would lie awake in her bed and sometimes hear the solitary bark of a coyote or a fox, or the raspy snarl of a wildcat—but she'd never been fortunate enough to catch a glimpse of them.

A small stream ran through the woods. In some places it was narrow enough to jump across, while in others it had to be waded. Mia liked to visit the spot where a family of beavers had built a dam, creating a large pool of dark water. She was not allowed to swim there, although it looked especially inviting on hot summer afternoons.

"You can't go in," her mother warned her repeatedly. "There are poisonous water snakes that will bite and hurt you."

Mia had never seen any snakes—neither in the woods nor in the pool. But she obeyed her mother, and was content to sit on a large rock overlooking the water. She enjoyed spotting fat frogs in the shade beneath the plants, watching the beavers come and go on their mysterious errands, following the unpredictable moves of a dragonfly and counting the different birds that swept down for a fast drink and splash.

In the summer of her thirteenth year Mia began to sense that things were changing, but she couldn't say how or why. The woods no longer seemed quite as interesting, and she felt lonely as she walked through them. At times she felt sick, but it was not like any illness she'd had before. It came for no reason, it would go away before it got too bad to stand, and then it would drift over her again some while later. It was like a fog inside.

"Stay away from that pool," her mother warned her. "The air is bad, there are bugs and snakes. It's not good for you."

But the air didn't seem that bad to Mia, and the bugs didn't bother her. She noticed that she actually felt a bit better when she was sitting on the rock by the water.

One very hot afternoon Mia decided to go in—just to cool off for a minute. First, she watched carefully for a long time. The pool was dark and still. There were no snakes, and the water bugs stayed in the shady areas around the edge.

Mia took off her clothes and hung them over a low branch on a young tree. She stepped cautiously into the water. She felt a few slimy rocks, and then her feet slid into a mixture of mud and sand. It held, and as soon as she got used to it she found that it felt good. Mia advanced slowly into the pool, testing the way with each tentative step. She stopped when she reached the point where the water was just over her waist. Then she eased down and floated on her back.

Mia pushed herself gently and moved her hands, adjusting her position so that she saw nothing above her but the sky, no trees, nothing from the land, only that brilliant cloud-free purple-blue expanse of sky. She felt wonderful. The water was lovely. Cool and shimmery, it made her think of liquid mint all over her body. Mia closed her eyes and drifted happily. She would open her eyes briefly, a quick peek—and to see nothing but deep sky was like being in a perfect dream, as if she were the only living child in the world, and the world was hers.

It took a while before Mia noticed the touch on her body. A very light, feathery sensation that tingled her skin. It seemed to be part of the water itself, but gradually she realized it was something separate. Down her back, between her legs—it was an unusual but strangely pleasant feeling. Mia thought that she was probably brushing the fronds of a delicate underwater plant.

She opened her eyes again, and this time she was saddened to see that the perfect sky was now different. A jet had penetrated it, a tiny white pinhead with a long wispy tail. It was so high that Mia couldn't even hear it, yet to see it was bad enough. It would be gone soon, but her private dream was spoiled.

Mia became more aware of the way her body was being touched. It no longer felt as if it could be a mere plant. The whole back of her, from the neck to the ankles, was being kissed or nibbled, or so it felt to Mia. Minnows? She knew that if she dunked her bare feet in at the edge of the stream minnows would soon come to investigate. Their touch tickled her toes.

She raised her head and looked down across her body, and saw a snake move through the shallow water across her belly. She put her legs down, kicking to find the streambed. The water was full of snakes all around her. They brushed against her skin, seeming to caress her. There were dozens, perhaps hundreds—

Mia let out a squeal of panic and thrashed through the water toward land, swinging her hands to push the snakes away from her. She crawled onto dry sandy ground, scurried back several feet and sat with her arms clamped around her knees. Her body trembled as she watched the water fearfully. The pool was now still and dark again. The snakes had disappeared from sight.

You must never return to that place, Mia told herself as she thought about it in bed that night. Her mother was right. There were snakes. It was a dangerous place. The pool was different, no longer the serene hideaway she had known.

Mia had not told her mother what happened because there were no bite marks on her body, and she felt all right once her nerves settled down. No damage, a lucky escape. It would only serve to upset her mother, and there was no need for that.

Besides, the more she thought about it the more Mia realized that nothing bad had taken place. The snakes had touched her for some time before she even noticed them. They hadn't done a thing to harm her in any way. The thought of it was disturbing, but in fact the experience had not become unpleasant until she actually saw it, saw herself there with the snakes—only then did she go into a panic.

Mia tried not to think about it anymore.

Three days later, she went back to the pool. She crawled in the bushes until she found the small strip of sand by the water's edge where she had taken refuge the last time. It was hidden by thick branches of foliage reaching out from the ledge above. Mia would not go in the water again, but she liked that place and she wanted to watch the pool.

After a while, she took her clothes off and put them away to one side. She stretched out on the sand. It felt good. It felt both cool and warm at the same time, since some sunlight filtered through the overhanging leaves. A breeze like baby's breath came and went, stirring the fine soft hair on her arms and legs.

Mia.

Her mind rolled in a lazy swirling dream. Her skin tingled in every pore. She knew vaguely that she was not alone, but she didn't mind. She sensed them as they came around her, and moved gently over her. They slid between her toes and fingers, curling in her ears. They were large and small, long and short, and they felt sleek and light, but strong. They swarmed into her mouth, filled her nostrils, and yet she was not alarmed—Mia seemed to breathe with or through them.

She was dimly aware that she was being lifted and moved, and then she felt a brief shock as she entered the water. Floating. They teemed and coiled all over her. Like jewelry, like a second skin, like a new body. They seemed to hold her in place, and she felt *one* touch her between the legs. Her eyes opened and Mia saw dark blue sky everywhere, and that was good, and then she let her eyelids fall shut again as she floated on the dream. And now the *touch* moved inside her, filling her. A skin storm raged all over her body, a slickness blossomed within her, and Mia could feel it as a presence in her belly, a taste in her mouth, a dull metallic clamor in her ears.

A hand gripped her hair and lifted her head up. In a daze, Mia caught a glimpse of her mother, saw a long flash of silver in the air, heard a violent eruption of water. She was spattered by gobs of what felt like molten iron. Her mother's voice roared in the chaos, but Mia couldn't understand it. Mia's skin fell away, and her body turned to light that scattered in the red air.

"Mia."

She opened her eyes. She was at home, in her own bed. What had happened? Mia felt different. Her mother smiled at her, and stroked her hair and cheeks. Mia expected a stern lecture, or at least an argument. But all her mother would say was: "You almost drowned. Thank God I got there in time. Oh yes, you very nearly drowned. My poor little girl."

In a few days Mia began to regain her strength. Nothing was said. Her mother was always smiling and cheerful, as if she knew that Mia no longer had to be told to stay away from the pool. In her bed every night Mia couldn't help thinking about it. She saw the pool in her mind as it was that day her mother saved her. It was red and oily with blood, and pieces of dead snakes floated on the surface.

A huge sadness stayed with Mia for some time. It filled her heart at every odd moment when she had nothing to do. She cried, but she could never say why. Sometimes it was nothing more than a couple of tears that surprised her as she worked in the garden, or she might wake in the morning and find her pillow drenched.

It was early on just such a morning when Mia heard herself moaning and crying. She twisted and turned in her bed, but could not seem to escape from a troubled sleep. She felt caught in a wet and sticky cocoon. She struggled against it but it seemed to be all a part of her. Then it suddenly ripped away from her, and she managed to open her eyes.

"Mia!"

Her mother had yanked the sheet away. There were two little snakes on Mia's belly. Her skin was stained with blood, and the bedding was soaked. Her mother tottered back a step, then turned and ran from the room. The snakes moved up Mia's body and kissed her face with their tongues. She took them in her hands and held them to her chest. Then she saw her mother returning—her face twisted with anger, a large knife in one hand.

"Oh, no."

Mia hurried to the open window. She touched the snakes with her lips and then gently flung them out into the air, as far from the house as she could. When they began to tumble back down they seemed to turn into a soft shower of silver rain that sparkled in the early morning sunlight. It vanished in an instant.

Her mother came and looked out the window, slapping the palm of her hand with the flat of the knife blade.

"Too late," Mia said.

WAX

Kevin Sweeney and Dale Jensen journeyed halfway around the world to investigate wax. This particular wax didn't travel well, no matter how carefully it was transported. In Manhattan, Sweeney and Jensen saw little of interest in it. The crude figurines and bizarre masks were dull and brittle, crumbling easily into dust. They felt grainy to touch, and had no luster. They smelled stale and looked like the kind of junk you might find among the bric-a-brac at a flea market.

But then a company chemist melted some pieces of the wax in a pan on a hotplate, and when it had cooled sufficiently but was still fairly liquid, Sweeney and Jensen dabbed their fingers in it. The wax felt wonderfully silky. It didn't sit in a hardening glob, but actually seemed to be absorbed into the skin, and Sweeney felt a sudden, lovely sensation in his fingertips. The wax also had an elusive but attractive fragrance—subtle, insinuating, and undeniably arousing.

The first analysis was tantalizingly imprecise: some mix of bee and tree waxes, blended with several herbs and/or spices, plant colorings—all no doubt of local origin and character. There might well be some profitable application. An exotic facial mask or creme, skin toner or rejuvenating balm.

Revlon wanted to know more.

Sweeney and Jensen based themselves at the Aurora Hotel in Rezpor. It was a rambling old relic with large rooms and noisy air-conditioners, but it was the best in the teeming city and adequate for their needs. They hired a guide-driver who wore a different Bulls T-shirt everyday and insisted on being called MJ. He was friendly and helpful, and his English was good—aside from the one time he tried to translate the names of various wildflowers and plants.

Within a few days MJ had taken them to several wax producers in the region. They were not proper businesses, but rather small family operations in ramshackle barns and sheds. The men cooked up batches of wax, the women shaped and set it as masks for local religious use or as figurines and jewelry. It was, after all, just wax, but the results were very impressive. The colors were vibrant and had an inner glow. The wax in its finished form was hard, almost gem-like, yet it had a sensuous feel, and the fragrance was even more attractive than it had been in the New York sample.

The local waxmakers were not secretive. They happily took Jensen's money and attempted to explain their work fully. But their measurements were maddeningly vague and casual—add a bit of this, throw in some of that, etc. The molten wax simmered slowly in iron kettles on charcoal fires for "a while" or "a couple of hours" or "a few hours." It was frustrating, but Jensen collected numerous plastic bags of ingredients, took photographs and dictated cassettes full of detailed observations, descriptions and notes as they went from one place to another.

At the end of the first week Sweeney and Jensen felt they were ready to refine their investigation. Jensen would focus on the bee-keepers and the special wax distilled from tree sap. Both were cru-cial to the process. Sweeney would work on the equally important spices, wildflowers and herbs. To assist him in this area, MJ intro-duced Sweeney to a young woman named Bija, who came from a family of waxmakers. She was a schoolteacher, said also to be well-versed in the old Khalkist religion and rituals in which the wax played an important part.

Jensen's research took him some distance up the vale to an iso-lated glen that produced the most highly regarded beeswax in the region. He was away from Rezpor for several days. During that time, Sweeney and Bija sat on the wide veranda of the Aurora every afternoon, sipped iced tea and talked. She was very helpful, her English was excellent, and she clarified much of the uncertainty regarding the ingredients and the waxmaking process. Sweeney accumulated extensive notes.

He also found her charming, irresistibly attractive. His personal life had been largely vacant for some time, his one early and short marriage long since consigned to history. He was 37, and had got-ten used to the idea of intimacy as an occasional, brief incident, a passing diversion. His work was interesting and well-paid, but in all these years he had not met a woman who held his attention for very long.

Bija was younger—and exotically sexy, with long black hair, gold-brown skin, dark eyes that flashed and glittered like black-blue opals. She had a full round shape. She seemed to like Sweeney immediately. On the second day he was sure of it. The third after-noon, Bija happily allowed him to take her arm when they went for a walk before they had drinks and dinner together in the hotel restaurant.

Later, when he thought she was about to thank him and say goodnight, and he was trying to think of how he could prolong the evening with her, Bija surprised him with a suggestion of her own.

"I have something very special I want to show you," she said as they stood in the cavernous lobby. She gestured with the thin attaché case she was carrying. "But not here in public, and I cannot take you to my home."

"Let's go to my room," Sweeney said to her without hesitation. "We can have a little nightcap, as well."

Upstairs, as he poured the drinks, Bija put the attache case on the coffee table and opened it. She removed a piece of chamois that had been folded loosely in the shape of a rough square. She set it down and carefully began to unwrap it. Sweeney sat beside her on the lumpy sofa. His eyes widened.

"These are the real masks," Bija said softly. "Made of the finest wax. So far, you have seen nothing like this."

They looked remarkably human. Sweeney was shocked when he held one and felt how soft and supple the wax was in his hands. The mouth and eyes were empty, but the lips felt warm and bouyant, almost moist, a remarkable illusion.

"Once a year," Bjia continued, "people in the villages used to put these on for a few days and nights, a religious festival, and they became someone else. They would not go to sleep. They would just love and play, like the children of gods. You know? It was for celebration and renewal."

Sweeney nodded. Mardi Gras, Carnival—no doubt it was pretty much the same all over the world, the oldest party in human history. He had many questions about the wax, but no desire to ask them right now. His fingers lightly stroked the mask. The coloring and texture were utterly amazing. Bija took the mask from his hand and gently pressed it to his face. It stayed in place, seeming to fit and become part of him at once. His face felt as if it suddenly came alive with pulsing electricity, and the fragrance was dizzying. It was like some new level of sensory awareness, he thought—slowly, with difficulty, his mind in a swirling haze.

Bija put on the other mask and moved her face very close to his. Sweeney kissed her, their faces seemed almost to merge. It was as if he not only experienced his own sensations—but hers as well. And knew it was the same for her. No kiss had ever felt so intimate, so exquisitely rich, so full of all-consuming triumphant pleasure. Sweeney was aware of taking her in his arms, his hands unhooking the back of her caftan—and then all thought became unnecessary and vanished like mist in the sun, as he touched Bija's skin. It was so beautiful, so unbearably beautiful...the touch of desire, and true intimacy that had always been beyond reach.

"My God! My God!"

Sweeney awoke suddenly at the sound of Jensen's voice. Late afternoon sun filtered into the room. How long—all night and into the day? Sweeney was lying on his bed, Jensen standing a few feet away. Jensen staring. Sweeney's mind could barely focus, but then he realized Bija was still lying in his arms. Or he was lying in hers, in her body. Her skin was sticky wet on his, he was coated with her, her ruined features and flesh melting, flowing together in their long embrace.

"Help me..." Sweeney gasped, and then blacked out.

Jensen took care of everything, rolling up the sheets in a thin blanket and then somehow disposing of them. He scraped and washed up Sweeney. He doled out tips to the chambermaids and others on the hotel staff. It was nothing, no problem at all. Sweeney was in a fog until a day or two after they were both safely back in New York. Even then, neither of them mentioned it, and Sweeney could not form any coherent thoughts about what had happened. Or had seemed to happen.

They had a few days off to get over the trip and the jet lag. Sweeney needed them. He didn't feel great, he was tired, weak, oddly nervous. When Jensen phoned on the weekend, he didn't even ask how Sweeney was. He just reported that they had to see Rod Zinko on Monday morning. Zinko was a high-up in product development and he wanted to thank them for their efforts. It was too early to tell, of course, but there might be something of use in that wax. The meeting would be short and sweet, the way such corporate ceremonies always were.

People in the office told Sweeney how well he looked, how good the trip must have been—which was funny in more ways than one. He still felt like crap. But he smiled stiffly and nodded, then took the elevator up to Zinko's suite. Jensen met him in the spacious anteroom.

"Okay?"

"Yeah," Sweeney replied with a nod.

"Good. We'll glide through this and then how about we head off for an early drink and lunch?"

"Sounds good to me."

"Sparks okay? Dark and cool and quiet."

"Sure."

Rod Zinko's personal assistant appeared and led them in. The office suite seemed dark, in spite of the floor-to-ceiling windows. Sweeney followed half a step behind Jensen. His steps felt tottery.

Zinko popped out of his leather chair and came around to the front of the large elegant table that served as his desk. He was very jolly. He was saying this and saying that, but Sweeney couldn't quite make out the exact words—they sounded muffled and warped to his ears.

Jensen first, then it was Sweeney's turn. Zinko clapped him on the shoulder as they shook hands. Sweeney was dazed, it felt like his whole shoulder had crumbled inside. He saw Zinko's expression, and looked down. In Zinko's hand were three of Sweeney's fingers, broken off and crumbling. Sweeney moved his head with difficulty and gazed in stark wonder at his own hand. He saw his pinkie fall off and break up in small clumps of granular powder when it hit the highly-polished oak floor.

Curing Hitler

My name is Jurgen Bausch and I was born in 1893 near Aachen. My medical studies were interrupted by the Great War, and in the summer of 1918 I was re-assigned to the military hospital located in Pasewalk. Until that time I had served as a medical assistant in field hospitals not far behind the front lines.

The hospital at Pasewalk was designated for the treatment of military personnel who were mentally and emotionally disturbed as a result of their exposure to the horrors of combat. These cases ranged from mild and transient shell-shock to deep and permanent psychosis, and they exhibited a variety of behavioral symptoms that in their own way were every bit as devastating as the sheer bloody carnage I had witnessed in the field.

Unfortunately, the hospital served in practice as more of a processing center than a true treatment facility. New patients arrived daily, so there was never enough time and space to give proper attention to them. The shortage of skilled practitioners resulted in long work hours for everyone. Much of our time was spent merely trying to prevent outbreaks of the grossest abuse among the patients—including violent aggression, degradation, mutilation and self-destruction.

It was essential that we transfer patients out as quickly as we received them, otherwise we would have been overwhelmed by the tide of human debris. Thus, a patient would first be stabilized with a sedative, if necessary, and a diagnosis would be rendered, often based on the most superficial observations. The paperwork would be completed and then the patient would be pushed on to any appropriate destination we could find—the immediate family or closest relatives, a rehabilitation center, another hospital, or, in the worst cases, an asylum.

Nonetheless, a certain small number of patients remained at Pasewalk for a few weeks, even a month or more. Those cases were neither too degenerative and hopeless nor too slight, or for some other reason had been deemed worthy of more substantive treatment by the presiding medical officer.

One such case, in which I played a small role, was that of an enlisted corporal, Adolph Hitler, who came to us in October of 1918 and stayed until the end of that fateful November. By then, of course, the war was over and Germany had lost.

My chief duty at Pasewalk was to assist Dr. Albert Stadler, who was in charge of Ward 2. Stadler was an able physician and a good man whose special interest was disturbed states of mind. He was thoroughly familiar with the emerging theories of psychology, and had acquainted himself with the techniques of psychoanalysis, some of which he tentatively approved. He had not taken a formal training course in it, but he had read widely and in some of our private conversations he expressed a belief that after the war it would become the dominant force in the diagnosis and treatment of most mental disorders.

Stadler was unsparing in his devotion to work, and he could be found on the floor or in his little office on the ward at all hours of the day or night. He once told me that he found it hard to sleep, no matter how tired he was, because he hadn't been able to see his elderly parents, his wife or his children in more than a year. Life was very difficult in Germany, and like the rest of us, he worried constantly about his loved ones. The conditions at Pasewalk were debased, the work tedious and demoralizing, but for a man of Stadler's undoubted abilities the ward was his only escape from worry and insomnia.

I was familiar with Hitler. He had distinguished himself in the modest role of messenger between units along the front lines, and he had been blinded by an exploding gas grenade. At a field hospital they found that there was nothing organically wrong with his eyes. He could see if he truly wanted to, therefore he must either be a malingerer or have some other—mental, emotional—disorder that was complicating his recovery. There was no valid medical reason to discharge the patient to civilian life, so our task was to resolve the matter and return him to his unit.

There was no question about his blindness. Both Stadler and I had observed instances of Hitler's being the unhappy victim of minor abuse occasioned by his inability to see. Once, a group of patients tricked him into falling down the stairs leading to the lower floor. Another time, a patient urinated on Hitler's face while he sat on his bed staring vacantly into space. Malingerers know how to avoid suffering such indignities.

It wasn't long before Hitler became a nuisance, and the ward officers began urging us to move him out. He was "difficult," he spent much of his time haranguing his fellow patients on whatever subject crossed his mind—the evils of tobacco and alcohol, the Jews, the war, communism, history, and so on. Much of it was the usual litany of complaints heard from soldiers of nationalist or rightist beliefs, and in a way they mirrored those voiced by the left. The common room in every ward was a bedlam of conflicting views and factions, much as the whole of Germany would become in the following years.

After a few unpleasant experiences, Hitler assembled around himself a small group of protectors and admirers. They enjoyed his rants and approved of what he said. They read the newspaper aloud to him and relished his sarcastic comments. Keeping all of the cliques like this from each other's throats was a significant part of our everyday work.

But perhaps what most unsettled us about Hitler's presence were his nocturnal ramblings. The man seldom slept, only nodding off for a few minutes now and then, accumulating at most between two and three hours of "false sleep" over the course of a twenty four hour period. At night, when the ward was much quieter and most of the patients were either asleep or lacked the energy to leave their beds, Hitler wandered alone. Up one corridor, down another, around the empty common room, through the aisles of beds and cots. It was as if, having nothing better to do, Hitler had decided to memorize the place and thus circumvent the limitations of his blindness.

Stadler and I had noticed this behavior. We would be taking care of paperwork in his office, late into the night, or relaxing for a few minutes, and we would hear the slow, deliberate shuffle of Hitler's flimsy slippers on the linoleum down the hall. Then, a moment or two later, he would appear, standing like a ghost at the open door of the office. Stadler and I would remain silent, perfectly still, staring at him. Hitler's gaze would be fixed on nothing. He would stop for a couple of seconds, and then resume his meandering way.

"He isn't ready to be cured yet," Stadler told me.

"Why not?"

"His blindness is hysterical in origin and the insomnia is a secondary effect. He's usually uncooperative when I question him but I've managed to learn a few things. Before the war he had no skills, no talent, no prospects, nothing. He lived poor, in city parks and culverts, occasionally at a men's shelter. But the war changed all that. For the first time he had a sense of purpose, and he performed well enough to be decorated, which gave him his first taste of genuine accomplishment. But after four years it's not so easy to maintain the same perspective. And then, suddenly the war strikes directly at him. He's gassed, blinded. But he's not regarded as a hero or a victim, which is probably what Hitler expected. No, they tell him he's malingering. And so, now, he's lost his sense of place and his focus. The problem, I think, is that some hidden part of him secretly enjoys this nowhere state he's in, and so his mind refuses to address the difficult issues he faces. We must bring him to that point. When we do, he will see again."

It wasn't my place to disagree, but I had my own thoughts on the possible nature of Hitler's affliction. An encounter I'd had with him one night made a strong impression on me. It was after Stadler and I had shared a late drink. As sometimes happened, he dozed off on the sofa in his office, so I headed to my own bed in the hope of finding a few hours sleep. Hitler was near the doors to the common room, and he stopped when he heard me.

"Who's that?"

"Bausch."

"Bausch." I had reached him by then, and beneath the light in the ceiling I saw a smile on his face, not a pleasant smile at that. "How can you cure me if you can't sleep either?"

"I can sleep," I said. "What are you doing?"

He gave a slight shrug. "Waiting?"

"For what?"

"If you know, my dear Herr Bausch, please tell me."

He delivered these few phrases slowly but in a rhythmic flow that was almost musical, his voice soothingly bemused—and yet, there was a gravelly undertone, an implicit taunt.

What disturbed me more, however, was the sight of his vacant eyes in the glow of the ceiling light. Hitler was standing with his face slightly upturned, as he usually did when moving around the ward. I knew that he had particularly bright blue eyes, but that was the first time I'd observed them so closely. They made me think of the eyes on Greek statues, blank, empty of any human expression or depth, but somehow so arresting we find it hard to turn away from them. The cold gem-like blue fire that shimmered in Hitler's eyes only enhanced the strange effect.

I finally realized that I'd been standing there for several minutes, simply staring at him, or his eyes. Hitler hadn't moved at all in that time, as if he knew exactly what was happening and liked it. I felt weak, drained, almost too tired even to breathe anymore. I felt that if I stayed there any longer I might sag to the floor in a coma. I forced myself to wake up a little, enough so I could brush past him and find my way to bed.

"Bausch," he said with a soft laugh. "Get some sleep."

I was exhausted after a sixteen-hour workday, followed by a few glasses of wine, and now I was further unsettled by the eerie emptiness of that brief encounter. And yet enough of my mind was still functioning. I had noticed something and would remember it the next day. Hitler had stopped at exactly the place where his blind upward gaze was pointed directly at the light fixture built into the ceiling. Without realizing it himself, he was beginning to respond to shades of darkness. He was beginning to see again. On his own.

A few days passed before I had the time to give this matter proper consideration and discuss it with Dr. Stadler. He tended to discount its importance, but he did conduct a new examination of Hitler's eyes. The tests, which I observed carefully, showed no organic damage—and no apparent reaction at all to a variety of light stimuli. Hitler was surprisingly cooperative throughout and seemed quite disheartened by the results.

So my theory was shot down, but Dr. Stadler was delighted by Hitler's reaction. For him to be discouraged was a sign of hope. It meant that the patient had reached the point where he wanted, at least subconsciously, to be cured. Now, perhaps, he could be led across the threshold.

A few days later, Dr. Stadler instructed me to retire to my bed early in the evening and sleep. He would need me later that night, and I had to be fully rested, awake and alert. I met him in his office at two a.m. As instructed, I had taken care not to go near Hitler on the way in or inadvertently let him know that I had returned to the ward. I settled comfortably on the sofa just behind and a little to one side of the desk. I was not to betray my presence by any movement or sound.

"Here we are now," Dr. Stadler said gently as he steered the patient into the room a few minutes later. "Here's a chair. Sit facing forward. That's it."

Dr. Stadler took his own seat. The only light in the room came from a gooseneck lamp on the desk, and now Stadler turned it around so that it was shining directly on Hitler's face. Stadler and I were in darkness. The light had no effect on Hitler, who sat with his face turned slightly upward. I had a clear view of him from just a few feet away, and already I found it hard not to stare at those brilliant eyes.

"Are you all right?"

"I would be, if I could see."

"Yes, and the time has come for the two of us to sort things out. You can't remain here indefinitely. They've got you pegged as a malingerer and probably a coward."

Hitler's cheeks flushed with anger.

"But your service record is exemplary," Dr. Stadler went on. "No one with a history like yours suddenly turns into a coward or a malingerer. Their diagnosis is wrong on all counts."

Hitler relaxed slightly, as his sense of honor was restored. "And yet," he said, "the condition persists."

"Your blindness is real."

A tremor of anxiety. Hitler now appeared oddly vulnerable. "Will I ever see again?"

"Only if you truly want to. Physically, there is nothing at all wrong with your eyes."

"Of course I want to see. But—how?"

"Hold out your hands. That's it, lean forward a little and rest your arms on the desk."

Dr. Stadler reached across the small desk and took Hitler's hands in his own. I could see that he held them tightly.

"Now listen carefully. I can't give you a full and proper course of treatment here, but I can give you the key. Then it's up to you, if you decide to use it. Life has failed you. First the world around you, and now more recently the war itself. The gas grenade was the final straw, triggering your blindness. But this blindness is in fact a defensive mechanism, a kind of shield constructed by your mind to protect you from further insult. We know that such reactions are a form of hysteria, but they can be overcome. Most of all, it requires will and courage, and I know from your record that you have the will and the courage necessary to succeed. *To see.* And then *not* to resume your past life, but to create a new life for yourself, your *real* life."

What increasingly alarmed me about all of this was not that I thought it was incorrect—I did, but that only meant it would be a waste of time—but the reactions occurring in the patient and the physician. Hitler appeared to shine with new confidence, while Dr. Stadler's speech grew slower and more disconnected. It was as if he were drunk, or drowsy, and in the process of falling asleep. I recognized this as the same thing that had happened to me the night I met Hitler outside the common room, and even then I could feel the same effect within myself, though it was weaker, probably because I was seated several feet away.

"It's there within you," Stadler continued. "Find the will to break through the curtain that blinds you. Summon the courage to see what you face, and then to face down what you see." After another pause, Stadler asked, "Do you hear me?"

"Yes," the patient replied.

"Do you understand it?"

"Yes."

"Will you...."

But at that point Dr. Stadler's head nodded forward onto his chest. I couldn't move. Hitler gently pulled his hands away and turned his head in my direction. His eyes appeared as vacant and unseeing as ever. I couldn't tell if he sensed my presence, not that it really mattered anymore. Slowly, he swung his head back toward the desk and the still form of Dr. Stadler.

"Get some sleep."

Then he stood up and walked out of the room. As a matter of fact, I fell asleep right there, on the couch. Dr. Stadler and I were both awakened a few hours later by the usual morning chaos breaking out across the ward. We didn't get a chance to discuss the session. Hitler, for his part, continued to move around like a blind man, delivering his endless harangues by day, roaming the corridors like a ghost at night.

Three days later, everything changed. As it happened, both Stadler and I were in the common room. An NCO rushed in, a piece of paper in his hand and the look of death on his face. He read the announcement of the armistice. The war was over. There were tears of joy, of sorrow, of anger. We all feared for the future, knowing not what it would be but that it would be difficult. My eyes scanned the room and I spotted Stadler. He gave a shrug and a forlorn smile. He made his way across the room to me, took me by the elbow and invited me to his office for a drink to mark the mixed blessings of the occasion. The ward officers and patients could fend for themselves. The noise was ferocious.

As we were leaving the room, we noticed Hitler in his usual corner, surrounded by his set of chums. Copies of the armistice announcement were being passed around. Hitler snatched one. He read it, his face coloring. He tore the paper to shreds and then launched into one of his loud rants.

"...Germany in ruins...."

"Well, he can see again," Dr. Stadler said as we stepped out of the room. "That's something, anyway. I wonder if he realizes that he's about to become unemployed again."

Years later, Dr. Stadler died in mysterious circumstances. His offense, I believe, was telling Hitler that he suffered from hysteria. To Hitler that was a grave insult.

For myself, I still believe Hitler was blinded by that gas grenade. It was a genuine injury, but his eyes were not damaged permanently. His system recovered at its own pace. The attitude of a patient is a critical factor in determining whether recovery will be speedy or slow. Clearly, Hitler's attitude was no help in regaining his sight—until someone or something came along, enabling him to find the inner strength and will that would carry him across the final barrier.

Whether it was Dr. Stadler and his mistaken "cure," or if it was the armistice ending the war, the horror of defeat—I don't claim to know. Maybe Hitler simply recovered on his own.

It probably doesn't matter.

All I know is that there are still moments when I lie in the dark and see those beautiful and unbearably empty blue eyes, and slowly I feel the life begin to drain out of me again, and I hear that low insistent voice as surely as if it were happening to me all over again, and it says, "Bausch, get some sleep," and I wish I could.

Ghost Music

I never wanted to tell this story, but there's no longer any point in sitting on it. I'd like to think that it might serve as a very small footnote to a very small entry in music history, but that seems rather unlikely.

Does anyone still remember Eric Springer?

Do you know who Mandy Robbins was?

A couple of months ago I was skimming *The Times* and saw the brief news item about the train wreck south of Cairo. The usual disaster in an under-developed country, dozens of people dead. I took it in and quickly passed on without a second thought, but a short while later I received a telephone call from an old friend in London. Did I know that Mandy Robbins was on that train, and had died in the crash? I was stunned. No one had heard from her in ages, though at various times rumor had it that she was living in a dark apartment in Buenos Aires, or a tiny cabin in a remote Norwegian fishing village, or a villa on a resort island in the Adriatic. But no one really knew, and after a while the stories dried up. We all more or less forgot about her, or we filed her away among our less happy memories—with Eric.

Mandy Robbins was en route to Luxor when the train accident occurred. Twenty years later, she was still running.

I live in Dutchess County now, about seventy miles north of Manhattan. I edit (and write most of) *Tonal/Atonal*, a monthly newsletter. My articles and reviews also appear in several other publications that cover 20th century music, and my monographs on Hartmann and Lutoslawski have sold well to libraries throughout the world. I'm working on Arvo Part now, and I teach a course at the local high school. It all adds up to a reasonable income and I suppose I'm happy enough in my A-frame. I own about 5,000 CDs, records and tapes, as many books, a superb stereo system, and I occasionally have an affair with a divorcee.

You know, it *is* a life.

But in 1976 I was living in London and I sincerely believed in the importance of great art, literary and musical. There were classics, old and modern, and they truly mattered—perhaps more than anything else. A new composition by Berio was greeted as an event of quasi-religious significance. Art was in some ways more real than life itself, I thought. Back then, I hadn't yet given up on myself, though I was already beginning to cobble together a sideline career as a commentator rather than a composer.

Eric Springer was an old friend with more talent and better luck. I was thrilled when he wrote to say he'd be coming to stay in London for several months. We hadn't seen each other in a while, though we kept in touch with postcards. Eric's Variations for Piano and Oboe had been heard on a late-night FM station in California by a young producer who decided to use it in his next film. *No-Hopers* was a cult success and the soundtrack sold quite well. Eric had already earned a measure of critical praise as a promising young composer, but now he had the added pleasure of an unexpected payoff from the world of popular entertainment.

He was coming to London to write a quartet, commissioned by the Claymore Foundation, and to be with the new love of his life. Mandy Robbins was then 23, attempting a comeback in a career that had never quite happened. She'd been a bright young prospect as a violinist at the age of 14, but the assorted stresses of high expectations, touring, and family problems had combined to derail her. At 18, she packed it all in and took a couple of years off to put her life in order. Then she began slowly and carefully to make her way back as a performer.

By the spring of 1976 she had done well enough to have a new agent and a challenging but very sweet job: she would perform the Berg Violin Concerto at the upcoming Proms. A friend and wealthy patron offered her the free use of his house in London, and she intended to spend four months mastering the technically difficult and emotionally taxing composition. It would be her breakthrough concert. There was talk of a live recording, and a contract for studio albums later. Mandy would also be the star soloist at the debut of Eric's quartet, sometime in the future.

Eric and Mandy, Mandy and Eric. When I met them at Heathrow in late April of 1976 the air seemed charged with the excitement of their romance and the dazzling music they were setting out to create. It all seemed to be coming together for both of them and I was swept up in it as well—happily so. I felt privileged to be the friend at hand.

They quickly settled into their new home, a Georgian brick house in one of the narrow streets behind Edwardes Square, on the edge of Kensington and Earl's Court. The owner had spent a small fortune renovating and redecorating, and it featured a music room with a Bosendorfer grand on which Eric could help Mandy rehearse, using a piano reduction of Berg's orchestral score. There was a separate den with a spinet in the converted basement, where Eric could work on his own composition.

It was ideal for them, and by happy coincidence I was living in a tiny flat behind the Olympia, a short walk from their place. We spent a lot of time together in the early going, as I showed them around London, took them on pub outings, introduced them to Indian food, and helped them find some of the less obvious sites that they were interested in seeing—like the modest house in Chelsea where Peter Warlock came to his sad and lonely end, and the rather dreary old pile that Edward Elgar had lived in, near the North End Road.

Eric and Mandy both took to London at once, they loved going for long walks around the city, and they soon began to talk about the possibility of finding an affordable place of their own after the Proms and staying on indefinitely.

I liked Mandy from day one. She was obviously intelligent, especially about music, though she wasn't nearly the compulsive talker on the subject that Eric and I were. She was petite, and still had a look of girlish prettiness about her, but you would occasionally catch a brief glimpse of adult sadness in her eyes when something was said that brought an unhappy memory to mind. I knew that she had struggled to escape a possessive father who'd attempted to control every aspect of her life and career; she was eventually successful in breaking away, but she still carried the emotional scars.

Most of the time, however, Mandy was buoyant and energetic, fun to talk to and be with, and it was very clear to me that she cared deeply for Eric—and that he felt the same about her. He had found her at exactly the right time in his life.

Eric was fast approaching thirty. He'd been something of a playboy for rather too long, and was in danger of being written off as an underachiever. He had never produced as much new music as some people felt he should. Now he was apparently making real progress at last. The movie success and the Claymore commission both helped enormously, but Mandy was the vital factor. She gave him love and a sense of stability, for what was perhaps the first time in his life. The two of them shared an ambitious vision—they wanted both greatness for each other in music, and to have a great love affair together forever.

Well, why not? At that age we all want everything, and we can't imagine why we shouldn't get it. I was beginning to sense my own limitations, but I still believed in Eric. And the first time I saw Mandy strike the violin strings with the edge of her hand in the famous "warm-up" of the Berg piece—a kind of firm but very delicate chopping motion, an incredibly difficult thing to do properly—I believed in her as well.

Eric and I were sitting on the small patio outside the Lord Edwarde one balmy evening a few weeks into their stay when I got the first indication that there were problems. Eric seemed to be distracted and had little to say. Mandy, who was not one for the drink anyway, had stayed home to take a hot bath; lately, she was being bothered by aching muscles in her shoulders and legs. Eric said she was rehearsing too much, and there may have been a minor disagreement between them.

I was sympathetic, but I sensed there was something else on Eric's mind. He was a tall, sturdy guy, but that evening he sat hunched over his pint in a way that suggested defeat. He looked like one of the dazed old-timers at Ward's. He had even gone for three or four days without shaving, which was not his style. We chatted fitfully for a while, and then I asked about his quartet. If there was trouble, it had to be with the music.

"Want to read some of it?"

"Of course, I'd love to."

I'd been looking forward to the moment when Eric would show me some of his new work. He reached down and unzipped the slim briefcase he always carried with him, fished out a few sheets of music paper and handed them to me. He had a smile on his face, but there was something sour in it.

The first page bore the hand-printed title "Quartet" and the dedication "for Mandy." My eyes scanned down the page and across the staves. I was amazed. It was pre-Serial, in fact it seemed to be pre-Romantic—an altogether astonishing turn back to the past for a composer like Eric. Another shock: the quartet opened with a *basse danse.* It was incredible. Nothing in his previous work had ever looked in this direction. But I was going too fast to hear it in my mind. I started over again, caught it—and a tremendous sense of confusion washed through me.

"You're quoting Warlock," I said without looking up.

"Am I," Eric said with a hollow laugh.

"This is his Capriol Suite."

"I know."

It continued for the next five pages, what was then the only fairly well-known piece of music composed by Peter Warlock, circa 1926. The restless flurry of notes ended abruptly in the middle of the seventh page, with a large "X" scrawled across it, and the words SHIT SHIT SHIT.

"I don't understand," I said.

"Neither do I."

"Surely you don't mean to quote at this length, and here at the very beginning of your own work."

"No, of course not."

"Well...?"

"I'll tell you what's really kind of scary about it," Eric said, staring at his pint. "I've worked on that for weeks, ever since we got here, but it was only the other day when I realized what it was. Until then I had no idea." He looked up at me. "I honestly thought it was all mine."

I let that pass for the moment because I couldn't think of a thing to say. All composers and writers are influenced by those who came before; as they mature they outgrow their influences and find their own voices, or else they come to a dead end. But this was not a case of excessive influence. Eric had Peter Warlock's music note for note, as far as I could tell.

"That's not scary. Embarrassing, maybe."

"Yes." He smiled sheepishly. "It is embarrassing."

What *was* scary, I thought but did not say, was that this was all he had to show for a month of steady work.

I told him not to listen to any other music (except the Berg that Mandy was practicing) and to begin again on his quartet. We both knew that the history of great works of art is littered with false starts. Or as Edward Albee said, you nose around and nose around like a dog, until you find the right place to squat. Eric was clearly relieved when I brushed aside the incident.

Privately, I was disturbed, and I knew he was too. Why else would he even show me those self-damning pages? And how could it be explained? Eric had been living quietly with Mandy for all of that month, up to nothing worse than a few pints at night after a long day's work—and who could begrudge him that? I understood influence, but how anybody could virtually transcribe the work of another person and not know that they were doing it is beyond me. Yet I had no doubt Eric was being truthful.

A few days later, on the weekend, the three of us went up to Portobello Road and poked around among the flea market stalls. I didn't find anything, but Eric bought Mandy a lovely silver charm of a cat, sleek and vaguely Egyptian, with a fleck of amber inset as an eye. It came on a thin chain, and Mandy immediately put it on around her neck. Mandy was very fond of cats, and if she and Eric stayed on in London they intended to get one.

We had a pleasant pub lunch on Church Street, and while Eric was at the bar buying another round I asked Mandy how her work on the Berg concerto was coming along.

"The music's fine, and I love it, but it's so demanding, and my body is behind schedule." She sipped her spritzer (as usual, the only one that she would have). "My legs get very sore after I've been standing for a while, and I seem to get tired quickly." I nodded. For the concert soloist, physical training and stamina are every bit as important as they are for the athlete. "But I'm following an excellent program of exercises, so hopefully I'll be in peak condition by the end of August."

"Good. I'm sure you'll be fine," I told her. "And how is Eric's work? He seems cheerful enough, but he hasn't said very much to me about it."

Mandy's face brightened. "I heard some of it last night and it was gorgeous. And I'm not just saying that, it really was the most beautiful music I've heard in ages."

"What was?" Eric asked before I could speak. He was back at the table with two fresh pints.

"The theme you were working on last night," Mandy said.

"Oh, yes." Eric smiled at me, looking pleased with himself. "She's right, too. It's the best thing I've ever done."

"Great," I responded. "I can't wait to hear it."

By the time we got back to their place Eric and I were quite jolly with beer and Mandy was tolerantly amused. I insisted that they both give me at least a brief preview of their work before I tottered off home. Mandy took out her violin while Eric poured a very ordinary scotch for the two of us.

Some people don't like Alban Berg. They just don't get that whole second Viennese school. But I find his music heartbreaking, especially the Violin Concerto, his own farewell to life. Mandy nearly had me in tears within a few moments. She only played the final part, the adagio, but that was enough. She sat down with a wince and a groan, and put her feet up on a hassock. I told her how good she was, several times. Then Mandy and I badgered Eric to play a bit of his new music. It didn't take much. He seemed genuinely eager and he stepped briskly to the piano.

"Remember, it's just an idea I'm fooling around with," Eric told us. "And you must hear it in strings."

He began to play, taking up his theme and exploring it, much as a jazz musician will improvise around a song line. It was far from developed, still spare and skeletal—but Mandy was right, it was a gorgeous idea that just hinted teasingly at rich colors and deeply moving harmonies.

Eric played for about ten minutes. Mandy and I clapped, and he grinned as he flopped down in the armchair and reached for his whiskey glass. I came up with some encouraging words and somehow managed to hide the huge distress I felt.

I still wasn't quite sure what he'd been playing, but I knew that I knew it—and it wasn't Eric Springer's music.

My knowledge of 20th century music is far from encyclopedic. I'm patchy on the Americans, Scandinavians, Russians, the Spanish and much of the rest of the world. But in 1976 I was really into British composers, particularly the more obscure ones lost in the enormous shadows cast by Vaughan Williams and Britten (since then I've concentrated on the Germans and East Europeans).

The next day I could still hear the theme in my head, and I began to work out what it might be. By late that afternoon, I at least had a pretty good idea of who the composer was. I dreaded speaking to Eric about it, but there was no choice in the matter. I rang and asked if I could stop by, knowing that was the time of day he usually finished working.

When I got there, Mandy was out and Eric was ready to go for a walk and a pre-dinner pint. That was fine with me, but first I had him play the theme for me again. He had developed it quite a bit in only twenty four hours, but hearing it again merely served to confirm my suspicions. While we were out walking I spoke in a general way about the music and how it was so different from his previous work. We went to the Britannia in Warwick Road.

"Now," I said after we'd taken our first sip of Young's, "I have to tell you what I don't like about it."

"Okay, fire ahead."

"It's by Ernest Moeran," I said. Eric stared at me as if he couldn't believe what I'd just said. "I'm pretty sure it's from his String Trio, composed in 1931. That, or his Violin Sonata of 1923. Anyhow, I'm certain it's E.J. Moeran."

"I've never even heard of him," Eric insisted anxiously, his face flushed and agitated. "And I'm damn sure I've never heard a note of his music."

"I believe you, but...."

"You must be wrong, you've got to be."

"Check it out yourself," I said. "And do it before you play or show that music to anyone else, because you'll be embarrassed, and you might even find yourself with legal problems."

"Jesus." Eric sat back, worried and subdued. "What's going on here?"

"I don't know."

"Who the hell is Ernest Moeran?"

"A minor English composer," I explained. "Born 1894, died 1950. A few of his works are of real, lasting quality. He's the kind of composer I love to find, overlooked by most people." At that point, I hesitated. But I had to go on. "When I first got into Peter Warlock seriously a couple of years ago, I came across Moeran. He and Warlock were very close friends."

Eric stared at me.

I did not tell him the saddest details of all about Ernest Moeran. We never got around to them, or maybe I just didn't want to risk making matters worse for Eric. That in 1950, at the age of 55, on one of his many trips to Ireland, Moeran was found dead in a river, apparently the victim of a heart attack. Or that in 1926 Moeran had a colossal failure—he could not complete work on a symphony that had been commissioned by the Halle Orchestra. Or that his friendship with the remarkable but very strange Peter Warlock had nearly destroyed Moeran's life while he was still a young man. In fact, there were people who knew them both and who believed that the best thing that ever happened to Moeran was the mysterious death of Warlock himself in 1930.

I didn't see Eric again until the end of the following week. I knew he would need some time to sort himself out, and I had to put my own thoughts in order—or at least try. I used the time to do a bit of research on Peter Warlock, but that didn't help me understand what was happening with Eric. The only explanation I could come up with was that he had to be going through some kind of mental breakdown. That he did know the Moeran piece, as he'd admitted he knew the Warlock, and he had begun to re-compose them both in the mistaken belief that they were his own—as a result of some deep confusion or psychological crisis.

But, aside from the music itself, I had seen nothing in his habits or behavior that would support such a theory. He appeared to be fine in all other respects, and Mandy had given no hint of troubles with him. All I could think was that something bizarre happened whenever he sat down at the piano to compose—perhaps the pressure to justify such an important commission became too great to handle, and his mind lurched off on its own, dredging up music he knew but dissociating it from its source.

Every Friday I spent a couple of hours at Bush House editing and polishing the English translations of emigre texts broadcast on the BBC World Service. It was a handy job, and it eventually led to my interest in the so-called dissident composers from the Eastern Bloc, like Gorecki.

Eric phoned, knowing I'd probably be there. He asked me to meet him at a place called the New Ambassador Club, which turned out to be a humble drinking den up one flight of stairs on Orange Street. I have no idea how Eric found such a place, or became a member, but he was at the last table at the back.

I almost didn't recognize him. The four-day stubble was now about two weeks old and had been shaved down to form an emerging goatee and a disconnected mustache. That was startling enough in itself, because Eric had never sported facial hair. But he also looked thin and gaunt, his skin was grey and his eyes were tired. Obviously he wasn't eating or sleeping properly.

"All right," he said, after fetching some ale. "I've got a problem. I know I heard Warlock last summer at the Hartt School. Maybe it was the music, or his odd name, but I was curious to see the place where he died shortly after we got here."

"Yes."

"And maybe Moeran was on the same concert program. I don't remember it, but maybe he was. That has to be what happened— how else would I pick up their music?"

"I'm inclined to agree."

"But that kind of music doesn't even interest me," Eric said with exasperation. "It never has. Tone-color, lyrical harmonies and the old modes. It's an *old* language."

"I know," I said. "That's never been your style."

"So why is that all I can do now? When I sit down and write or when I fool around on the piano, the only thing that comes out is that kind of music. And then I realize what it is, and I have to throw it out and start all over again."

"Do some exercises in dissonance," I suggested.

"I've tried," Eric told me. "But whenever I consciously try to set off in a particular direction I immediately come to a dead end. I get nowhere." He leaned across the table and spoke in an urgent voice. "I've been here going on two months now, and I've written nothing of my own. Not one note."

"It sounds like writer's block," I said sympathetically. "I guess the only thing you can do is to keep working until you work your way out of it. And you will, sooner or later."

Eric looked as if he didn't entirely believe me. In fact, I wasn't sure I believed it myself. Eric had another theory. The success of the movie soundtrack had somehow leached away at his self-confidence. He was afraid of not being taken seriously, of being dismissed as a popular hack. His quartet would be an easy target for that charge from people who resented his windfall, and fear of this was now blocking him creatively.

There may have been a small grain of truth in what he said, but there was also a large blob of paranoia. The music community didn't follow him that closely. Eric was just one of many young composers with true potential but a tenuous hold on the art, and he was not yet the focus of widespread interest.

"That's a stretch," I told him. "The movie money started to come in a couple of years ago. It's in the past now, so you can forget about it. And there's no point in worrying about what the critics will say about the quartet until you finish it. You have a massive case of self-consciousness, that's all, and the way out of it is to keep working. You'll break through."

Eric thought about that for a few moments, and then he said, "Tell me more about Peter Warlock."

"This is not really about Peter Warlock," I said. "This is all about you, and your music."

"I know," Eric replied. "Still...."

"Well, he was a brilliant scholar and a very good composer," I said. "Some of his songs are among the best in English music. He was born in 1894, and his real name was Philip Heseltine. But his music criticism offended so many people that when he came to the point of publishing his own music he decided it would be best to use a pseudonym. No one—"

"Look at that," Eric interrupted. "He was so worried about what people would say that he took another name."

"Yes, but it didn't work. People soon knew that Warlock was Heseltine. By the way, nobody seems to know how he came up with that name, but he had a strong interest in the occult, and there were stories about experiments with satanism and drugs. Warlock certainly had his darker side. Some people remember him as being distinctly sinister and he was prone to extended drinking binges. E.J. Moeran was so much under Warlock's influence that he shared a place with him for a while, but eventually he realized that the life-style was destroying his work and ruining his health, and he had to get out. But there were other people who said that Peter Warlock was essentially warm and caring, a very good friend, and that his occasional outbursts of wildness were merely a release from the intense pressure of work. When it came to his music, it seems he was a hard taskmaster on himself."

"Why did he kill himself?" Eric asked.

"We can't be sure he did. The gas valve was very loose, and it may be that he stretched out for a nap, and a leak did him in. On the other hand, his personal life was troubled, his finances were always in bad shape, he suffered bouts of depression, and he thought he was a failure. His music bucked the trends of the day— this was 1930—and he thought he was going nowhere. He did mention suicide to a few friends, and later they regretted not taking him seriously. The inquest returned an open verdict, but that was probably an act of kindness. From all the evidence, it certainly does look like suicide."

"He was what, thirty six?"

"Right, and it's only just in the last few years that people started listening to him again and liking what they hear. He had an intense, charismatic personality, there's no doubt about that. Most people who met him either hated and feared him, or else they simply adored him."

"Hmmn." Eric shrugged. "Sometimes I think there's a weird story behind every composer who ever lived—except Sibelius, of course." I laughed. "Warlock sounds as peculiar as they come, but what he has to do with me, I have no idea."

"I'll tell you one more thing about him."

"What?"

"He was tall, like you," I said. "Some people described him as Mephistophelean in appearance. I've seen a photograph of him, and they're right about that. He had a mustache and goatee, just like the ones you've sprouted."

Events got in the way and I wasn't able to see Eric or Mandy for another two or three weeks after that. I did speak to him on the phone once and he assured me that he was at last beginning to make a little headway with his work. He sounded distracted, and I took that to mean that his mind was entirely on his music. The next time I called I got Mandy. Eric was out. He went out every day late in the afternoon and came back late at night, usually in a boozy state. When he worked, the music she heard was not music at all, just doodling at the keyboard. She was worried.

A few days later she rang and asked if I knew where he might be. She was in a state, and I got the impression that he had not been home at all the night before—or if he had, he'd gone out again. It was early evening and she couldn't stand waiting there alone, not knowing where he was or when he might return. I tried to calm her down and promised to look for him.

I didn't think there were very many places Eric might wander to, since he still wasn't terribly familiar with London. I tried his little drinking club in Orange Street first. He wasn't there but the large woman behind the bar told me that he had left about an hour ago, with a lady friend.

I tried the French and a couple of other pubs in Soho before I found him at the Colony Club. It was even drabber than the New Ambassador, but it had a better clientele—literary publishers, free-lancers, the art crowd arrayed lovingly around Francis Bacon and Lucian Freud.

Eric was off in a corner at a typically rickety table with a woman dressed entirely in black. She had a long, horsy face, and long, straight blonde hair. Her name was Gillian, or Francesca. They were both moderately pissed and they each thought the other was wonderfully amusing, I most amusing of all. It took me one round of drinks and not much effort to detach Eric, and I got him into a taxi. He was humming like a tractor, but unfortunately it was nothing more exalted than the refrain from "Lola."

"What the hell are you doing?"

"I'm turning into Peter Warlock." He laughed.

"No you're not," I told him. "You're just acting like a big child—dodging your work, leaving Mandy alone for hours on end. It's stupid, Eric, stupid and uncalled for."

"Maybe he's taking me over." Another laugh.

"Why would he bother?" I snapped. "Peter Warlock is resting happily in his grave, his reputation is secure."

It turned out to be a vicious remark, and I was immediately sorry I'd made it. We were miserably silent the rest of the way. I went in with him to say hello to Mandy. Eric smiled and gave her a kiss on the cheek, and then sloped off down to his study in the basement. Mandy was in tears, obviously not in the mood for much talk. The front room was a bit messy and I noticed that she was still moving very stiffly.

"Where was he?"

"Having a drink at a club with Francis Bacon." It's amazing how you can find the gloss when you need it. "Wait till tomorrow to have a chat with him. I'll do the same in a day or two. He's just having a hard time getting going with the quartet, but he'll snap out of it soon enough."

"I hope so."

"You'll see."

"George, thank you so much."

"Not at all. How're you feeling, love?"

"Otherwise?" A faint sardonic smile. "Still sore and achy, but I'll be okay. As soon as Eric gets back to normal."

I went straight round to the Black Hart in Earl's Court Road and had two quick shorts. There is a natural instinct to assume the best about our friends, and a concern about how much you can interfere in their lives before you go a little too far, and they shut you out. I feared greatly for Eric—that he was using his music troubles as an excuse to fritter away his time on clubbing, boozing and chatting up the dollies. He could easily wake up one morning soon and find that he'd blown the Claymore commission and lost Mandy, and I couldn't imagine how he would recover from two such devastating, self-inflicted failures.

I walked home that night trying to figure out how I might be able to get through to Eric, to shake him out of his funk without alienating him. I had no idea that it was already far beyond me. Even now, looking back twenty years later, I wonder. Weren't the signs all there, waiting to be seen? Shouldn't I have known what was really going on? But I didn't see, I didn't know—or if I did, some part of me must have been unwilling to face it.

Eric seemed subdued when I met him two days later. He had a slightly disheveled look about him, his clothes were rumpled and his hair was brushed back in slick clumps that tended to separate and dangle down on the side of his face until he shoved them back again. Eric wanted to go for a pint but I wouldn't, so we sat in the sun at Holland Park, which only made him look more bedraggled and forlorn.

I can't remember much of what we said, but it wasn't of any special importance. I was going to Italy for a few days to do an interview with Luigi Nono. Eric gave me some very good questions to ask, which showed that his critical thinking was still in fine form, and that cheered me somewhat.

He didn't attempt to explain or apologize for the evening I brought him home from the Colony. He didn't refer to it at all, and neither did I. I've never seen any point in rehashing boorish or childish behavior. Since then, of course, I've often wondered about everything we left unsaid.

I wish I'd given in a little and gone along to the Britannia or the Black Hart with him for a pint. But I wasn't in the mood, I was trying to discourage him from the beer, and we always want to believe there will be time for another pint, another day. But when we parted on the High Street a short while later, it was the last time I saw Eric Springer alive.

I rang them two or three times after I returned from Italy, but no one answered the phone. I meant to go around, but I had a number of assignments to catch up with, and so the days stretched into a week. It was about eleven o'clock one morning when I got the call. At first the voice was so faint that I almost hung up, thinking no one was there. But then I caught it—not much more than an exhalation.

"Mandy? Is that you?"

"Can you...help me."

"I'll be right there."

I'd never heard a human voice sound so weak and helpless. I think I ran all the way from my flat to their house. I tried the door at once, and found it unlocked. I shouted for both of them as I went into the front hallway, but got no response.

The front sittingroom was empty, and the main music room as well—I hesitated there just long enough to glance at the loose pages of sheet music scattered around the place, hoping that some of it might be Eric's quartet, but it was the Berg score. Plates of half-eaten fast food had been left on the floor and perched on the arms of chairs, looking as dry and hard as wax imitations.

I hurried downstairs to the room where Eric worked. It was dark, and there was a damp chill in the air. It reeked of stale tobacco. I turned on a table lamp and saw some ashtrays full of cigarette butts. There were a couple of virtually new pipes on a side table. Eric had never smoked, and I was sure I'd never told him that Peter Warlock did, both cigarettes and a pipe.

There were no books, tapes or records in the room, it was as simple and austere as a monk's cell. A chaise—for one frantic second I thought I saw Eric stretched out on it, the thin blanket tucked up under his chin, just as they found Peter Warlock. Eric wasn't there, but there were more loose sheets of music scattered all over the place. Each page was clean and unmarked, lined with blank staves that lanced my heart.

Just as I got back to the ground floor, I heard a noise from upstairs. I found Mandy in the main bedroom. She was curled up beneath a sheet, barely conscious. Her face was desperately pale and her hair clung to her face in sweaty snarls. She saw me, but she didn't seem to register who I was.

"Help...Eric...."

"It's all right, love," I told her. "Eric's not here at the moment. He must have gone out."

"Eric...."

"No, it's George," I said with a grin. I sat on the edge of the bed and stroked her face lightly. "You're not well, are you? Have you seen a doctor?"

"George." Her eyes found me then. "I can't move."

"Why—"

At that moment I noticed Mandy's legs poking out from under the sheet, and I was horrified. Her toes were curled tightly and her calves appeared to have shriveled. I pushed the sheet up and saw the same slack and wasting flesh all along the lower part of her thighs. I could barely find words to speak.

"Mandy, what—"

It was absurd, but thoughts of Berg and his Violin Concerto suddenly swarmed in my mind. The piece Mandy had been preparing to play in the last week of the Proms. I've always thought of it as Berg's farewell to life, since it was all about both life and death, and Berg died (his own bizarre, absurd death) within a few months of completing it.

But there was another person involved. Manon Gropius, the lovely young daughter of close friends and a special favorite of Berg's. At the age of 18, just before Berg was commissioned to write the Concerto, Manon lost her long and heroic battle against the ravages of polio. Berg was deeply moved, and dedicated the Concerto to her—"to the memory of an angel."

Now, staring at Mandy's legs, I felt a confusion that seemed to boil up out of my bones and surge through me, leaving me dazed and paralyzed. Finally I heard Mandy's faint voice again.

"Save Eric."

"He's not—"

"The kitchen."

I seemed to come back into my own body then and I raced down the stairs. I hadn't even thought of checking the kitchen at the rear of the ground floor. It had a gas stove. The door wouldn't budge. I was sure I could smell gas. As I rattled the doorknob uselessly, I noticed something hanging from it. The thin silver chain with the charm that Eric had bought for Mandy at Portobello Road, the Egyptian cat with the amber eye.

In a moment of awful certainty, I knew I'd never told Eric the single most revealing detail about Peter Warlock's death, the sign that strongly pointed to suicide rather than an accident. A few minutes before he stretched out on the chaise and tucked the blanket up beneath his chin, Warlock had taken his cat and put it safely outside the room. It was the cat's frightful wailing and mewing that eventually drew the landlady's attention.

I got Mandy out first. While the neighbors looked after her and alerted the police and fire brigade, I went back for Eric. I expected the house to blow up at any moment. I took a chair and smashed the kitchen window, unlocked the outside door, got in and turned off the gas. I waved a towel around, trying to clear the air. I had to step outside twice to overcome dizziness, but then I was finally able to go to Eric.

He was slumped back in a chair, his head pointing north, his feet crossed at the ankles and propped on the edge of the wooden table. He looked for all the world like someone who'd just dozed off while waiting for the kettle to boil.

But his lips and cheeks were as red as a tanager, and there was about his mouth the slightly bemused smile of the dead.

I visited Mandy at St. Mary Abbot's Hospital, and I saw her again shortly before she left London. She recovered quickly from what the doctors said was probably a psychosomatic illness. She wasn't having any of that, and neither was I, but there seemed no point in trying to argue otherwise—with anyone.

Mandy and I, sadly, found that we had little to say to each other. It was as if we both wanted, or needed, to retreat from a terrible experience we had shared unwillingly. I felt more than a little guilty for not paying serious attention to what had been happening to her, so preoccupied was I by Eric's situation. She scratched the Proms, of course, and disappeared. I have no idea whether any of the rumors I occasionally heard about her over the years were true, but she never performed in public again.

If Eric Springer is remembered at all today—by people who never knew him—it is probably not as the promising composer of the plaintive and Webernist Variations for Piano and Oboe, but as the composer of a sweetened-up movie theme based on it.

Notes

"(his own bizarre, absurd death)"

Not long after he completed his great Violin Concerto, Alban Berg (1885-1935) suffered an insect bite on the back. From neglect or mistreatment, it formed an abscess. Berg was so poor at the time that he and his wife attempted to lance it themselves. They used toenail scissors. Berg's condition worsened steadily and he died soon after he finally entered a hospital. No effort was made to determine the exact cause of his death but it was most likely due to blood poisoning.

"To those whom God has forsaken is given a gas-fire in Earl's Court."—Patrick Hamilton, *Hangover Square*

I came across this line several years after Eric's death, and for obvious reasons it made a deep impression on me.

Hamilton is probably best-known as the author of the plays *Rope* and *Gaslight*. He hated the movies that were based on them. His novel *Hangover Square* is set in Earl's Court on the eve of World War II. It ends with the hero killing two people and then taking his own life—by gas—after leaving a note asking the police to look after his cat. Oddly enough, when the novel was filmed this character, who had nothing whatsoever to do with music, was transformed into a homicidal composer.

Years earlier, Hamilton had been struck by a car and seriously injured. He recovered, but his face was disfigured. He took to wearing a grotesque artificial nose for a while. This accident contributed enormously to the alcoholism that eventually killed him. It occurred in the narrow side street directly behind the house in which Eric Springer died, years later.

LULU

It seems to me that there can no longer be any choice between enduring the torment of reality, of false categories, soulless concepts, amorphous schemata, and the pleasure of living in a fully accepted unreality.

—Joseph Roth, *Flight Without End*

I never met my grandfather, Leo Kuhn. He refused to come to America and live with us, despite repeated invitations from my father (his son), preferring to spend the last years of his life in the small Vienna apartment that had been his home since the end of World War II. Leo still had a few old friends there, and he lived with his memories. My father visited him twice, the second time accompanied by my mother. While they were there, late in January of 1961, my grandfather passed away quietly in his sleep one night. He had been in gradually declining health for some time. He was 66 years old.

Leo Kuhn, according to my father, was "a half-assed writer" who had published a lot of things back in the '20s and early '30s, but had never quite amounted to anything. He wrote short stories, articles, poems, topical essays and impressionistic sketches that appeared in the ephemeral press. What my father meant, I learned much later, was that Leo was impractical and never really earned a steady income. He was one of the many who, when young, manage to survive on the fringe of the literary world. You don't get paid much but you don't need much, and money doesn't seem to matter anyhow. Your writing does appear in print, and for a while at least, that's enough to sustain the hope that you will eventually mature into a writer of lasting significance.

Once you pass into your thirties, however, and have a wife and perhaps even a child or two, it becomes much more difficult to maintain this kind of life, even if history does not intervene. Leo knew important people and he was in fact well-connected, but he never managed to produce the great novel or stage play that would transform his career in a single stroke. Most likely he never had it in him, or perhaps the immediate demand for the next short piece and the next small payment kept getting in his way.

Vienna in those days, even with all the chaos and suffering that followed the Great War and the collapse of the Austro-Hungarian Empire, was still a lively city, fermenting with rich artistic and intellectual activity. My impression is that right up until the very last minute Leo spent most of his waking time at places like the Cafe Griensteidl and the Cafe Central, seated at a table in a corner, consuming endless cups of coffees, smoking one cigarette after another, and dashing off yet another feuilleton by day, then drinking wine or pilsner on into the night with friends and acquaintances from that floating world. Over the years he came to know, at least on a nodding basis, such figures as Schnitzler, Hofmannsthal, Musil, Werfel, Perutz, Zweig and Schoenberg—a stunning array of cultural titans.

Eventually, however, history did intervene. Karl Kraus once described Vienna, that City of Dreams, as "the proving ground for world destruction." The rise of Nazism in Germany and its rapid growth in Austria made it increasingly difficult for Leo to sell or publish his work. His wry humor and sarcasm had been displayed countless times in print, making serious enemies whose day would soon be at hand. And in any event, he was a Jew.

Several months ago, I came across some of Leo Kuhn's papers. A few diaries, notebooks and files of yellowed clippings that chipped off at the edges in my hands. They were in the attic. My father had just died and I was clearing out his house. I was annoyed but not entirely surprised that he had kept the existence of these papers secret from me for so long. I'm an associate professor of German Literature, I can speak, read and write the language fluently. My doctoral thesis was on the patterns of social unreality in von Doderer's *The Demons* and *The Waterfalls of Slunj*. My father certainly had to know that this material would be of tremendous interest to me, not only for any footnotes it might add to a particularly fascinating period of European literary history but also for whatever it could tell me about my own grandfather.

Over the years, however, I had come to understand that my father harbored a lot of anger and bitterness toward Leo. It had to do with their flight from Austria. Both Leo's family and that of his in-laws were reasonably well off. They had some relatives already in America, and apparently they had few illusions about the turn history was taking. Quietly, unobtrusively, they disposed of all their major assets and managed to transfer most of their funds out of the country. Family members made their way out of Austria in small groups over a period of time, usually on what were described as "holiday" or "business" trips from which, of course, they had no intention of returning.

No doubt some very substantial bribes were paid to facilitate all of this, but it was remarkably successful. By the early spring of 1938, when Austria became a province of the Reich in the *Anschluss,* most of my grandfather's and grandmother's families had already made it to the United States. Leo was not among them. He refused to believe that such drastic action was necessary. He thought that fascism was destined to fade quickly and that he was clever enough to weather the squall. He would somehow keep his contacts, he would write under pseudonyms, and he would emerge well-positioned in the aftermath of the storm. He did agree that his wife and their three-year-old son (my father) should leave with the others, and he promised to follow them if that truly became necessary.

Just a few months later, however, when he suddenly had to flee Austria in the aftermath of *Kristallnacht,* Leo went to Paris. The Nazis would subsequently chase him from that temporary haven, but then he found shelter in the south of France and remained in hiding there until the Liberation. He never did make any real attempt to reach his family, not even after the war, when Europe was in ruins and there was no point at all in trying to persuade them to return from America. In a sense, what Leo did was effectively to abandon his wife and son—or at least that is how my father apparently grew up seeing it.

All through my own childhood, no one spoke of these things. Not my father, not my mother, none of my cousins, my uncles or aunts. My grandmother died long before I was born—but even her cancer failed to bring Leo across the ocean. I'm sure my father regarded that as the final, unforgiveable sin.

Years later, shortly before her own death, my mother did tell me that Leo was a black sheep figure in the family, an alcoholic, a foolish self-centered man who cared only for himself and for his writing, who would not change himself or his ways in order to reunite his family, even when he knew that his so-called "career" was marginal and his writing had no enduring value. He preferred to remain in postwar Vienna, clinging to his ghosts and tattered illusions.

That is probably not an inaccurate portrait of Leo, but it is incomplete.

Working only in my spare time, it took me months to decipher and read all of his surviving papers. The printed matter was occasionally interesting but did nothing to change the assessment that he was a minor writer, an adequate journalist who could not shake the notion that he was destined for higher things. Leo's handwriting was cramped and hasty, his words were long dark blots that reminded me of atonal note clusters and feverish, tortured music.

After the war, he wrote and published many short trivial things, but he kept coming back to one story, which he never finished. It was meant to be an account of his friendship with Joseph Roth in Paris, particularly in the weeks leading up to Roth's death there in 1939. Leo had known Roth in Vienna years before, but they did not become close until Leo arrived in Paris in 1938. Roth had been based there since 1933, having left Germany the day after Hitler took power.

Joseph Roth was very much the kind of writer that Leo Kuhn always wanted to be, and Leo adored him. Roth's haunting, elegiac novels, such as *The Radetzky March* and *Flight Without End*, captured both the fallen world of Austro-Hungary and the bleak estrangements of life in the Empire's wake. He was a major author, though his work has never found much of an audience in English, and, unlike Leo, Roth's extensive journalism never got in the way of his serious fiction. He wrote fifteen novels in the last fifteen years of his life, despite the fact that his personal circumstances grew increasingly nightmarish. His wife went mad, he was hounded by the Nazis, he was frequently destitute, and he was a determined alcoholic, right up until the day his heart finally gave out.

It seems to me that Leo could never make up his mind as to exactly what kind of piece he wanted to write about Joseph Roth. Some parts read like notes for a straightforward memoir, while other passages have the feel of fiction. Even with all that we do know about Roth, it is still impossible for me to be sure how much of what Leo wrote was true. At one point he cites Gautier's famous account of Gerard de Nerval as the literary model he would follow, but sometime later he appeared to change his mind, drawing black lines across whole paragraphs and scribbling brief, contradictory messages to himself.

—No, not an elegy

—This is a ghost story

—Inner story only

—Roth's ghosts were *real*

—Not right, be factual!

—Real love or mythic love

And so on. I often think of Leo Kuhn sitting alone in his small apartment, struggling through the whole drab decade of the 1950s with the numerous elements of his story, trying to force them together into a coherent whole. He failed, and I wonder why. If nothing else, Leo was a competent writer, he understood basic structure and he had a workable command of language. Furthermore, it gradually became clear to me that he had *all* of the story. Perhaps he simply could not bring himself to finish it, to let go of it. Perhaps he needed it as a continuing presence, to be worked on and lived with for the rest of his days. Or perhaps he was helpless, possessed by a story that was a kind of demon he could never exorcise.

Not surprisingly, I have the same kind of problem. This is not an essay or a memoir, nor is it fiction, though it undoubtedly contains some of all three—and I have no reliable idea which parts are which. A large part of it derives from Leo's own first-hand observations, but nearly as much of it draws on what Roth told him, and neither Leo Kuhn nor Joseph Roth were completely reliable.

I am attempting to put the pieces together now, both for Leo and for myself. I believe this is the story that ultimately cost my grandfather his family.

By the time Leo arrived in Paris in April of 1938, Joseph Roth had long since fallen into the final pattern of his life: writing and drinking, furious bouts of the one followed by furious bouts of the other. He had spent some time in Brussels and Amsterdam, but he always returned to Paris, where the largest community of exiles from Germany and Austria had gathered. They subsisted in a dreamlike state of hope, waiting for reality somehow to annul itself so that they could resume their true lives. Roth saw them—and himself—as lost ghosts who linger on, incapable of accepting the fact that they had died and this world was no longer theirs.

Roth's circle of friends and acquaintances had shrunk practically to none, by his own choice. A woman named Sonja lived with him on and off. When she was there, Roth seemed to pull himself together. He ate better and would write a great deal in a short period of time. But sooner or later Sonja would disappear for a few days, and Roth immediately lost interest in anything. He made the rounds of the cheap bars and taverns in the neighborhood, drinking away the days and nights until Sonja came back to rescue him again.

Leo had taken a single room in a house owned by an elderly Russian, just around the corner from the rue de la Vieille Lanterne, where Roth lived in a small apartment. The first few times they met, their conversations were brief and civil, but Roth clearly intended to keep to himself. Gradually, however, Roth began to accept Leo as more than just another neighbor, and to feel comfortable with him. They shared a common past, in a way. Leo was friendly but respectful, and made no demands or judgements. In fact, he was always happy to accompany Roth on his regular drinking excursions. They were the only times when Roth really seemed to relax and would allow himself to speak freely.

Their friendship was cemented on the night when the German stranger came up to them on the street as they were making their way from one tavern to another. The man wore a hat and overcoat, and he was smoking a flat Turkish cigarette. He was young, his skin was waxy smooth and his eyes were clear.

"Ah, the good Herr Nachtengel," Roth said sarcastically.

"Are you well, Herr Writer?" the German replied. "I hope you're taking care of yourself. We don't want anything to happen to you." A mirthless smile appeared on the man's face. "Someone of your great—stature." It was obviously an insult, both personal and literary. Roth was comparatively short, and he had no international profile in the way that an author such as Thomas Mann did.

Leo had barely taken in this brief exchange when the man turned to him and smiled coldly. "How nice to meet you at last, Herr Kuhn."

Roth grabbed Leo's arm and they brushed past the German. Leo was quite startled that the man knew him by name. A few minutes later, when they were alone in the back corner of a basement bar, Roth explained patiently that there were scores of German agents in Paris, each of them keeping track of numerous exiles, waiting for the time when scores would be settled. There would never be mercy for those who had committed political or cultural offenses.

"You're on their list, same as me," Roth said with a faint smile, and then he laughed. "But cheer up. At least it's a sign that you did something right somewhere along the way."

Roth, who had never known his own father, was Jewish on his mother's side, but it was his writing that singled him out for special attention. His fiction was not at all directly political, nor did it espouse a certain cause. Instead, Roth chose to examine the effects of history on the lives of individual characters. His primary focus was always on the human. But as far back as 1923, in his very first novel, *The Spider Web,* he had written presciently about the extreme nationalist gangs and private militias forming throughout Germany, and in that serialized tale he had even made specific mention of Adolf Hitler, who was then still largely an unknown figure outside of the right-wing netherworld. The Munich Putsch, in which Hitler attempted to seize control of the Bavarian state goverment, did not take place until November of 1923—ten long years before he finally became *fuhrer* of all Germany. But Roth's early reference to him was the kind of thing that Hitler would neither forgive or forget.

That night was also the first time Leo spoke with Sonja. Roth got so drunk that Leo had to help him make it back to his apartment, and she was there when they arrived. It was obvious that she had just returned, and Roth was clearly very happy when he saw her. "My lover," he said again and again, as he held her in a clumsy embrace. "My muse." However, as soon as he sat down on the chaise, he leaned back, closed his eyes and passed out, his breathing loud but regular.

"Thank you," Sonja said to Leo as she led him to the door. "He will be all right, now that's he's home."

She was short and no longer quite young, but still very attractive. Her hair was black, or a very dark brown, and it was cut short in a style that had gone out of fashion several years before. Her body was slim but pleasingly rounded. Her skin was very pale, yet as bright as alabaster. Her eyes had such a penetrating quality that Leo suddenly felt awkward and quickly turned away. He sensed some special power in her presence, a quality of strength and relentless honesty—although, the next day, he wondered if that wasn't just a wine-induced fantasy.

"I'll look in—"

"No, please don't," she told him. "He'll be writing."

"Of course."

"You're a writer, too, I can tell," she added, moving closer to Leo. "So, you understand. He needs to use his time."

"Yes." His throat was tight, he felt very warm, and he wanted to touch her, a thought—a sudden desire—that shocked him. "Of course."

"Time to do his work, to write."

Leo nodded, mumbled something, and left. The next day he woke up with his head full of dreamy, confused images of Sonja. It was difficult to understand why, since he had been with her for only a few moments. It had to be some implicit sexuality, the unspoken frankness in her eyes—the way she had looked at him. Certainly she was attractive, and he'd consumed a good deal of wine. Most likely he had gaped at her without even realizing it. Rather than act embarrassed or shy, or pretend that she hadn't noticed, her expression, her response, was to direct it right back to him—as if to say, Yes, and so?—forcing him to confront himself and his uncertain impulses.

It was disconcerting, all the more so the day after. Leo had no intentions toward the woman, and he would never want to disrupt Roth's personal life in the least way. He admired Roth so much that at times he even felt guilty about drinking excessively with him. Wouldn't it be better, after all, if Leo could persuade Roth to drink less and write more? But to do so would cost him Roth's friendship, that was quite clear. One time Roth told him, "I drink as atonement, otherwise I would not continue." Leo didn't fully understand exactly what Roth meant—that he would not continue to drink? write? live? When he asked, Roth frowned in irritation, gave a shrug and said, as if it were self-evident, "Continue."

In any event, Leo firmly believed that all serious writers sacrifice parts of their personal lives in order to accomplish what they do, and that the resulting work must justify the price paid.

That afternoon Leo made the first entry in his "Roth" notebook. But the first name that actually appears in it is Sonja.

Leo saw her again a few days later. It was growing dark at the end of the afternoon and he had just posted another pseudonymous article to Vienna. These harmless pieces on Parisian culture and social life still brought him a small return, but the market for them was vanishing quickly. Few in the Reich wanted to read or hear anything even vaguely positive about the French, no matter how non-political the topic might be. But Leo was not about to start writing the kind of anti-French nonsense that was now so much in demand in Germany. There were already plenty of literary whores working that dismal street, and it appalled him.

Leo saw Sonja emerge from the narrow Rue de la Vieille Lanterne, and he instinctively pursued her. A moment later, he caught up with her and they walked together for a while. Whether she spoke German or French, her pronunciation was exact but unaccented, almost characterless. She was at ease in both languages, so it was impossible to guess where she came from originally. But the pure sound of her voice was lovely to the ear, soft and rich. *Every time she spoke, I wanted to lean closer, to get as close as I could and let her voice wash over me,* Leo wrote.

The facts tumbled out hurriedly in his notebook. She told him that Roth had just fallen asleep after a long night and day of writing. Now he would be asleep for many hours, perhaps right through to the next morning. Roth's work was going well but it was very difficult and painful for him.

And when he slept like that, Sonja had to get out of the apartment—she had to live, breathe, relax. Roth knew, he understood her. All he wanted was for her to be there the next day, to come back to him when he had to start work again. Out of some peculiar need, he simply couldn't write without her nearby, and if she did not return after a while he would give up, go out and start drinking again.

Leo found all this fascinating, but it baffled him. Why did she leave and not come back for days on end? Their relationship appeared to have some mysterious aspect, but Leo would not dare ask either of them about it. He could only hope to learn more in time, for he was certain that it was a key element in any understanding of Roth and his great work. As for Sonja, she was quite intriguing in her own right, and Leo immediately enjoyed being in her presence. Nor did it escape his notice that she seemed quite happy to be with him.

After they had walked a short while it became apparent that Sonja had no particular destination in mind, so Leo took her to a brasserie he knew that served decent food and wine at working-class prices. It was as if he had taken her home. She relaxed at once, threw her wrap off her shoulders, and her face appeared to be lit up from within. He seldom needed to speak. She told him that she was a singer and had performed in numerous nightclubs in Germany and France, though not so much lately. She'd had a string of lovers, each of them worse than the one before. They were businessmen, schemers, criminals, and they had led her into trouble with the police at one point. She had used many different names, mostly to do with her stage act—Sonja, Kristen, Nelly, Mignon, among others. But all of that was in the past now, and she could only be interested in men who created, not destroyed. Men who wrote or painted or made music. Joseph Roth was small and unsightly, he had somewhat bulging eyes, his hair was disappearing, and his body was a wreck from years of heavy drinking. But he created, the fire in him was true and good, so Sonja would give him whatever he wanted and needed. After all the pain and trouble she had been through, she thought that love was an illusion, a fantasy—but one that was still, sometimes, worth the imaginative effort. Leo didn't know what to make of all this. She seemed both sophisticated and naive at the same time.

But it didn't matter. By then he was completely under her spell. The fire in her dark eyes, the way her hair moved as she spoke, her voice stirring him, seeming to speak right into his mind, the line of her throat, the way her breasts filled out her simple blouse, her small delicate hands—everything about her was so soothing and pleasing to him. He felt happily drowsy, from the food and wine and the heat of the nearby coal-fire, and he didn't want to move. It had been a long time since Leo had last enjoyed the company of a woman, much less one who made him feel thoroughly at ease, as Sonja did.

His wife—and this was the only direct comment I ever found by Leo about my grandmother—was a good woman, but she understood little of who he was and what internal forces drove him.

As the evening went on, Sonja even appeared to grow younger. There was more color in her cheeks, her manner became more animated and girlish, but never loud or silly. It was delightful. *I realized that what I felt—in a genuine physical sense—was nothing less than the surging energy of life itself, radiating from her like heat and light from the sun,* Leo noted without irony the next day.

"Show me something you wrote," she said when they left the brasserie and were walking along the street. "Please?"

"All right," Leo replied after the briefest hesitation.

His room was small and chilly, but he lit a fire and poured some schnapps for both of them. She stood by the fire and quickly scanned a short tale of his that had been published the year before. When she put the magazine down on the table, she smiled at him— a smile that made him feel very good since it seemed to signal her approval of what he had written. They sat on the lumpy old chaise in front of the fireplace, the only suitable furniture, and almost at once Sonja raised one leg and swung herself around so that she was sitting on his lap, facing him, her legs on either side of his. Her hand stroked his cheek and teased his hair, she sipped her schnapps and then ran the tip of her tongue along his lips. She must have noticed the sudden conflict in Leo's expression, for her smile grew wider, and there was a measure of good-natured sympathy in it.

"Don't worry," she said. "He doesn't need me this way."

"He called you his lover."

"For him, love is only spiritual now. He's fighting death."

"Even so...."

"It's all right," Sonja assured him. "And you *do* need me this way. Don't you?" Her smile now naughty and complicitous. "No point in denying it."

"Already you know me too well."

"Leo, be bad with me."

She unhooked a couple of buttons on her blouse, took his hand and slid it inside, pressing it to her breast. She leaned closer, until their foreheads touched, and her mouth licked and nipped at his. Somehow, the glasses were quickly set aside, she had his pants open, and she pulled him into her. Their passion was as fierce as it was swift in its consummation.

"Give me a name," she whispered to him, after.

"What?"

"Give me a special name, so I'm yours alone."

"Oh, I don't know...."

"No one else will ever hear it," she insisted. "All those other names I've used were spoiled by other people. Except for Sonja, but that belongs to Joseph, you know."

"Lulu, that's who you are," he said, surprising himself.

"Ah, that's the first name I remember from childhood! I used to think it was so old-fashioned, but now you've rescued it for me." She kissed him.

"Where were you born?"

He felt her body shrug in his embrace. "Orphaned, I suppose."

Then desire intervened, slower this time but more powerful than before, a long, devastating yet beautiful expression of the lonely hunger and deep need within both of them.

Leo awoke cold and alone in the grey dawn. He crawled into bed and soon fell asleep again, waking late in the morning. He fretted through the rest of the day. He was too tired to work properly, but he jotted down brief notes to himself and worried about his friendship with Roth. Leo reminded himself again and again of what she had said: *He doesn't need me this way.* Nonetheless, it was imperative to keep this sudden liaison secret. There was no way of knowing how he might react. It would be bad enough if there were an angry break between Roth and Leo, but far worse if this interfered with Roth's work.

But Leo couldn't stay away, he wanted at least to see her again as soon as possible. That evening he knocked on the door of Roth's apartment, and a shouted voice invited him in. Roth was at his small rickety table, writing. Sonja sat on the rug at his feet, her head resting against his knee. Roth stood up and crossed the room to talk with Leo. He was working, quite busy, no time to spare just now, but perhaps in a few days he would meet Leo and they would go out for a drink. Leo understood, of course, and encouraged Roth to push ahead with his work. At one moment in the brief conversation, Leo's gaze drifted past Roth's shoulder to Sonja, who was still sitting on the rug. At once, her hands moved and touched her breasts, cupping them, and her face lit up with a large smile. She was so naughty! Leo had to look away immediately, and he was relieved that Roth apparently hadn't noticed anything unusual in his expresssion just then.

Two days later, in the early afternoon, his Lulu came to him and stayed for several hours. This soon became the new pattern in Leo's life. She would come to him whenever she could. Sometimes they went out to eat and drink, but time was so precious that they usually stayed in his room and made love, later resting in each other's arms before the fire, then making love again as often as they could before she eventually had to leave. She was a wild, imaginative lover, desperately needy but also infinitely giving. It was as if Leo had discovered true passion and desire for the first time in his life— and discovered, as well, that there is no end to it, no logical conclusion, that it goes on and on as long as there is life and imagination to illuminate its perpetual labyrinthine turns.

"Where did you go?" he asked her one day.

"When?"

"Those times when you used to leave Roth, and be gone for a week or more. Where were you, what were you doing?"

A child-like pout. "It doesn't matter." Then she smiled. "That's all over, finished. When I leave him now, it's only to come to you."

"Yes, but—"

"Shhh," kissing him again and again. "Just fuck me."

Leo's need was as great as hers, and the more he had of his Lulu the more he wanted. When she wasn't there with him, he soon grew restless and he found it hard to concentrate on his work. He constantly felt tired, or lazy, and could lie on the chaise for hours, half-awake, recalling previous meetings with Lulu or trying to imagine what delights the next one might include. At times he scolded himself for acting like a lovesick boy, but then he would think: *Yes, I am. So?*

Leo continued to see Roth fairly regularly, but there was a distinct change in Roth's behavior. Now that Sonja no longer left him for very long, he was able to get more writing done. But drink was still an essential part of his life, so he drank some as he wrote, and once a week he went out for an extended binge with Leo that would last from early in the evening until nearly dawn. In spite of this, he did look a little healthier, or perhaps more at peace in some way, and Leo later observed in his notebook that his affair with Lulu was, ironically, secretly, having a beneficial effect on Roth.

Like a man putting his affairs in order, Roth carefully began to share more of his past life with Leo. After the Great War, he had married—too soon, he later realized. His wife, Frieda, was a good person, not unintelligent but a middle-class daughter who aspired to a settled home life. She would make a good mother. She may have fallen in love with the idea of marrying someone who would eventually become a famous and successful writer. Roth was still at a loss to explain why he had married her, except that perhaps Frieda represented some image of stability he felt necessary in his life at that time.

In practice, the reality was quite different for both of them. He soon found her uninteresting and complacent, even tiresome in her petty ways. But Roth could always escape, and did. Frieda was trapped in their apartment, left alone for days and nights at a time while Roth roamed the countryside on journalistic assignments or simply caroused in the cafes with his friends. Fear of how others would react, and perhaps a sense of her own failure as a wife, prevented Frieda from sharing her situation with anyone or doing anything about it. The powerful social constraints of her conventional upbringing and her own fragile nature only made matters worse, and Roth returned home one morning to find her curled up on the floor, peeling and eating wallpaper. She never completely recovered, and in time had to be placed in an institution. A couple of years later she contracted some illness, and died.

Roth never forgave himself. He found a new sense of urgency in his work, but writing was not an escape. He also took to drinking in a new way. It seemed to him that alcohol was a fitting, fine and ultimately final punishment. He would yield himself to it, and carry out the sentence. From that time on, his whole life became a kind of macabre race in which the goal was to write as much as he could and also to destroy himself in the process.

If Leo saw any parallels between Roth's personal life and his own, he did not enter them in his notes. I have to believe that he thought about them, was even haunted by them, for the rest of his life. It seems to me that Roth and Leo had both sacrificed their wives (and in Leo's case his son), probably without giving it much consideration at the time. They had chosen the artistic, literary life, and had lived it exactly as they saw fit, in a typically youthful and unfettered spirit—regardless of the consequences for those who were closest to them.

Roth subsequently had one romantic affair, with a young actress and writer named Irmgard Keun. They were together for a couple of years, drifting from one European city to another (outside of Germany). Their relationship was passionate and stormy, and ultimately doomed. She couldn't bear to sit by and observe Roth's self-destructive descent, nor could she save him from it. Finally, as much at his insistence, she pulled away and left him. Roth told Leo that he thought of Irmgard as his only "true" love, but that he accepted losing her—it was a necessary part of *his* sacrifice.

[Irmgard Keun was another of those whose names were on a German list. She fled Holland when the Nazis invaded in 1940 and escaped to England, where she remained until her death in 1982. Her best novel was published in an English translation as *After Midnight,* Victor Gollancz Ltd, 1985.]

Sometime after that, Roth wandered into a dingy cellar bar in Montmartre, where he sat and drank, and watched and listened as a young woman "who was no longer quite so young" sang that most poignant and bitter song of abandoned love, *Surabaya-Johnny*. She told him later that he was the only one there who paid any attention, and that his eyes were "big and wet" when she finished. She wore a black slip. She said her name was Mimi. Before long, however, Roth began to call her Sonja.

He told Leo that without her he no longer had enough strength or will to write a single sentence.

Leo and his Lulu continued their affair, and it would seem that Roth never found out about it—or if he did, he never let on. By his own account, Leo was happier than he had ever been. She was a joy as well as a pleasure, child-like, almost innocent, but at the same time a profoundly erotic woman to whom nothing was new or forbidden. She was as much a fantasist as any storyteller, though her imagination expressed itself in who and how she was on any given day. Thus, her presence always had about it an air of anticipation and unpredictability that Leo found compulsive and addictive.

But there were certain worrying signs that he wondered about. She always came to him in a tired, pale condition. This was understandable, since she spent so much time sitting up with Roth as he wrote, and obviously there was nothing healthy about that way of life. They all were poor, ate badly and drank too much. All the same, he was shaken one time when, after making love, they were huddled beneath the blankets, luxuriating in their nakedness together, talking quietly about nothing in particular, and she suddenly murmured, "He's killing me, you know." But when he sat up in concern and asked her what she meant, she passed it off lightly. "Nothing, really. Not like that! It's just that at the end of each session, I feel like I've worked as hard as he has. I'm so exhausted I feel dead. That's all."

It pleased Leo to see how quickly she was transformed whenever she was with him. The color would begin to resurface in her cheeks, her eyes grew brighter and her whole body brimmed with new energy. It was nothing less than the power of love and passion, visible to the naked eye, the two of them drawing new life and vigor from each other every time they met. And if their trysts generally left Leo in a similar state of exhaustion, so much so that even the following day he could barely do one hour's work, he was not bothered in the least. He willingly and completely surrendered himself to *the magic of Eros*. But Leo was still capable of giving the matter some practical consideration.

"You must live with me."

For once, she looked surprised. Then sad. "I can't. I belong to him, and I wouldn't do that to him. This is all you and I can have."

"He's going to die soon," Leo said. "You know it, too."

"Don't speak like that."

"And after the war, whenever it comes—"

"Please!" Now her expression was pained. "Don't write endings for us, not even imaginary ones. You have a wife and child somewhere, another life, and sooner or later you'll want it back. That is what the end of the war will mean to you, whenever it comes."

"No, no—"

"Don't," she cut him off. "It hurts too much."

"I'm sorry. My poor Lulu."

Then she showered his face with kisses, teasing his mouth. "Think of me as your dream lover. I only want to give you pleasure. Be happy with me."

He was. He even began to think that he would be happy to die with her, as life without her had become inconceivable to him. The day after a long encounter with Lulu, he would lie in bed or on the chaise for long hours on end in a kind of daze, his body weak, his mind adrift on a sea of images. It was hard to form clear thoughts. Much of this time was a blissful quietus, the aftermath. But one small part of his brain continued to ponder the internal dynamics of their situation, and Leo's notes reflect a deep-seated uncertainty.

Today she spoke to me of Courtly Love. It is deeply carnal, its whole point is consummation in body as well as spirit. For centuries the Church and society have worked strenuously to de-sexualize Courtly Love and turn it into some harmless, chivalrous claptrap. True Courtly Love is subversive, a threat to the existing order. Tristan went against the King. Women had the power to pick and choose among men, to decide their own fate.

Courtly Love is, by definition, adulterous.

Tristan possessed Isolde in the flesh—but could not keep her.

Leo asked Lulu what all of that had to do with the two of them. She said that their love was like Courtly Love, freely given with no expectation, and thus pure in and of itself. She wanted him to know how much she cherished it.

Does she really understand? Leo asked himself later. *She has her hand on the truth, but perhaps does not entirely grasp it. Any good student of medieval history knows that the ultimate goal of Courtly Love is not sexual, nor is it even spiritual. The true goal of Courtly Love is death.*

Novalis: "Our love is not of this world."

Toward the end, Leo's notes were obsessive on the subject of death. He believed that talk about Courtly Love was simply part of the fantasy that Lulu spun for herself and for him, and as such he enjoyed it. But death was the kernel of truth in the fantasy, and Leo saw it differently, though in equally mythic terms. He began to ruminate about the role of the Muse. Sonja was Roth's Muse. Roth sucked the life and creative spirit out of her, which was why he could write so much and so well when she was with him, and could not when she was away. The Muse gave, but her giving was also a real sacrifice of herself.

The other part of the dynamic (to stay with Leo's term) was his relationship with Lulu. His dream lover. She was right about that, there truly was a dream-like, unreal quality to the passion they shared. It was a kind of mutual fantasy, in which he and Lulu could escape the disappointing world outside for a little while, and flee into the realm of pure desire. It was a fantasy he cherished.

But Leo could also see the weak point in the equation. His life force was being drained, and it was the only one that was not being replenished adequately. The situation could not continue this way indefinitely. The inexorable conclusion was death—his. Whether Leo truly believed this is impossible to say, but he did write this astonishing note: *If Roth were healthier I might have to decide whether to kill him, but as it is I can at least hope to outlast him.* Perhaps he was looking ahead to the prospect of Lulu becoming his Muse. But then he would have to face the question of where she would turn to draw strength in order to feed and inspire him in his work. There would have to be another "Leo," another lover. He had worked himself into an intellectual corner with heartbreaking implications. All of Leo's knowledge and understanding had turned poisonous, and he wanly noted: *If it proves necessary, I will submit. Roth is worth it. Lulu is worth it.*

All of this seemed quaint and amusing, the first time I read it. People take things so seriously, and years later it looks so different. Few of us can relate now to that time and place, that distant, dead culture. But these were very intelligent and gifted people, better-educated, thoughtful, questioning in a way that quite escapes us now— we have an answer for everything we ask, lucky as we are.

The more I stared at poor Leo's words, his clotted handwriting, the more I followed his tortured chain of thought—the more I sympathized with him and even came to believe him. Or at least to believe that he believed. If I could understand him, then I could forgive him for not being in my life. And the truth is, I wanted to forgive him, for Leo, like Joseph Roth, had chosen a remorseless faith in literature and its necessary way of life—which I secretly shared, but lacked the courage and foolishness to attempt.

Things played out his way, in a sense. On the last afternoon of what Leo called his "only genuine life," Lulu came to him and they passed a few hours in the most intense lovemaking, pressing the far edge of violence and unfathomable need, an experience that left them both in tears of joy, incapable of speaking until the time came when she had to leave. Roth would finish his book that night. He told her to ask Leo to join them the next evening to celebrate.

I understood: Roth had known all along.

The following afternoon, when he knocked on the door of Roth's apartment, there was no answer. Perhaps he had come too early. He tried the handle, and the door opened. Yes, there they were. Roth was asleep on the chaise, and Sonja was asleep in the narrow bed in the far corner of the room. Leo was about to back out quietly when Roth suddenly groaned and stirred. There was something vaguely alarming about the noise Roth made, so Leo carefully approached. Roth's eyes stared at him, and Leo had never seen such anguish. Roth's hand moved, barely. Leo interpreted it as a beckoning gesture, and he moved closer.

"I'm dead." Roth's voice was a feeble whisper.

"Lulu."

The word may not actually have escaped his lips, but Leo spoke it, and he turned immediately to the bed. He rushed across the room. She was there, he saw the blankets mounded up over her body. He recognized the beautiful curve of her hips, the correct length of her slender frame. He even saw, he was sure, the slight rise and fall of her shape as she breathed, deep in understandable sleep. When Leo put his hand on her shoulder, his memory-sensation was true, he knew exactly how her shoulder felt and recognized it again. But when he gently pulled back the layers of cheap fabric, they fell away from his hand. He uncovered nothing but the bottom sheet, which still bore the impress of a small body. Leo touched it, and he thought he could detect a fading warmth. But all the sheet held was dust and lint and bits of human grit. He pressed his face to the bed, and—oh God, yes—he could smell her in the most intimate way, as he had tasted and smelled her in love.

But she was gone, like a bed-ghost (*Bettgeist*).

Roth was still alive, and in agony. Leo hurried and performed the necessary function of getting help. Roth was taken to Saint-Jude, the nearest hospital for the poor. Strangely, Leo had no trouble sleeping that night. He left the door to his room unlocked, but he had no visitor. Lulu did not magically appear. Leo was allowed to see Roth the next morning. He was in a ward filled with dozens of patients, all from the bottom of French society. The conditions were mean and the pervasive smell was terrible. Roth had no strength left in him, almost no life at all. Only his lips and eyes moved a little. His large eyes were yellowish and his face appeared to have collapsed into itself. For several minutes he merely gazed at Leo, and his expression was impossible to decipher.

Finally, Leo found a few words. "Did you finish it?"

"Yes."

"Good. I'm so happy to hear that."

"Kuhn."

"Yes?"

"You're looking at the saddest man in Europe."

Then his eyes closed. Leo waited until he was sure that Roth's breathing continued. He smiled and patted Roth's hand. *No,* he thought as he turned away and started to leave. *Nobody so close to death can be that sad.*

Leo left his door unlocked again that night, probably still hoping somehow that Lulu would return to him. But she didn't. It was nearly noon when he awoke the following day. He felt rested, better physically now, though his heart was still sick with disappointment and sorrow.

As he was leaving to go to the hospital again, Leo almost walked right past a man lingering on the sidewalk. But there was something familiar—and then the man smiled and stepped closer.

"Herr Kuhn, how nice to see you again." The German agent.

Leo started to continue on his way. He had seen this man a number of times over the months. Leo refused to speak a word to him. But now the German reached out and took hold of Leo's arm.

"Just to save you the inconvenience," he said. "Your friend Herr Roth died this morning. No doubt you were expecting this, it's hardly a surprise, considering the foolish way he lived. One evening I saw him sitting alone in Bernier's—in the rue de Faubourg, do you know it?—and I thought to myself, this is a man who died a long time ago but doesn't realize it. Nobody reads his sort of thing anymore now, do they? What do you think?"

Leo freed his arm and hurried away.

He remained in Montmartre, living in that room, until the following year, when he left for the south shortly before the Nazi occupation of Paris. He left just before dawn, successfully dodging Herr Nachtengel.

Joseph Roth's last novel, *The Legend of the Holy Drinker,* is now regarded as one of his finest works. It is a tale of atonement and redemption. Roth was 44 years old when he died.

My grandfather, it seems, also drank heavily until the end of his life. But I don't think his drinking served the same purpose as Roth's. It seems more likely to me that Leo used alcohol as a consolation for the loss of Lulu, and perhaps also for the failings of his career as a writer—he was never the writer he wanted to be, and surely he understood that.

Yes, yes, I know she is gone, if indeed she was ever there. And I know she will never come back—I tell myself this everyday. But the rest of me is not convinced. So I light the fire every evening and try again to put the words in order. Perhaps if I get the magic pattern right, it will summon her back. My Muse, my lover—I have no life without her.

Romantic nonsense, the delusions of an old man—I suppose they are. But I can understand his desire to believe now. Leo never gave up on the only two things that really mattered to him after he left Germany: his Lulu and his writing. Naturally, he couldn't stop working on her story—their story. And he remained faithful to her hopeless plea: "Don't write endings for us."

Every time I sit down to write an essay, a report, or even a harmless little tale of my own (none of which has ever been published), I think of my grandfather. His irrational faith in the rightness of such work pleases me. I see it as a gift from him to me—one that certainly skipped past my father. But it is a gift of very mixed qualities. And, I remember my mother's warning to me.

Dawn is often at hand when I finish writing. I can make out shapes in the thick grey light. I go to bed, and see once again the shape of my lover beneath the blankets. I know so well the curve of her hip, the length of her body. Sometimes the lingering darkness fools me and for an awful moment I may not see her hair on the pillow, and my heart races as my hand reaches to touch her.

Nightsuite

An abyss yawns open in my soul and a cold blast from the hour of God brushes my pale face.

—Fernando Pessoa, *The Book of Disquiet*

ONE

Every Tuesday around eleven he went to the Paradiso. It was the quietest night of the week at the restaurant, and he knew he would be able to sit alone at one of the small tables in the secluded back section without being distracted by a crowd of people. Later in the week this area was always full of young couples, and there was a smiling pianist who played romantic show tunes.

In its decor and narrow L-shaped confines, the Paradiso was something of a relic from a previous era. It was located on the top floor of a five-story building and had to be reached by a slow cage-lift. At street level, only a small brass sign indicated its existence. Nonetheless, the Paradiso had a certain loyal following.

The banquettes were made of cracking maroon leather and the walls were hung with inexpensive prints of 18th century hunting scenes. The floorboards creaked beneath old forest green carpeting that was laced with brown paths worn between the tables. With its plain white linen and slightly pitted cutlery, the Paradiso suggested a private club lingering in gradual decline.

That night, his peace was disturbed by two young women who came in and unaccountably chose to sit at the table closest to his. They appeared to ignore him and they were not loud, but the one who did most of the talking spoke in tones of such quiet intensity that it was impossible for him to ignore her. He nearly wished that the restaurant were busier, so that her words would be swallowed up and lost in the anonymous chatter of a crowd.

He glanced at them briefly a couple of times. He didn't know them, and yet there was something not entirely unfamiliar about them. The one who talked was blonde, rather small and slim, but attractive. She smoked Dunhills, one after another, tapping them loosely on the edge of the glass ashtray and occasionally making a tight gesture in the air with one of them. The sound of her voice surprised him with its richness and plaintive elegance. Her voice and gestures made him wonder if he had seen her somewhere once before, perhaps even there in the Paradiso.

"He told me that as soon as I came into his life, he started to die. As if I were actually consuming him. But it wasn't me, it was his own need that ate him up from within. His need was so very great, you know. If you could somehow measure need, it would be impossible to measure the need that possessed him. I was only the object of his passion. I wouldn't say I caused it, but that it was there in him all the time, and then he found me, or I found him, and that opened the door.

"Not that I minded, of course. It was exactly that fire that drew me to him in the first place. I could feel it, like some kind of feverish heat that radiated off him whenever I was in his presence. It was so physical, I could feel my skin tingle when he came close to me. He would look at me, and it was as if the blood began to sing in my ears and head and heart. He would touch me, just on the arm or the small of my back, and I would become wet for him. The power of his desire was vast. It was the most intensely sexual relationship I could ever imagine. You have no idea. That's what I miss most, now. The physical.

"Should I tell you this? One time, he looked up at me and said, when I put my tongue inside you, I do so not only to give you as much pleasure as I possibly can, but because I have to taste you, I have to take your taste inside me. He said, I breathe in your scent and it becomes part of my blood.

"Later, he told me it was *all* imagination. We have to imagine and create, we have to fantasize, or there's nothing. Passion, desire, romance—those things don't exist unless we make them happen. We dream them into being, he said. Most of all, love. Love doesn't exist unless we conjure it up ourselves, out of thin air. Well, he thought that way, and of course I didn't tell him otherwise. It doesn't matter how we explain such things to ourselves, really. It doesn't change anything.

"I know, passion can be so silly, and desire merely animal, like an adult form of childishness. Self-absorbed, limited. I know, I know. But do you care? I don't. He was right about that—what else is there?

"No, I didn't devour him and he didn't devour me, though it often seemed as if that's what we were doing to each other. Maybe he was right, in a way, and we were exhausting our imaginations together. At the time, however, I don't think either of us believed it could ever end. I suppose there *is* a rhythm and a natural course to these things. Eventually you notice that something seems slightly different, in you or in the other person. But perhaps that, too, is just something we imagine.

"You know, I told him that he would begin to lose interest in me. Once he had had enough. Naturally, he denied it. Impossible. Never happen. I knew that he felt he had to say that, and I didn't mind. There were certain things we both had to say, in order to keep it alive. Even if you sense inside that they're not entirely true, you forgive the other person. You feel grateful, because it's necessary. Everything we imagine is a kind of elaborate lie, if you want to see it that way. But it's always better than the alternative. He said the same thing to me, that I'd lose interest in him. But he had no clue, he didn't know me at all.

"My need was far greater than his.

"You wonder how it ended. I can tell you what happened. You start saying things you don't mean to say. I tested him. I said, you'll never leave your wife and home for me, you'll never leave the life you have. And he came to me one night and said, you see? I have. He said, yes, you see, I have. He said, there's nothing left for me out there, that world has fallen away. I only have *here* and *now*, he said. I can only *be* here with you.

"And he stayed with me from then on, for all the time we had left. We spent every minute together that we could. Almost every minute.

"But some part of him was still that other person, the part that haunted him for what he'd done. And is passion really endless? Perhaps we used it up, perhaps we exhausted it in each other. If you truly reach the end of it, is there ever any way back? I don't think so. Not anymore.

"I left him alone for a while. At the time, it seemed necessary for both of us, but that was a mistake. I should have stayed with him, every minute. We should have stayed together. Now all I can think is, I wish I had been there with him. They never would have found him like that. The way he was."

The women had finished their coffee and were preparing to leave. He could not bring himself to speak, and in any event he wouldn't know what to say. For no sensible reason, he felt a baffling sense of forlorn exaltation.

They never would have found him like that.

"If love is real, that's why I loved him so much," she was saying. "Because he was willing to give all of himself to me. Because he died for me."

TWO

Later, it all seemed as vivid and unreal as something imagined.

His zone was mostly clear. People had been leaving all day, their vehicles crammed with televisions and computers, favorite clothes and boxes of important papers. He seldom needed to say anything to them. They knew what was going on. They knew the way out. Everyday life had suddenly been curtailed, deformed, forced into certain narrow limits.

There was so much electricity in the air that he could hold his bare arm out and watch the hair on it stand up and sway wildly. The sky was a yellow-green that was always on the verge of being suffused with blackness. Dust floated horizontally on arbitrary streams of wind. There were brief random outbursts of cold rain, and hail that fell as BBs, marbles, golf balls and sometimes large amorphous grey clumps with the weight and texture of wet cement.

The land was so flat you could see trouble coming from far away. It was not at all uncommon for people to sit outdoors in the summer and watch a tornado make its uncertain march across the plain, miles away. There was always a danger that one might blow right into town, but in his life that had never happened.

Now, however, everything was threatened. This storm was of a different magnitude altogether, freakish and unforgiving, a monstrosity. It produced bizarre effects—sucking the moisture out of your throat and nostrils, floating fireballs that drifted through the streets like lost balloons, lightning that forked up out of the ground and quivered and danced for minutes on end, air so green or yellow that you thought you'd fallen to the bottom of a strange sea, devastating micro-bursts. This demon storm, with exquisite slowness, was now rolling over the town.

By the time he knew he had to leave, the Jeep was dead, its battery or wires fried. His cell phone connected to nothing. The walkie-talkie produced mere static. There were other emergency volunteers in the area—or had been. Perhaps they'd all left by now. Not that he needed their help. He'd been trained. He knew what to do if he were trapped in town. How to protect himself. Survive.

The debris flying through the air was getting bigger and more dangerous. Broken boards, pieces of twisted metal, salvos of shattered glass. There was a roaring buzzing clatter in the distance—he couldn't see a funnel cone, but the sky had turned so inky there that it was impossible to make out anything clearly.

He hurried out of the blast, into a side street, and that was when he saw the young woman. Her long flowing blonde hair was the only note of color in the grey scene. She was walking calmly away from him. He thought he'd checked all of these buildings earlier and found them empty. Perhaps she had been hiding, and was now foolishly trying to flee. He called out to her, but the wind erased his voice instantly. He ran after her, caught up with her, and grabbed her shoulder. She didn't appear surprised to see him.

"What are you doing?" he asked loud enough to be heard over the rising noise that swirled around them.

"I want to see the storm."

"You can't do that." He shook his head forcefully. "You've got to get inside and take shelter in a basement until this is over." She said nothing, but merely stood there, gazing intently up at him. Hazel eyes flecked with a few tiny shards of amber. Hair windblown, charged with electricity in the air. She was barely twenty, he would guess. He grabbed her by the arm. "Come on with me."

He pulled her along with him as he went inside a stone building in the middle of the block. He found the stairs that led down to a reassuringly deep cellar. It was quite dark, but a little greyish light filtered in from low basement windows that were still unbroken. As soon as they got there, she huddled close to him.

"Hold me."

"We're okay now," he told her. He wasn't at all sure that they were, but he was pleased by the conviction in his voice. "We'll be safe here."

"I'm not scared," she said. "I'm excited."

She held his hand to her heart, and he could feel it drumming. Then he also became aware of the soft curve of her breast. Her body pressing lightly against his, so many points of contact—each one like liquid light flowing into him. Her face rested on his chest and he imagined he could feel her breath on his skin. He didn't want to move away from her.

"You're so excited too," she said. Her hand opened his pants and reached inside, holding him. "That's okay. I know how much you want me. You don't have to say anything. I want you, just as much."

She was small and light, and she seemed suddenly to climb up onto him in a quick easy movement. He was aware of his hard cock sliding up between her thighs and moving smoothly into her. The same exhalation seemed to come from both of them at that moment. Her body gripped him. Her arms and legs tight around him. He moved with her and in her.

When he opened his eyes, they were lying together on an old blanket on the stone floor. Her hair was fanned out across his chest. Then he could feel her lips and tongue on him. She sat up and leaned over to kiss him, her lips glistening.

"Taste the two of us together," she said.

His fingers in her hair, he pulled her mouth to his, licked and kissed her, and pushed his tongue in deeply to dance with hers. He wanted her again.

"I want you again," she said, her voice a long soft cry in his ear, as he became a gorgeous rush inside her.

He couldn't move until, later, he realized that she was leaving. Hurrying up the stairs without a word. *No.* He tried to call out to her his throat was dry and he couldn't speak. He stumbled to his feet and ran after her. The front door was open, banging in the fierce wind. As soon as he looked outside he could see that the storm was all over them now, exploding the town piece by piece.

Then he saw her, walking purposefully the way she had been going when he stopped her. The swirling gale pulled her ahead a few steps, then stopped her for a second or shoved her sideways, but she continued. He ran out into the middle of the street. Dust blew in his eyes and bit his skin. He opened his mouth to call out to her, but his throat was filled with the taste of dry earth, and he couldn't make a sound. He plunged ahead, using his arms to protect his face and head from the objects flying by, some of which grazed and staggered him.

He was aware of the huge blackness overhead, but there on the ground he seemed to be enveloped in a sickly yellow-green light. Then he saw her again, not so far ahead—or rather, he saw the momentary flash of her pale skin and blonde hair as she disappeared around the corner and into a whirlwind. He was at once terrified for her, and yet hopeful.

Without hesitating, he rushed after her.

This happened to him in a town he had never seen before, and in a part of the country to which he had never been.

THREE

She looked like someone he once had known.

The moon was ruby-gold the night he left the house for the last time. He had no intention, no plan. He had gone for a walk like this many times before on pleasant summer nights, when the air was just cool enough that he wouldn't break a sweat, or there was a light breeze ruffling the leaves.

The neighborhood looked different at night, and after walking for a while he would sometimes find himself in a part of the city he didn't know very well. It wasn't a problem, however. Sooner or later he would come to a familiar street, or spot some building he recognized, and then the rest of his route would fall in place.

That night his idle stroll was disturbed when he came around a corner and saw a young woman walking along not far ahead of him, as if she had just emerged from one of the buildings on that street. She had fair hair and a slender but attractive figure. He instinctively slowed his pace to match hers, so that he would not pass her by. He trailed along behind her in this way for some little while, moving farther away from the center of the city, into a decayed area of grimy warehouses and older homes, many of which had been converted into cheap apartments or else simply abandoned. Here, every street was dark, few cars drove past, and there were no people about. He began to worry for her. It seemed to him that she didn't belong here, at least not by herself and not at this time of day. He would feel better when he saw her enter a brightly-lit house with other people obviously present inside—her family, or some girlfriends she shared an apartment with, perhaps.

Instead, she slipped through a broken chain-link gate and went inside a small one-story building that had originally been a garage. The house that probably once stood next to it was gone, burned or demolished, it's foundation now partly filled in with gravel and trash. The wide door in the front of the garage was boarded over with corrugated sheet metal. The woman had used a narrow door in the side of the building, and she left it open. The interior had been completely dark, but now he saw the dim flickering of candlelight within.

Only to make sure she's all right, he thought vaguely as he approached the open door. He peered inside. She seemed to be waiting for him. She was wearing a loose robe, and she sat on a large mattress that was covered with a wrinkled but clean sheet. The fat candle sat on a cinderblock a few feet away from her. She smiled when she saw him step inside the door. Without thinking about it, he pushed the door shut until it wedged tightly in place. She opened her arms to him, and he saw the lovely inner curves of her breasts.

"Oh, lover," she said. "Every day I stop and think about how empty our lives would be if we'd never found each other. How empty our lives *were*."

He didn't know her at all, and yet he felt as if he'd already known her a long time. There was an implicit intimacy between them that felt exactly right. He crossed the small room and sat down beside her. She took him in her arms and cradled his head between her breasts. The first touch of her skin on his seemed to bathe his whole body in comfort and relief. Oh yes, he thought dimly, this is what I have missed. This is what I have gone searching for all those times I never even knew I was searching for anything at all. When I walked alone in the night.

Her hand opened his shirt and undid his pants. He nestled closer to her and listened to her heart beating. His face took in the soft fullness of her breast, and his lips found her nipple through the thin fabric of her robe. Then he noticed something else—the rich sweet scent of her. He moved lower, closer to it, until it seemed to fill his nose and head, dizzying him. He felt as if he were floating serenely on a river that never reached the sea, but he was also hard and heavy with desire.

"Taste me," she said. "And then fuck me so I can feel how much you really need me and want me."

He tasted her, and was thrilled to see how much pleasure he gave to her. He knew immediately that he could never have enough of this. And when he entered her, he was like a sleeper rolling, tumbling into a long beautiful dream.

"I don't want to leave," he told her sometime later.

"You don't have to."

"Can we stay here?"

"Here, or anywhere."

"You see?" He smiled at her. "I told you. That I would come to you like this." His own words shocked and thrilled him. "That I would be yours, and you would be mine. That I'd leave everything else behind for you."

She smiled at him. "When did you tell me that?"

"The first time I saw you."

"Ah, yes. And what else, my lover?"

"I'll die before I go back."

"I know you do love me," she said. "And I love you."

He stood up and went to the foggy window. He heard her move along the floor and come up low behind him. She pressed her face to the back of his thighs, her hands snaking round his hips. Once again the gift that she was blossomed warm and sweet within him, and he would surrender himself to her.

Outside, the bright sun glittered harshly on vacant ground, light bouncing aimlessly off the broken surfaces. No matter where he looked, he saw nothing. No houses, no buildings, no streets, no cars. No people. Nothing at all. It was just as he'd thought all along. She was all he had, his dream lover. Without her, he would cease to live.

There is nothing, unless I can imagine and see it.

Grateful, eager to fly and storm and disappear into her again, again and again and again, he turned around.

Figures in Scrimshaw

Nina Ghent was still working in the same waterfront bar when I arrived in the city to research and write about the crimes of five years ago with which she had been so closely associated, though never charged.

A while back I had written a feature about the short life and grisly death of a teenager who had been a witness in a murder case. The article was subsequently reprinted around the country, film rights were sold and a TV-movie was made. I'd been looking for another such story ever since, and I thought I'd found one. There are so many crimes, but so few interesting ones.

The Denmark Inn was an old Victorian house that had been turned into a bed and breakfast. Like the neighborhood around it, the Inn had a faded and somewhat seedy look about it. I told the landlady, Mrs. Jamie Grey, about my project, and she agreed to help me. I was counting on her as a primary source of information. She gave me the same round tower room that Richard Kellogg had stayed in during his fateful visit to the city. It was not especially attractive or comfortable. The air felt musty, the furnishings were well-worn and there were predictable prints of sailing ships struggling against stormy seas. The front window offered a narrow view of the harbor a block away, at the bottom of Denmark Street.

I came in the off season and was the only guest at that time, so Mrs. Grey insisted that I dine with her the first evening. She served a fair chicken Florentine, and we were quickly on a first name basis. One other person lived there, an elderly man I knew only as Joe, who helped out around the house and did the yardwork in exchange for room and board. He ate by himself in the kitchen, and when I spoke with him later in the course of my stay he had nothing useful to say. Jamie, however, was eager to tell me what she knew, and she knew a lot.

She thought Richard Kellogg was hopelessly Romantic. The son of a wealthy family, he had graduated from Brown and kicked around for a year or so. He had no urgent need to work or settle anywhere. One day, he saw Nina Ghent's photograph in a tacky true crime magazine, and immediately packed his suitcases and drove the four hundred-plus miles here to meet her and "hang out with her," as he explained it to Jamie. Richard said that Nina's photograph "spoke to him," that he was "irresistibly drawn" to her and that her life was "fascinating."

I was familiar with that part of the story from the news reports I'd read. I had to smile at myself, though—I didn't tell Jamie that I too had first been drawn to this case by a photograph of Nina Ghent that I had seen in a similar true crime magazine, one which covered the incidents leading to Richard's death. I knew what Richard meant, I'd felt a little of the same tug. Even in photos of rather poor quality, there *was* something hauntingly attractive about Nina's face.

The earlier story, the one which caught Richard's fancy, was about the time when Nina's then-boyfriend Andre was gunned down on a Sunday afternoon in the middle of the city. His BMW was sprayed with bullets. Nina was sitting next to him, and was wounded in the neck and left forearm. Andre was said to be involved in a number of criminal acitivities including drugs and prostitution. Nina was described as an expensive call girl, well-known at the convention center hotels, until she had been promoted to the dubious status of Andre's girlfriend.

A year or so later, when Richard arrived on the scene, Nina had come down in the world and was working as a hostess at a girlie joint called the Sand Bar. It had an odd mix of convention traffic and a local biker crowd. Nina had a new boyfriend, of sorts, a biker named Zach who worked there as a bouncer but was suspected of being involved in more serious, criminal endeavors.

According to Richard, Nina fell in love with him. More likely, Nina and Zach planned to squeeze as much money as they could out of Richard, and then drop him. But something else happened, it all played out differently.

One night Zach and some of his pals turned up at Nina's apartment. It's not clear what, if anything, Richard and Nina were doing at that moment, but there was a scene, a scuffle, and shots were fired. Richard and Zach both died, the other bikers took off, and Nina was in a state of hysteria when the police arrived. Later, she gave a statement in which she said that Zach had been in a drunken, jealous rage, and that he and Richard had shot each other more or less simultaneously. Richard apparently had already acquired his own handgun somewhere along the line, and his fingerprints were indeed found on it.

"I warned him over and over again," Jamie said. "But he wouldn't listen. He wanted to live his life like a movie. You know, a kind of romantic thriller. He wanted to be like a Bogart character, a man who moved in a dangerous world but could take care of himself. He was a grown man, but still a boy in ways, still very naive. You can't fool around with people like that for very long without paying a price. I didn't see that much of him, but I liked him. As soon as Richard fell for *her*, he would be out late most nights and came back here around dawn, to sleep during the day. He loved that night world."

She shook her head slightly, a sad expression on her face. I nodded as if in agreement, but my thoughts were elsewhere. I didn't care about Richard Kellogg, or Zach, or Andre. Oh, they were part of the story, of course, but to me they were just arrows showing the way. The real story was Nina Ghent. I had seen her picture and I felt her spell. Men and boys died violently around her. She *had* to be a terrific story, if only I could get it out of her.

I walked to the Sand Bar that night. It was right down on the old quay but out a little from the center of the city, and it was larger than I expected. There were two pool tables to one side and a drinking area around the long bar. A small raised stage was used by the girls who danced and undressed down to their thongs. They came on every half hour or so and performed for about fifteen minutes, two at a time. If you went through the swinging saloon doors you would find yourself in the dimly lit back room, which had three or four banquettes. That was where one of the girls would bring you for a private drink, a lap dance, whatever you could afford. There always seemed to be three or four girls floating around in the bar.

Nina wasn't there. A bartender thought it was her night off. I struck out on each of the next three nights too. Somebody thought she had come down with the flu, or a cold. I would retreat to my room at the Denmark, buzzed from a little too much beer and frustrated by my lack of success. I would stare at the grainy photo of Nina in *Master Detective,* and wonder.

During the day I cruised around the city and jotted down notes. I spoke with a few cops and lawyers and newspaper reporters, filling in minor details. It was good use of my time, but it yielded nothing new or essential.

In the evening, over dinner, I chatted with Jamie and nodded dutifully at her inevitable warning that I should be very careful. She was somewhere in the vague zone of her mid-to-late-thirties, still attractive, slim and fit, with medium length hair. Sometimes I would be aware of her looking at me in a way that made me wonder, her gaze lingering, her smile very warm. She had an air of stalled sensuousness, but I couldn't decide what to do about it—so I did nothing.

The fifth night, a Sunday, I finally found Nina. The night before, the Sand Bar had been packed, noisy and very unpleasant. Now I was happy to find that there was hardly anyone in the place when I arrived. The bartender immediately waved to me, as if he had an important message.

"You still looking for Nina?"

"Yes."

"She just got here. She'll be out in a minute."

"Thanks."

I bought a beer and waited nearly twenty minutes. She came out of the staff room behind the bar, and glanced around. The bartender said something to her and nodded toward me. She put on her best business smile and approached. She still looked like the younger woman in the magazines, but there were also clear signs of wear and tear on her face when she got close enough. I knew she was only 27, but her eyes were older. The other women at the Sand Bar looked younger and more girlish—but in spite of that, less attractive than Nina.

"Hi, baby. You looking for me?"

Her voice was surprisingly light and sweet, nothing like the nightclub Dietrich voice I had imagined, corroded by tobacco and booze. Naturally I had to buy her a drink—several, in fact—to get to talk with her. We sat in the main bar, but at a table by the far wall. I explained who I was, what I was doing, and I made my best case for her cooperation. I explained that I would not pay her, but said that the story would be told with or without her help, and that she might as well get her side of it on the record. I promised her a full and sympathetic hearing. I emphasized that I was less interested in crime than I was in her personal story.

I expected her to say no at first. I expected an argument about money and possibly even some threats to my health. But as I spoke, she seemed to be paying only partial attention to my words, as if her mind were wandering to other matters. She studied my face, her eyes worked on mine. She sat very close to me and I could feel her warmth. She was wearing a dress that was little more than a short slip, black and lacy. I was very aware of her slender thighs, of the stimulating juniper fragrance about her, of her full breasts beneath the flimsy maroon satin fabric. But I knew why I was there. I finished my little spiel and waited for her to respond.

"God, you're hot. You know that?"

I thanked her. I hadn't heard that in quite a long time—not even from a businesswoman. I said, "But I really do want to talk to you about all of these other things. Not here, of course. I want to take notes, maybe tape—"

"It would be a lot better if we moved in there." She nodded toward the room with the banquettes. She leaned even closer to me and her voice was low and conspiratorial. "It would look better. Give me some money."

The only other people in the place then were a few bikers, but I could easily see them as a part of the prevailing scheme of things. So I bought another round of drinks, and I made a bit of a show giving Nina some money, in case somebody there was watching us. We went to the banquette at the far end of the back room. The jukebox boomed and echoed.

As soon as we sat down, she let herself slide back against me. She put one arm around my shoulder, raised her feet onto the seat and let her slip slide up her legs. She rested her head on me and began kissing my neck.

"We have to play the part," she told me. "So you might as well enjoy it. You make me wet, you know. Nobody does that here. Go ahead, baby. Touch me and see for yourself."

I let my hand rest on her bare thigh and kissed her lightly. It was not that I didn't want to do more—I certainly did. She was incredibly sexy—her voice, her wide deep eyes, her gorgeous skin. But I knew that this sort of thing could only get in the way of what I wanted to accomplish, and I made a serious effort to maintain control of what I said and did.

"When can we talk?"

"It's not safe."

"I'm not worried about that," I insisted.

"Ah, you love me too. Richard loved me, you know."

"Did you love him?"

"Of course. But listen, we can't talk here. Wait for me on Antwerp, the street behind this one. Fifteen minutes. I'll tell them I'm still sick. I'll be driving a silver Audi. Wait under the overhang at the $10 Shoestore."

She drove too fast and she suspected that every car in the rear-view mirror was following us. Her boyfriend, Lester, was very jealous. The only reason she had anything to do with him was because a woman needed protection, and she didn't have much choice in the matter. Not that she lived with him all the time. She still had her own place, but they had a kind of arrangement. She was with him, and that was known to all around the city. It was pretty much like with Zach and Andre. But, what can you do?

"Hey, baby, sit closer." Nina reached across my body and grabbed my right hand, placing it between her legs. She was wet. She slammed her foot down on the accelerator. "*In me—Oh*...God I love that when I'm driving. You're so good, you've got that magic...*touch*."

As soon as we were inside her apartment, Nina dropped her handbag on the coffee table and pulled me down onto the moss green shag carpet. I didn't bother to think about it anymore, I was so caught up with her. I realized that this is the way she is—you're drawn to her, and her reality overwhelms you completely, absorbing you into her larger self. And you go with her, you give in happily—I knew I was exactly where I wanted to be.

"Come on, baby, *fuck* me so I *feel* you."

The door slammed open. Lester lurched in. He was very large and very angry. I couldn't understand what he was saying, but I didn't care. Nina scrambled on the floor, screaming.

"He'll kill me! He'll kill me!"

She was tearing frantically at her handbag, and then a small pistol spun off her fingertips and thumped on the rug. I saw Lester stepping slowly toward Nina, raising his arm. He was holding a large ugly old revolver. I snatched up Nina's gun and fired at him—surprisingly, the bullet hit him in the middle of his large stomach. This only seemed to annoy him, and he began firing at me. I held my arm steady and just kept squeezing the trigger. His belly erupted, his eyes narrowed, he fell backward.

"It's okay, it's okay," Nina told me, her voice simmering with hysteria. "Get out of here *now*. I'll handle it. I shot him. Self-defense. *Get out, baby!*"

I stood up. "Can I see you tomorrow?"

"You *do* love me," Nina said. *"No!"*

In fact, I'd been shot twice. One bullet had ticked the flat of my left shoulder, while the other had left a short furrow in the fat just above my right hip. I smiled as Jamie leaned over me, scouring my torn flesh with antiseptic. Somehow I had found my way back to the Denmark on foot, and she took over from there.

"It happened in Lima," she told me. "We'd been married for six years. No kids yet, we weren't ready for that yet. We loved this house. We were renovating it slowly, at our own pace. Keith was an investment banker, and his special area was South America. He'd been there dozens of times, but this was the first trip I got to go on with him. Anyhow, one day I was supposed to meet him at a bank, and we were going to go for lunch. It was one of those big posh banks, right in the center of the city. I was sitting there, waiting for him, and I looked up and saw him walking toward me. I remember the marble floor was so shiny. Then the shooting started. Stupid me—can you believe this? I hadn't even noticed that the bank was being robbed. Some terrorists. But the army had arrived and all hell broke loose. I heard the shots erupting. Keith—the spray went right through him, like a dotted line. I'll tell you. I've been over this so many times, I've played this scene out in my mind again and again—it's just *empty* now. It's over with, it's done. It happened, and I'm still here. You know?"

I nodded. I put my hand on the small of her back and patted her gently, as if to console her. I didn't know what to think. I was injured and I was dazed. But I did have certain insistent thoughts and feelings.

Jamie had been there when her husband was shot down. Later, she'd been there when Richard Kellogg turned up in search of his own violent destiny. And now she was tending to my wounds. She was wearing an extra large men's pajama top. I caught the delicate scent of star jasmine. Her hair was loose and slightly mussed, but the soft light from the table lamp brought out its dark reddish glow.

"How do you feel?"

"Okay."

She finished bandaging me. "Are you sure?"

"No."

"What is it?"

"You."

"Me?"

"You make me hot."

Jamie smiled as I put my hand on the back of her head, my fingers in her hair, and I pulled her face toward mine.

▲ ▼ ▲

Jamie was in tears. A couple of months had passed. I was back. This time I intended to stay. I'd brought my things in a rental truck.

"You're going to die," she moaned. "With *her*."

I took her in my arms, comforting her, kissing her brow. I held her tight and brushed her hair from her face.

"Look," I said gently. "I told you. I'm just going to *talk* with her. She's a story to me, that's all. But it's still the same story, and I have to go with the story."

"You were awesome, baby, awesome. I'm going to give you such incredible pleasure—pleasure until you can't bear it anymore. And then I'll keep on until you beg me to stop, and maybe I won't even stop then."

I smiled. We were in a rest area off the highway a few miles outside of the city. Just playing it safe, no particular reason. Evening, the sky full of beautiful purple clouds and golden light, the taste of recent rain still in the air.

"Before the cops got there, you know what? I was wet. I was thinking of you and playing it all back again in my head."

I saw the car come rushing off the highway. I watched the gravel fly through the air as the car skidded close to her car, which was parked behind mine. I carefully raised my arm from around her shoulder, at the same time opening the door.

One man coming.

Nina was screaming. I pushed her down below the car window, out of the line of fire. I jumped out and immediately hopped a couple of steps off to the side. My arm came level and I saw his belly on the sight.

I felt a jab somewhere. *Good.*

In the Desert of Deserts

Drive at night, somebody told me in Laghouat, and at first I did. But that advice was only good as long as I knew where the road was. The road was quite fair over some stretches, but then it would peter out, fading into the surrounding terrain, becoming invisible until it reappeared a mile or two farther on. That was all right too, if I didn't stray dangerously. A sensitive driver can tell where the road ought to be even when it isn't.

But I found it maddeningly difficult to follow the trail at night. My vision was restricted to the range of the headlights, and I had no useful sense of the landscape. At one point on my first night out I was driving along cautiously when the powerful beams of an oil supply truck lanced the darkness. The truck went by, nearly a mile away from me. *That* was where the road was, I realized unhappily. A trucker could make the desert run at night because he'd done it so many times he knew the way instinctively, but it was impossible for a first-timer to travel like that. I decided to travel the rest of the way by daylight.

Besides, there was more to the challenge than just making it all the way to Niamey. I wanted to experience the Sahara at its most difficult, as well as to enjoy it at its beautiful best. It would be a shame to drive through the desert mostly at night, and come away like some empty-handed thief.

I spent much of the second day in Ghardaia, where I topped up the water and petrol tanks. I gave the Range Rover a careful examination, and was satisfied. I checked the spare parts list, but I already had everything on it. I had done these same things the day before, at Laghouat, only a hundred miles away. But this was my last chance to correct any problems or pick up something I might need. Ghardaia has supplies, equipment, skilled mechanics and even cold soda. The oil pipeline runs nearby. It's a fairly busy town, considering the fact that it's located out on the edge of the edge.

I don't distrust people but I slept with one eye on my Rover and its load of supplies. I was up before dawn, feeling as eager as I was nervous, and I left Ghardaia when the first infiltration of grey light began to erode the blackness. Now the crossing was truly under-way.

I was travelling south through the Great Western Erg, and my next stop was In Salah, more than three hundred miles away. This would be the easy part of my journey, I reckoned. The desert was immediately fierce and formidable, but I knew there was an oasis at El Golea and some kind of a military outpost at Fort Miribel, both of which were on my route.

South of In Salah the terrain would become much rougher, the climate even more hellish, and although in theory there were more villages in that part of the country I knew that they would prove to be fly-speck settlements that offered little. I had been told that in the Sahara what you think you see on a map is usually not what you find on the ground. I had no fear of dying of thirst or starvation, nor even of heat, but I did worry about a mechanical breakdown that could strand me indefinitely in some heat-blasted cluster of huts on the far side of nowhere.

At first I made relatively good time, but by midday the road deteriorated predictably and I had to drive more slowly. After a break for lunch I proceeded, and soon got stuck. The sand in the Sahara can be deceptive and treacherous. One moment it may be as firm and hard-packed as an old gravel road, and then it will turn into something like dry water, all but impossible to stand in or move through. My right rear tire slid into just such a hole, and it took me nearly two hours to extricate myself with the help of aluminum tracks.

Even so, I felt reasonably pleased by the time I decided to stop for the night because I had experienced no major trouble and nothing unexpected had come up. I picked a place where the road was clearly visible, then pulled off about a quarter of a mile to set up camp.

That last night of peace I fancy I absorbed something of the remorseless clarity of the Sahara. This is a world composed of a few simple elements—sand, air, the disappearing sky, then the blue, red, yellow and white stars—but each one of them is huge in its singularity. They are so vivid and immediate that after a while they begin to seem unreal to the human observer, like stage props for a drama that never happens and involves no one. In the Sahara, it is said, God talks to himself. I had not come to the desert looking for any mystical fix or tourist inspiration, but I did find something like joy in the loneliness and insignificance it constantly threw in my face.

I ate, cleaned up, drank a single neat scotch and then slept well. It was chilly, but I had of course expected that and was warmly wrapped, and if there was any night wind it didn't disturb me at all.

Before dawn, as I prepared to leave, I found the footprints. I knew at once that they were not mine.

I almost laughed. I felt a little bit like Robinson Crusoe, shocked, amused, fascinated. After the initial wave of reaction passed, I began to feel uncomfortable. Crusoe had a pretty good idea of what he was up against, but the footprints I'd discovered made no apparent sense. For one thing, they shouldn't have been there at all.

They formed a counter-clockwise trail, roughly in the shape of a circle, around my little camp. They looked like the tracks of a solitary adult male wearing ordinary shoes and walking at an ordinary pace. The footprints stopped twice, overlapping tightly before continuing, as if at those two points the unknown visitor had paused to stare and think for a moment. It was disturbing to know that he could only have been looking at me as I slept just a few yards away, inside the circle.

I calmed down after a few minutes. The headlights of an oil company truck passing by on the road must have caught part of the Rover in the darkness, and the driver stopped to investigate. It was so obvious, I felt silly. The fact that I could see no trail to or from the circle was strange, but a breeze could have hidden them or perhaps the driver had walked a particularly hard-packed stretch of ground that would show no footprints.

Once I was on the road again I thought no more about it. My progress was slow because the wind started up and the road became more difficult to follow. It was a long day, hot and demanding, but late in the afternoon the conditions changed abruptly, as so often happens in the Sahara. The wind died away and at the same time I hit a good section of the road. I covered more ground in the last four hours than I had in the previous eight.

This time I camped a little farther from the road, beyond a ridge, where no headlights could spot me. I didn't like the idea of anyone sneaking up on me in the middle of the night, out there in the depths of the desert. My vehicle and equipment were worth a small fortune, and the next person might not think twice about bashing my head in and hiding them. He could always return later with a partner to collect the goods. The chances of anybody else finding my remains would be virtually nonexistent.

I felt so secure that I was not at all prepared to come upon anything unusual the next morning, but I did. The same unmarked heels and soles, coming from nowhere, going nowhere, but circling my ground, stopping once or twice.

I was shaken. I didn't want to be there anymore, and yet I sat down. It was as if I could not bring myself to leave. I had to reason my way out of this threatening situation. Whoever had left those tracks couldn't have followed me on foot because I had come too many miles yesterday. He could have followed me by car, or truck, or even on a camel, but surely I would have seen him at some point, and if he stayed too far back he couldn't be certain of finding the point where I left the road for the night.

Besides, why would anyone bother to shadow me like this? To approach me in the darkness, but then do nothing? If he intended to attack me he could have done so twice by now. The whole thing made no sense at all. It was precisely the fact that nothing had happened that worried me most. It seemed somehow more menacing, as if I were being monitored.

Could it be a Bedouin, a nomadic Arab? It seemed unlikely. I'd been told that they travel in clans and that they seldom come through this part of North Africa. There's nothing for them here and it isn't on any of their usual routes. Besides, I doubt that the Bedouins wear ordinary Western-style shoes.

I put my hand to the ground and touched one footprint. Yes, it was real. I was not hallucinating. I traced the indentation in the sand. He had big feet, like me. I placed my right foot next to one of the footprints. Nearly a perfect match. However, my high-top camping shoes had corrugated soles, and no heels.

It was theoretically possible that I had made the footprints in the middle of the night, because I did have a pair of ordinary shoes packed away in the Rover, but I simply couldn't believe it. I had absolutely no recollection of taking them out, putting them on, walking the circles, obscuring my tracks back to the van, and then packing the shoes away again. Not the slightest glimmer of any such memory. If it was my doing, asleep or awake, I was well on the way to losing my mind.

But isn't that what the desert is supposed to do to a person who wanders through it alone? Madness creeping in, like the sand in your socks. I told myself it wasn't possible, at least not in the first three days out of Laghouat. All that desert mythology was nothing more than a load of romantic rubbish.

Nonetheless, I decided to push on all the way until I got to In Salah. I stopped only to eat and drink, and to let the engine cool down a little. I got stuck a couple of times but never lost the road, and I made pretty good time. The changes in the Sahara were largely lost on me, however. When my eyes weren't fixed on the road ahead they were glancing up at the rearview mirror. But I never saw another vehicle or person.

When I reached In Salah I was so exhausted that I slept for eleven hours. I spent another day working on the Rover, stocking up on supplies, and enjoying the break in my journey. I even had a stroll around the town, what there is of it.

And I decided to change my plans. Instead of heading south, through the moderately populated mountains of the Ahaggar, as I'd originally intended, I would now turn west to Zaouiet Reggane and then drive south through the Tanezrouft all the way to Mali, and from Bourem I would follow the course of the Niger River on into Niamey. The net effect would be to shorten my journey and make it less scenic but also perhaps more challenging. The Tanezrouft is vast, empty and closer to sea level, therefore hotter than the Ahaggar. The oil trucks don't run in that part of Algeria. Some people believe that the Tanezrouft is the worst part of the whole Sahara Desert.

So why do it? I don't know. I must have been thinking that no one would dare follow me across the Tanezrouft. Before I left In Salah I bought a gun, an ugly Czech pistol. I don't know if I was indulging my own crazy delusions, or pursuing them.

These actions and decisions of mine had an irrelevance that I could not completely ignore. It was as if I sensed that I was merely distracting myself with them, and that they didn't really matter. If the man was real, he'd be there. And if he was other than real, well, he might be there anyway.

One hundred miles south of Zaouiet Reggane, I awoke. I went out about fifty feet, looking for the footprints. Nothing. So I went a little farther, but again found nothing, no sign, no mark, that didn't belong to that place. I broke into a trot, circling my camp site, scouring the ground as I went. Still nothing of an unusual nature.

I ran right past it, then stopped sharply, one foot skidding out from under me as I turned back. Even then I didn't see it, I smelled it. And, as the saying goes, I thought I saw a ghost. A pencil-line of blue fluttering in the air. It was smoke. In the sand were two footprints, just two, not my own. The same shoes. The heel marks were so close they almost touched each other, but the toes were apart, forming a V on the ground. It was as if the man had squatted on his haunches there, staring at me while I was sleeping. Nearby, a discarded cigarette. It was still burning, almost to the filter now, and it had an inch-long trail of intact ash. I don't smoke.

I touched the smoldering tip just to convince myself that it was real, and it was. I jumped up and looked around, but there was no one in sight for half a mile in any direction. I'd chosen a natural basin, so there was nowhere to hide and even if someone was lying flat and trying to insinuate himself into the sand he'd still be easily seen. There was no one. No tracks. Just me and those two footprints, and the cigarette.

I picked it up and examined it carefully. Any trademark had already burned away, but there was enough left for me to see that the cigarette had the slightly flattened, oval shape that is more common to the Middle East than Europe or America. But that told me nothing. I wish it had lipstick on it.

I say that, but I drove scared, and the farther I went the more frightened I became. There was nowhere on the entire planet I could feel safe, because I could drive until I passed out and I would still be in the middle of the Sahara. When I reached Bidon 5, a desperate little waterhole, I sat off by myself and let the engine cool for three hours. They thought I was another of those wandering Englishmen who go to the most awful places in the world and then write articles about it for *The Sunday Times*.

I considered driving on, but common sense finally prevailed and I stayed the night. I must have been even more tired than I thought, for I slept late into the morning and no one bothered to wake me. Early starts are like a matter of religion to me, but I felt so much better, refreshed, that I wasn't annoyed. Besides, I had plenty of time. The change of route gave me an extra three or four days.

I was also encouraged by the fact that I was approaching the southern limits of the Sahara. Another three hundred miles, and I would be rolling through the grassy plains of Mali. When I got to Bourem I might even take a side trip and visit the fabled city of Timbuktu, a center of Islamic teaching in the 15th century. I have heard that Timbuktu is just a dull and decayed backwater of a place nowadays, but I was tempted to take a look. How could I come to within a hundred miles or so of what was once regarded as the remotest spot on earth, and pass it by?

But I still had the last of the Sahara to deal with, and the road soon disappeared. My progress was slow, I got stuck and had to dig my way out several times, and the heat was devastating. I pushed on, regarding the desert now as nothing but an obstacle to be overcome as quickly as possible. Mileage is deceptive because the road, when you haven't strayed from it, meanders this way and that in its endless pursuit of firm ground, and one hundred miles on the map is usually a hundred and twenty five or thirty on the clock. I think I reached the border, or even crossed it, when I had to stop for the night. Another day, a day and a half, two at most, and I would leave the Sahara behind me.

This time I parked only a few yards off the road. There was no traffic at all this far south so I had nothing to fear in that respect, and the sand was too treacherous to risk venturing into any farther than necessary. I checked the air pressure in all of the tires, checked my gun, had a glass of scotch, and got into my sleeping bag.

It was still quite dark when I awoke. Just like in a film, my eyes opened but the rest of my body didn't move. I was lying on my side, and I knew immediately that I was not alone. My mind wasn't working yet, I was still in a fog, and at first I thought I saw a single red eye staring at me from some distance away. It was the glowing tip of a cigarette, I realized dimly. I couldn't make out anything of the person who held it. I was overcome by a wave of choking fear that seemed to be strangling me from within. A dozen hungry lions circling closer wouldn't have frightened me as much as that burning cigarette did.

I had the gun in my hand, my elbow dug into the sand. I was still lying there in my sleeping bag, and I forced my drowsy eyes to focus on the tiny red speck of fire. A moment later it traced a gentle arc, came to a stop, and then brightened sharply. As he inhaled, I squeezed the trigger. The explosion seemed distant, a curiously muffled noise that might have come from another part of the desert. I shut my eyes, having no idea what had taken place, and I fell back into sleep.

The brightness woke me later. I didn't believe anything had actually happened during the night because my memory was blurred, dream-like, unreal. The gun was where I had put it when I got in the sleeping bag last night, between carefully folded layers of a towel on the ground nearby. If I had fired it at some point in the night, surely I wouldn't have put it back so neatly.

But when I sat up and looked around, I saw the body. I felt calm, yet desolate. He was about twenty yards away. I got to my feet and walked slowly toward him. My shot had been true, like a sniper in one of the old European wars. The slug had smashed his face into a bowl of bloody mush.

His hair was black and curly, his skin olive-colored, and he wore a plain white short-sleeved shirt, faded khaki slacks, and a pair of ordinary shoes. A man so dressed, on foot, wouldn't last more than a few hours in the desert. His presence there was such a vast affront to sanity and nature that I felt a flash of anger. It gave way, a moment later, to cold helplessness.

I found a few loose cigarettes and a box of matches in his shirt pocket, but he carried nothing else on his person. I don't smoke, but I took them. I checked inside the shirt collar but it had no label or markings.

It seemed to me that I would never know who this man was, or how he came to be in the desert with me, what he wanted, or why I had been compelled to kill him, so I got my shovel and buried him on the spot. Dead bodies are supposed to be heavy and cumbersome but he felt as light as a bundle of sticks.

Somewhere along the way in Mali I gave up thinking about it. There was nothing to do, there were no answers to be discerned in the lingering confusion of fact and fear. Guilt? No. I've seen enough of the world to know how superfluous human life really is. I drove, losing myself once again to the rigors and pleasures of simple movement.

Bourem offered little, Timbuktu less. I looked at the dust, the mud, the crumbling and overgrown buildings that seemed to be receding into prehistory before my eyes, and I left. In Niamey I relaxed, celebrated and got laid. I made my way eventually down to the beaches at Accra. I ate with Swedish and German tourists who fretted about the unofficial fact that ninety percent of West African whores are HIV-positive.

That didn't bother me. I drank bottled French water with my scotch, but I also busied myself with the women. Day after day, night after night. There's not much else to do, except drink and lie about. Besides, there are moments in your life when you just know you're meant to live.

"Why?"

Ulf was a well-meaning, earnest and somewhat obsessive Swede who had developed a spurious concern for my reckless behavior. I shrugged absently at his question. He wanted an answer but I did not care to mislead him.

"Regardless."

Ulf had money and nothing to do, nowhere to go, like me, and so we drove to Abidjan, then Freetown, finally Banjul. I enjoyed his company, but by the time we were in the Gambia the charm wore thin and I was eager to be alone again. Still, I agreed that Ulf could tag along as far as Dakar. He was still with me days after that, as I approached Tindouf far to the north.

"I'm heading east," I told him.

"But it's just a short run to Marrakesh now." Ulf was quite disturbed. He consulted the map. "There's nothing to the east, only the Sahara. No road. Nothing."

"There's always a road."

Ulf hired someone to drive him to Marrakesh. I stayed on in Tindouf for a couple of days, working on the Rover and restocking my supplies. I was serious about driving east. True, there was no road, but I believed I could make it anyway. I had it in mind to reach Zaouiet Reggane, four hundred miles away, and then take the road south until I found my campsite near the border. It was the last arc in a big circle.

Why indeed? At times I was crazy with disbelief. I thought I had to return to the spot and dig up the dead man, just to make sure that he was real. The missing bullet in my gun was not good enough, nor were the stale cigarettes I still carried with me. I had to see the body again. In some strange and unfathomable way, the rest of my life seemed to depend on it.

But there were moments of clarity too. I was caught up in a senseless odyssey. I could ramble around Africa until I died, of old age or stupidity. I argued with myself, dawdled, hung on for days in the soporific dullness of Tindouf. I dreamed of the dead man's hands reaching up out of the sand to strangle me, like some corny turn in a horror movie. I dreamed that the grave was still there, and I found it, but it was empty. Most of all, I imagined that I would never locate the place again, that I would just burn and blister myself to a blackish lump as I dug pointless holes in the desert.

I did, after all, drive east. A few miles from the village, the ground became tricky. I pushed on, often swerving one way or another on an immediate impulse. Progress was slow. Late in the afternoon, I had a sense that I would never make it anywhere near Zaouiet Reggane. Then all four tires sank into a trough of very fine sand. I got out. The Rover was in it up to the axles, with no chance at all that I could extricate it by myself. I reckoned I was between twenty and twenty five miles east of Tindouf, which was a long one-day walk. I prepared to spend the night there. I would set off early and reach the village by nightfall. I would return the day after, with helpers, and we would haul my vehicle onto solid ground. They would laugh, I would pay, and later I'd drive to Marrakesh, perhaps catch up with Ulf, and that would be the end of it.

I woke up in the middle of the night. Unable to get back to sleep, I pulled on my jacket and walked into the chilly darkness. I didn't go far. When the dim outline of the Rover began to fade in my vision I stopped. This is what he saw, I realized.

I was still fogged with sleepiness. I sat on my haunches, with my heels together and toes apart. It's often rather bright in the Sahara at night, when the stars form a brilliant skyscape, but some high thin clouds now cast everything in shades of black. The Rover was an inky lump against the charcoal expanse of sand. This is what he saw.

Without thinking, I took one of his crumpled cigarettes from my jacket and lit it. I didn't inhale, but puffed at it, and the glowing red tip only seemed to emphasize the blackness around me. I imagined a shape stirring out there, mysterious and unknowable, secure in the anonymity of the night. I imagined it noticing me behind my tiny pinpoint of fire, fixing on me. As if I were the only stain on all that emptiness. And then I thought that maybe I had been wrong from the beginning.

It was like looking deeply into your own eyes, and finding nothing there.

Nocturne

In the calm of his middle years, O'Netty made it a point to go for a walk at night at least once a week. Thursday or Friday was best, as there were other people out doing things and the city was livelier, which pleased him. Saturdays were usually too busy and noisy for his liking, and the other nights a little too quiet—though there were also times when he preferred the quiet and relative solitude.

He enjoyed the air, the exercise, and the changing sights of the city. He enjoyed finishing his stroll at a familiar tavern and sometimes seeing people he knew slightly in the neighborhood. But he also enjoyed visiting a tavern that was new to him, and observing the scene. O'Netty was by no means a heavy drinker. Two or three beers would do, then it was back to his apartment and sleep.

O'Netty went out early one particular evening in September and found the air so pleasant and refreshing that he walked farther than usual. A windy rainstorm had blown through the city that afternoon. The black streets still glistened and wet leaves were scattered everywhere like pictures torn from a magazine. Purple and grey clouds continued to sail low across the darkening sky. Eventually he came to the crest of a hill above the center of the city.

He decided it was time to have a drink before undertaking the long trek back. He saw the neon light of a bar a short distance ahead and started toward it, but then stopped and looked again at a place he had nearly passed. The Europa Lounge was easy to miss. It had no frontage, just a narrow door lodged between a camera shop and a pizzeria. The gold script letters painted on the glass entrance were scratched and chipped with age. But the door opened when O'Netty tried it, and he stepped inside. There was a small landing and a flight of stairs—apparently the bar was in the basement. He didn't hesitate. If it turned out to be something not for him, he could simply turn around and leave, but he wanted at least to see the place.

The stairs were narrow and steep. The one flight turned into two, and then a third. O'Netty might have given up before descending the last steps, but by then he saw the polished floor below and he heard the mixed murmur of voices and music. The bottom landing was a small foyer. There was one door marked as an exit, two others designated as rest rooms, and then the entrance to the lounge itself. O'Netty stepped inside and looked around.

The lounge could not have been more than fifteen feet by ten, with a beamed ceiling. But there was nothing dank or dingy about the place. On the contrary, at first glance it appeared to be rather well done up. It had a soft wheat carpet and golden cedar walls. There were three small banquettes to one side, and a short bar opposite with three upholstered stools, two of which were occupied by men a few years younger than O'Netty. Along the back wall there were two small round wooden tables, each with two chairs. Table lamps with ivory shades cast a creamy glow that gave the whole room a warm, intimate feeling.

There were middle-aged couples in the back two banquettes but the nearest one was empty, and O'Netty took it. The bartender was an older man with gleaming silver hair, dressed in a white shirt, dark blue suit and tie. He smiled politely, nodded and when he spoke it was with a slight, unrecognizable accent. O'Netty's beer was served in a very tall pilsener glass.

The music playing on the sound system was some mix of jazz and blues with a lot of solo guitar meditations. It was unfamiliar to O'Netty but he found it soothing, almost consoling in some way. He sipped his drink. This place was definitely unlike the average neighborhood tavern, but it wasn't at all uncomfortable. In fact, O'Netty thought it seemed rather pleasant.

After a few minutes, he realized that the other people there were speaking in a foreign language. He only caught brief snatches of words, but he heard enough to know that he had no idea what language it was. Which was no great surprise. After all, there were so many European languages one almost never heard—for instance: Czech, Hungarian, Rumanian, Bulgarian and Finnish. O'Netty concluded that he had come across a bar, a social club run by and for locals of some such eastern European origin. Before he left, perhaps he would ask the bartender about it.

Although he couldn't understand anything the others said, O'Netty had no trouble catching their mood. Their voices were relaxed, lively, friendly, chatty, and occasionally there was some laughter. It was possible for O'Netty to close his eyes and imagine that he was sitting on the terrace of a cafe in some exotic and distant city, a stranger among the locals. He liked that thought.

Some little while later, when O'Netty was about halfway through his second glass of beer, he noticed that the others had either fallen silent or were speaking very softly. He sensed an air of anticipation in the room.

A few moments later, a young man emerged from the door behind the bar. The music stopped and everyone was still and quiet. The young man came around to the front of the bar. He could not yet be thirty, O'Netty thought. The young man swiftly pulled off his T-shirt and tossed it aside. He was slender, with not much hair on his chest. He kicked off his sandals and removed his gym pants, so that he now stood there dressed only in a pair of black briefs. The other two men at the bar had moved the stools aside to create more space.

The young man reached into a bag he had brought with him and began to unfold a large sheet of dark green plastic, which he carefully spread out on the floor. He stood on it, positioning himself in the center of the square. Then he took a case out of the bag, opened it and grasped a knife. The blade was about eight inches long and very slightly curved. The young man's expression was serious and purposeful, but otherwise revealed nothing.

What now, O'Netty wondered.

Let's see.

The young man hooked the tip of the blade in his chest, just below the sternum, pushed it in farther, and then carefully tugged it down through his navel, all the way to the elastic top of his briefs. He winced and sagged with the effort, and he used his free hand to hold the wound partly closed. Next, he jabbed the knife into his abdomen, just above the left hip, and pulled it straight across to his right side. He groaned and dropped the knife. Now he was hunched over, struggling to hold himself up, and he could not contain the double wound. His organs bulged out in his arms—liver, stomach, the long rope of intestines, all of them dry and leathery. There was no blood at all, but rather a huge and startling cascade of dark red sand that made a clatter of noise as it spilled across the plastic sheet. The young man was very wobbly now, and the other two at the bar stepped forward to take him by the arms and lower him gently to the ground. The young man's eyes blinked several times, and then stayed shut. The other two carefully wrapped his body in the plastic sheet and secured it with some tape they got from the bag. Finally, they lifted the body and carried it into the room behind the bar. They returned a few moments later and took their seats again. Conversations resumed, slowly at first, but then became quick and more animated with half-suppressed urgency.

After a while O'Netty finished his beer and got up to leave. No one paid any attention to him except the bartender, who came to the end of the bar for O'Netty's payment and then brought him his change.

"By the way, sir, in case you don't know. You can use the fire exit. There's no need to climb all those stairs."

"Ah, thank you," O'Netty replied. "It *is* a lot of stairs."

"Good night, sir."

"Good night."

The fire exit opened onto a long metal staircase that brought him to a short lane that led to a side street just off one of the main avenues in the center of the city. It was already daylight, the air crisp and fresh, the early morning sun exploding on the upper floors of the taller buildings. O'Netty stood there for a few moments, trying to regain his bearings and decide what to do.

Then he saw a city bus coming his way, and he realized it was the one that went to his neighborhood. It must be the first bus of the day, O'Netty thought, as he stepped to the curb and raised his hand.